Cursed with a poor sense of d[illegible]
to read, **Annie Claydon** spent [illegible]
lost in books. A degree in Eng[illegible] followed
by a career in computing didn't lead directly to her perfect job—writing romance for Mills & Boon—but she has no regrets in taking the scenic route. She lives in London: a city where getting lost can be a joy.

Karin Baine lives in Northern Ireland with her husband, two sons and her out-of-control notebook collection. Her mother and her grandmother's vast collection of books inspired her love of reading and her dream of becoming a Mills & Boon author. Now she can tell people she has a *proper* job! You can follow Karin on Twitter, @karinbaine1, or visit her website for the latest news—karinbaine.com.

Also by Annie Claydon

Risking It All for a Second Chance
From the Night Shift to Forever
Stranded with the Island Doctor
Snowbound with Her Off-Limits GP

Also by Karin Baine

The Nurse's Christmas Hero
Wed for Their One Night Baby
A GP to Steal His Heart
Festive Fling to Forever

Discover more at millsandboon.co.uk.

CINDERELLA IN THE SURGEON'S CASTLE

ANNIE CLAYDON

SINGLE DAD FOR THE HEART DOCTOR

KARIN BAINE

MILLS & BOON

First published in Great Britain 2023
by Mills & Boon, an imprint of HarperCollins*Publishers* Ltd,
1 London Bridge Street, London, SE1 9GF

www.harpercollins.co.uk

HarperCollins*Publishers*
1st Floor, Watermarque Building,
Ringsend Road, Dublin 4, Ireland

ISBN: 978-0-263-30594-4

01/23

This book is produced from independently certified FSC™ paper to ensure responsible forest management.
For more information visit: www.harpercollins.co.uk/green.

Printed and Bound in Spain using 100% Renewable Electricity
at CPI Black Print, Barcelona

CINDERELLA IN THE SURGEON'S CASTLE

ANNIE CLAYDON

MILLS & BOON

To Charlotte.
In gratitude for your company on the journey.

CHAPTER ONE

THERE WAS JUST one thing to keep in mind while negotiating a path through one of the main London stations late on a Friday afternoon. Watch your ankles.

Grace Chapman had arrived just in time to get some coffee from one of the stands at Paddington Station, before catching her train. This was the first surge of the evening—people who'd left work a little early to miss the rush hour, and get a head start on wherever they were going for the weekend. She'd paused, studying the departures board, and someone had rammed an overnight case into her left ankle.

'Sorry.' The word floated back at her over the woman's shoulder. No time to stop when you were hurrying to meet whatever delights the weekend might hold.

'That's…' Grace shrugged. Clearly it didn't much matter to the woman whether it was all right or not.

Perhaps she really *was* becoming invisible. Lost amongst the ranks of an army of carers, who didn't have too much time for social engagements, and so were tactfully left out when friends made their plans for the weekend. It felt sometimes as if she was fading in front of everyone's eyes.

Grace sighed, rubbing her ankle. This was what she'd decided to do. What she *wanted* to do. She'd stood too long now in front of the board, looking at the names of towns and cities that she wouldn't be going to, and there was no time for coffee.

There would be plenty of opportunity to grab a drink and let her mind wander when she was on the train. Grace started forward, weaving through a stream of people coming the other way, and made her way along the platform to the correct carriage for the seat she'd reserved.

This week the train wasn't too crowded, and the group of four seats had just one man sitting in the window seat opposite to Grace's. She gave him a brief smile as she sat down, stowing her bag into the overhead rack, and caught the fleeting impression of a pair of bright blue eyes before she looked away again.

It was tempting to take a second, much longer look. But this was *her* time. The next five hours down to Cornwall was when no one else needed her attention and Grace was alone with her thoughts. She pulled a journal from the outside pocket of her handbag and opened it, in the universal traveller's signal that she wanted to be left alone. The train jolted slightly as it began to pull from the station, gathering speed as it started its journey out of London.

'Page twenty-seven.' The voice had a touch of warm humour about it that made it impossible to ignore. The man's hand lay on an open magazine in front of him, and reading upside down made it clear to Grace that he was perusing the same medical journal that she'd just taken from her bag.

'Good article?'

He smiled, and she felt a sudden flush of something she'd left behind a long time ago. Something she had no time, or inclination to rekindle.

'It's interesting.'

'Thanks. I'll check it out.'

The man opposite her nodded, picking up his copy of the journal and flipping through the pages. It appeared that was the sum total of any effort he was going to make towards a conversation, and that suited Grace just fine. Only…

There was something about him. Something in that smile that made her want to talk. The first thing she'd noticed about him—those jewel-like iridescent blue eyes—seemed to sparkle with humour. His short corn-blonde hair might have put him amongst the surfers who spent their weekends in Cornwall at this time of the year, but there was something about the set of his jaw that indicated purpose rather than sunshine.

He caught her looking at him, over the top of her journal. Time to look away again, but a different and stronger instinct compelled her to meet his gaze. When a smile began to play recklessly with his lips, she couldn't quell the desire to return it.

'I'm thinking…orthopaedic consultant?'

'Right in one. Reasons?'

'You have a subscription to an orthopaedics journal…' She nodded towards the cover of his copy of the journal, which had a bar-coded sticker in the corner, the same as hers. 'And you're wearing a suit.'

A very good suit. The hand-stitching on the lapels, and the way it fitted his broad shoulders made that clear.

That put him somewhere around the level of a consultant, despite the youthful ebullience of his smile.

'I could be on my way somewhere that demands a suit.' He was teasing now, and Grace felt a thrill of excitement run up her spine. She moved, trying to disguise the forbidden frisson, laying her journal down on the small table that divided them.

'On a train that arrives at nine o'clock in the evening? You'd be late. And you have a slight crease.' Grace nodded towards his right elbow, starting to like this game very much.

He chuckled suddenly. 'Fair enough, an all-day suit and an orthopaedics journal. Although I've been in surgery today, which you couldn't have been expected to know.'

She might have, if she'd dared look at his hands before now. Perfectly clipped nails and the look of softness that came from frequent moisturising. The patch of dry skin on the side of one of his fingers, no doubt the result of scrubbing, put the seal on the deduction.

He was looking at her now, with an assessing gaze. Grace resisted the impulse to pick up her journal and hide behind it, wondering if he'd felt quite as naked as she did now.

'Orthopaedics, naturally.' He smiled down at the journal in front of her. 'I'd say rehab, because of the article you've just been reading. And your shoes tell me that you're on your feet most of the day...' He frowned, clearly working his way through all of the options in his head.

He'd noticed the comfortable fabric-topped trainers, then. Since her feet were hidden under the table now, he must have been watching as she'd made her way to her seat, and somehow the thought made Grace feel even more naked. Gloriously, refreshingly naked, as if she'd thrown off her clothes to bask in the sunshine.

'I'm going to take a wild guess and say physiotherapist.'

There *was* a hint of something deliciously wild in his smile. Along with something that stepped back and observed carefully before getting his guesses exactly right. If she'd met him in another life…

This life was what Grace had. This moment, and this train.

'Good guess.'

'And you're on your way back home. Visiting someone?' He shot her an apologetic look when she raised her eyebrows, as if he knew that maybe he'd gone a little too far. 'There's some Cornish in your accent.'

She'd started this game, and she could hardly object to his having picked up the trace of Cornwall in her tones, that ten years living in London hadn't yet been able to quash. All the same, it took a practised ear to notice it, which meant he was probably from Cornwall as well, even if there was no hint of that in his speech.

'I'm going to see my grandmother. She's getting a little frail now and needs someone to keep an eye on her, so my sister and cousins take care of her during the week and I visit at weekends.'

If she said it like that, the schedule seemed less punishing. More like weekends away instead of the increasingly hard work in making sure that Gran was well cared for. But it didn't look as if he was falling for that, because his mouth twisted, his gaze softening into a look that somehow indicated he understood just how difficult this was.

'You're Cornish too?' With any luck, he'd pull out his phone and show her pictures of the wife and gorgeous family that were waiting for him there. That would fix the fantasies that were beginning to form in her head, and they could spend the rest of the journey in pleasant conversation. Or silence. Whatever worked.

'Well spotted. I didn't think my accent resurfaced until after Exeter.'

His smile contained a hint of self-effacing humour. His phone was concealed on the small table under his copy of the journal, and he picked it up, seeming to scroll through pictures to find his favourite one. Here it came…

'Here's my reason for being on the train.'

He handed her the phone and Grace felt her eyebrows shoot up. No sunshine or happy smiles, just a stone building that looked like a converted barn, surrounded by trees. There were cars and vans parked outside and it had the air of a place of business.

'What's this?' Grace narrowed her eyes, trying to read the sign that stretched over the top of the glazing on one side of the building.

'Swipe right.'

Didn't that mean you were about to fall in love? The twitch of his lips indicated that the implications of his comment hadn't escaped him, and his shrug disclaimed the nod to online dating. Grace couldn't resist swiping to the next picture.

'Oh! That's beautiful!'

He smiled. 'There are a few more…'

She wanted to linger over the picture. The glass vase, covered in swirling shades of blue, gave the impression that the sea had somehow risen up and was in the process of forming a perfect spherical structure. Grace swiped back to the picture of the building, enlarging it so that she could read the sign.

'You're a surgeon who moonlights at a glass factory?'

He laughed, nodding. 'Improbable as that might sound, yes. It's actually my father's glassworks. He died a year ago and I'm doing my best to keep it afloat.'

'I'm sorry to hear that. That your father died, I mean…'

'Thank you.' He pressed his lips together for a moment, the shadow of grief darkening his face. But it seemed he didn't want to dwell on the hard things in life any more than she did. 'Take a look at what we do…'

Grace flipped through the pictures, one by one. Everything and anything you could make from glass was represented, all imbued with a liquid motion that made the pieces seem alive. Light and colour, fashioned into something that you could reach out and touch.

'These are amazing.' Words didn't really cover it, but perhaps her expression did, because he returned a gratified smile. 'Your father made these?'

'He established the style and brought craftsmen together who could make it a reality. We're carrying on that tradition. All of the pieces that you see there have been made in the last year.'

'They're beautiful. I can see why you want to keep things going.'

He nodded. 'We have artists who have worked there

for twenty years. My father died suddenly, and they thought that the best thing they could hope for was that I'd sell the place to someone who might have some intention of keeping some of them employed. I wanted something a bit better than that, for them and for my father.'

'And so you've taken over the running of the place?' It seemed like a huge task—the kind of thing that would split someone in two. In comparison, looking after her grandmother at weekends sounded like a relatively simple proposition.

'For a while. We're working towards making it a place that's run by the people who work there, but that takes time. We have to develop management skills and decision-making processes if it's not all going to fall apart as soon as I walk away.'

'That sounds really hard.'

'Most things that are worth it come with their share of difficulties.' He shrugged. 'Would you like something to drink from the buffet car?'

Grace did want some coffee, even if it was tempting to take a little longer looking over the photographs. She laid the phone down, reaching for her bag to find her purse, and he shook his head and got to his feet.

'Stay here and keep an eye on my things. I'll go…'

Penn McIntyre hadn't got any further than the titles of the articles on the pages in front of him, the words swimming in front of his eyes in a mess of fatigue. He'd had a couple of patients cancel their appointments this afternoon, and got an earlier train, which meant that he'd be down in Cornwall before midnight. He was so hungry for a good night's sleep.

And then… Then an angel had dumped her bag in the rack above his head and squeezed into the confined space. He'd caught a brief glimpse of light blonde curls and green eyes, before good manners had made him look away.

But the woman really must be an angel, because she came with small miracles. It was impossible not to notice that she was reading the same orthopaedics journal that he was. And since this edition had only come out today, she probably hadn't got to page twenty-seven yet. When he'd caught her looking at him over the top of the pages, he'd taken a chance…

Suddenly, he was wide awake, as if her mere presence had just effected that good night's sleep that he so craved. Another miracle. Then she'd bettered it, when she smiled back at him and replied.

She looked tired, too. Not that Friday evening, long week kind of tired, but the kind of fatigue that grew over months. Penn reckoned that the weekends away that she dismissed as little more than visits to her grandmother, were more draining than she let on. He hadn't experienced the demands of caring for an elderly relative, but he was quite aware of what they were.

He didn't have the time or the inclination to add another relationship fiasco to the succession of disasters that he'd already managed to chalk up against his name. But this, he could do. A train journey had a beginning and an end. It was an interval in time that didn't leak out into the rest of his existence. And the wish to spend that time with her was impossibly tempting.

As he queued for coffee, he realised that he didn't even know her name. That had seemed unnecessary, because there was the kind of intimacy between them that only came from chatting with a stranger. She must know how it felt, to tend to a patient and hear them confide their most private fears. To give a small part of yourself, supplying comfort and a way forward, and then bid a smiling goodbye at the end of a consultation. Couldn't they take a little of that kind of comfort for themselves, before they reached Cornwall and went their separate ways?

He picked up a couple of packets of sandwiches before ordering coffee and walked back between the rows of seats, balancing the two large cardboard cups carefully. Not daring to look at her until he reached the bubble of the seats that faced each other across the small table. When he did, the warmth of her smile hit him anew and he almost collapsed back into his seat.

She peeled the plastic top from one of the cups, and let out a sigh of pleasure. 'Chocolate sprinkles. I forgot to ask for them, thank you...'

Penn nodded an acknowledgement. He'd played it safe, and the other cappuccino didn't have chocolate sprinkles, so he could give her a choice. He opened the bag he'd brought.

'Sandwich?'

She hesitated, obviously as hungry as he was. 'I haven't eaten... Which one's yours?'

'Either one. You choose.'

She chose the ham and cheese, then dipped her hand into the bag on the seat next to her and produced her purse. Penn shook his head, and she ignored him, glancing at the price sticker on the sandwich packet, and sliding a ten-pound note across the table towards him. Penn felt in his pocket for some change and when he put the coins into her hand, she shot him a reproving look, clearly knowing that he'd given her too much.

'I don't know your name.' She asked the obvious question, and Penn felt his heart sink as a little bit of the everyday intruded.

'Penn.' Maybe first names *only* would be enough of an answer for her.

'Short for…' She stopped, giving him a querying look as he held up his hand.

Most people he met didn't assume that Penn would be short for Penrose, even if there weren't too many likely alternatives. But the old Cornish name would be more obvious to someone from Cornwall.

'Yeah. It's a family name.'

'And kids can be cruel?' She twisted her lips in an expression of regret.

He supposed that it wasn't so difficult to work out. Only the long-held trauma of childhood bullying could make someone stop another person short before they got a chance to say their full name.

'Yeah. I've heard every creative alternative there is.'

'I think it's a great name. *Penn* is even better.' She smiled, holding out her hand. 'Hi, Penn. I'm Grace.'

The train seemed to be travelling twice as fast as it normally did. One cup of coffee and a sandwich, and London was a distant memory as they sped through the countryside, stopping only at the major stations along the way.

A lot had happened in those few short hours. Penn was a rare creature. Someone who listened carefully and thoughtfully, but who seemed unafraid in speaking his mind, including his own experiences. They'd talked about growing up in Cornwall. He was an only child with divorced parents who had largely remained on amicable terms, and his time had been split between running barefoot on the beach while in the care of his father and wearing shoes in the company of his mother.

'She has a love of the arts and a very full social calendar. And an inability to sit still for very long...' He smiled, clearly remembering the round of galleries and interesting places that he'd described with a great deal of affection.

Grace allowed herself to venture back into her childhood in rather more detail than usual. Her story of the picture-perfect village became a little closer to reality, fleshed out with real people and situations that weren't always flawlessly perfect.

'My mother has ME, and there were times when she wasn't well and just getting out of bed was an impossible effort for her. I was the eldest and I learned how to cook and shop and look after my little brother and sister.'

Penn nodded. 'You were the helpful child of the family?'

Grace hadn't thought of it quite like that before, but he was right. She'd been proud of the way that she had helped her mother, and felt very grown up when she walked down to the village shop after school, with her purse and shopping bag.

'Gran did a lot too, and my dad would take over when

he got home from work. And people in the village used to keep an eye on us. They all knew that there were times when Mum wasn't well.'

'But you came up to London to study?'

'Yes, my brother and sister were older and could fend for themselves by then. I was thinking about staying at home, but I got an offer from a good university in London, and Mum and Dad encouraged me to spread my wings a bit. It was Gran who finally persuaded me, though.'

'She sounds like an important person in your life.'

'Gran was the one who always had time for me. When I was little, she used to take me out every Saturday afternoon and we'd have the best adventures together, then go back to her cottage. In the summer, we'd have sandwiches for tea in the garden, and in the winter, we'd toast muffins by the fire.'

'And she gave good advice?'

So many people failed to see that Gran hadn't always been old, and that she'd once been a force to be reckoned with. Penn made that leap smilingly and with no apparent effort.

'Excellent advice. She told me that I might fall in love with London, or not. And it didn't matter either way. If I could honestly say that I'd never regret not giving it a go, then I should stay put.'

Penn chuckled. 'So of course you took up the place.'

Grace shrugged. 'What else was I supposed to do? I thought that London would be all bright lights and interesting places, but I was really miserable at first, living in cramped, noisy student accommodation and not knowing anyone. Then in my second term, I discovered that I was starting to really like it.'

'There's something about the anonymity, isn't there? Feeling at home amongst strangers.'

'You like that?' Grace wondered why he'd wanted to be anonymous, when all she'd really wanted was to be seen and accepted for herself. Maybe Penn's seemingly throwaway comment about the *helpful child* wasn't too wide of the mark, and London had been the escape from the universal success and approbation she'd found in being the one who'd helped her mother so much.

He waved his hand, as if trying to dismiss his own feelings. 'I guess I'm just spending a bit too much time trying to be visible at the moment. Taking over the glassworks, talking to everyone in an effort to find a way forward…'

That felt like the truth, but not all of it. Grace let it go. They were virtual strangers, only bound together by opposite seats on a train. Finding that they had some things in common didn't mean that they felt the same about everything.

'You're a surgeon who doesn't like talking to people?'

He laughed suddenly. 'No, I do as much talking as I can with my patients. I'm a lot more comfortable with that, though. Medicine was what I always wanted to do.'

'I'm happy with what I do too. I never get two days that are quite the same, and every patient's different as well.'

'I'll take that as a recommendation. You must be good at your job.'

It was a nice compliment, and Penn seemed to really

mean it as well. He asked about her work and Grace described the clinic in Camden Town, where she worked with people who'd suffered injuries and illnesses, anything from sore muscles to road accidents and strokes. He listened carefully, asking questions and seeming to store her answers away for future reference.

In answer to Grace's question, he told her that he split his time, three days a week at a central London private hospital, and two days a week at the hospital where he'd trained as a surgeon.

'It's a good balance.' He must have seen her raise her eyebrows in surprise. 'I learn a lot from each.'

His appetite for learning seemed unquenchable. Penn seemed to want to know and understand everything, and she felt her own curiosity growing. He was accomplished, good-looking, and he had a kind of magnetism that made conversation with him so very easy. Why would someone like him value invisibility?

He lived alone, in a part of London that screamed understated wealth, telling her that he considered himself lucky when Grace mentioned that Holland Park was a very nice area, and leaving her to guess that there must be money somewhere in his family. Then he adroitly managed to ask, without really asking at all, about her living arrangements.

'I was in a relationship, but it broke up a year ago. My partner said he was happy with my going down to Cornwall at the weekends, but it turned out to be more difficult than we thought.'

That was the sanitised version. Jeremy's unspoken proviso was that if she was away at weekends, every moment of her time during the week should be spent on him. He'd even pressured her to stay home a few times, when it was far too late for Grace to make alternative arrangements for Gran's care. The most hurtful thing was the jibe he'd thrown when she'd apologetically told him that she had to go. He earned more than her and surely her time was bought and paid for already.

'I'm sorry to hear that. That must have been a painful time for you.'

'I just wish I'd known where we stood, right from the beginning. Then it wouldn't have felt quite so much like a balancing act.'

He nodded. 'I know what you mean—about the balancing act. I think there has to be at least one thing in your life where you stand your own ground. One thing that's yours and you don't compromise on.'

That sounded like something to think about. Maybe not now, because she wanted to savour Penn's company. 'How about another cup of coffee? I don't compromise on that.'

He laughed suddenly, clearly realising that she was intent on lightening the mood. 'Good choice. I don't either.'

'We've time for a second cup before we get to Newquay.' She got to her feet, taking her purse from her bag before he got a chance to move.

If you only had one more minute, what would you say?

They seemed to be hurtling towards Newquay at the speed of light. At this rate, the one minute would have passed in silence, while Grace was still working out what would or wouldn't be appropriate.

Then Penn took the matter out of her hands. As the

train slowed before pulling into the station, he gathered his belongings, turning to take the booking card from the back of his own seat. He glanced at it quickly and then put it into his jacket pocket.

'You're on this train every Friday evening?'

Grace nodded, feeling her heart thump in her chest.

'Me too. I'll book this seat again next week.'

Before she could say anything, he'd walked away, between the rows of seats towards the queue that was already forming to get off the train. The doors swished open and Grace craned to see him step down from the train and walk away.

No goodbyes on the platform, then. No trying to put into words what this journey had meant, and probably embarrassing herself in the process. No turning to leave, wondering if he was watching her go.

Grace reached for the booking card at the back of her own seat, and stowed it carefully away in her bag.

CHAPTER TWO

MAYBE PENN HADN'T made the invitation clear enough. Or maybe he'd been too pushy about it and should have left things to fate. Whatever. He usually got a later train down to Cornwall on a Friday evening, but he'd asked his secretary to arrange his diary so that he could leave in time for the one that Grace would be catching. All he could do now was wonder whether she'd take his suggestion and book the seat opposite his.

He'd spent some time wondering whether this was wise, because it was starting to feel a lot like a date. But, however sparkling the hours promised to be, no one in their right minds asked someone to spend five hours on a train with them, before going their separate ways. Least of all Penn McIntyre, the twenty-second Lord of Trejowan, whose title carried an expectation that he'd always find the right venue for an unforgettable evening.

But the train had been like a breath of fresh air. Full of emotional honesty and without the weight of the previous twenty-one generations of his family, which had put an unbearable pressure on so many of his relationships. He'd neglected to mention the castle, as well…

It was ironic that ownership of the castle by twenty-two generations of his family was all about continuity, because its curse had followed him through his life so consistently. Bullied as a child, then mistrusted as a teenager. However hard he worked, there was always the suggestion that everything he achieved was the result of privilege. And if that hadn't been enough to break his heart, the one woman he'd loved enough to want to marry had insisted that the Penn McIntyre who made his living as a surgeon wasn't enough for her, and the man she really wanted was Lord Trejowan.

The details he'd chosen to omit from his conversations with Grace mattered, because they were all about the unbreakable threads that had run through his life. And however much he told himself that it wasn't a matter of deceit, it just hadn't come up in conversation yet, he knew that wasn't true.

But Grace had seemed content within their bubble of anonymity, and for the moment, Penn allowed himself to ignore what might happen when it broke. He was too busy looking forward to Friday evening.

He hurried through Paddington Station, wondering if Grace would be there. When he boarded the train and caught a glimpse of her blonde curls, at the far end of the row of seats, his heart leapt in his chest and he felt as if he was fighting suddenly for air.

Slow down. His hand moved to the small package in his laptop bag, checking for the hundredth time that it was still there. And then he left all of his hopes and fears behind, stepping into the warmth of the small shining world that seemed to centre around Grace.

'Hi. You made it, then?' She smiled up at him as

he leaned over to stow his weekend bag in the overhead rack.

'You did too…' He smiled back and sat down. Grace pushed one of the cardboard cups in front of her towards him.

'Since we didn't compromise on coffee last week… You'll join me?'

That would be an uncompromising and effusive *yes*. Penn leaned back in his seat, lost in her gaze as he nodded his thanks, and took a sip. Her eyes seemed greener than he remembered them and more beautiful.

'I have something for you, too.' He took the package from his bag and slid it across the table.

Something about the way that her hand jerked back, as if she was wary of accepting anything from him, made Penn glad that he'd decided to dispense with wrapping paper and a box. Remembering the way she'd refused to allow him to buy her even a sandwich last week, he'd made do with bubble wrap, reckoning that gave the impression of a passing gesture rather than something that he'd chosen very carefully.

'What is it?'

'You could always open it and find out. It's just something I picked up at the glassworks.'

His casual shrug obviously made Grace feel a little better about the gift that was trying so hard not to *be* a gift. She peeled the sticky tape off, turning the package in her hand carefully to unwrap it.

'Oh! It's beautiful!' The small blue glass dolphin shone in her hand as she inspected it carefully. 'It looks just like a real dolphin as well… This is just the way they move.'

Grace's own lustrous gaze, which put the beauty of the glass to shame, had seen the whole point of the piece, straight away.

'Phil, the glassmaker who made it, is an avid dolphin watcher. He prides himself on accuracy, so he'd be pleased to hear you say that.'

She held the dolphin up to the light, shards of blue reflecting across her face. The urge to touch her skin was almost irresistible, but Penn knew that he *must* resist if he wasn't going to spoil everything.

'Is that the way you do things? People make whatever they want to make.'

'Not exactly. We have a signature style, and some kinds of things sell better than others. But within that, there's plenty of room for individual glassmakers to do their own thing. Phil likes dolphins. Phoebe, on the other hand, makes orchids. She says it's a good excuse for filling her house with real orchids, but I suspect she'd do that anyway.'

'And that's how it worked when your father was in charge?'

Penn shook his head. 'No, my father was a glassmaker himself, and so he designed and made everything and the other glassmakers just followed his patterns. We decided that we needed to change that and that each person working at the glassworks would be encouraged to develop their own pieces, alongside the ones my father designed.'

'When you say *we*...?'

'It's not a euphemism for *I*. There's a staff meeting every month to talk about how everyone wants to go forward. We discuss everything and make decisions together.' Penn had modelled his approach around his own experience. Every member of the medical teams he worked with was valuable and should be heard.

'Whatever you're doing, it's working. This is gorgeous.'

'Thank you. I'll let Phil know that you like it.'

He settled back into his seat, pleased with Grace's delight at the gift that was masquerading as anything but a gift. And just when his defences were down, she innocently asked the question he'd been dreading.

'It must have been marvellous growing up with all of this around you. Your family lived at the glassworks when you were a child?'

'No, when my parents' marriage broke up, my father left and lived at the glassworks. There's a cottage behind the barn.' His surgeon's coolness cut in suddenly. Each word was capable of wounding, but he knew exactly where and how to cut.

'And your mother lived nearby?'

'A little way along the coast. It was pretty remote. That's one of the reasons she left and came to London.'

His answers had the desired effect. There were no actual untruths there, but they didn't contain the words *lord* or *castle.* And Grace latched on to the London part of it, commenting that it must be nice to have his mother in the same city.

'Yes, it is.' Penn began to relax again. Crisis averted. 'So what have you been up to this week…?'

Grace had spent the whole week looking forward to meeting Penn on the train again. And as soon as he'd arrived, the slow pace of anticipation had turned into the rush of squeezing everything into these short hours with him.

She was a little embarrassed that she had nothing to give him apart from a cup of coffee, in return for the beautiful glass dolphin. But she'd been thinking a lot about what he'd said last week, wondering where *she* stood her ground and refused to compromise. Grace had come to the conclusion that it was here… These hours on the train were hers, and she wanted to spend them with Penn.

That felt like a risk. She'd ended up giving all the time she had to Jeremy, and he'd still done the sums and reckoned it wasn't enough.

Penn seemed so different, though. His account of a creative disagreement at the glassworks was making her smile, when she saw one of the guards working quickly along the aisle between the seats, speaking quietly to the passengers. She caught the word *doctor* and laid her hand on Penn's arm, quickly jerking it away again when she'd realised what she'd done. It had been the first time they'd purposely touched, although the cramped space under the table between the seats had occasioned a little frantic shuffling of feet and apologetic smiles.

He turned, and Grace heard the words again.

'Is there a doctor...?'

Penn's arm shot up, beckoning to the guard, who hurried towards them.

'I'm an orthopaedic surgeon, and my friend's a physiotherapist. Can we help?'

Friend… One new word to add to the pleasure of the journey, but that would have to be later, because it looked as if there was some urgency to the situation.

'Thank you.' The woman was clearly trying not to alarm anyone, but shot Penn a look of grateful relief. 'Someone's fallen and hurt themselves. We'd be grateful if you could help.'

Penn was already out of his seat and the guard pointed back in the direction she'd just come. 'They're three carriages down. You can't miss them. I'll gather your things and bring them down.'

Grace quickly showed the guard which of the bags in the overhead rack were theirs. 'Thanks. Don't let that break, will you…' She pointed to the glass dolphin that was still unwrapped on the table, shooting the guard a smile, and then hurried after Penn.

A path opened up in front of them, people moving out of their way. Maybe it was the fact that they must already know that there was some kind of medical emergency on the train. Maybe it was Penn's measured but purposeful air. Grace breathed a few thank-yous as they went, keeping up with his hurried trajectory.

At the end of the third carriage, there was someone lying in the aisle, one guard kneeling beside him and another keeping watch over the carriage. People had been cleared from the seats around them, and those seated further up were craning their necks to see what was going on. Penn reached into his pocket, then showed his identification.

'Mr McIntyre. Thank you for coming. The gentleman tripped and fell on the way back from the restaurant car, and he's hit his head. He's been unconscious for a few minutes and we put him in the recovery position. The on-board medical kit is right there…' He gestured towards a bag on one of the seats.

Perfect. Someone who knew what to do and could communicate the relevant details. And then move out of the way. The guard stepped back and Penn knelt down in the confined space. The man was young, about Grace's own age, and was lying on his side with a small pillow under his head.

'How long has he been unconscious?'

'I…don't know.' The guard looked around. 'Anyone…'

'Five minutes.' A voice came from one of the seats and a woman's face popped up from behind the headrest. 'I timed it.'

Good thinking. Grace wasn't sure she'd remember to look at her watch the next time she saw someone crash to the ground, but it was what Penn needed to know.

'Great, thanks.' Penn's attention was on the man on the floor, who seemed to be coming round now. 'Anyone know his name?'

There was silence, and Grace bent down, careful not to bump against Penn's arm as she felt for the inside pocket of the man's jacket. Her searching fingers found what she was looking for, and she withdrew his wallet, then opened it and pulled out a driver's licence.

'Thomas Stanford.'

'Thank you.' One brief flash of Penn's smiling blue eyes, before he turned his head again, and gently tried to rouse the man. 'Thomas… Thomas…'

No reaction. This wasn't looking good. Grace handed the wallet to the guard for safekeeping and Penn looked up at her again.

'Try him, please.'

Why? Grace could ask questions later. Penn's quiet assurance told her that he had his reasons.

'Thomas… Tom, open your eyes.'

The man's eyes fluttered open, and Grace bent a little further forward. 'That's right. Look at me.'

He seemed to be able to focus on her face, and Grace smiled. 'Is it Tom, or Thomas?'

'Tom…'

'Hi, Tom. I'm Grace. My friend's a doctor and you're in good hands.'

That word again. Penn had used it first, but she thought she saw his lips curve into a smile as she took his lead, cementing the relationship.

Tom was coming back to them, slowly but surely. Penn was busy, monitoring his pulse and checking for signs of injury to his head. Then he asked one of the guards to go and find something they could use as a cold-pack, and fetch a blanket if they had one. Tom's gaze moved to him, and Penn started to go through the checks for a concussion, holding up one finger and then three.

'My leg…' As Tom was becoming more and more aware, he began to move, clearly in pain. It was important to keep him as still as they could…

'Grace?' Penn must know that she'd been letting him take all the decisions, but he also knew there was no need to tell her what to do next.

She nodded, carefully examining Tom's legs, looking for any sign that he was bleeding. When she got to his knee, Tom cried out, starting to move again, and Penn tried to calm him and keep him still.

'I think it's his right knee. I can't really tell, but he

may have dislocated it when he fell. It seems to have reduced back into place spontaneously but the kneecap's slightly misaligned.'

'Okay, thanks.' Penn addressed the guard again. 'How long until the train can stop?'

'Twenty minutes, we're going to make an unscheduled stop at the next station. We've called ahead and the emergency services say that an ambulance will be waiting.'

Penn nodded. They were travelling through open countryside, and there would be no benefit in stopping the train here, where an ambulance would have difficulty getting to them. The quickest way to get Tom to hospital was to keep going until they reached the next town.

But there were so many unknowns. Had Tom tripped over and knocked himself out as everyone seemed to assume or was the fall the result of something else? A lucid interval, where someone regained consciousness and seemed to be recovering but then slipped back into unconsciousness, was unusual, but it happened. In this confined space, and without the ability to fully examine him, Grace's own assessment of Tom's knee was open to question, and Penn's decisions about what to do next were based on incomplete information.

But he didn't show any uncertainty. He was reassuring and gentle with Tom, checking for any signs of an underlying condition that could have caused the fall without alarming him. The two guards were following his quiet instructions to the letter, confident in his leadership.

He turned to her, speaking quietly. 'I'll keep monitoring Tom and you see what you can do to make his leg more comfortable before we have to move him. Agreed?'

A good leader communicated with those around them, particularly when working with an untested team. Although it felt as if three cups of coffee and a train ride had told each of them all they needed to know about the other. They both knew that it was likely Tom was concussed, and keeping him still and calm was important.

'Yes.' She flashed him a smile and Penn nodded, twisting back round to speak to their patient.

Grace sorted through the various shapes and sizes of bandage in the first aid bag, and sent one of the guards to procure newspapers, which could be rolled and flattened as makeshift splints. Tom cried out as she positioned and dressed the leg, but Penn was helping him to breathe through the pain, leaving her to do what she needed to do as quickly as possible.

The train began to slow as they approached the station. Announcements were made, reminding people that this was an unscheduled stop and asking them to make way for the ambulance crew. When Grace looked up, she saw a flash of yellow and green on the empty platform. Penn turned, giving her a relieved smile.

Penn McIntyre. It had hardly registered when the guard had looked up from his ID and mentioned his name. Her friend. As the ambulance crew boarded the train and Grace stood back to let them through, it hit her. She had a moment now to shiver with pleasure at the thought.

Penn was quickly bringing the ambulance crew up to speed and the guards moved to block passengers from this section of the train, addressing the few inevitable grumbles about the delay. Pain relief was quickly administered and then the difficult process of manoeuvring Tom onto a stretcher and off the train was considered.

Grace saw their bags sitting on one of the nearby seats, and picked them up, ready to follow while Penn helped the ambulance crew. Suddenly, she was bathed in the warmth of his blue eyes as he stepped back for a moment to give them more space to work.

'Don't you have people waiting for you at the other end? You could stay on the train.'

Tom didn't need her now, and there *were* people who depended on her waiting in Cornwall. But her cousin always stayed with Gran until Grace arrived and… She wouldn't mind waiting and Grace wanted to see this through.

'You're throwing me off the team?' She smiled up at him, and Penn gave her a sudden grin.

'Never…'

CHAPTER THREE

The ambulance crew was well practised at this, but a little help didn't go amiss when faced with getting a patient out of a tight spot. Penn helped to carry Tom off the train and to the waiting ambulance, feeling warmth spread through him as he glimpsed Grace getting off the train behind him, carrying their bags.

He shouldn't feel this. Shouldn't want her to change course in order to be with him, but she'd given him no choice. He could no more have thrown her off the team than flown in the air.

Penn turned his attention to giving the ambulance paramedic a full résumé of all he'd observed, then grasped Tom's hand in one more reassurance before he climbed out of the ambulance. Grace was sitting on one of the benches on the platform, her gaze fixed on the departures board.

'How long to wait until the next train?' He sat down beside her.

'Only half an hour, but it's already showing as delayed by ten minutes, because of the unscheduled stop. And it's a slower train, so we'll be arriving in Newquay at least an hour late.'

'Do you need to call someone?'

She nodded, took her phone from her bag and got to her feet as she dialled, wandering a little way along the platform, as if to separate him from the conversation she was about to have. The way that Penn separated her from everything else that was going on in his life, keeping the time he spent with Grace pristine and unsullied.

She ended the call, turning to walk back to him. 'My cousin's staying with Gran until I arrive. Apparently they've just started to watch a film on TV, so she says she'll get to see the end of it.'

'It's just you and your sister and cousins who care for your grandmother?'

She nodded, sitting down on the bench next to him. Grace was well named, always so precise and graceful in her movements. That might be explained by her training, but in truth it was unquantifiable. Balance, light and movement that even the finest glass couldn't represent, and which gave him the audacity to imagine a caress. The train had pulled away now, and in the still air, he could smell her scent, curling around him in an exquisite embrace.

'Yes, Mum was determined that she wanted to help, but she's not well enough to be able to commit to a definite time each week. Dad goes round quite a bit—he does all the gardening and jobs around the cottage, and Mum comes with him to visit when she can. My brother lives in America with his wife, so he videoconferences every week.'

'It's great that she has you, and that you're all so committed to her care.'

Grace shrugged. 'There was never really any question in our minds that we wanted to do it. Gran was there for all of us in different ways when we were growing up, and I guess what comes around goes around.'

Not always. But the idea seemed important to Grace. Penn stretched his legs out in front of him, looking up at the darkening sky. Just enjoying her presence.

'You can spill now. Why did you want me to speak to Tom?'

'It worked, didn't it?' He shot her a smile. Grace hadn't asked at the time. She'd just trusted him and done as he'd requested.

'Yes, but what made you think it would work?'

'I've seen unconscious patients respond to one voice and not another before. Different tones and types of voice reach different parts of the brain.' And Grace's voice… It seemed to be able to reach all of the pleasure centres of *his* brain.

'That makes sense.' Grace smirked at him. 'Mr Penn McIntyre.'

'I'm feeling at a disadvantage now. Since I only know your first name.'

She hesitated, and Penn wondered whether she'd resist this small step towards intimacy. Sitting here on the quiet platform, nothing to do and nowhere to go, felt suddenly very intimate.

'Grace Chapman.'

Penn couldn't resist a gratified smile. The exchanging of names was something he did every day, but this was special. Having to wait for each new detail made it all the more entrancing.

'Nice getting to know you, Grace Chapman.'

'You too, Penn McIntyre.'

* * *

It was well past ten o'clock when they arrived at Newquay, and the windows of the train had been streaked with rain for the last fifteen minutes of the journey. As they got off the train, the skies opened and they both ran for the shelter of the canopy above the platform.

'Where do you need to go?' Rules were one thing, but Penn wasn't about to leave her alone on a dark and wet night. 'I dropped my car off at the garage last week, and they said they'd leave it for me in the car park.'

Alarm registered on her face. And something that looked like proud independence. Which was generally a good thing in Penn's estimation, but could be taken too far sometimes.

'Thanks, but that's okay. Gran's village is only a couple of miles out of Newquay and I can easily get a taxi.'

Right then. Second names were okay, but getting into his car was stepping over the boundaries.

'I've got a drive ahead of me, so a detour isn't going to make any difference.' He pressed a little, and Grace shook her head, thought turning into motion as she stepped back.

'In that case, you'd better get going. I'll be okay, honestly.'

'I'll wait with you then, until the taxi gets here.' The least he could do was to see her safely on her way.

'No.' That single word and the determined set of her jaw, didn't brook any further argument.

The tantalisingly slow progress of their friendship had just come to a halt. They'd both decided to keep whatever happened between London and Newquay separate from the rest of their lives. If Grace had applied that rule a little too over-zealously for Penn's liking, he could hardly complain.

'Will I see you next week?'

She smiled suddenly. At least he still had that, and he should be grateful. 'Yes. Same time, same place?'

'I'll be there.'

It almost physically hurt to tear himself away. Leaving any woman alone in the darkness, when his car was right here, felt like flying in the face of his principles. But Grace…

Penn jogged towards his car, pretending to avoid the downpour, but in fact wanting to give her as little time as possible to slip away from his line of sight. There were three or four cars, just leaving their parking spaces and about to drive past where Grace was standing at the station entrance, and his could be any one of them. He slung his bag on the back seat and closed the car door.

He could see her, standing under the canopy still, silhouetted in the lights. She was already on her phone, looking away from him towards the main road. Penn sat still, a shadow in the darkness.

He waited for ten minutes, expecting that at any moment Grace would catch sight of him and march towards the car to tell him to leave. But then a taxi drew up outside, and he saw her run towards it, then bend down to speak to the driver briefly. Then she got in and the taxi executed a U-turn and drove back towards the main road.

Penn resisted the temptation to follow it. That was nothing but curiosity, and couldn't possibly be justified as concern for Grace's well-being. He made an effort not to look in the rearview mirror, to see which way the taxi would turn, and started the car. He had a weekend's worth of work and then another five days in London ahead of him before he'd see her again, and Penn was already missing her.

It had just been an offer of a lift. It had been dark and raining and maybe she should have taken Penn up on it. He'd walked away so quickly from her that it was impossible not to wonder whether he was angry. But Grace's first thought had been that this was a favour that would have to be returned. Jeremy's transactional view of relationships, again. Everything that was given had a price tag attached to it.

She'd got through the week without dwelling on it too much, but now, sitting alone on the train, it was all Grace could think about. It was possible that Penn had been delayed with a patient or his plans had changed—they had no way of contacting each other. It was also possible he'd been frustrated with her show of independence and decided to catch a different train. But there was still time…

Minutes had already ticked away, and she was down to counting seconds now. Then she'd have to stop hoping. Grace pressed her face against the glass, squinting along the platform towards the gates. He wouldn't be able to make it now. The last of the passengers were climbing hurriedly aboard.

Then she saw him. Slipping through the ticket barrier at the last moment, and running hard for the nearest carriage. Grace caught her breath. The doors closed and the train started to move, and she couldn't see at this angle whether or not Penn had been left behind on the platform.

She stayed in her seat, staring fixedly at the one that she'd hoped he'd be occupying by now. At least he'd been there and tried to catch the train. And maybe he'd know that she'd be in this seat every week from now on.

The connecting doors to the next carriage swished open and she jumped to her feet. Penn was looking a little breathless, but grinning broadly, and Grace couldn't conceal her delight.

'You *made* it.'

'Only just. I'm sorry to keep you waiting. I cut things a bit fine with my last patient this afternoon, and there were a few delays on the Underground as well.'

That didn't matter. Nothing mattered because he was here. The train swayed slightly as it began to pick up speed, and he reached out to steady her.

They were both off balance, and Penn grabbed one of the handrails, his other arm coiled around her waist. She felt the solid strength of his body against hers before she regained her footing. For two seconds, maybe three, she could have moved away but didn't. They were enough to cement the realisation that keeping Penn at arm's length wasn't as easy as she'd been telling herself.

'Sorry…' He was the first to apologise, and she felt herself blush.

'My fault.' Grace removed her hand from his shoulder, realising that her appreciation of his muscle tone was far from professional. She sat back down again, unable to resist watching Penn's smooth movement as he slung his bag into the overhead luggage rack.

Nice. Very nice. She wasn't entirely sure how she was going to meet his gaze now, though.

'I'm glad I did make it. I have a conundrum that I'd really value your opinion about.' He took his seat opposite her.

Thank you. His relaxed smile told Grace that even if he was aware of her embarrassment, he was ignoring it.

'Fire away…' Her voice sounded strangely normal, almost as if her heart wasn't thumping in her chest. 'Does it have to do with glass or surgery?'

'Neither. It's about physiotherapy. The patient I was seeing this afternoon has confronted me with a bit of an awkward situation, and I'd quite like to hear your professional view. Confidentially…'

'Of course.' Professional. Confidential. Two great words to remember when you were trying to regain your composure, and Penn was gentleman enough to use them.

'My patient is a young woman, who was referred to me for treatment at the private hospital where I work. I operated on her to repair a fracture in her forearm that had occurred in childhood and never healed properly. That all went extremely well, and I referred her on for physiotherapy to help her regain normal mobility in her wrist and elbow. She already had her own physiotherapist, a nice chap and very switched-on. I gave him a call then we exchanged a couple of emails and everything seemed to be going to plan.'

'And then it didn't?' So far Penn had described a perfect aftercare strategy.

'On Monday, my secretary took a call from her. She'd

had some kind of bust-up with her physiotherapist and she wanted an appointment to come and see me.'

Grace nodded. 'It happens. Different people prefer different approaches.'

'I called her back and there was a bit more to it than that. She'd had a nasty fall and cancelled the appointment she had the following day, because she was very bruised. When she emailed for another appointment, she got no reply, so she tried again and again got nothing back.'

'So… What? I'm confused. She was ghosted by her physiotherapist?'

'I'm not sure of the exact situation. She's not the kind of person to push things, so I called him to find out what was going on. He apologised, and said he's been ill recently and is having to take a break from work. He'd thought that he'd got back to everyone who'd contacted him.'

Grace frowned. 'Okay. That's unfortunate. I'm sorry he's not well, but it's really important to have some mechanism in place that will support your patients in these circumstances.'

'My thoughts exactly. So my difficulty is… I asked my patient if she'd be able to pop in today to see me for a chat, and she's adamant that she doesn't want another physiotherapist. I think she's got it into her head that she did something wrong, and she asked me if I could give her some exercises that she can do on her own.'

'You know as well as I do that physiotherapy isn't just a matter of giving someone a few exercises. You said she'd had a nasty fall. How badly did she hurt herself?'

'Badly. She fell a few feet onto concrete and landed

on her right side. She has a bruised shoulder and ribs and deep-tissue bruises on her hip. I operated on her left arm, and there's no sign of any damage there.'

Grace wasn't entirely sure how she could help with this. 'I can't add anything to what you already know in clinical terms, Penn. She needs therapy. You can't change your recommendations just because a patient doesn't like them very much, however understandable their attitude.'

He leaned back in his seat, pursing his lips. 'That's just the thing. I'm willing to compromise with her to get the best outcomes possible, but I also feel that pushing her a bit is the right thing to do. I know where to draw that line with surgery, but rehab's not my specialty.'

'Well, if it were me… First, I think the fall must have been very traumatic for her. You said that she'd been doing well, and suddenly she's hurt again and the achievements she's made must seem very fragile. She needs some solid encouragement right now, to boost her confidence.'

Penn nodded. 'And second?'

'Physiotherapy is a holistic approach that's centred around active engagement and trust. Your patient's embarked on that process with someone and then been let down, and if she doesn't want to start all over again with another physiotherapist then I can understand that.'

'What would your approach be, then?' His brow creased in thought.

The everyday process of swapping thoughts and talking through a way of encouraging someone, was so much more thrilling than usual. If it wasn't the train itself, then

Penn's blue eyes and the way his forehead creased when he was thinking would have to take the blame.

'I'd slow things down on the treatment front, just temporarily, and concentrate on how she's feeling. Give her some advice on how to maintain her progress in the short term and encourage her to talk through how she feels about what happened and how it's affected her emotionally. She may well come up with a longer term solution herself.'

'You're telling me that I should just support her, while she finds her own way forward?'

'My job's very different from yours. I wouldn't put a scalpel into a patient's hand.' Grace's joke provoked a smile in return.

'That's a relief. And you've given me something to think about. Thank you.'

She should let this go now. Penn would do the right thing and advise his patient well. But Grace knew what it was like to have your trust shattered, and helping Penn's patient regain hers felt like an acknowledgement that such a thing was possible. That she might be able to trust again too.

'If you want… I mean, if it's appropriate…' The words dried in her throat.

'If what's appropriate?' He seemed lost in thought now, but his eyes flashed a brilliant blue as he looked up at her.

'I'd be happy to meet her, just for an informal chat. If you think I could be of any help.' Grace shrugged, ready to hear him say that it wasn't a good idea. When she'd refused a lift from him, she'd already made it clear that their relationship should stay on the train. She regretted that now, but Penn could be forgiven for thinking that it was a lot simpler to just take her at her word.

He hesitated. 'I don't want to put you to any trouble…'

No. Of course not. It had been a bad idea.

'…which is not to say I wouldn't really appreciate your input. I can ask her how she feels about it, because I think it would be very valuable for her. As long as you're sure you can spare the time.'

This really wasn't about time. It was about whether Grace could trust herself—trust Penn—enough to step over the boundaries they'd made for their relationship. But there was a patient involved, and Grace believed that she could help. That was the one absolute in a whole sea of uncertainties.

'I'm sure.' She took her phone from her bag. 'I suppose we'd better exchange numbers, so you can call me.'

'I was thinking I'd ask you for your number anyway, so I could let you know if I couldn't make the train. This afternoon was too close for comfort.'

He knew. Penn knew she'd been waiting for him, and he wouldn't let that happen again. Grace felt a frisson of excitement as they exchanged numbers—one more everyday thing that was thrilling when she did it with Penn.

'Enough of work.' He laid his phone back down on the table. 'I'm going to insist that you let me buy the coffee this time, and you can give me the lowdown on what's been going on with you this week…'

CHAPTER FOUR

THE SLOW, EXCRUCIATINGLY hesitant move from getting-to-know-you to something more. It was killing him, but Penn couldn't go any faster, because of the ball and chain around his ankle. The better he got to know Grace, the more glaringly obvious it became that he wasn't telling her the whole truth about himself. Sooner or later, he was going to have to admit to the title and the castle, and he dreaded her reaction.

Maybe he should just trust her and tell her before it got to be an issue. But that was challenging, and it was easy to put it onto the back burner because there were so many other things clamouring for his attention.

He called his patient April, suggesting the way forward that he'd agreed with Grace. There was a short silence on the other end of the line.

'If I talk to someone then I'll be making a commitment, won't I?' April didn't sound all that happy at the prospect.

'No, you'll be talking to someone and asking whatever questions you want to ask, so that you can take control of the next stage of your recovery.'

Penn had always given his patients as many choices

as possible, but when it came down to it, he *was* the one holding the scalpel. He had to just trust Grace that this different approach was more appropriate for April's rehab.

'Okay. Sounds good, Mr M. Tell me where and when.' April's abrupt turnaround was a surprise, but he couldn't help smiling over having proved Grace right.

'I'll check on the best time and get back to you. When are you free?'

'I can make anytime…'

Penn reminded April about the need to keep doing her exercises while they worked on finding a way forward, and received a more enthusiastic response than he had the last time. Then he allowed himself the pleasure of calling Grace. The phone rang for a while before she answered, sounding a little breathless.

'Have I called at a bad time?'

'No. Another couple of minutes, when my next patient arrives, and it will be, though.'

Two minutes was fine. Glass half full.

'I'll make it quick, then. If you're still up for it, then April would like to discuss things with you.'

'Who? Oh—you mean your anonymous patient from the train.' Grace paused and he heard the sound of a keyboard. 'Okay, I've got my diary. How does Wednesday at five sound? I have a couple of patients later on in the evening, but I'll be free until six thirty.'

Which meant that Penn wouldn't be able to ask casually whether she could catch a bite to eat with him afterwards. Too bad. He supposed that he could have offered to meet up when she'd finished for the evening—everyone had to eat—but this week was shaping up to be busy, and he had a whole folder full of emails to write in connection with the glassworks as well.

'That's great, thank you. I'll be coming with her if that's okay.'

There was a short silence. 'Is there something you haven't told me, Penn? She's a friend of yours?'

It wasn't an unreasonable conclusion to come to. Private patients might expect their surgeons to have a little more time for emotional support, but this was above and beyond the call of duty. Grace was right to ask because if that was a factor in the equation, she needed to know about it.

'No, April's a patient. My thinking is more along the lines of *you* being a friend and wanting to learn a little about your approach.' Maybe he could snatch a few moments alone with Grace as well, to talk with her.

He heard her laugh. 'That's fine, knock yourself out. It'll be a lot better if she comes along with someone that she trusts and who can ask a few pertinent questions.'

'I'll put my mind to some difficult ones. What's the address?'

Grace rattled out the address and he snatched up a pencil, scribbling it down. They'd been talking for one minute. That meant that the second was still up for grabs.

'Thanks. I really appreciate this. Even if I do feel a little as if I've just handed over my scalpel to April.'

'Just this once, eh? We can't have you making a habit of it.'

'My thoughts exactly.' Penn wondered whether they were talking about patients or off-the-train meetings.

Grace laughed again. 'Well, I'll look forward to

seeing you… Oh, hold on… I'll be with you in a moment, Terry.'

Her next patient had obviously arrived and Penn turned the corners of his mouth down. He'd thought he still had thirty seconds…

'I'll let you go. See you on Wednesday at five.'

'Great. Thanks.' Grace ended the call, and Penn supposed she'd turned that shining smile of hers onto her patient now. He'd be much mistaken if she hadn't, and wondered whether the anonymous Terry was appreciating it as much as he should.

Two days. And in the meantime, he had patients to see too. Penn picked up the phone, calling his secretary to ask if Mrs Phillips had arrived yet.

Mia had great taste. But the pleasure that Grace would normally have felt when her colleague mentioned that she *loved* her blouse, and that the red and yellow ochres complemented her colouring perfectly, was tempered today by the thought that she'd taken every blouse she owned from the wardrobe and chosen carefully. If Penn noticed that she'd dressed up a little, then red and yellow ochre wasn't going to be a good look.

Trousers and soft trainers would dress it down again. And maybe she wouldn't be hunting in her bag for the lipstick she'd thrown in at the last moment before leaving home this morning.

At ten to five, her phone buzzed. Just a one-word text.

Coffee?

Grace supposed that she could accept that, since she was doing Penn a favour in chatting with April, and also missing her evening break. She texted back a thank-you and suggested that the coffeehouse next door to the clinic was the best in the area.

She retreated to her consulting room, gathered up the papers on her desk and then shoved them into the drawer. Grace was just wondering whether the plants looked a little as if they needed watering, when Penn appeared in the doorway. He was wearing a dark blue suit—immaculate as usual—and his customary grin, which always came with the suggestion that underneath the formality, he was a guy who liked nothing better than the open sky and the sunshine.

'Hello. This is nice… Plenty of light.' He scanned the consulting room, his gaze seeming to take in the large curved topped windows, the plants and the prints on the wall.

'We have the whole of the top floor here, so there's plenty of room to spread out a bit.' And bring a little of their own personalities into their consulting rooms. The way that Penn was looking around, obviously liking what he saw, was more gratifying than it ought to have been.

He nodded, turning to a young dark-haired woman who seemed intent on making herself inconspicuous at the moment. 'This is April Graham. April, this is Grace Chapman.'

'Hi. We got coffee.' April thrust a paper cup into Grace's hands and stepped back again, almost bumping into Penn. She was a whole head shorter than Grace, and her dark jeans and T-shirt emphasised her slim frame.

'Thanks. I could do with one right now.' Grace sat down in her own chair, swivelling it round to face the two visitors' chairs that were placed alongside her desk. April was hovering nervously.

'Come and sit down.' She pointed to the nearest seat, and April slipped into it. Either she was very shy, or she really didn't want to be here. Penn was being no help at all, striding over to the other side of the room and inspecting an ergonomic kneeling chair that was propped up against the wall.

'Coffee…!' Grace caught his attention, tapping her finger on the side of one of the remaining cups in the cardboard carrier, which April had slid onto her desk.

'Ah. Yes, thanks. Do these really help?'

'It's all about choosing the right chair for you. Some people find them very comfortable.' Penn must know that as well as she did.

'Hmm. What do you think, April?'

April smiled suddenly. 'We're not here to look at chairs, Mr M.'

Questions answered. April was shy, and Penn was just breaking the ice a little. Grace leaned back in her own chair. 'What do you do for a living, April?'

'Computer programmer. Mr M's been telling me that I should get a chair that helps me move around a bit. I spend a lot of time in front of a screen.'

'That's good advice. The right chair will make a difference to your shoulders as well as your back, as it helps you sit a little straighter.'

April straightened her back a little, not seeming to notice that she was doing so. She was anxious to please and clearly a little vulnerable, despite her attempts to convince Penn that she could do without any more help. Grace reached for her cup and took a sip.

'I hear you've had a pretty hard time recently. An operation on your arm and then a bad fall.'

April flushed. 'It wasn't so bad…'

'It's hard, though. Just when you're working to get better.'

April grimaced, giving a small nod.

'Can you tell me a little about how you fell?'

April hesitated. 'I thought you'd tell me what you could do to help.'

Grace glanced up at Penn, who was quiet now, leaning against the deep windowsill, sipping his coffee. His almost imperceptible nod told her that he was happy with the way things were going and wasn't going to interrupt.

'Yes, that's the aim. But first of all, I need to know what you feel you might need some help with…'

April had told Grace the whole story, including quite a few details that she'd left out when Penn had first heard it. Grace had been right—April needed to get this out of her system first, so that she could start to engage with a treatment plan again.

When April had asked whether Grace could see her for physiotherapy, she'd shaken her head. 'I'd really like to, but I want to suggest something else to you that I think might be better.'

'Okay.' April looked at her queryingly.

Penn was all ears as well. This hadn't been the intended outcome of this evening's chat, but he'd assumed that Grace wouldn't say no if she was asked to take April on as a patient.

'I'd like you to see my colleague Mia. She and I work together quite a bit, and I think that her particular approach might suit you. And if Mia's not in the clinic and you need some advice, then I'll have access to your notes, so you can always speak to me.'

Genius. Grace was giving April a framework of more than one person that she could come to. After she'd been let down, it was exactly what she needed to help build her confidence.

April nodded. 'Yeah. That actually sounds great.'

'Okay.' Grace reached forward across her empty desk, took two mini presentation folders from a bundle of information materials on the windowsill, and handed one to Penn and the other to April. 'There's information about all of our therapists in there, along with some blurbs about how we work and so on. Have a read through it and talk it over…'

April opened the folder, and then closed it again. 'I think I'm good with making the appointment right now.'

'Why don't you have a word with Mr M about it first? See what he thinks…' A slight smile hovered around Grace's lips as she glanced at him.

Penn smirked back, wondering if it would be construed as flirting if he responded by calling her *Ms C*. 'If you're both happy with the arrangement, then I think it's an excellent way forward. I'll email you through an information release form, April, and once you've signed it, I'll get your notes and X-rays sent over.'

Grace nodded. 'Good. Our receptionist's not here at the moment, but you can give her a call between nine and five on weekdays and make the appointment. I'll speak with Mia in the morning and let her know what's going on and we'll take it from there…'

Penn had mentioned that there was *another matter* that he needed to speak to Grace about, and then walked April down to the front door of the clinic. His first glimpse of her on the train always made him smile, and even this short parting was enough to remind him that she really was more beautiful every time he saw her. That instinctive attraction was now accompanied by trust and professional respect.

'What does April really think? Is she happy with everything or was she just being nice?' Grace had guessed that he'd taken the opportunity of walking April to the door to ask how she felt about the decisions she'd made.

'I'm no longer the first call she makes when she has a problem. She's found someone else.' Penn chuckled. 'For which I'm profoundly grateful, by the way.'

'That's fine with me. She can call me anytime she wants. I just don't want you to think that I took advantage of the situation to pick up a new patient. I didn't expect April to make a decision on the spot.'

'I'm not thinking anything—other than this is the right thing for my patient, and so I'm happy with it.'

'Okay. Was that the other matter?'

Penn sat down in the seat opposite her. 'I can't make the train on Friday. I'm scheduled for a complex reconstruction surgery.'

She nodded, giving him a brittle smile. 'And it'll take a while.'

'May well do.'

'Never mind. I'll see you next week maybe?'

Did she care? Was she as disappointed as Penn was that they wouldn't have the time together that was starting to become as essential to him as breathing? It was difficult to tell. Grace's face had suddenly become impassive.

'I'm sorry. I've started looking forward to our train journeys together.' Perhaps if he gave a little, then Grace would give a little back.

'You shouldn't be sorry…' She spoke quickly, laying her hand on his arm and then thinking better of the gesture and moving away from him again. 'You should never apologise because you can't be somewhere. You have responsibilities and you can't be in two places at once.'

She seemed so earnest all of a sudden. Grace had said something about a partner who resented her being away from home so much, and it seemed as if he'd touched on a sore spot for her. *Very* sore, if the look on her face was anything to go by.

'By *sorry* I meant that I regret that I won't be seeing you, because I wanted to.' Maybe that was giving away a little too much, but he couldn't bear Grace's sudden dismay.

Then she smiled. 'I regret it too. I've been enjoying our train journeys together.'

In which case, he could ask what he wanted to ask. 'But since next Monday's a bank holiday… If you're not working or looking after your grandmother, I was wondering whether you'd like to visit the glassworks. We're running our first open day.'

She thought for a moment.

This was more excruciating than being fifteen and asking someone out on a date. So many more unknown factors. So much more that could go wrong. But it was a crucial first step towards letting Grace see the side of his life that he'd kept secret.

'That would be really interesting. Yes, I'd like to come. Will you text me through some directions?'

'That's great. It starts at ten, but you can drop in at any time. Or I can pick you up?' Penn remembered the last time he'd offered her a lift and wondered if he'd gone a little bit too far.

'Thanks. I may take you up on that. We'll arrange a time at the weekend?'

'Yes, let's do that.' Penn got to his feet. 'I'll look forward to seeing you then.'

'Me too.'

Her windows overlooked the street, and if he punched the air and ran as soon as he got to the front door of the clinic, Grace might see him. He'd wait until he got to the corner…

CHAPTER FIVE

'WHAT DO YOU wear for an open day at a glassworks?' It was a knotty problem, and so Grace decided to go to the one person who was sure to know. Mia always dressed appropriately.

'Anything. Apart from sequins.'

Grace frowned. 'This is a serious question, Mia.'

'And it's a serious answer. I wore an antique top with sequins to a posh barbecue once. Sequins used to be made of metal and they actually get slightly warm if you stand too close to any source of heat. I imagine that would be something to take into account if you're going to be around a furnace.'

'Okay, gotcha. I won't ask to borrow your sequinned top.'

'I've got a nice summery one made out of broderie anglaise. The holes aren't too revealing and it goes with anything—you can dress it down with shorts or jeans, or up with a skirt. I'll bring it in tomorrow and you can try it on if you like.'

'Would you mind?'

'No, course not.' Mia grinned. 'I have more clothes than I can wear anyway, and you should get out more.'

'Because I sit around doing nothing, most of the time?' Grace joked. Mia was one of the few friends who seemed to realise that her time with Gran wasn't just a weekend break, but actually involved quite a lot of hard work.

Mia wrinkled her nose. 'Because you don't. Everyone needs some time for themselves.'

The top was duly tried on and loved, and Grace stowed it away carefully in her weekend bag. The five-hour journey down to Cornwall seemed very long without Penn, but she had the bank holiday Monday to look forward to. She stayed with Gran on Sunday night, and her cousin arrived bright and early as agreed, so that Grace could catch the early-morning bus into Newquay to meet Penn.

She was glad she'd decided to dress the top down, with cargo shorts and flat leather sandals. It was the first time she'd seen Penn out of a suit and…

Oh! Well-worn jeans and a pair of green baseball shoes. A green T-shirt, which showed off a pair of strong tanned arms. He was leaning against a shiny black SUV in the station car park, his face tipped up towards a cloudless sky, his blonde hair ruffled and shining in the breeze. There were no words for this feeling, just a sudden constriction in her throat that told Grace that this was just about as good as any man could get.

'Hi. How was your weekend?' He turned to her, smiling. Grace began to feel a little dizzy.

'Good. Yours?'

'Busy. I made the mistake of thinking that an open day was just a matter of turning up and opening our doors, but apparently there's a lot more to it than that. You have to have T-shirts…' He gestured towards the back seat of the car, where there were two boxes labelled with the name of a local printer.

'You've got T-shirts? Let me see…'

He opened the passenger door and Grace climbed into the car, catching the scent of leather seats. Penn got into the driver's seat, and reached back to open one of the boxes. Taking out a plastic-wrapped T-shirt, he handed it to her, and then started the engine.

'Nice logo.' As they drove out of Newquay, Grace was inspecting the printed logo on the back of the shirt. The design had the same curved, almost molten quality as the glass dolphin that now sat in pride of place on her mantelpiece at home.

'Yeah, the old one was becoming outmoded, so we decided to have something new. Everyone produced a design…apart from me, of course, because I'm no good at anything like that… And there was a vote and a prize for the winner. I think they've turned out well.'

'They're great. So along with keeping the place running, you've rebranded everything?'

He laughed, turning onto the main road that led out of Newquay. 'It was rather more evolving than rebranding. We had a load of boxes and carrier bags with the old design on them, and we used those up first. What we do now is have a plain box with the name of the glassworks on it, and we add a sticker that gives the name of the particular craftsperson who's made the piece. Change in emphasis.'

'So you're no longer the figurehead?'

There was something about the word *figurehead*

that Penn seemed not to like, as he pulled the corners of his mouth down momentarily. He was such a natural leader and it was a shame he didn't seem to want to acknowledge it.

'Times change. My father came to Cornwall from Scotland and set the glassworks up from scratch. He loved Cornwall, and many of his glass designs were influenced by what he saw around him, but it was all very much a product of his own vision. We can't keep trading on his reputation, though. We have to move forward and create something new.'

'Your mother isn't interested in the glassworks?'

'No, it's not really her thing. The divorce was partly because my father reckoned that making glass was a far better use of his time than being a husband. After they split up, she never set foot in the place and now that she's moved to London she has nothing to do with it.'

That choice. Running a glassworks or being a husband. Penn had taken on a lot, and Grace wondered whether that was a choice for him as well. Maybe it was a choice for her too, that she hadn't really acknowledged. Being busy was one very good reason not to have to think about the horrors of dipping her toes back into the dating pool.

They were on the main road, heading south, and Grace realised that she had no clue where they were going.

'Where *is* the glassworks exactly?'

'It's a few miles outside Truro.'

'And you came all this way just for some T-shirts?' Grace hadn't realised that they'd be going so far.

'T-shirts are important. And it would have taken you ages on the bus.'

* * *

The glassworks looked better than it did in the picture on Penn's phone. A cloudless blue sky didn't hurt, and nor did the sweep of the hills. They'd driven along a one-track road with lay-bys dotted along the way for cars to pass each other, then into a wide valley, where a group of low-lying buildings nestled together. Penn drew up next to the front entrance, waving a hello to a couple of people who were crossing the parking area.

'This is lovely.' The slate roofs and stone walls, some covered with moss and climbing plants, were a mixture of old and new but seemed entirely at home together. Even the glass fascia covering one side of the building seemed to reflect the colours of the surrounding countryside.

'The site was derelict when my father came here. Just an old barn, which now houses the shop and the office suite. There are a couple of cottages at the back, but the glassworks itself is new.' He beckoned for her to follow him, walking around the side of the barn. The buildings at the back were arranged around a paved garden area that was the centre of early-morning activity, chairs and tables being set up around a large awning, which sheltered an empty food display unit.

'One of the local tea shops is providing catering. We'll be having glass-blowing demonstrations throughout the day in the workshop, and there's a local potter coming to do some hands-on demonstrations for the kids—she'll be in the barn, out of the way of the furnaces.'

'And that's where you stay, when you're here?' Grace

pointed to the two cottages, which stood at a slight angle to the paved area, to afford some privacy.

'Yep, the one on the left. We use the other one for storage. My kitchen's been co-opted for catering purposes for the day.' He waved to the two women who had just appeared at the front door, carrying trays of sandwiches and cakes, and one of them called back a greeting as they navigated their way past the exuberant summer growth in the small front garden.

'I can't wait to see glass being made.'

'That's something special. I'm just hoping that people will come. We won't be starting with the demonstrations until eleven, so perhaps you'd like to see a little more of what we make in the meantime? We've set aside some space in the shop to show off a few of our larger, exhibition pieces.'

'I'd love to. Lead on…'

The floor-to-ceiling glazing in the shop filled the area with light, and the exposed roof beams gave a feeling of space. Several glass sculptures stood on display to the left of the entrance, and on the right shelves were stacked with smaller pieces that were for sale. A young dark-haired woman sitting in the far corner jumped to her feet when they entered.

'It's okay, Em, we're not customers.' Penn grinned at her. 'This is my friend Grace. Grace, this is Emma.'

'Hi, Grace. Can I show you around?' Emma's broad Cornish accent and her lively smile made Grace feel instantly at home.

'I don't want to take up too much of your time…' Grace hesitated, looking up at Penn. Maybe he had a different task in mind for Emma.

'That's okay. I'm an ambassador.' Emma flashed a smile in Penn's direction.

'But you'll take people's money if they insist.'

Emma rolled her eyes. 'Of course I will. But this is a no pressure environment.'

'Yeah, okay.' Penn chuckled. 'Emma's been reading up on this.'

Clearly Penn's guidance had come into play somewhere as well. Emma's ownership of her job was exactly in line with what he'd spoken about when he'd talked about the changes he was making here.

'Well, if you have the time, I'd love to take a tour.' Grace didn't want to discourage Emma.

'Right then. If you don't mind, I'll go and get the T-shirts and hand them around.' Penn grinned at them both.

'No problem. There's lots to see.' Emma beamed back at him.

'What colour do you want, Em? Blue, green or pink?'

It was obviously a rhetorical question, because Emma was wearing a plain pink T-shirt, her hair caught up in matching pink clips. She gave a mock sigh. 'Oh, I don't know. Whatever you think…' Emma beckoned to Grace to follow her on the first leg of her ambassadorial tour, and Penn retreated, laughing.

The tour was actually very interesting. Emma's knowledge about glassmaking techniques made it clear that she'd spent time in the workshop, watching the glassmakers, and she and Grace swapped opinions about the pieces they liked the best.

'The ones over by the window are lovely.' Grace wandered over to the clear glass bowls, alive with sunlight.

'Yes, I like them too. If you get them at the right angle, you sometimes see rainbows.' Emma held one of the bowls up to the window, turning it in her hands before passing it to Grace.

A movement outside distracted her. Penn was standing by the open back door of his car, obviously sharing a joke with two other men. One of them reached into the car and pulled out two of the T-shirts, one green and the other dark blue. The men seemed to be comparing the colours, and the blue was handed to Penn while another green one was retrieved from the box in the car.

Good choice. Blue would go with his eyes. Then one of the men pulled his own shirt off to don the new one, and Penn and the other man followed suit.

It was an unselfconscious, natural moment, warmed by the sun and prompted by the idea that no one was around to stare at them. But Grace was staring. Penn's suntan reached right across his shoulders and back, and when he raised his arms to take off his T-shirt, Grace could see the movement of muscle beneath the skin.

She wrenched her gaze away from him, glancing at Emma. She was staring too, although it appeared that neither of them was going to admit to it. The men were still talking together, but all that Grace could see was Penn's smooth, powerful movement as he'd pulled off his T-shirt.

'You wouldn't think it, would you? He's so down to earth…' Emma murmured, almost to herself.

'Wouldn't think what?' Grace fixed her gaze on the bowl in her hands.

'You know. The thing about being a lord. Having a castle.'

Penn? Grace froze, wondering how to ask without making it obvious that she didn't have a clue what Emma was talking about.

'He's a good boss though?'

'Yeah, he's a great boss. Old Mr McIntyre was really nice, but you had to do things his way. Penn asks us what we think.'

'And he inherited his title from his father?' Maybe it was in name only, and the castle was a few tumbled stones on an acre of land in Scotland. A girl could hope…

Because the alternative was beyond imagining. She and Penn were becoming friends, and he accepted that she didn't have much time to spare, because he was busy too. Grace had even been falling prey to thoughts that maybe—just maybe—something more than friends might be possible, although she wasn't sure how that would work in practice. But if Penn really was a lord and had an actual castle, then he must already have all the things he could ever want. She'd be back in the situation she'd been in with Jeremy, trying to make up for all of the things that she couldn't give and feeling backed into a corner by his demands on her.

'No, not his father. His mother.' Emma frowned. 'I'm not sure how that works. I thought it was fathers and sons. Anyway, he's got the castle to prove it. Even if he never talks about it.'

'No, he doesn't, does he? I wouldn't stop talking about it if I had a castle.' Grace shamelessly fished for more information.

'No, me neither. Especially one that big. We went

there on a school trip when I was little and it was amazing. Have you been?'

'No, it's never really come up. We're both pretty busy.'

Emma nodded sagely. 'Yes, it's a lot of work here. You won't tell him I said about it, will you…'

Maybe some of Grace's horror had seeped through and shown on her face. Emma seemed suddenly uncomfortable.

'No, of course not. It's our secret. I know he doesn't much like talking about it.' She could say that without any qualms, because Penn had carefully neglected to even mention it. She hadn't known him all that long, but she'd told him things that she never talked about to anyone and she'd thought that Penn had done the same.

'Yeah. Thanks.' Emma looked up as the glass door swung open at the other end of the shop.

'I hope you don't mind pink…' Penn was grinning, holding a pink T-shirt.

'I'll manage.' Emma shot Grace a smile. 'I'll just go and put it on…'

Penn handed over the T-shirt and Emma disappeared through a door behind the cash register. He sauntered over to her, and all that Grace could think was that his clear blue eyes weren't really windows to his soul after all.

'What do you think?'

'The glass is lovely.' The smile on her face felt as if it was going to crack and shatter into a thousand pieces any moment now.

'I'm glad you like it. We have a lot of very talented people here.' He paused for a moment, looking at her.

Maybe the cracks really were there and beginning to show. 'Everything all right?'

'Yes, fine. Emma's really very knowledgeable and the glass is beautiful.'

Penn nodded. 'If you've seen enough, I've got to go round and give out some more shirts—would you like to come and meet a few more people?'

'Later perhaps. Emma hasn't finished her tour yet, so I'd like to stay here…'

'Okay.' He gave her another questioning look, but Grace refused to respond. 'I'll be back in time to give you a tour of the workshop, before the demonstration officially starts.'

'That's great.'

Grace watched him walk away. She could ignore this, put on a smile and get through the day…

Just the thought of it told her that she couldn't. She'd hardly been able to get through a two-minute conversation without Penn noticing that there was something wrong. Maybe he thought that a castle was an unimportant detail in his life, but for Grace, it changed everything. There was no balance in their relationship any more. Penn wasn't the hard-working surgeon who was struggling to keep his father's glassworks afloat in his spare time. He was a man who had the kind of power that she couldn't imagine. The kind of power that Jeremy would have relished and would have made sure that Grace took notice of.

Penn already had enough power over her. She'd already missed him during the week, and felt devastated when she'd thought he wasn't going to make the train. Already thought about him in the quiet moments before she went to sleep every night. She had to stop this and stop it now.

Before she had time to cry at the thought, Grace slipped through the glass doors of the shop. She wouldn't be missed. Emma would probably think she'd gone somewhere with Penn. And Penn was out of sight now. Walking across the deserted car park, she made for the shelter of the hedgerows on either side of the narrow access road.

CHAPTER SIX

SOMETHING WAS WRONG. Grace had given him the kind of look you'd give your worst nightmare when he entered the shop, and the insincere smile she'd quickly replaced it with was even more chilling.

He'd wondered whether Emma had overdone it a bit in her role as ambassadorial sales representative, but Emma was a lot more sensible than that and Grace had been determined to stay in the shop and finish the tour. It occurred to him that someone might have said something to her about his title, but Penn dismissed the thought as both unlikely and slightly paranoid. Everyone here knew about it, but they were a little more interested in his father's legacy than his mother's.

His determination to pursue the friendship meant that Grace would have to know sooner or later. But the plan had been to show her the things that really mattered to him and then tell her himself.

He walked over to the workshop and handed out a few more shirts, before putting the box down so that everyone could just help themselves. Something was wrong, and he couldn't stop his head from swimming with possibilities until he found out what. Penn made his way back to the shop, forcing himself to smile before he walked in.

Emma was sitting alone at the cash desk.

'Hey, Em, have you seen Grace?'

'No, she wasn't here when I got back. I thought she was with you. Maybe she's gone over to the workshop?'

'No, I've just come from there.' Penn wondered whether Grace had gone through to the offices, but couldn't think of a reason why she would have done so. 'She wasn't upset about anything, was she?'

Emma thought for a moment. 'No, she was fine. She really loved those glass bowls by the window.'

Penn waited, sensing from Emma's frown that there was more.

'I may have said the wrong thing, though. Not on purpose…'

A lump started to block Penn's throat.

'We were just chatting, and I said that you were really down to earth, even though you're a lord…' Emma twisted her face in an agony of embarrassment.

He couldn't bring himself to chide Emma—this wasn't her fault. Penn shrugged, flashing her a smile.

'I can't imagine why that would have upset her. And thanks for the compliment.'

'Really?' Emma didn't look entirely convinced.

'Yeah, really. Down to earth is good. I'll go and find Grace. Give me a call if you need anything, eh?'

'Will do. If she comes back, I'll tell her you're looking for her…'

Grace knew. All that Penn could think about were the childish jibes, aimed at the posh kid with the unusual name. The people who'd seen only his title, and treated him as if he'd never had to work for anything in his life. The women who'd seen only the castle, and not the man he wanted to be.

Just when he'd thought he'd found his place in life. He'd left the castle behind, and worked hard to gain the respect of his colleagues, his patients and the people here. Penn's growing confidence had allowed him to speak to a beautiful woman, sitting opposite him on the train, and it hurt more than even he'd expected to think that he might have been mistaken when he felt that Grace saw him for who he really was.

He walked through to the office suite that occupied the other half of the barn, looking through each of the open doorways, and climbed the stairs to his own office on the first floor. His father had created this space up in the old hayloft, and it afforded privacy and also the ability to see everything that was happening in the complex of buildings if you opened the glass door that led out onto a narrow balcony. When Penn was a child, he'd worked out where he'd be hidden from his father's gaze and the shouted instructions from above.

But Grace had no such expertise. She didn't know that if you wanted to traverse the road that led to the glassworks without being seen, you had to walk on the other side of the hedge. Penn thought he saw a trace of anger in her determined gait.

Rage made him suddenly catch his breath. This wasn't fair, and it couldn't be happening… Plainly it was, but this time, Penn wasn't going to retreat from it without putting up a fight. He marched downstairs and made for his car, for once ignoring the other claims on his attention. They could wait.

She was still walking, and when his car approached her from behind, she had a more distinct air of anger about her. Fair enough. Penn was angry too. She heard the engine behind her and turned, ready to step back to let the car pass. Penn wound down the window.

'Grace!'

'I'm going now.'

That was something. She clearly wasn't going to bother with explanations or excuses, so he wouldn't have to work through those before they got down to her real reasons for leaving.

'If you want to go anywhere, it's three miles to the nearest bus stop. At least let me take you.'

'I'm fine. Go back. You've got things to do.' She'd turned and started walking again, throwing the words over her shoulder.

If she'd thought about it, then she'd have realised that turning the car in the narrow lane was going to be tricky. Not that Penn had any intention of doing so until he had an explanation. He edged the car forward, keeping up with her.

'I saw Emma. She said that she told you...' Penn couldn't quite bring himself to say the words *lord* or *castle*, although he knew that they were at the heart of this.

Grace stopped suddenly and turned. 'It's *not* Emma's fault.'

'Of course it isn't. It's mine...'

'Too right it is. When exactly were you going to mention that you're a lord and that you live in a castle? Did you imagine that I wasn't going to find out?'

'I don't *live* in the castle. I stay at the glassworks when I'm in Cornwall.' Penn bit his tongue. He was splitting hairs, because he did legally own the castle, and he had an apartment there even if he seldom used it.

Grace folded her arms, glaring at him. 'And that makes all the difference, does it? And before you say that I haven't told you where I live, that's because there's an unspoken assumption that it's somewhere *ordinary*. A castle isn't ordinary and it's something to mention.'

Penn wondered if getting out of the car would give Grace the opportunity to turn and walk away from him again. But she'd obviously decided to stand her ground, so he risked it.

'Why don't you just *listen* to what I have to say before you judge...?' He broke off as another car came down the lane, in the direction of the glassworks. 'Stay there.'

He got back into the car, then backed into a lay-by so that it could get past. Grace appeared to be going along with his instruction to stay put, but from the way she was looking at him, that had nothing to do with any acceptance of his actions on her part. Fair enough. He'd done the wrong thing and he owed her an explanation.

She waited as he got out of the car and walked back towards her.

'Look, Grace. I'm sorry I didn't tell you but... I wanted you to know me and that's *not* who I am. It's not what's important to me. I just wanted you to see the things that are, first.'

'Oh, and you think I can't make my own mind up about that?'

'It's the first thing that most people I meet see about me. I wanted you to look past that.' This wasn't working. Grace seemed even angrier now, if that was at all possible.

'So you just went ahead and judged me, did you? You couldn't give me the benefit of the doubt and find out what I had to say about it. That's what really hurts, Penn.'

Her words stung. What had seemed like a simple act of self-defence did have an element of arrogance about it.

'What *would* you have said, then?'

She flushed suddenly, shaking her head. 'Honestly… I don't know. Hiding it has made it seem more important and I can't get my head around it. I don't know how to react now…'

That was fair. A lot fairer than he'd been with her. He'd backed Grace into a corner, and he could understand now that maybe her only way out had been to walk away.

'I hear what you say, Grace, and you're right. I made a decision not to tell you because of what you might think of me, and that says everything about me and nothing about you. I apologise. Unreservedly.'

Her face softened suddenly, and her eyes filled with tears. 'Apology accepted. Maybe I overreacted—'

'It's okay not to like it. I don't.' Penn shrugged. He could see that Grace *didn't* like it all that much, and he wanted to know why.

Another car was speeding down the lane, travelling

faster than it should. Grace seemed too miserable to even notice and Penn instinctively pulled her to one side against the hedge as the car drove by, gone before he could turn and shout to the driver to slow down.

Then, none of that mattered, because Grace hadn't moved away from him. She was in his arms, her shoulders heaving from emotion. The one thing that Penn really needed now was a train…

There was somewhere they could go to be alone, though. Away from the insistent tug of the everyday world.

'Can we talk, Grace?'

She nodded, and he took her hand, grasping it tightly in his and leading her along the road for a few hundred yards. After climbing the padlocked gate, he held out his hand to help her and she brushed it away.

'I haven't lived in London for so long that I can't climb a gate, Penn.'

'No. Of course not. I just wanted to…' Help? Be a gentleman? He wanted all of those things, but he wasn't sure how to phrase it without upsetting Grace any more than he had already.

But now that they were alone, the easy-going atmosphere of the train seemed to have reasserted itself. Grace reached out, putting her hand on his shoulder before she stepped down on the other side of the gate. Looking around, she took the same direction that Penn had reckoned on, along the side of a field of maize, careful to keep to the grassy path between the crops and the hedge. She sat down on an old weather-bleached log, which Penn remembered from when he was a child, taking this route to avoid notice.

'Is it okay for us to be here?'

'Yeah, this is a footpath.'

Grace nodded. Penn sat for a while, waiting for her to say something, and when she didn't, he spoke.

'I'm not going to make excuses, Grace. Those train journeys we shared were really special and I should have had more respect for them. And for you.'

She nodded thoughtfully, gazing out over the rippling maize. 'They *were* special, weren't they? Something outside our everyday lives.'

That was exactly the way Penn felt. He wondered if he might back-track and change the *were* special back to *are* special.

'May I tell you a little about myself?'

Grace turned, the hint of a smile on her lips. 'It's time we knew each other a little better.'

That was all he could ever have asked of anyone. 'I'm the twenty-second Lord of Trejowan. I inherited the title when I was twenty-five, from my mother...'

'How does that work? I thought titles passed down through the male line.'

It was an old story, and not particularly interesting. But at least they were talking, and he wanted to show Grace that he wasn't going to conceal anything from her in the future.

'Most do. But the way a title is inherited is determined by the letters patent and ours are unusual. It's all about a king wanting to provide for the daughter of a favourite mistress... You want me to elaborate?'

Grace laughed. 'You can sketch the family scandals out for me later. Just tell me the upshot of it.'

That was something of a relief. 'Thanks. What

it means now is that the eldest child, irrespective of whether they're a boy or girl, inherits the title when they're twenty-five.'

'Which is what happened to you. Didn't your mother mind?'

'Not in the least. She took the whole thing pretty seriously when I was growing up and used to do a lot at the castle—she loves the theatre and the arts, and she was always putting on workshops and exhibitions to encourage young artists. But as soon as I was twenty-five, she gave me a series of lectures about the responsibilities I was taking on, and promptly moved to London. I wasn't too impressed by it all since I was in the second year of my foundation training as a surgeon, so I had plenty of other things to do. My mother was delighted at the prospect of reliable plumbing.'

Grace smiled suddenly. 'Who can blame her? The castle's not in very good shape, then?'

Penn tried to think about the place impartially. 'It's in great shape for its age. It's big and it has some beautiful apartments—I have one and my mother has another. I don't go there much.'

Her eyes were full of questions. Here, in the sunlit bubble that had formed around them, it seemed okay to answer them.

'When I was a kid, it wasn't all that easy living in a castle. I used to get teased a lot over my name and the school bullies all felt they needed to take me down a peg or two.'

Grace's eyebrows shot up. 'And you thought I might be a school bully?'

'Never crossed my mind. But…things have a way

of changing but staying the same. Now people tend to either like the idea of my title a little too much and I can't work out where I fit into that, or they assume I've never worked a day in my life to get what I have now. I've been privileged, for sure, but some of it I've earned for myself.'

'So you'd rather just be the surgeon that I met on the train?'

That was all he wanted to be right now. The guy that Grace had met on the train. An ordinary person, who'd fallen into conversation with the most special woman.

'That would be my preference.'

'So I won't call you *sir*, then?' Grace was joking now, but even so Penn winced.

'I really wish you hadn't even considered the idea.'

She nodded. 'My turn to apologise. And I'm sorry that I just walked away from you. I can see now how hurtful that must have been.'

'It was nothing I didn't deserve.'

She reached for his hand, and Penn felt the inevitable rush of mindless pleasure as Grace wound her fingers around his. 'I overreacted and that was everything you didn't deserve.'

'It doesn't matter…'

Penn felt the constriction in his chest begin to ease, and with it his curiosity grew. What could mean so much to Grace that it had provoked tears?

She took her hand from his and he didn't dare reach for her, even though he craved that small contact. Then he felt her fingers on the side of his face, tipping it round to meet her gaze and leaving him helpless in the warmth of her eyes.

'You don't get away with taking all of the responsibility, even if you might like to. I have a…reluctance to take help from anyone.'

He chuckled. 'Now, tell me something I haven't already worked out for myself.'

'It matters to me, Penn. You're a man who gives help in all kinds of ways, and I'm only just realising how much power you have. I'm not comfortable with that. It means a lot to me to be on equal terms with people.'

'You think we're not on equal terms?' Penn shot her a disbelieving look.

'Remember I said that I had a relationship break up, when I first started looking after Gran?' Grace's hands were clasped tight in her lap now. 'We'd been together for two years. I brought Jeremy down here for a week's holiday and everyone really liked him…apart from Gran, that is.'

'She had some advice for you?'

Grace nodded. 'She generally does. She said I should be careful, because he was the kind of person who was completely focussed on getting what he wanted. I didn't listen, because things were great between us, and his ambition didn't seem to be a bad thing. He has a job in finance and he earns a lot more than I do…'

'Does that matter?'

'I didn't think so. I'm not exactly struggling, but I have to watch the pennies a bit—I'm on my first mortgage. I couldn't afford the kinds of places that Jeremy wanted to go, but he said that they were his treat. I didn't reckon on the fact that he knows how to create a balance sheet.'

Now Penn was completely lost. 'I'm sorry. What do you mean by that?'

Grace sighed. 'He works long hours during the week. When it first became obvious that Gran needed round-the-clock care, I discussed the idea of my coming down to Cornwall at weekends, and he said it was fine with him. He was sure that I'd make up for it by being in London during the week. I thought it was just his way of saying that he loved me…'

Cold fingers gripped Penn's heart. 'But it wasn't?'

'He winds down after work by going out. He'd be home at about the time I was going to bed, and expect me to stay up, eating and drinking with him. Or he'd call, wanting me to join him somewhere. I changed my own work schedule as much as I could, making appointments later in the day, so that I could get enough sleep. But it was exhausting and it wasn't enough for Jeremy. He said I owed him more and he wanted me to pay the debt that I'd incurred.'

The chill was spreading and Penn shivered. A balance sheet… He couldn't even ask but maybe the silence, so full of questions, spoke loudly enough for Grace to hear it.

'He came home one evening, with a *present*.' She turned the corners of her mouth down, gesturing air quotes. 'He said that if I wasn't around at the weekends, I could make up for it by making weeknights special. It's not that I'm averse to trying something new but…'

Grace fell silent as Penn shook his head, motioning for her to stop. 'Please. I'm begging you, Grace, don't ever feel you have to explain and don't ever try to justify yourself.'

Her beautiful eyes softened, taking on a darker shade of green. 'You're right. We don't need details—they're embarrassing.'

Penn was on sure ground now. 'That's not what I meant. I'm sure you've had as many conversations about intimacy in the course of your work as I have, and there probably isn't much that could embarrass either of us. I don't want you to explain because I've heard you say that someone tried to coerce you and I believe you. That's enough.'

She nodded. 'Thank you. It took me a while before I could use that word… Coercion.'

'You can now, though?'

'Yes. Seeing that what Jeremy was doing wasn't out of love, but that he was just manipulating me into a position where I felt I couldn't say no… That was a big step for me.'

Penn couldn't ask, but he craved one word. No. Had Grace told her partner no?

She smiled suddenly, as if she could see his thoughts, leaning towards him to brush his arm with her fingers. 'I said no. That was the beginning of a very swift ending. I came back from Cornwall the following weekend and he was gone.'

'I'm glad to hear it.' The sudden relief gave him the courage to ask another question. 'But how does my being a lord have anything to do with this?'

Grace shrugged. 'All I could see in that moment… when Emma told me…was that you're someone who can give the people around him anything. You have a castle and a glassworks, people who depend on you in every area of your life. I'd promised myself that I'd never entertain another unequal friendship, and this one… It seemed like one where you had everything to give and there was nothing I could give in return. I just panicked.'

Penn considered the idea carefully. The balance sheet was still there in Grace's thinking, and that was a natural reaction to what she'd been through. He was having difficulty getting his mind around it.

'If I had to reckon it up, I'd tell you that you'll never have anything other than an unequal friendship with me, because you give me more than I could ever hope to give in return. But that's not helpful, because it assumes that we have to keep count. That's something I'm not prepared to do.'

She laughed suddenly. 'I like the way you think, Penn. If you could remind me of that on a regular basis then I'd appreciate it.'

He suspected that he might have to. Grace's sense of worth as a child had come from what she could do for the people she loved, and her ex-partner had taken advantage of that. Change was hard and it took time. He was a work in progress as well. But it seemed that Grace was willing to wait for him. It would be his privilege to wait for her.

From the sounds of it, a small procession of cars was going past them now. Grace turned, but the hedgerow was too dense to see the road.

'You should be getting back. It seems the open day's getting off to a good start.'

'If you still want to go home then I'll take you.' He should offer her that, even though he wanted Grace to stay more than anything else he could think of at the moment.

'I'd like to stay…'

'I was hoping you might. Thank you.'

She didn't seem in any hurry to move, and Penn wasn't either. Grace leaned a little closer, her shoulder touching his. He dared to put his arm lightly around her shoulder, and she moved closer still.

This was what words couldn't adequately say. It was forgiveness and the beginnings of a new trust, snatched from the jaws of anger and defeat. It was the sweet promise that he felt every time Grace touched him.

'Shouldn't we be getting back?' The way she turned the corners of her mouth down at the thought allowed him to reject the idea.

'This is more important. Everything else can wait.'

Her hand wandered a little, resting lightly on his knee. Everything she did seemed even more exquisite in this quiet seclusion.

'That's the nicest thing you could have said, Penn.'

CHAPTER SEVEN

THEY'D SPENT HALF an hour in the sunshine, so still and quiet together that even the birds seemed to forget that they were there. Being close to Penn felt so right, exactly where she was supposed to be, and when they dawdled their way back to his car, Grace slipped her hand into the crook of his arm, holding tightly on to the gorgeous feeling of togetherness.

It ended too soon, leaving just the sweet aftertaste of his smile. When they returned to the glassworks, Penn had more than one person wanting to see him, the most vociferous of whom was Emma.

'Penn, it's heaving with people in the shop. I left Phil in there to keep an eye on things while I was gone, but he's going to the workshop in a minute to start a demonstration. They've got plenty of people there, and I'm all on my own and I *need* a bit of help.'

'Okay. Coming now, Emma.' Penn shot Grace an apologetic look and gestured to the other three people, who had their own questions for him, to walk with him. Two were answered immediately, and Penn stopped in the doorway to give more detailed instructions to the third, giving Grace the opportunity to follow Emma into the shop.

'What can I do, Emma?'

Emma puffed out a breath, looking round. 'We really never expected it to be this busy. Particularly not at this time in the morning. It's only eleven o'clock…' She turned to wave a thank-you to a man in overalls, who was just leaving. 'But you shouldn't be helping, Grace—you're a guest.'

'It's okay, Em.' Grace heard Penn's voice behind her. 'If Grace would like to help, we're not going to stand on ceremony.'

Penn had clearly been listening to what she'd said to him. Nothing she did here would be entered into any balance sheet, and that gave a brighter lustre to it all.

Emma shot her a grateful look. 'I suppose… Do you know how to operate a till? I could wrap everything and…' She glanced up at Penn. 'Could you deal with anyone who has a question?'

'I'm happy with that.' Grace replied quickly. It was more than ten years since she'd worked in the village shop on Saturdays, but how different could it be?

The first customer was easy. Emma called out the price of a glass penguin that she was wrapping, and Grace managed to hit the right button to open the till and counted out the change, before thanking the customer for their purchase. But the second wanted to pay by card…

She felt Penn gently nudging her out of the way, and she nudged him back a little less gently. 'Just show me how to do it, Penn.'

'Sure you don't want to change your mind and get a cup of tea?'

'Positive.' She smiled at the customer. 'Sorry about this. The boss is getting under our feet again.' Grace heard Emma snort with laughter.

'Okay. You just need to scan the barcode before Emma starts wrapping things up.' Penn unwrapped the bowl that Emma had just swathed in tissue paper and gave it to Grace.

'Gotcha. I didn't do that the last time. It was a penguin.'

'Never mind, I'll make a note on the stock list.' Penn waited while Grace scanned the barcode and handed the bowl back to Emma.

He plucked a card from the wrapping area and handed it over to the woman who was waiting to make her purchase. 'This tells you a bit about the craftsperson who made your bowl.'

'Ah, thank you.' The woman smiled. 'It certainly is lovely.'

'Thank you. One of my favourite designs too…' Penn turned to Grace, showing her how to use the card reader. While she waited for the authorisation, he nudged Emma. 'Stickers, Em.'

'Oh! I nearly forgot.' Emma pulled a box of coloured stickers out from under the cash desk, then carefully applied the right one to the box. 'All these people, it's messing up my process…'

'That's okay,' Penn murmured to her. 'You know what to do, just slow it down a bit.'

He was a surgeon and used to working under pressure. That showed, because Penn was managing to keep the line of customers happy, calm Emma down and show Grace how to take the payments, all at once and with apparent ease. The queue at the cash desk began to dwindle, and when they'd served the last customer, Emma puffed out a sigh of relief.

'Thanks, Penn. That was all a bit frenetic.'

'Don't let the size of the queue spook you, Em. Just work through it one person at a time. It's always quicker that way.' He turned to Grace. 'Are you quite determined not to have any fun at all on your day off?'

Grace folded her arms resolutely, and heard Emma giggle behind Penn's back. 'I'm having fun, here with Emma. There are people over there who look as if they're just bursting with questions. You can go and help them if you want something to do...'

At one o'clock, a young woman and man turned up from the workshop to relieve Emma for lunch. Penn prised her from her post, telling her that she wasn't to come back for another hour, and Emma promised him that he'd be sorry if anything was broken in her absence, before pretending to flounce away.

Grace followed him over to the paved area, which was full of people eating and drinking in the sunshine. A middle-aged woman, who looked rushed off her feet, saw them coming and picked up a tray from under the counter.

'There you go, Penn.' She ignored the queue, carrying the tray straight over to him.

'Thanks, Judy. What's the damage?' Penn felt in his pocket.

'Put your money away, Penn. We've already made

more than we usually do for the whole bank holiday weekend at the tea shop. Consider this a small thank-you.'

'It's my pleasure. This is really not necessary…'

Judy dumped the tray into his hands and walked away, ignoring Penn's protests. He walked over to the serving area and picked up a couple of paper serviettes, and Grace saw him slip a note from his pocket into the tips box.

'You just couldn't resist, could you?' Grace couldn't help letting him know that she'd seen him do it.

Penn shrugged. 'Why should I get things for free?'

Because he was the boss here, and he'd given Judy a solid business opportunity by asking her to come and do the catering. Grace wondered whether that could be construed as taking advantage of his position, and whether his refusal to do so showed that her fears about him really were groundless. There were no free tables, and so they sat down on the grass together.

'We're never going to manage all this.' The tray was full of plates, containing sandwiches and scones, with little pots of jam and cream.

'Just do your best.' Penn straightened, waving his hand to a young woman who was walking across from the workshop, hands plunged deep into the pockets of her overalls, her red hair untamed and glinting in the sun as if she'd just shaken it loose around her shoulders.

'Phoebe… Grace.' He made a quick introduction, and Phoebe gave a bright smile.

'I love your flowers.' Grace remembered that Phoebe's name was on the orchids in the shop. 'I've been selling quite a lot of them today.'

Phoebe grinned. 'That's what I like to hear.' Penn motioned to her to join them and she sat down on the grass.

'Help yourself.' Penn indicated the sandwiches. 'Can I get you something to drink?'

'I'll just take a large gulp of your water if you can spare it.' Phoebe grinned and Penn handed over the bottle of spring water that he'd just opened.

'How are the demonstrations going? I'm sorry I haven't been around much this morning.' Penn shot Grace a glance that told her he wasn't sorry at all, and pleasure tingled down her spine.

'They've been great.' Phoebe reached for a sandwich and Grace handed her a paper plate. 'I thought that it would be a bit challenging, everyone just sitting staring at you while you try to get on and do what you normally do. But it's been nothing like that. We've had loads of questions. Next time we do it, I think we should pick someone from the audience to make something as part of it.'

Penn thought for a moment. 'Good idea. We'd have to think about safety considerations, though.'

Phoebe nodded. 'If I get together with Phil and make up a plan…?'

'Yeah, do that. I'll take a look at it.' Penn grinned. 'So there's going to be a next time?'

'Ha!' Phoebe snorted with laughter. 'I don't think you're going to have much choice in that—everyone's talking about it. Anyway, we've got the T-shirts now, so we'd better use them…'

They'd finished their lunch and, with Phoebe's help, managed to clear the tray. Penn had started to head back to the shop, suggesting that Grace might like to catch up with Phoebe, who was heading to the workshop for her next demonstration.

'But I've learned how to do payments now! This isn't good management, Penn. You don't teach someone how to do something and then send them off to do something else.'

'It's not management at all. You're a guest. And Emma should have a chance to grow into her role a little.'

'So you're just going to throw her in at the deep end and hope?'

'No, I'm going to go over there and demonstrate a few people management skills. Emma's already catching on, and when it starts working for her, she'll have no hesitation in asking me if there isn't something else I might be doing.'

'You're saying that helping isn't necessarily going to help Emma.'

The look of quiet amusement on Penn's face told Grace that was exactly what he was saying. A balance sheet was far too simplistic a thing to apply to the way that he operated.

'I'm saying that I'm really grateful for your help at the shop because at that point we couldn't have coped without you. Now you're *wanted* in the workshop.'

Wanted rather than needed. Penn was definitely making a point and Grace cordially ignored it, even if it did prompt a bloom of warmth in her heart. 'I'll see you later, then.'

Phoebe had clearly added a new step to her demonstration, and involved the small group of people standing behind the temporary barriers between them and the furnaces, asking them to choose the design and colours of the piece she was going to make. It was fascinating, watching blobs of molten glass take shape, and Grace stayed for the next demonstration as well. When Penn came to join her at half past three, she was flushed from the heat of the furnace and excitement in equal measure.

He'd promised to get her to her train on time, and there was no talking him out of driving her back to Newquay, stopping outside Gran's cottage on the way so she could pop in, fetch her weekend bag and say a hurried goodbye to Gran and 'See you next week' to her cousin. Penn parked outside the station, then got out of the car to come with her to the platform.

'You're seeing me off, then?'

'I'm so glad you came.' He was suddenly serious. 'It's a long time since I've sat on the edge of a field and passed the time of day.'

They hadn't spoken about that. It had been too special for the hurried conversations that went on in the glassworks.

'Maybe we should do it again. Without the shouting…' Grace's embarrassment resurfaced as she thought about how she'd just walked away from Penn, without hearing what he had to say first.

He made a show of weighing the idea up. 'Strictly between you and me, I rather appreciated the shouting.'

They probably wouldn't have talked the way they had without it. Grace nodded. 'That can be your job the next time, then. I'll bring sandwiches.'

He laughed. 'Done. See you on Friday? Same time, same place.'

It was a regular date now. Friday evenings on the train were something to look forward to, and it would give Grace a little time to get her head around the idea that if Penn had turned out to be a little different to the man she'd thought, that wasn't necessarily a bad thing.

'I'll be there. Thank you so much for today, Penn. The glassworks is a very special place.'

'My pleasure. I hope you'll visit again.'

'I will.' Not because of the glass. Maybe Penn needed to know that. 'They have so much respect for you there, and it's not because you're a lord. It's because of all you've done.'

The look in his eyes told her that he *had* needed to hear someone say that. She smiled up at him, standing on her toes to brush a kiss against his cheek in a friendly goodbye.

Then suddenly, everything changed. All of those stolen glances, the times when they'd lingered in each other's smiles, and Grace had wished that she might have met Penn sometime in another life when there was nothing to keep them apart… When their lips met, she could feel the heat and the yearning that had made these last few weeks into a delicious slow burn of something that was a great deal more than friendship.

And then Penn stepped away.

'I'm… That was presumptuous. I'm sorry.'

'Did it have anything to do with castles or balance sheets?' Grace reckoned not, and she couldn't leave things on this note.

'No, it most certainly didn't.' He reached for her again and this time he initiated the kiss. Hot and sweet, and it lasted until the clamour of her train pulling up at the platform tore them apart.

'Friday…' She picked up her bag, backing away from him. Still weak-kneed and almost tripping as she got into the waiting carriage.

'Friday.'

It was an effort to turn away from him, but when Grace scrambled across empty seats to the window, Penn was still there. His fingers brushed his mouth, as if their kiss was something precious that he intended to keep. Grace's hand moved to the window, her palm pressed against it in a silent signal that all she wanted to do was touch him again.

Penn waited on the platform, until the train drew away. When she could no longer see him, she picked up her bag and found the seat that was booked for her. The journey ahead of her seemed an endless torture of having to sit still and wonder whether that kiss had been the best thing that had ever happened to her, or the biggest mistake she'd ever made.

No, it wasn't a mistake. A little too soon maybe, when they both had so many reasons to be cautious. Giving a little piece of herself to Penn felt different from all the times that she'd allowed Jeremy to take those pieces from her, but it still made Grace fearful.

There was still so much that they didn't know about each other. But that kiss had been the one perfect thing that gave Grace a reason to seek a better future, even if all the odds seemed stacked against it.

The rosy glow that seemed to surround the glassworks on his return wasn't all just a trick of the light. This *was* the closest he had to a home in Cornwall, and he was accepted here. Penn spent Monday evening helping clear up the inevitable mess from the open day, which gave him a chance to work without having to think about what he was doing.

It was becoming harder and harder for Penn not to see Grace as his ideal woman. She was warm and kind, smart and outspoken. She didn't seem to care one way or the other about what he was, only who he was. But there were other reasons for walking away from someone who was weighed down by a title. Maybe she didn't want to spend her time running from it the way he did, or being confronted by other people's assumptions. Penn knew how much that hurt, and he wanted more than anything to protect Grace from it.

And she'd been so badly hurt already—not just hurt but abused and betrayed. Penn wanted to kick something in frustrated rage when he thought about that, and instead had managed to drop one of Phoebe's flowers on the floor of the workshop. Breakages in the glassworks were something that happened all the time. The feeling that a part of Grace had been broken was a matter of far greater concern.

But still he couldn't forget that kiss. Wrong place maybe, and wrong time, although perhaps the train had arrived at precisely the right time, before they had both blundered into something that neither of them was ready for yet. All the same, it had been a precious glimpse of what he and Grace could be to each other.

He took the late train back to London, falling into exhausted unconsciousness for the whole of the journey. Then, after a few hours in his own bed, Penn went back to work, feeling ready for the challenges ahead.

Grace had texted him, saying that April had made an appointment with her colleague and the consultation had gone well, and the resulting conversation of one-line messages lasted for days. Their friendly to and fro had put their relationship back on firm ground, where a kiss might be acknowledged but not acted on, and it had got Penn through a difficult week at work. But now, at last, the Friday afternoon train beckoned.

He made it with ten minutes to spare. Penn found Grace sitting in her seat with a frothy cappuccino and an almond croissant on a paper plate in front of her. The dark rings that so often shadowed her beautiful eyes had disappeared and she was relaxed and smiling.

And something had changed. Grace rose to brush her lips against his cheek in greeting, and when she pushed a paper carrier bag back across the table towards him, their fingers touched. Little things that might be lost in the context of friendship, but with Grace they held the scintillating promise of a relationship that might go far beyond that.

'Hey. Good day?' Penn opened the bag, finding coffee and an almond croissant inside.

'Good week, actually.'

'Yeah? Tell me about it. I could do with some good news.' Grace was the very best of news, all by herself, and whenever she was there, his day automatically became brighter and better.

'What's up, Penn?'

He shook his head, taking his coffee from the bag. 'Just...some days are better than others.'

She leaned back in her seat, folding her arms. 'But you can deal with that all by yourself. Clearly.'

He was learning fast, and not talking about things wasn't the way to go with Grace. All the same, she seemed in a more relaxed frame of mind than usual and he didn't want to spoil that.

'Tell me about your week, Penn.'

Showing weakness or pain might be a mistake when you were faced by bullies or people who didn't understand what your priorities were, but with Grace… She could take weakness and turn it into something strong. She broke off a small piece of her croissant, put it into her mouth and waited.

'Okay, you win. The surgical procedure I did yesterday was pretty tough.'

'How so? Didn't it go well?' She took a sip of her coffee.

'It went very well…' The image of the small form on his operating table, who was far too young to ever have to be strong, flashed in front of his eyes. 'My patient was just four years old.'

Grace turned the corners of her mouth down. 'What was the procedure?'

'She was in a road accident. Both of her legs were broken, one was a compound break, the bone was shattered. One hand had multiple fractures as well. The hand surgeon and I were both working on her…'

'To minimise the amount of time that she was under the anaesthetic?'

Penn nodded. 'Yeah. We had to plan things very carefully. How much we needed to do straight away and what could wait. How much stress the procedure would put her body under.'

He pinched the bridge of his nose between his thumb and forefinger. This was exactly what he'd signed up for. Complex procedures, patients who'd been badly injured. Keeping a cool head through all of it, maintaining his concentration.

Grace reached across the table and took his hand. 'What's her name?'

It wasn't about names. It was about doing his job, mending what was broken and then moving on to the next person who needed him. Staying strong, which largely meant staying silent when the cases that tore at his heart came along.

'We're both done with work for the week. We can be as human as we like on our own time.'

Penn couldn't help a smile. When her fingers tightened around his in response, he didn't just feel the thrill of having her close. He felt the warmth of being human, in a world where he never really seemed to be on his own time.

'Sophie. Her mother was injured in the same accident but not as badly—she's in hospital at the moment, but we'll be releasing her in the next couple of days. Her father is…struggling obviously, but he's been amazingly strong. He only leaves Sophie's bedside to go and visit his wife and give her news. I saw Sophie and spoke with both her parents this morning and…she's got a long way to go. But things went well yesterday and I really think she's going to make it.'

'That's great. I'm so glad you were there for all three of them, Penn. Sometimes that takes its toll, doesn't it?'

'Yeah. Sometimes I need to remember that.'

Grace shrugged. 'We both do. What was it you said about taking a break every now and then?'

'This *is* my break.' He had Grace, even if they were separated by a table. Penn was beginning to really dislike the table… But he could still catch her scent and see her eyes. And she was giving him the time to acknowledge that even if he was unswerving in his concentration when he was working, he could still feel something when he wasn't.

'I'd tell you about my week. But I don't want you to think I've been relaxing too much while you've been working so hard…' She turned the corners of her mouth down.

'Tell me about it. Spread a bit of happiness why don't you.'

Grace gave him a luminous smile and his heart jumped suddenly, pumping warmth and feeling into his body. They both knew how to acknowledge the bad things, and then move on. That was all part of the job. Maybe he should extend that principle to the rest of his life, because Grace always made him feel that anything was possible.

Grace had been to see a film with Mia during the week, which had felt like a delicious and rather daring evening out, rather than what it was, which was an acceptance of a casual invitation on Mia's part. But Penn listened, laughing as she outlined the plot.

'So…let me get this right. Everyone thinks that the wretched, bullying uncle has been murdered by his nephew. But the detective immediately knows that he's innocent because…' Penn shrugged in disbelief.

'It was a bit more textured than that. But yes, it did have quite a bit of jumping to conclusions that I couldn't really follow. The setting was beautiful, though. An old stately home in the wilds of Yorkshire.' Grace ventured a teasing smile. 'You know the kind of thing.'

Penn shot her a wry look. This was the first time that she'd alluded to anything that might be even vaguely connected with his title, and Grace wondered whether she'd gone too far. It seemed to be a very sore point for him.

Then he grinned. 'We have murders all the time down at the castle in Cornwall. That's why I never go there. I reckon I'd be the first to fall foul of all the intricate plots going on. It's a lot safer at the glassworks.'

Grace wondered whether she'd ever get to actually see the castle. It didn't really matter either way, but she was still a little curious and wanted to know everything about Penn.

'Wise move. Although you might turn out to be the one who solves all the murders. Surgeon turned part-time detective.' Penn would make a very good hero.

'I think I'll stick to what I know. So how about you? Did the world suddenly crumble just because you took an evening off?'

'Funnily enough, no. Although my flat's looking a bit the worse for wear since Thursday evening is usually my cleaning and ironing night. So it'll be double bubble next week.'

Penn chuckled. 'I should send my cleaner round to give you a hand. She'd be thrilled. She's always complaining that I don't make enough mess, largely because I'm hardly ever there. She told me the other day that I was threatening her livelihood.'

A lump suddenly lodged in Grace's throat. He could do that, couldn't he? She imagined that Penn's house in Holland Park was just as nice as the location sounded, and it made sense that he had a cleaner because there were so many other things Penn needed to spend time on. But the idea that a word from him could eradicate the pile of ironing from her life and render her kitchen spotless was uncomfortable. What would be an adequate gesture in return?

She shouldn't think like that. Penn clearly didn't, but then he didn't have to. He didn't have to count his own generosity, and he couldn't understand how it might erode her own feeling of independence.

'Sorry…' He'd seen that he'd said the wrong thing and looked suddenly embarrassed. That wasn't fair—he shouldn't have to apologise for what he had.

Grace reached across the table to brush the back of his hand with her fingers. 'It's a really nice offer. I might even take you up on it one of these days.'

He knew full well she wouldn't, but his face softened into a smile. 'So tell me about the rest of the film. Who really *did* do it?'

'It was the family solicitor…' Grace jumped as her phone rang, still nervy over the sudden realisation that she and Penn still had a way to go before they could be entirely comfortable with the differences in their lives. She picked it up, checking who was calling.

'Sorry, this is my sister. I'd better take it…'

CHAPTER EIGHT

BAD MOVE. ALTHOUGH it seemed that Grace had forgiven him for the reckless offer of help. But now she was frowning as she listened intently to what her sister was telling her on the phone. The colour, draining from her face, told him that whatever this was about, it wasn't good news. Penn focussed his gaze out of the window, trying vainly to give her a measure of privacy.

She ended the call, before putting her phone slowly down onto the table between them. Penn thought he saw tears in her eyes, but Grace brushed them away quickly. He wondered how he could ask, after having got things so wrong just moments ago.

Thankfully he didn't have to.

'It's my gran. They think… I mean, they probably know, but they're waiting until they have the X-rays to confirm…' She swallowed hard. 'She's broken her hip.'

All of Penn's coping mechanisms clicked in. 'When did this happen?'

'My cousin was there this afternoon, and she'd left Gran watching TV while she went to make some tea. Gran decided she had something to say that wouldn't wait, and she fell on her way into the kitchen.'

'And she's at the hospital?'

'Yes. They've taken her to the main unit in Truro, and my cousin called my sister from there, so that she could let me know.'

So there was no news yet on her grandmother's condition. Penn knew that must be agonising for Grace. 'She's where she needs to be. That's good.'

'Yes…yes, that's right. She's where she needs to be.' Grace's fingers were moving nervously across the small table and she started to fold the napkin on her plate, then put it carefully into her empty coffee cup. The paper plate got the same treatment and then she reached for Penn's napkin.

This must be killing her. Her gran was hurt and there was nothing that Grace could do to help. In the confines of the train, she couldn't even work off her nervous energy by going for a walk. He let her collect up everything on the table, before stowing it into her cup and then into the paper carrier bag, but when she took a tissue from her handbag and started to wipe the table, he caught her hand.

'It's clean enough, Grace.'

Grace nodded. She sat still for a moment and then looked at her watch. 'I just… You know what the risks are to elderly people following hip fractures.' Her lip began to quiver.

So did Grace. There wasn't any point in glossing over them, because all of Grace's training was telling her to weigh up the facts.

'Yes, I do. Surgery carries an increased risk for the elderly, and that's something we can't do anything about. But you know the right questions to ask, and you can make informed decisions about what comes next for your gran.'

She nodded, pressing her lips together. 'Yes…yes, there is that.'

'And rehab isn't always straightforward either. Someone of your gran's age can't bounce back the way that younger people can, and she needs very careful assessment and a lot of encouragement to get back on her feet again. But she has one big advantage there, too. She has you, and you know exactly what's needed.'

Grace was trembling now. He caught hold of her hand, trying to steady her, and she curled her fingers around his tightly.

'I… I don't know if I can do it, Penn. She's not a patient to me… She's my gran.'

'That's right, and knowing everything that can go wrong is making things worse right now. But it's your strength as well. If your gran was my patient, I'd be looking at things overall and seeing you as someone who could make a real difference to her recovery. You can be prepared for the worst, but you need to focus on the fact that your gran may well come through this much better than you expect.'

'Honestly…?'

'I'm not even going to answer that. You know how to assess the situation as well as I do. Grace, it's okay to be worried…' If she was going to do it, she may as well own it. His words brought the flicker of a smile to her lips.

'Okay. Thanks. I'll do my worrying here on the train perhaps. When I get there, I can think about the questions I need to ask.'

'That sounds reasonable. Where are you meeting your sister?'

'Jessica's going to the hospital. She's Gran's named welfare guardian, but she doesn't make medical decisions without discussing them with me. I said I'd be there as soon as I could, but I don't think they'll be doing any more than stabilising her and doing some tests this evening.'

'No, I doubt they'll be referring her for surgery before tomorrow, but they'll be doing all they can to get everything in place tonight. I'll take you to the hospital.'

'But...' Her eyes filled with tears. Grace was obviously struggling with this and the easiest and best thing to do was insist.

'I keep my car garaged near the station during the week, and I'm heading towards Truro anyway. And maybe I can help you answer any questions that your family has. I am an orthopaedic surgeon, after all.' And her friend. Penn would claim that privilege if nothing else.

Grace heaved a shaky sigh. 'Yes. Thank you. I'd be really grateful if you'd stay for maybe fifteen minutes and just explain everything.'

She was on autopilot. But Penn didn't really care how or why she'd said *yes*. He just wanted her to say it.

'That'll be my pleasure. Now, how about taking another breath? Because it'll be a while before we get to Newquay...'

He'd insisted they eat something while they were on the train, because it stopped Grace from looking at her watch every five seconds, and he didn't know if they'd get an opportunity later. She was obviously worried, but Grace had recovered from the shock of her sister's call, and when she called her sister back to let her know that the train was on time and she'd be at the hospital in less than an hour, Penn was gratified to hear that she also passed on the information that he would be there too.

'Jessica asked if I'd found you on the train.' Grace smiled at him. 'I told her no.'

'Although strictly speaking, I suppose you did.' Penn chuckled. Being found on a train by Grace had been challenging but it had worked out pretty well so far.

'I guess so. Although not today. I wouldn't want her to think I've been hunting down stray orthopaedic surgeons and kidnapping them.'

'No. That might create a panic in the medical community.' He wouldn't resist a kidnapping if Grace could be persuaded to give it a try. Maybe not this evening, though.

The train arrived in Newquay bang on time, and the drive to the hospital took only twenty minutes. Grace followed the texted instructions from her sister, and Penn found himself in a waiting area for the orthopaedics ward, being introduced to three young women who were very obviously related to Grace.

Jessica's smile was a lot like Grace's. Mags, Grace's cousin, had her green eyes, and her other cousin Carrie had her light-blonde curls. Only Grace had the magic of all three. Plus, that indefinable something that Penn couldn't explain, but always made Grace the only woman in the room.

'I should have watched her more carefully.' Mags had been with her grandmother when she'd fallen.

'It could have been any one of us.' Carrie put her arm around her shoulders, but Mags seemed inconsolable.

'You can't always apply the same cause-and-effect thinking to injuries in older people. It's uncommon but a hip fracture can occur spontaneously, and in those cases, the fall is a result of the fracture, not the cause of it. In any case, there were probably a number of different factors that contributed to her injury.' Penn tried to give whatever comfort he could.

'Yes, that's right.' Grace added her own voice to the reassurances. 'And Gran has osteoporosis, remember. You can't watch her every moment of the day, Mags. None of us can. If we stopped her from moving around, that would only make it more likely that she'd be injured, and she'd be miserable as well.'

Mags shot a questioning glance in Penn's direction, and he nodded, wondering if Grace minded that her own very sensible advice seemed to need his confirmation at the moment. But her smile gave no hint that she did.

'We've seen the doctor.' Jessica took a piece of paper from her pocket. 'We didn't understand everything he said, so Carrie asked the questions and I wrote his answers down.'

Penn chuckled. 'I so wish all of my patients' families were this well-organised.'

'That's Grace's doing,' Mags spoke up. 'She said we should each take different jobs and responsibilities, whatever we could manage, and stick to them. That way we get some time off.'

It was a good strategy. Penn had heard a lot of carers say that the most difficult part was never being off duty. Grace had proposed a solution to that, which seemed to be working. Each of the women was responsible for different days and different aspects of their grandmother's care, and if they stuck to that and worked together then they all got to keep the rest of their lives.

'We're lucky to have each other,' Grace murmured, leaning forward and taking Jessica's written notes, putting them into his hand. Apparently he'd just been co-opted into the group and this was *his* job now.

He scanned the handwritten notes, which were separated by bullet points. 'Grace could answer all of these…' He didn't want to make her feel that her own expertise was being disregarded.

'You do this kind of procedure every day, so you have a much better appreciation of the practicalities than I do. If you don't mind…' Grace leaned back in her seat, suddenly looking very tired. It occurred to Penn that for the time being she really needed to be just another concerned relative, without the responsibilities of her own medical knowledge.

'It's my pleasure.' Penn turned his attention to the first bullet point. 'So your grandmother's already had an X-ray and it appears she has a femoral neck fracture. The femoral neck is right below the ball-and-socket joint between your pelvis and femur…'

'That's your femur.' Mags was looking confused already, and Grace leaned forward, tapping the long bone that ran from her cousin's hip to her knee.

'Right. Gotcha.'

'Depending on where the fracture is, and whether the blood supply to the top of her femur is damaged, the surgeon will do either a full hip replacement, a half hip replacement or they'll stabilise the hip with a metal screw and plate system while the bone heals naturally. Does that say "hemiarthroplasty", Jessica?' Penn pointed to Jessica's second bullet point.

'Yeah. The question marks are because I didn't know how to spell it. He seemed pretty certain that this was what they'd do.'

'It would have been a lot better if he'd just said half hip replacement.' Penn always tried to avoid medical terms when talking to relatives, because giving them long words that they didn't know the meaning of didn't help when they were already in a stressful situation. 'Let me explain a little about what that entails…'

He'd gone through everything on the list, carefully explaining what it all meant and what they could expect at each stage of the process. At the end of it, everyone still looked worried, but Jessica, Carrie and Mags looked much less confused. That was generally the best that Penn could hope for, because worry was a natural reaction.

Carrie fished in her bag, then took out a foil-wrapped packet that turned out to be homemade fudge. Everyone helped themselves, clearly craving something sweet.

'I should have thought to ask before now. Have you eaten, Penn? I've got some pasties in my bag. I made a whole batch of them this afternoon and I grabbed a few when Jessica called…'

'No, that's…' Penn saw Carrie's face fall. 'On second thoughts, I am a bit hungry.'

'There you go, then.' Carrie beamed, dipping her hand into the capacious holdall that looked as if it contained all manner of useful things, and produced another foil-wrapped packet that was slightly warm to the touch when she handed it over. Grace shook her head when Carrie proffered a second pasty, and Mags said that she thought she could manage one now.

'So what are we going to do now?' Grace asked. 'Have they said anything about what's going to be happening tomorrow?'

'They said they'd be monitoring Gran overnight, and depending on her condition generally, they may operate tomorrow.' Jessica shook her head. 'It all seems to be happening very quickly…'

'That's good.' Penn interjected. 'Early surgery generally has better outcomes, as long as there are no other factors that make it necessary to wait.'

Grace nodded. 'Gran's in pretty good health generally, so I guess it may well be tomorrow. I'll get back here for eight o'clock and see if I can find out what's happening and let you all know.'

'You're staying at Gran's?' Jessica asked. 'You're welcome to stay with me, of course, but it's a bit of a trek here from Tintagel.'

'Or you could share my sofa bed with Mags…' Carrie offered, then turned to silence her sister when she opened her mouth to protest. 'No arguments. You're coming home with me. You've had enough of a scare already this afternoon, having to cope with Gran falling like that, and I'm not having you spend tonight on your own at home.'

Grace nodded in agreement with Carrie. 'I think it'll be easier in the morning if I stay at Gran's. If you don't mind dropping me off there on the way home, Jess.'

'Of course not. As long as you don't mind being

there.' Jessica got to her feet. 'The nurse said that I could check in with her to see how Gran's doing before we go.'

Everything seemed to be agreed. But however sensible the arrangement seemed, Penn didn't like it. Grace would be all right staying at her grandmother's house, but he doubted she'd get much sleep. And the glassworks was only a few miles down the road…

Jessica was making her way over to the double doors that led to the ward entrance. Mags had decided that she didn't want the pasty after all, and Carrie had put it back into her bag before going with her sister to find a lavatory. It was now or never.

'You're welcome to stay with me, in the cottage at the glassworks. There's a spare room and it's closer to the hospital.'

'Thanks, but it's a little remote there. I can get a bus into the centre of Newquay, and then on from there to Truro.' She gave him a half-hearted smile that left Penn with the distinct impression she was making excuses.

'I was thinking that you might find it a little upsetting, being alone at your grandmother's.'

'I'll manage. You've been too kind already, Penn, and I really appreciate everything you've done.'

He didn't want to hear this. If Grace couldn't tell the difference between his offer of a room for the night, and the conditions that her ex-partner put on whatever he gave to the relationship…

'I really *haven't* been too kind.' He caught sight of Grace's dismayed expression and bit his tongue. She was under stress and picking arguments with her wasn't the right thing to do. Nor was putting her under pressure to do what he wanted her to do, even if he did think it was best.

'I'm sorry, Penn.'

Her eyes filled with tears. He'd done this. Penn tried, convicted and sentenced himself.

'No—I'm the one who should be sorry. It's best that you do whatever you feel most comfortable with.'

He looked up as Jessica walked towards them. He would have liked to make a more fulsome apology, but time had overtaken them again.

'I spoke to the nurse and she says that Gran's sleeping peacefully.'

'Good. That's very good.' Grace smiled encouragingly at her sister, even though she must know as well as Penn did that her grandmother would have been given drugs to ease her pain, and sedated was probably a more accurate description than sleeping.

'She said that the doctors will make a decision tomorrow about the op. That's not going to happen until after nine at the earliest.'

'Okay, I'll be here for nine and I'll let you all know what's happening as soon as I do.'

'I'll come as soon as I've got the kids sorted out. I expect either Carrie or Mags will too, if not both. Are you ready to go?'

'Penn's offered me his spare room for the night. He's only a few miles down the road. I may not be needing a lift…' Grace looked at Penn questioningly, and he nodded, grinning back at her and thanking his lucky stars that he'd stepped back when he did. The fact that her decision had made him very happy was less important than the thought that she'd made her own choice, without too much pressure from him.

'Okay. That honestly sounds a lot cheerier than being on your own at Gran's.' Jessica gave him a bright smile. So much like Grace's, apart from the fact that it didn't make his stomach lurch. 'I can't thank you enough for everything, Penn. I feel so much happier about Gran now that I've got a better idea of what we're up against.'

'My pleasure. If you have any other questions, Grace has my number and you're welcome to give me a call.'

Jessica grinned. 'Thanks, I may well do that. You two had better get going now, and get a decent night's sleep. I'll wait for Carrie and Mags and let them know what's going on…'

She'd almost lost Penn. Again. Grace had seen the hurt in his eyes, and he had every right to feel wounded. It was fine for her to feel all the things that she felt, but suggesting that Penn was anything like Jeremy wasn't fair. She was beginning to believe that she could leave that hurt behind, and moving forward was something she really wanted to do.

When Penn tucked her hand into the crook of his arm, she hung on to him tightly as they walked in silence back to the car. The overwhelming feeling that Penn was there and that he would keep her safe, allowed her to relax a little and begin to hope for the best for Gran.

As he drove up the narrow lane that led to the glassworks, she saw that the gate into the car park was closed. Beyond that, a light from the barn glimmered in the darkness.

'Someone's working very late, aren't they?'

He shook his head. 'We have security on-site at night. My father used to reckon that his presence alone was enough to put off the most determined burglars. That actually might have been the case—he had a reputation for being fierce at times and no one ever did break in. But the place is empty on weeknights now, so I had a good alarm system installed and there's a guard who comes in.'

He stopped in front of the gate and a light flipped on from somewhere over their heads, illuminating the car. Grace jumped, blinking, and Penn wound the car window down, then leaned out towards the intercom.

'Evening, Arthur.'

'Evening, Penn. Welcome home.'

The gate swung open in front of them, and Grace saw a portly figure in one of the windows of the barn, watching as the car drove past. Penn waved and the figure returned the gesture.

He drew up outside the two cottages, switched off the engine and turned in his seat. 'I'll give Arthur a call and let him know that I have a guest, so you won't be challenged in the morning. He's a good guy, one of four ex-policemen who got together and set up a security company. They advised us on our security system as well. You'll be safe here.'

Grace had no doubt of that. Maybe Penn's insistence on making the point was more to do with letting her know that she'd be safe with him.

'I wouldn't be here if I didn't feel safe with you, Penn. Sometimes I can be a little too defensive.'

He shook his head. 'You have every reason to be. You've been hurt.'

'Never by you.'

His eyes glistened in the darkness. For a moment, it seemed as if he would lean forward and kiss her, and Grace wouldn't have stopped him. But Penn was too much of a gentleman. He must know how she was feeling and he wouldn't take advantage of her desperate need for comfort.

He got out of the car, fetched their bags from the back seat and led her towards the cottage, stopping before he opened the front gate. 'Watch out for trailing branches. I've been meaning to cut some of the shrubs back for ages, and they're getting a bit out of control.'

Penn led the way, holding some of the larger branches back for her. In the darkness Grace could smell the heavy scent of flowers. Inside the cottage was white-painted, comfortable and attractive, but anonymous. He showed her upstairs, put her bag on the bed in a crisply tidy room and then closed the curtains.

'Are you going to sleep tonight?'

She felt crushingly tired and wide awake, all at the same time. When Grace looked at her watch, it was almost midnight.

'I could lie down for a while.' Her back ached as well, from the tension.

He nodded. 'The kitchen has—' he shrugged '—things you'd most likely expect from a kitchen. Same goes for the bathroom, which is the door on your right. Help yourself to anything you want.'

'Thank you. It's very…' She gave him a silencing

look when he opened his mouth to speak. 'It *is* very kind of you, Penn, and I'm grateful.'

He grinned suddenly. 'My pleasure. Get some sleep if you can…'

CHAPTER NINE

SHE'D LAIN AWAKE, going through all of the things that might go wrong with a hemiarthroplasty. All of the things that might go right, and what needed to be done afterwards, the care and encouragement, getting Gran mobile again. The exercises that she would recommend and how she might tactfully check that Gran's physiotherapist was up to scratch on the latest research.

Then, suddenly she was sitting up in bed, wide awake. Penn had just stepped back from the bedside, moving the cup of coffee away from her flailing arm, and the room was bathed in sunshine.

'What…what's the time?' Grace rubbed her eyes, looking around for her travelling alarm clock. She was sure that she'd put it on the nightstand, but it wasn't there now.

Penn picked it up from the floor with his free hand, then put it back in its place, along with the cup of coffee. She *needed* coffee, and Grace grabbed it, taking a mouthful.

'Nearly half past eight.'

He didn't sound as panicky about that as Grace felt. 'What? I'm going to be late…'

'No, you're not. Fifteen minutes to shower and dress—I'll have a takeaway cup and breakfast ready for you by then—and fifteen minutes to get to the hospital. We'll be there bang on time.'

We'll be there? At the moment, Grace couldn't really object to that, because there was no other way she'd be at the hospital by nine. She lay back against the pillows, closing her eyes.

'Hey… I'm not leaving until I see you standing up.'

Grace jerked back into wakefulness. It was a good strategy on Penn's part. She could go right back to sleep without too much prompting.

'Didn't my alarm go off?'

'Yep, I heard it at half past six. You must have slept through it. Or woken up and thrown it across the room.'

Probably the latter. Grace wondered if she'd broken it.

'On your feet.'

Grace sighed and got out of bed. Penn's grin broadened suddenly.

'What now?'

He shrugged. 'Nothing. I've always rather liked pink elephant pyjamas.'

She pulled a face as he turned to walk out of the room. Penn could be the most exasperating man alive when he put his mind to it, and even that made her feel better about the day ahead.

He was as good as his word. She showered quickly and dressed, then found Penn waiting for her at the bottom of the stairs, a bag in one hand that presumably contained coffee and something to eat, and his car keys in the other. They made the hospital in ten minutes, and by nine, Grace was standing outside the orthopaedic ward, pressing the entry buzzer.

She waited for a while at the desk, and a senior nurse came to tell her that Gran had had a good night and that the consultant would be making a decision about when to operate this morning. Visiting hours were from ten o'clock, and she could see Gran then. Grace texted Jessica to let her know, as she walked back to the waiting room.

He was eating a shiny red apple, and even that wasn't the most tempting thing about him. Penn always looked effortlessly gorgeous, and if every hair wasn't tamed into place, as it usually was on the train, then that just made him look even more desirable.

Exhaustion was the only explanation for being able to actually sleep in the same house as someone with that kind of sex appeal. Or maybe—as she'd slipped under the covers of the comfortable, fresh-smelling bed last night, Grace vaguely remembered letting out a sigh. In the quiet of the anonymous, perfectly tidy cottage, she'd felt…safe. Because Penn was there, and he'd make everything all right.

'What's the story?' He reached into the breakfast carrier bag and handed her an apple. Red, shiny and tempting, but even so Grace took a bite from it.

'She had a comfortable night. I'm taking that to mean that she has a sufficient amount of pain relief.'

'That's always a plus. It's not an easy thing to get right.' Penn had clearly decided on taking a positive outlook, but it was still reassuring to hear him say it. 'No word on whether they'll operate today or not?'

'No, the consultant will be seeing her this morning and making a decision. The nurse seemed to think they would be going ahead with the surgery this afternoon.'

'Good. Nurses usually know what we'll decide before we get a chance to even examine a patient. When can you see her?'

'She said to wait until ten, when visiting time starts. They're still dealing with breakfast and medication at the moment.'

Penn nodded. Clearly he thought that everything was going as it should, and that was an enormous relief.

'It's odd, isn't it?' He stretched his legs out in front of him, taking another bite of his apple. 'This visiting business. Whenever someone says *"The consultant will decide"* I keep thinking that I ought to be somewhere in that loop. Only I'm not. I'm sitting in a waiting room, eating an apple.'

It was a good look for Penn. Grace had to admit that.

'Yes, I know what you mean. I'm getting a new appreciation of the job that visitors do. I generally concentrate on my patients, and anyone else that's hovering around is secondary. The nurse this morning... She asked me if *I* was all right.'

'First thing of value that I ever learned at medical school.' Penn grinned. 'Nurses know everything. I'd be asking how you were doing as well, even if you clearly don't think that's a pertinent question. Being a carer is a tough job, and you and your sister and cousins are going to be a big part of your grandmother's recovery.'

'To be honest with you, I'm looking forward to having something to do. This sitting around is exhausting.' Grace puffed out a breath, wondering if a few stretching exercises might make it all a bit easier. 'Shouldn't you be going? I expect you have things planned for today.'

'I'm okay here for a while.' Penn looked around the empty waiting room as if there was nowhere he'd rather be and took a bite of his apple.

'Go, Penn. I know you're busy and Jessica's on her way. She'll be here in an hour.'

'You're the support crew for your gran today?'

'You noticed?' Grace had been wondering what Penn thought of her sister and cousins last night, all worried and emotional and yet somehow getting to the right place in the end.

'You're all pretty organised. In a disorganised kind of way.'

'I think *flexible*'s the word you're looking for, isn't it?' Penn nodded and Grace smiled. 'We're all in different places in our lives. Jessica's children are of school age and her husband's able to look after them while she's at Gran's, but she lives further away, so she does her two days with Gran and then steps back, apart from spending time on the phone keeping everyone up to date with what's going on. Carrie's a single mum, so she can't stay with Gran overnight, but she does all of the cooking and shopping.'

'Lucky you. That pasty was very tasty.'

'Yes, Carrie's a good cook. Mags is on her own and works from home. She's a web designer, so she can take time off during the week to look after Gran. I take the weekends so that they all have a break.'

'And when's *your* break?'

'During the week. It's not as if the others don't have

things to do when they're not at Gran's. When I say *break*, I mean doing something else.'

'Ah. Yeah, that's my definition of *break* as well.'

'Physician, heal thyself. Or define your own break, Penn.' He had as little time for himself as she did.

'Fair enough. I probably should go and take a break at the glassworks…' He hesitated and then asked the question that Grace was hoping, against all of her better instincts, that he might ask. 'Is it more convenient for you to stay over at mine tonight? You'd be welcome.'

Those better instincts were telling her to say no. But Grace could get used to the feeling of safety and serenity that she'd encountered last night at Penn's cottage, and rejecting his offer seemed like a final admission to herself that she'd never be able to truly reject Jeremy's attitudes. Meeting Penn had made Grace realise that she was strong enough to at least try.

'Thanks. If it's no trouble… I'll probably be here all day, but I can pick up something for dinner on the way back.'

'I usually just order a takeaway. That might be easier.'

'I'm getting a bit weary of eating food that fits into a container. I'd like to cook.'

He chuckled. 'You've got a point. If you feel like it, a home-cooked meal would be really nice, thank you.'

Penn didn't have to be there with her for Grace to feel his presence. He'd asked her to let him know what was happening, and when Gran was taken into the operating theatre at noon, she called him. Jessica had spoken to Carrie and Mags and had another list of questions for Penn, and Grace waited impatiently while he went carefully through the answers. Then, finally she had a chance to speak with him alone, while Jessica wandered away from the bench outside the hospital building, composing the text for their cousins.

She called again after Gran had been brought back to the orthopaedics ward, and while Jessica was sitting with her. Gran had come through her surgery well, and the doctors and nurses were pleased. Grace walked into Truro and then back again to the hospital with her shopping for a final check on Gran and a lift back to the glassworks with Jessica.

'So you're cooking for him?'

'It's the least I can do.' Grace couldn't ignore Jessica's knowing look. 'Cooking for someone isn't necessarily an act of foreplay, you know.'

'Works every time for me and Justin.'

'So I gather. Has it occurred to you that some of us like to just cook and then eat for its own sake?' Sometimes Jessica thought she knew everything about relationships, even if she was Grace's younger sister. Since she and Justin were astonishingly happy, maybe Jessica *did* know a bit more than Grace did. However much she denied it, cooking for Penn was special. Everything she did with him was special.

'You could do a lot worse. Lord Trejowan…'

'How do you know that?' Grace hadn't mentioned it, and she was certain that Penn wouldn't have.

'I mentioned him to Justin last night, saying how great he'd been. He said that the name rang a bell and so we looked it up on the internet.'

Grace was beginning to see what Penn was up against.

He'd spent time going through all of Jessica's questions, and Jessica had thanked him, telling him she didn't know what they would have done without him. But the first thing she'd thought to say to Grace was *Lord Trejowan*.

'You haven't told Carrie and Mags, have you?'

'No! I'm not a gossip.'

'Well…keep it quiet, would you? Penn's worked hard to be a surgeon and that's what he wants to be.'

Jessica nodded. 'Yeah, I can see that a title and a castle… Have you *seen* the castle?'

'Jess, please…'

'Okay.' Jessica held up her hands in an expression of laughing surrender. 'We'll forget all about the castle. He's a kind man, and that means a lot. And breathtakingly easy on the eye.'

Grace couldn't deny that. She nudged her sister's elbow, smiling back. 'Are you going to give me a lift now, or do I have to get a taxi?'

When they reached the glassworks, Grace waited for Jessica to turn in the road and drive away, before she approached the intercom at the front gate. Before she got a chance to work out which button to press, a voice sounded, making her jump.

'Good evening, Ms Chapman. I'll come and help you with your bags.'

The gate swung open in front of her, and before Grace could reply that it wasn't necessary and she could carry her own shopping, the intercom clicked off. As she walked across the car park, she saw a stocky, smiling man heading towards her from the barn.

'I'm Arthur.' He held out his hand and Grace decided that giving him just one of the bags would be enough.

'Grace.'

'I'll be keeping an eye on the place tonight. So if you see any lights in the barn, you don't need to worry, it'll be me.'

Grace had been thinking of sleeping, in preference to looking out of the windows. But it was nice of Arthur to mention it. He was cheerful and smiling, but there was a trace of assurance about him that made Grace suspect he was good at his job.

'Thank you. Penn tells me you're an ex-policeman.'

'Yes, twenty-five years. I'm a bit too young to retire, so I got together with a couple of mates I'd been on the force with, and we set up our own security business. Working nights suits me. It gives me a bit of time during the day to spend with the grandkids.'

Arthur stopped suddenly, putting the bag he was carrying down and opening the gate to the small garden in front of the cottage.

'This is as far as I go. It's as far as any of us go. We like to give Penn a bit of space.'

Grace imagined that Penn was very grateful for that. He had little enough time to himself at the moment, and it was a nice gesture. Grace picked up the bag, then stepped onto the front path.

'Thanks, Arthur. Have a good night.'

'You too, Grace.'

The scents of last night were an undisciplined riot of colour this evening. It was a real cottage garden, planted to be self-seeding and involve a minimum of work, although the shrubs and climbing plants did need to be cut back. As she walked up the garden path, the front door opened and Penn appeared. Suddenly, all of her attention was sucked away from the flowers, from Arthur's watchful kindness and from the beauty of this quiet place. Even the ever-present worry about Gran seemed to recede a little.

This felt suspiciously like coming home.

It had been a tiring night. And an even more tiring day.

Penn had lain awake last night, listening for sounds of crying or pacing, or anything else that might suggest Grace was awake and needed some comfort. Quite what comfort he was going to give hadn't featured too greatly in his thinking, because he was determined not to invade any of her space, so hugging was out of the question. Although when he'd seen her in pink elephant pyjamas, the temptation to hug her had been almost irresistible.

He'd spent much of his time in the shop this morning, working out what needed to be made next week to replenish their stocks. Then he'd gone to his office, and instead of sitting down behind the desk, he'd thrown himself down on the long leather sofa that had been his father's one nod towards inviting anyone into his minimalist lair. Mostly it had been used for sleeping after his father had been working late, and the walk across to the cottage was too far to contemplate.

Penn had slept soundly for three hours, his phone balanced on the square arm of the sofa so that it would wake him if Grace called. When she did, he'd spoken with her for half an hour and the news had been good. That, more than anything, had restored him to wakefulness and he'd taken the accounts with him back to the cottage to await her arrival.

Grace never just *arrived* anywhere. She seemed to burst into the space around him, bringing the kind of light and colour that he had thought that only glass could create. He followed her into the kitchen and watched as she unpacked her bags, stowing an extra pint of milk away in his otherwise empty fridge.

'How was your day?' He leaned in the open doorway, which gave her the run of the kitchen and also allowed Penn to indulge in his new favourite pastime of watching every move she made.

'Gran came round from the anaesthetic well, although she's still pretty dopey. But she knew that Jessica and I were there, and we got her to drink a little juice.'

'Sounds good. You'll be going back tomorrow, I take it?'

'Yes. I may just go in the morning, and Carrie or Mags will go in the afternoon. What about your day?'

'I spent most of it in the shop.' Penn decided to leave out the unscheduled nap. 'We were busy… A lot of people who'd heard about the open day came to take a look. They're going to be busy in the workshop next week if we're going to keep pace with the demand.'

'That's great. It sounds as if things are really taking off.' Her smile chased away all of Penn's reservations about that. Grace always made him feel that impossibilities were just challenges.

'Our next job is to meet the demand. No one wants any of our standards to slip. We're not a production line. Every piece is different.'

'So you'll be busy for a while longer.'

'I reckon so. Are you going back to London tomorrow evening?' Perhaps he should take the car and drive them both.

'I haven't made my mind up. I called my boss at home today and she said that I could take a week's compassionate leave. But I feel I should go back to work.' She turned suddenly. 'I can't decide what's best. What do you think?'

The agonising tug of war between staying uninvolved and getting involved vaporised suddenly. Nothing could withstand the heat of Grace's gaze, or the way that it made him feel.

'I think… Take the leave.'

'That's what you'd do?'

'Trick question. No, probably not. I'd be thinking in exactly the same way you are and trying to do two things at once. But there's such a thing as pushing yourself too hard, and that's not going to benefit you, your patients or your boss.' He grinned at her. 'You asked me what I thought was best.'

'Ah. Glad you cleared that one up.' She smiled back at him, before turning to the shopping bag on the counter.

'Can I suggest a compromise, then?' Penn wasn't going to give up that easily. 'I've got a videoconferencing set-up in my office, which allows you to change the camera angle and focus with a remote control. It's great for presentations and such like, and it would actually be really good for speaking with your patients because you're not tied to a desk. It'll never replace actually seeing people, but it'll work for one week and allow you to check in with people. Your colleagues can fill in with people who need an in-person consultation or an examination, but it'll probably take quite a bit of the load off them.'

'So, I could come to the glassworks during the day and use the equipment?' Grace was thinking about it…

'Why don't you just stay here? I won't be around, but there's security at night and plenty of people at the glassworks during the day. You can drop me at the station tomorrow and use the car during the week to get to the hospital. You might even find you have time to just sit in the sun, or go for a long walk in the countryside.'

She turned, staring at him. 'That sounds…rather too good to be true.'

'And so you're thinking of reasons why you shouldn't do it.' Penn could save her the trouble. He knew exactly why Grace didn't want to go for the idea.

'And I dare say you have a theory about what they might be?' Her eyes were dancing with humour.

'First, you do what needs to be done, and you're not used to taking the easy way out. Second, you're still a little hung up over this business of the balance sheet. Which I don't blame you for, by the way. I just wish I could convince you that no one's keeping count.'

Grace pursed her lips. 'I'll do you a deal. My worst nightmare for yours.'

'What's my worst nightmare?' He had a few. Right now, losing Grace came at the top of the list.

'Take me to the castle. Your castle. Next weekend. You have the door key?'

'You want to go there?' That ranked pretty high on his list of nightmares, because he'd already lost too many people to the place. Penn had stood by helpless, watching it take people that he loved from him, as its quiet grandeur suddenly became more important to them than he was.

'Yes. I'm curious.'

Okay, he'd go for it. It was a risk but Grace had trusted him, and he should return the favour. 'It doesn't actually have a door key, though. Think drawbridge and a padlock and chains.'

'It has a moat!' Grace's eyes lit up. 'Tell me there are water lilies and we can go paddling.'

No one had asked that before. Penn wondered if there was time to install a few water lilies before next weekend, and decided that Grace would just have to take the castle as she found it.

'No water lilies, sorry. It's a bit deep for paddling, but I suppose we could sit on the edge and dip our feet in.'

She actually looked disappointed. Penn wondered whether the treasures of the castle would make up for that and rather hoped they wouldn't.

'Do we have a deal, then?' She walked across the kitchen, holding her right hand out, and Penn took it.

'Deal. So what's for dinner?'

'Homemade hamburgers, pan-fried chips and salad. It's not as fatty as it sounds.'

'Once in a while's okay. Shall I open a bottle of wine?'

'No, not for me. I'll either fall asleep or start crying…' Grace turned the corners of her mouth down. The worry over her grandmother was never too far beneath the surface, even if she did try to hide it.

'Yeah. On second thoughts, I might, as well. Let's just eat and have an early night, shall we? Tomorrow's another busy day.'

And it seemed the next week was going to be make or break. But it was the only way forward for them. Penn just had to trust and hope that it wouldn't break them.

CHAPTER TEN

It had been a challenging week. Gran was recovering well and already able to walk a few steps, and it had been decided that she should go to rehab for a while, before she went home. Like all decisions, it hadn't been as simple as it sounded, and Grace had had to work very hard to get everyone on the same page.

Penn had been right. She'd needed to be here. He'd been right about the videoconferencing as well. His assistant had shown her how to use the camera and the large wall-mounted screen, and it had been a good way of monitoring her patients and alleviating the workload for her colleagues while she was away. A couple of her regular patients had even suggested that it was a lot more convenient for appointments when just a progress report and some advice was necessary.

She'd slept better than she had in a long time, in the comfortable bed with the windows open to the sounds of the countryside. She'd gone for a few walks, and sat in the workshop with Phil, watching while he fashioned dolphins. And she'd made progress on another little project that she hoped Penn would like when he returned.

He'd called to say that he'd be back on Friday evening. And just in case she'd thought he'd forgotten about the bargain they'd made, they could visit the castle on Saturday afternoon if she was free.

She drove into Newquay to meet the train that arrived just after ten on Friday. The thrill of seeing his silhouette against the lights of the station wasn't unexpected, but it always took her slightly by surprise, as if every time she saw him was always the first. When he got into the passenger seat of the car, his smile had much the same effect.

'Am I late?'

'No, you were on time. The train was four minutes early.'

'Good journey, then?' Grace started the car and concentrated on turning in the road, so that she didn't have to think about how tempting it was to take the cliché of picking him up at the station a little further and kiss him.

'Long and boring. I had to resort to reading this from cover to cover.'

He unfurled the magazine that was rolled into his hand, showing her this month's edition of the journal they'd both been reading when they'd met. Had it really been a month? So much had happened and yet it had flown by.

'Anything good in there?'

'Page twenty-seven. Very interesting article.'

He remembered. Grace remembered every word of that first conversation too.

'I'll have to borrow yours. Mine will be on my desk at the clinic.'

'So how was your week?'

Grace puffed out a breath. 'Gran's recovering well.

She'll be released from hospital in a day or so, and she's going to rehab. It wasn't an easy decision.'

'That may well be the best thing for her.'

'Yes, I think so too. Jessica, Carrie and Mags don't. They think that we'd be able to look after her at home. And of course Gran wants to go home, so that doesn't help things. I agree with her doctor that her recovery needs to be guided for a little while longer.'

Penn nodded. 'You're right, of course. Sometimes it's difficult to see that when you want everything to go back to normal so much.'

'Yes, it is. And to be honest, practically speaking, it's been an easy week for all of us, because Gran's being looked after in hospital. I had to put my own guilt over that to one side and make the decision on what I know medically. I persuaded them in the end, but when I told Gran…' Grace felt her chest heave with emotion. 'When I told Gran, she cried.'

'That must have been very tough for you.'

'We talked it through and I told her that I'd gone to see the place and everyone has their own room and there's a nice garden. They even have a hairdresser who comes in on Wednesday afternoons, and that was a big plus point for her. But I never wanted to be the one that told Gran she couldn't go back to her own home, even if it's just for a little while…'

Tears began to mist Grace's eyes and she blinked them away, keeping her mind on the road.

'And how's the videoconferencing working?' He seemed to sense that it was time to change the subject.

'Good. That's all very good. The set-up in your office is great. I called up my boss to show her how it all worked and she was really impressed.'

Penn nodded, smiling. 'And hopefully it gave you the opportunity to keep up with things at work *and* get some time to yourself?'

'Yes, it's been good.' Time to herself had forced Grace to stop and think about a few things, but she'd save that for a conversation when she wasn't driving. 'So tell me about *your* week.'

'Busy, mostly. One thing after another, with not much time to breathe. But Sophie's doing well.'

'You've been going to see her, then?' Of course he had. Penn might like to pretend that he was all about practicalities, but he'd shown himself to be perfectly capable of impractical acts of kindness.

'Yeah. I took her one of Phoebe's orchids…'

'Penn! You're such a softy.' Yet another quality she liked about him. 'Did she like it?'

'She loved it. Phoebe was really pleased too, when I called her to let her know. She said that she might think about how we could do that kind of thing more often.'

'So she and Phil are cooking up a plan behind your back?'

Penn smiled. 'Let's hope so.'

They were approaching the glassworks now, and Grace wound down the car window, waving in the direction of the concealed camera. The light flipped on, and Arthur's chuckle sounded from the intercom as the gate opened.

'Come on in, dear.'

As she drove past the barn, giving Arthur another wave, Penn chuckled. 'He doesn't call *me* dear…'

'You don't bake cupcakes for him.'

'No, that never occurred to me. So how *was* the oven?'

'It still had one of the stickers inside from when it was new. I didn't notice it until after I switched it on, and by that time, it was half melted and I had to scrape it off.' Even the little annoyances of life had been an odd kind of pleasure. Doing things that she didn't actually *need* to do but wanted to do.

'So you're not going to believe that I kick back and bake cupcakes every now and then?'

'No, you'll have to come up with another imaginary hobby. Cupcakes are all mine.' Grace parked the car, but as she went to switch off the headlights, Penn reached across, stopping her.

'What have you done, Grace?' There was a hint of tension in his voice.

'You said…' He'd said that the front garden had needed attention and she'd gone out on a warm evening and done some weeding. It had looked so much better that she'd kept going, cutting some of the shrubs back from the path the following evening. Maybe that had been a mistake, and Penn liked the untamed look.

'No, I didn't. I don't remember saying that the cottage was yours on condition that you did a little gardening.'

So *that* was his problem. 'I like gardening, and I don't get to do it at home.'

He narrowed his eyes. 'I'm just trying to work out whether that's really the point. It looks great, by the way.'

'Well, that's something. And since when do you

get to judge? You're the one who scatters dolphins and flowers around to all and sundry.'

'No one else gets dolphins.' He grinned suddenly, and Grace shivered as tingles ran down her spine. The dolphin was special to her, and it was nice to know that it had been special to Penn as well.

He pinched the bridge of his nose with his thumb and forefinger. 'Okay…rewind. Thank you, it's a really nice gesture, and I'm sure you enjoyed doing it a great deal. I'll admit that it'll be a relief not to get slapped in the face by foliage whenever I forget to duck.'

'And thank you again for letting me use the cottage. It's been a really nice opportunity to take some time for myself and settle my mind. I'll admit that while I enjoyed the gardening, I also reckoned it was the least I could do in return.'

That hadn't been so difficult. The warmth in Penn's face as he nodded a smiled acknowledgement made her feel that the bargains she made with him didn't ever come with a hidden price. She switched off the headlights, and as her fingers fumbled to release her seat belt in the darkness, Penn got out of the car, then made for the driver's door to open it for her.

'Penn, could you…' He was a shadow in the scented warmth of a summer's night, and Grace couldn't stop herself from reaching to touch him. 'I really need a hug.'

His arm curled gently around her waist, and his fingers spread across her back. An irresistible impulse drew her closer and she heard Penn catch his breath.

'What's all this about, Grace?'

'It's just… I've had time to myself this week and…

Does it make any sense if I say that I'm feeling the difference between good things and bad again?'

He chuckled. 'Makes perfect sense to me. When you're overwhelmed, you don't dare feel the bad and so the good loses its lustre as well. Stress makes it all just something you have to get through before you go on to something else.'

Penn felt it too. That was no surprise—his schedule was punishing. 'This week, I've started to want the good things again. Things I can do that are just for my own pleasure.'

She felt him take a breath and he hugged her tight. 'I think that's called self-love, isn't it?'

'Yes, I think so. I'm surprised that you do. You're not exactly a poster boy for being proud of what you were born with.'

That made him laugh out loud. 'I'm hoping you might discover the knack of it and let me in on the secret.' Grace felt his lips against her cheek, lingering just a moment longer than they should.

One moment more. One more stolen kiss that she dared to plant a little closer to his lips. And then they drew back from each other, as if in silent agreement that any more would catapult them beyond the point of no return. The downward quirk of Penn's lips told her that he regretted not being able to take that step as much as Grace did.

'I saved some cupcakes for you.' She smiled up at him.

'You did? That was going to be my next question. I'll enjoy eating them.'

Grace laughed. She slipped her hand into the crook of his arm, letting him lead her towards the garden gate.

Penn had slept soundly last night, even if the prospect of the castle was beginning to loom. When he woke, something about the quiet of the cottage felt like home.

He had to finally admit that he was in a relationship with Grace. They shared their thoughts and fears, nurtured and encouraged each other. Penn lived for the times he was with her, and he seemed to be able to make Grace happy too. Sex wasn't everything…

Penn stretched his arms against the pillows. Even if sex wasn't everything, he still spent quite a bit of time thinking about it. But he could wait, until the time was right.

Grace had already left for the hospital, but when he went downstairs, there was a note on the refrigerator door in the kitchen, which said she'd be back by noon and was an obvious hint that he should be ready by then for their outing to the castle. He'd put their bargain to the back of his mind this week, but now it seemed all-important because this obstacle had to be climbed before they could risk getting any closer. Terrifying, and yet full of the wild promise of Grace's smile.

He could either sit here and daydream all morning, or work his fears and desires out of his system. Penn made coffee and set off on his morning rounds. A little different from those at the hospital, but the net effect was still much the same—he got to see how everyone was doing and made himself available for anyone who wanted to talk to him.

The workshop was unusually busy for a Saturday.

Hours at the glassworks were flexible, but everyone here had responded to the success of the open day and the sudden dip in stock levels and were working hard to make up the shortfall.

'Any chance of a hand here?' Phoebe called over to him. Penn was used to fetching and carrying for the glassmakers. He'd done it for his father when he was little and he enjoyed being part of the process.

'Sure. What do you need…?' Penn picked up a pair of the thick gloves that protected glassworkers from burns, along with an apron and face shield.

'If you could take a few things through for annealing.'

Phoebe was clearly on a roll this morning, and when she was, there was no one faster. Phil's measured style suited the subtle swirl of his own pieces, and Phoebe's speed seemed to bring her brightly coloured flowers to life.

He started to carry finished items through to the large annealing oven, where glass would be cooled at a consistent temperature to harden it. Stacking the oven was a skilled job in itself that Penn had learned when he was just a teenager, working here with his father, and the craftspeople here trusted him to do it.

After an hour, he called for everyone to take a break. Busy was one thing, but safety was everything, and he'd noticed that a very recent recruit to the glassmakers' ranks had been cutting corners. He beckoned to Phil, who seemed to know what Penn's concerns were already.

'Andy's a good lad. He cares about what he does and he's got…something.' Penn nodded. The *something* that

Phil was referring to was that indefinable thing that made a good glassmaker. Everyone here recognised it.

'But he's rushing.'

'Yeah, I know. The place he came from is all about productivity.'

'That's all well and good, but I won't have him compromise on safety. His or anyone else's.'

Phil nodded. 'I'll have a word. Are you around today?'

Penn looked at his watch, feeling suddenly guilty, torn between feeling he ought to be here and wanting to be with Grace. 'For another hour. I was hoping to get away this afternoon, after twelve.'

'No matter. I just wanted to talk to you about the proposal you made.'

'Yeah? Thought any more about it?' Phil was the undisputed boss in the workshop when Penn was away. Everyone knew that. Penn had suggested that they might regularise the situation by giving him a pay rise and a job title that expanded his role a little.

'I had a word with Jeannie. She says that I speak pretty well about glassmaking.'

'She's right.' Phil's wife was the practical one of their partnership. 'You're the best advocate for our work there is, because you don't even know you're doing it.'

'And I wouldn't mind having the authority to make a few changes in the workshop.'

Penn laughed. He was in the habit of automatically agreeing to anything that Phil suggested, so nothing much was going to change there.

'So you think you might give it a go?'

'Maybe.' Phil obviously wasn't going to make a final

commitment just yet. 'I'd like to go through everything with you in detail first, though.'

Penn should make himself free. This was obviously something that was important to Phil. Habit made the offer linger on the tip of his tongue, but Grace… Grace seemed to be pulling at his sleeve, telling him that there was more to life than just work.

'Uh… I don't suppose you're here tomorrow, are you?'

'It's Jeannie's birthday tomorrow, so I'm not going to be around. Anytime in the next couple of weeks maybe, eh?' Phil ambled away, clearly satisfied with the arrangement. Perhaps *now* wasn't quite as important a word as Penn had taken it for.

When everyone went back to work, Penn stayed in the open doorway of the workshop. All of the other glassmakers were going at their own pace, knowing that Penn's rule of safety first was the one that they should never break. But Andy…

Penn jumped as someone tugged at his sleeve. Grace was half an hour early, and just the sight of her made Penn wonder how he'd made it through the morning without seeing her. She was wearing a sleeveless dress, fitted at the top with a wider skirt that filmed around her legs, and Penn's overall impression was that somehow she appeared to be shining in the sunlight.

'New dress?' He cleared the lump from his throat.

'It's Jessica's. I didn't have many clothes with me when I came down here. She said it suited me better than it did her, and I could keep it if I wanted.'

Penn nodded, hoping that Grace would make the right decision. She always looked wonderful, but usually dressed for practicality. Something new, even if it had been given to her by her sister, seemed to be in keeping with a week that had held a few unnecessary pleasures.

'How did this morning go?'

'Really well. Carrie was the one who was most against Gran going into rehab, but she's been asking around in the village and one of her friends actually knows the place where Gran's due to go. Her mother was there after a car accident. So who should turn up at the hospital while I was there but the mother, whose name is Edna and has known Gran for years. Edna was telling Gran all about the rehab centre and how much it helped her get mobile again, and by the time she'd finished, Gran had decided that she wanted to go after all.'

'That's nice of Carrie. Exploring the other option that she didn't agree with.'

'Yes, I'm really grateful to her for that. I feel much better about it all…' Grace jumped suddenly, her hand flying to her mouth. When Penn looked around, he started forward, but she caught his arm, because Phil was already dealing with the incident in the workshop.

'I told you not to rush, lad.' Phoebe had stepped back as slivers of molten glass skittered across the concrete floor, and she was nodding to emphasise Phil's point.

'Sorry, Phil. I was trying to keep up.' Andy gestured towards Phoebe.

'Phoebe's an experienced glassmaker, and she goes at her own pace. You're still learning and the first and only thing you need to keep your eye on is safety.'

Phil turned, calling for everyone to stop and waiting while the glassmakers finished what they were doing.

'We've got a way to go to make up on the stocks. But we all know that glass takes its own time, and if I find that anyone's produced more than they usually do today, it'll go straight in with the cullet.'

Penn saw Phoebe's eyes widen, but she nodded in agreement with Phil.

Grace tugged at his sleeve. 'What's the cullet?'

'Waste glass. Putting a perfectly good piece in with the cullet is about the most shocking thing you can do…' Penn murmured back.

'Ah. Go, Phil,' Grace whispered.

'Fair do's, Phil.' One of the other glassmakers spoke up and everyone else agreed.

Penn saw Andy apologise again to Phil, who had the trace of a smile on his lips now. He seemed to be offering to show Andy a few things, and the lad grinned, accepting gratefully and standing next to Phil as he began to demonstrate some of his own techniques.

'You're staying, aren't you?' There was a trace of disappointment in Grace's tone, but she'd understand. If things needed to be done here…

Suddenly, he knew. If there had been any real issues around workshop safety, then he would have been compelled to stay, but Phil had things under control and everyone already accepted his authority. And he wanted this time with Grace. Even though it seemed like a terrible risk and his instinct was to put it off as long as possible, he knew that the longer he put it off, the greater the risk. If Grace was going to surprise him, and fall prey to the castle's malevolent spell, it would be better to know now before he started to fall in love with her.

It was already too late to worry about that, because

he'd started to fall in love with her some time ago. And if love meant trust, he should show a little of that too. He had to trust Phil and the other glassmakers as well, because he couldn't be here seven days a week.

'Just for fifteen minutes, eh?' Penn looked at his watch. 'We'll go at twelve.'

That beautiful, sunny smile of hers nearly knocked him off his feet. 'You're sure?'

'I'll have a word with Phil first but…yes, I'm sure.'

CHAPTER ELEVEN

PHIL HAD TOLD him to go. Phoebe had whispered to him to go, because Phil always had everything under control and Penn would know that if he were here more often during the week. Penn lingered for another five minutes, and then Phoebe looked daggers at him and he walked out of the workshop. Grace seemed to have disappeared, and he took five minutes to freshen up and change his shirt, then found her waiting for him in the sunshine by his car.

'So it's a real outing?' She nodded at his shirt. 'Should I go and get my tiara?'

It was a harmless joke on her part, but it hurt. Penn gave her a wry smile.

'No, but you could give me a break.'

He drove south, towards the coast. Grace was quiet, perhaps sensing his nervousness. Or maybe she was a little nervous herself. She'd had her own reasons for not reacting well to finding out about his title.

They topped the brow of the last hill, and the castle came into sight below them. Situated on a long slope that meandered down towards the sea, grand in the sunlight. This was usually where the tour buses stopped, and Penn wondered if he should do so. The five round towers, joined by thick defensive walls to form a rough circle around the green at the centre, were all visible from here.

'Oh!' Grace clapped her hand across her mouth, her eyes suddenly wild with an emotion that Penn couldn't divine. 'It's…big.'

He decided to stop the car. No point in rushing towards whatever awaited them.

'What do you think?'

She turned to look at him. 'I don't really know. I didn't expect this, Penn.'

'What *did* you expect?'

'Um… I don't know that, either. It looks a bit scary.'

Yeah. Castles were meant to look scary. Penn reckoned that wasn't what Grace meant.

'Scares me too.'

She reached across, took hold of his hand and squeezed it. 'Let's storm it together, then. Safety in numbers.'

If she'd stay with him then that was all the safety Penn needed. He nodded, put the car back into gear and drove down the sloping road towards the castle.

By the time it loomed up next to them, she seemed to have regained her composure, opening the car window and looking up at the stone walls. She commented on the moat, seeming to thoroughly approve of it even if it didn't contain water lilies, and Penn drove across the wooden bridge that led to the entrance.

'Stop! Penn, please stop.'

He stopped the car. Grace got out, bent down to examine the sides of the wooden structure and then turned to him. 'This doesn't go up and down, does it?'

'No. The castle's open to the public from time to time, and having a real drawbridge isn't all that practical these days.'

'Oh.' She got back into the car. 'Well, never mind.'

Penn felt a smile tug at his lips. No one had ever been disappointed before that the drawbridge didn't go up and down, and he wondered whether Grace would have demanded a demonstration if it had. He drove towards the high gates, unlocked the smaller access gate incorporated into the bottom of one of them and then parked in the shade of one of the thick walls. Grace didn't get out of the car.

'There's no one here.'

'There might be. There are a few of apartments over on the far side, for the people who work here.'

'Are *they* here?'

Penn shrugged. 'No idea. It's Saturday. They might have gone shopping. Or gone to the beach or the pictures.'

The idea seemed to amuse her. 'Fancy living in a castle and going to the supermarket.'

There was no answer to that. Everyone needed to go to the supermarket. Penn reached for the glove compartment and took out the pair of binoculars that he'd brought with him. 'Here. You'll need these.'

He'd reckoned that Grace might like the battlements, and so he cut across the grass of the courtyard to reach the side that overlooked the sea, stopping when Grace bent to examine a tiny wildflower at her feet. His mother obviously hadn't been here in a while or she would have uprooted it ruthlessly, and Penn thanked his lucky stars that it had escaped.

'Emma said…' She pressed her lips together, obviously not wanting to get Emma into any trouble, and Penn smiled an encouragement, wondering what Emma *had* said. 'She said she'd been here on a school visit once. Is the castle open to the public on some days?'

'Usually, in the summer. It's been closed this year. We had some people in from one of the museums to open up some of the older parts of the interior, and it was decided it would be better to give them the run of the place. They've pretty much finished now, and we might open up again for the autumn.'

'That helps keep the place running?'

'It's mostly just so people can come and see it if they want to. My great-grandfather sold off most of the land that was attached to the place, and established a trust, which covers the costs of upkeep.'

'So…the land beyond the moat isn't actually yours?'

'He sold off the land that you can't see from here. Which isn't as far as it sounds because we're surrounded by hills.' Penn unlocked the door that led to the winding staircase that would take them up to the battlements.

Grace grabbed at her skirts as they stepped out into the stiff breeze coming from the sea. Rather than hold them in place, she pulled the sides forward to knot them together at the front. It was a practical measure, leaving her hands free for the binoculars, even if her normally brisk stride was slightly foreshortened. One more thing to love about her.

They spotted ships and pleasure boats, far out to sea, and then went downstairs to the large rooms below them, which had hardly changed since the castle had been built. But when Penn pulled the dust covers from some of the castle's greatest treasures, they didn't seem to impress Grace as much as the open air and a small flower.

'You've shown me lots of wonderful empty spaces. Where do *you* fit into all of this?'

As they wandered out into the sun of the courtyard again, Grace asked the inevitable question. But Penn's confidence was beginning to grow. Grace had shown a polite appreciation for the interior of the castle, a keen interest in the work of the museum, and she'd loved the view from the battlements. But the warmth of her smile seemed reserved only for him.

'I grew up in the apartment my mother now has, over there…' He pointed to a set of windows that ran across the main castle walls. 'When she decided I was old enough for a place of my own I ended up there.' He indicated one of the towers.

'You lived in a tower?'

'It's never been my permanent home. I came back for the holidays when I was studying, and I used to spend some of my weekends here. Now I always stay at the glassworks when I'm in Cornwall.'

That was partly a matter of time. Partly because he'd lost confidence in the idea that it was possible to be himself when he was here. But Grace's reactions and his own sheer longing that this time might be different had given him the courage to show her everything.

'Want to come for a cup of tea? At my place?'

'I could really do with a cup of tea right now.'

He led her across the grass and unlocked the door that led to the private staircase, which would take them up two flights to the side door that opened straight into his kitchen. Above that, the sitting room took advantage of the best views, and on the two floors below, there was a study and a bedroom. Grace stepped inside, looking around.

Grace wasn't sure what to expect from a castle's living quarters. She actually hadn't been sure what to expect from any of the afternoon.

She'd wanted to come here. She knew that it was a part of Penn's life that he wanted to keep hidden, and that had been an ever-present barrier between them, like a malevolent ghost at a banquet. The feeling that there was nothing she could give him only became more of a threat when she knew that there was a lot about his life that she hadn't seen yet.

She'd been very afraid, though. When he'd stopped the car, she'd almost got out and run, although there wasn't really anywhere she could run to. But his obvious feelings about the place, his admission that he too was afraid, had given her strength. If his invulnerability was unnerving, then his vulnerability only made her want to fight for him. With him.

The kitchen was large, completely circular and displayed the scrupulous cleanliness of somewhere that was cleaned every week and then not used. Sand-blasted stone walls gave texture and contrasted with shiny cream-coloured cupboard doors and a wooden worktop that curved around one hundred and eighty degrees of the space. On the other side, there was plenty of room for a sofa and shelves of books, and in the centre a huge island with space for sitting and eating.

'It's so light in here.' The large windows, looking

out to sea, were a surprise. 'I thought that towers had little windows.'

'They usually do. But this is a watchtower, looking out to sea. Originally they would have had wooden barricades that fixed over the windows, to shield the defenders from arrows, but the real point of this place was not to let anyone land or get close enough to fire arrows.'

'Hmm. I'm learning a lot about medieval warfare.' She smiled at him.

'This has been here since medieval times, but it really came into its own during the Tudor period, and they modernised it quite a bit then.'

'Ah. Tudors who had no hesitation in ignoring their history and installing a few mod cons.'

He chuckled. 'Yes. They were more interested in practicality. I don't have any milk, but I can pop across and see if anyone's in to borrow a cup full…'

'That's fine. I'll have some of the herbal tea—that looks nice.'

Penn made the tea, and led her up a curved stone staircase that was set into the wall, the treads covered with polished wood that matched the wooden handrails on the open side. The sitting room had the same large windows, perfect for looking out to sea, and a stone hearth, with leather sofas arranged around it. Curved shelving on the walls held glass and books, and there was a large statement piece to one side of the windows.

'That's beautiful.' Grace walked over to inspect the blue and white ripples that seemed to be begging her to reach out. 'Can I touch it?'

'That's what it's made for.' Penn seemed pleased at

her reaction. 'It was my father's favourite piece from all the things he made. He kept it in storage, but I had it moved here, because it's too big for the cottage.'

'It's nice that you have it on display. Something like this shouldn't be hidden away.'

'He'd be pleased to hear you say that. I don't know why he kept it in storage. It wasn't like him to do that.'

Grace had been looking carefully for Penn's reactions to everything she did, knowing that it would be so easy to say the wrong thing and hurt him. But the curves of the glass, the way that it seemed to swirl and revolve around the centre of the piece, reminded her of something.

'It looks…a bit like two people, in an embrace. There are no heads or arms but…' Now that she'd seen it, she couldn't unsee it.

Penn walked across the room and stood beside her, staring at the piece. 'You know, I think you're right. I never saw it before, but… To be fair, I don't remember this ever being on display, so I didn't see much of it. I just knew that he liked it.'

'Maybe your mother knows.'

'I doubt it. And even if she did, she wouldn't say. She and my father were perfectly friendly when I was growing up, not like some couples who dislike each other with the same fervour that they loved each other before it all went wrong. I always wondered how I came to be conceived amongst all that civility.' Penn chuckled. 'Maybe this is my answer.'

'Do you still want it in your living room?' Grace grinned up at him. 'I hope I haven't spoiled it by suggesting too much information.'

He thought for a moment. 'No, you haven't. I've always thought it was beautiful, and if there's a little love there as well, then that's nice. This place could do with it.'

Penn turned away from the swirling glass, as if looking at something that represented love could hurt him. Maybe this place wasn't meant for love. Grace could see how it might be overwhelming if it was the first thing you saw about Penn. But she'd met him on a train. Got to know him, and started to care for him deeply, in the anonymity of rows of seats and first names, where they could be themselves.

'Penn.' He was standing at the window, staring out, and she laid her hand on his arm, feeling the muscles flex at her touch. 'Why are you so afraid of this place?'

He turned to face her. 'Aren't you?'

'I was. But it seems that keeping my eyes on you makes it feel a lot less scary.'

'That's nice… *Really* nice. Not many people do that.'

'Then they're missing out on something special.'

'That's nice too.' He heaved a sigh. 'When I was at medical school, I asked a group of friends down here in the summer. We had a great time. We spent most of it down on the beach. But after that, there were a few comments. Then someone said that they expected I was getting good marks in my assessments because someone had put a good word in for me with the powers that be.'

'That's not fair. You must know it wasn't. You can't get anything you want just by knowing the right people any more.'

'That's not entirely true. It's surprising what some people will offer you when they know you have a title.

But yes, I do know that I had to work for everything I got educationally.'

'And professionally, as well.'

'Again, not entirely true. When I first became a doctor, I was offered a really good job at a private clinic, and when I questioned my mother, it turned out that she knew one of the trustees, who'd put my name forward. I turned it down, and the job I have now is one that I had to work and prove myself to get. Although some people seem to think that it just fell into my lap.'

'It didn't. That's what matters, Penn. That's all that matters.' Grace was beginning to see how this might eat away at a person. It had never occurred to her to check whether any of her own job offers had been because someone knew someone.

'Thank you.'

'No, Penn. Don't you *dare* thank me for saying what I know. And don't you dare think that this place is all I see about you. It's nice… It's big as well and I could see how someone might want to live here.'

'I wouldn't mind living here if it wasn't so remote. It's just too far from my job, and the life I've made. I thought I'd made it obvious what mattered to me and who I wanted to be but…' He shrugged. 'It was a long time ago.'

Someone had broken his heart. 'What happened? A long time ago.'

'I met someone. We did all the usual things, and after a couple of years, I asked her to marry me. She said yes, and that of course we'd be living down here.'

'Did she have family in Cornwall?'

'No, she was from London. But she reckoned that

if you *had* a castle then you were automatically going to live there. I tried to explain that sometimes living in a castle can be inconvenient, and suggested every compromise I could think of, but she wouldn't have it. She wanted me to give up my medical career and take over the day-to-day running of this place. I couldn't accept that and so she left. She said I'd let her down, because she'd dreamed of living here, ever since she'd first seen it.'

Grace knew what it was like to be given an ultimatum. She'd said no, but it had eaten away at her trust in the world.

'It's just one person's view of the world, Penn.'

'Yeah. As I said, it's a long time ago.' He didn't sound much convinced of that, and Grace didn't blame him. She'd finally understood the realities of his assertion that people didn't see him any more once they'd seen the castle, and they were heartbreaking. She could see why he would be cautious in starting anything new.

'Penn.' She stepped towards him and laid her hand on his chest. She felt him flinch, but then he laid his hand on hers as if the gesture were something precious. 'Look at me.'

His gaze found hers. She could see all of the passion in it that was thrumming through her own body. 'This place is a nice place, but that's all it is—just a place. It's you that I see.'

He took her hand in his, raising it to his lips. Then he wound his arm around her waist, kissing her.

As first real kisses went, it was exquisite. Passionate and full of longing, and yet taking nothing for granted.

'Would you… I don't want to push you, Grace, but would you consider…' He seemed unable to say it.

'You're not pushing me. Yes, I'd like very much to go downstairs with you.'

That meant the bedroom. He knew it meant the bedroom. After five weeks of keeping their attraction on a low simmer, it had finally boiled over and Grace imagined it was written just as clearly on her face as it was on his.

'I'd like…'

'Penn! You're really not very good at this, are you?' Grace knew why. It was fear, and she felt it too.

'No, not very. I can make you another cup of tea and then take you home if you want…'

At this rate, a girl was likely to feel that he didn't care. She knew that wasn't true.

'Or you can take me downstairs and make love to me. Which I would like a great deal more than anything else you could suggest.'

His smile told her all she needed to know. 'I would too.'

There was nothing hesitant about the way he kissed her once again, before taking her hand and leading her to the stairs. Winding down, past the kitchen, then to the bedroom.

All she could see was the bed. Penn stripped off a heavy bedspread, and she smelled the scent of fresh linen underneath.

'Stay here. I'll be a moment… Maybe two. I have condoms, but I'm not sure where they are…' He grinned apologetically and Grace kissed him again.

'I'll wait.'

When he disappeared through a door on the other side of the bed, the room resolved into sharp focus. A central wall bisected the circular space, the head of the bed against it. On either side were doors, which must lead to a bathroom and a dressing room, because there was no other furniture apart from two small bedside tables. The light from high windows was softened by fine linen net curtains, and shades of cream and brown gave the space a serene and restful air.

And there was just the bed. It seemed deliciously decadent. Grace sat down on it, and slipped off her sandals, the sound of drawers being opened and closed drifting through the open doorway. Then Penn appeared and she forgot about everything else.

'You started without me.' He nodded towards her sandals, before leaning over to tuck the packet of condoms discreetly under one of the pillows. Getting to her feet, Grace felt Penn's hands resting on her hips as she unbuttoned his shirt.

Undressing him was like opening the best Christmas present she'd ever had. His body looked good in clothes, and even better without them, strong and flawless. Apart from the scar on his forearm. Grace ran her finger over it.

'From the glassworks?' It looked like a burn.

'No, it was from an open fire, here. Christmas ten years ago.'

She bent to kiss the red puckered skin and heard him sigh, as if finally he was beginning to heal. Penn pulled at the zip of her dress, letting it fall around her ankles.

'Appendix?' He ran his thumb across her abdomen.

'When I was thirteen. Gran looked after me and it was the longest time I spent not thinking about jobs I needed to do.'

'I'm going to make you forget about everything else…'

'I already have…'

He was so gentle. So kind. In the depths of his clear blue eyes, Grace found everything she'd been looking for. Penn had struggled for so long to be accepted for who he was, and she knew that the only person he wanted to make love with was the woman she really was.

Penn was all she wanted. She told him so and felt his trembling fingers tracing across her cheek. Heard him promise that she was everything that he wanted. Reassurance gave way to passion and when he slowly entered her, she felt her body arch, ready to take everything that he wanted to give her.

She felt his hand curl around the back of her leg, pulling it upwards against his hip. Moving slowly, searching for something.

'Penn…?' They had this right already. So very right…

'Wait…' He smiled down at her. 'Stay with me, Grace. You know I won't hurt you.'

She'd never allowed a man to take control like this. Using his own body to mould hers and move it into the exact position that would give them both the most pleasure. But Penn had the same knowledge that she did—probably more. He knew just when a muscle would start to pull slightly, stopping the moment before it did. Just how far her body could go.

'Relax… Trust me.'

She could hardly speak, the feeling was so overwhelming. Couldn't answer him with anything other than a sigh. But she felt her body give itself up to him, and his smile told her that he felt it too. His hand slipped beneath her thigh, lifting her slightly, and sharp waves of pleasure began to roll through her.

'Penn. That's right... That's *so* right.'

'Nearly.'

There was more? Grace wasn't sure she could take much more of this. Then he moved again and she realised that she could. She could see a pulse beating in his neck. Feel the way he was hardening inside her. He must be close to the edge too, but still he kept searching.

She heard herself cry out. The sudden catch of his breath. For a moment he was still, letting them both feel the pleasure, and then he started to move, sending scintillating showers of feeling through her. His skin warmed beneath her touch and she felt her own heart thundering in her chest as she came so hard that she felt tears forming at the corners of her eyes.

And then she felt him come, swelling and pulsing inside her. The very angle and position that had given her so much pleasure allowed her to feel his, and that final act of intimacy was overwhelming.

She curled against him, and he held her tight in his arms, pulling the bedcovers over them to keep them warm.

'It's true what they say, Penn.' She snuggled against his chest. 'Orthopaedic surgeons really do rock.'

'Who says that?' He brushed a kiss against her forehead.

'Someone must. It would be unfair not to. We physiotherapists can rock a little too.'

She heard him chuckle softly, in an expression of pure contentment. 'I have no doubt of it. I'm really looking forward to finding out more about that…'

There was only one thing that rivalled the pleasure of having Penn push her further than she'd ever known she could go, and that was finding out just how far she could take him. Using her own insistent craving for him, to make him feel more and then feel it again a second time. They'd made love all afternoon and then slept a little, waking as the sun began to set.

'Is it time for us to go?' Grace didn't want to move, but the ever-present feeling that she should because there was somewhere that she needed to be, had begun to reassert itself.

Penn reached for his watch, which lay alongside the empty condom packet on the small table by the bed. 'Probably. Is there anywhere you need to be in the morning?'

Grace thought for a moment. 'No, not really.'

'There's nowhere I need to be either. We could stay here.'

'Suppose someone wants us?'

He shrugged. 'They'll call. Is your phone charged?'

Always. Grace reached for her bag, which had slid under the bed, and saw Penn's sticking out of the back pocket of his jeans, which also lay on the floor.

'Eighty percent.'

'I've got seventy-five. That'll be plenty.' He took the phone out of her hand, then placed it with his on the table. 'There's no food in the kitchen, but I'll go and get fish and chips from the village. I dare say there's a bottle of decent wine in the cellar to wash it down, and then we can sleep a little, or make love… Whatever we want. Maybe take a walk on the beach in the morning, and then drive back to the cottage for lunchtime.'

That sounded like pure bliss. 'But no one knows where we are.'

He leaned in and kissed her cheek. 'Isn't that one of the best parts of it all?'

CHAPTER TWELVE

PENN WASN'T SURE that he could say what he'd liked best about the last twenty-four hours. Sitting in the kitchen, wrapped in bath-robes and eating fish and chips, accompanied by a very decent bottle of red that he'd appropriated from the cellar beneath his mother's apartment. Showering with Grace, feeling the touch of her fingers as she soaped his body. Being able to hold her close and talk to her, as moonlight slanted across the floor of the bedroom towards them.

Making love had been the most physically pleasurable. Giving himself to Grace, knowing that she trusted him enough to give herself to him, had changed him in ways that he'd never thought possible, literally overnight. And when he thought about it, every moment of those twenty-four hours had been an act of love. Hiding away from the world, with the one person he wanted to be with the most. And finding that his worst nightmare had become a refuge, because Grace was there with him.

Of course there was a price to pay for it all. They'd stayed at the castle until the last moment, and as he'd driven back to the glassworks, Grace was already on the phone to her sister to check that everything was going to plan with their grandmother.

She'd changed her clothes and packed hurriedly, while Penn hurried over to his office to scoop up his laptop and the papers he'd need to take back to London with him, to work on if he got time during the week. Then they were back in the car again, making the London train with only five minutes to spare.

She leaned back in her seat, smiling at him as the train drew out of the station. Something had changed. She seemed more relaxed and somehow happier to plunge back into the rigours of the week ahead. Something had changed in him, too. Something that felt a lot like the first bloom of a precious new love.

'Was it worth it?' He asked the question, knowing how she'd answer but wanting to hear her say it.

'It was worth it.' Grace thought for a moment. 'How are we ever going to manage this, Penn?'

'I don't know. But we've made the time once and we can do it again. I'm pretty busy for most of the week…'

'That's okay. I will be too, but we can see each other next weekend.'

'Meet up on the train, on Friday evening.'

She smiled at him, and suddenly all of the difficulties seemed to be just difficulties and not insurmountable obstacles. 'Yes. We'll do that.'

Grace ran for the train, ducking in and out of the stream of people, all of whom seemed to be coming the other way. Her bag was heavier, because along with some things for Gran, she'd packed more clothes. In the mêlée, she caught sight of Penn running towards her.

'Ten minutes. Plenty of time.' When he reached her, she fell into his arms and he kissed her.

'I didn't want to miss it.'

He smiled down at her. 'Me neither.'

Hand in hand, they made the platform, stepping onto the train and finding their seats. He reached across the small table to take her hands in his.

They relaxed into the familiar bubble that had served them so well. And then the time that was just for her and just for Penn as well spilled over to the bedroom at his cottage. They spent twelve wonderful hours there, before it was time to race out of the door and drive to the rehab centre to see Gran.

It was a little nerve-wracking. Penn was coming with her and this was the start of making things official. Gran would undoubtedly tell Jessica, who would in turn tell Mum and Dad.

'McIntyre…' Gran frowned at him, before turning to Grace. 'Don't I know the name, dear?'

Grace shot an apologetic look at Penn, who was taking the comment better than she'd thought he would. Before she could think of a suitable answer, Gran supplied one herself.

'Are you one of *the* McIntyres? There was an old family… They were in the area for years. I forget the name… It was something else, and then McIntyre.'

Penn smiled at Gran. 'Yes, that's right. I brought you some McIntyre glass.' He proffered the box that he'd been carrying.

'Ooh, thank you, dear.' If Gran knew about the castle or Penn's title, then thankfully her attention had now been diverted to the box. She opened it, then carefully took out one of the four hearts that were inside.

'They're for your window, Gran. You can hang them up here and take them home with you when you go.'

'They're very pretty.' Gran turned the pink and white streaked heart over in her hands, almost dropping it, and Penn's hand shot out to save it.

'I'll leave you to hang them up.' Penn got to his feet. He'd been quietly taking in everything—the reception area, the corridors and Gran's small but cosy room. He was probably going for a nose around.

Gran might be vulnerable, and a little forgetful at times, but keep her in the present moment and she was still as sharp as a pin. 'Are you going to the gym, dear? Seems it's the first thing that everyone wants to see…'

'I'd be interested to see it. Will you take me?' It was important to keep Gran walking as much as she could manage, and Penn obviously wanted to see how well she was doing, as well as what the facilities here were like. Whatever else Penn was, he was still a surgeon.

Gran pointed to the notice on the inside of the door. Someone had drawn flowers around the edge of it, and it stated very clearly that she wasn't to walk outside her room unless she was with a nurse. Penn squinted at it and smiled.

'I'm a doctor. Will that do?'

Gran thought for a moment. There was nothing like a slightly forgetful ninety-year-old to take a person down a peg or two.

'A doctor's fine, Gran. Penn will make sure you don't fall.'

Gran nodded, getting to her feet, taking Penn's arm.

'This is nice, isn't it, Grace? I never thought I'd be escorted by a real lord. Turn right for the gym, dear.'

'I had no idea that Gran knew. I'm so sorry.' Grace walked to Penn's car with him. Hopefully Jessica wouldn't let it slip that she knew about Penn's title until she was officially told.

'That's okay.' Penn seemed unusually relaxed about it. 'My name tends to ring a bell with people in Cornwall, either because of the glassworks or the castle. And your grandmother knows a lot about local history. We had a very interesting conversation about crabbing pots while you were talking to the nurse. She was telling me that she remembers her father fishing with the old-style pots made out of willow.'

'Yes, she does. There's a picture of him somewhere, making one.'

'Really? That's a very rare art these days.' Penn seemed to find her own family more interesting than his own, even if his had a little more real estate attached to it.

'So what did you think of the place?' Grace got into the car.

'Great. The gym's good, and your grandmother's room is very comfortable with all the right mobility aids. They're getting everyone up and about as well. I was very impressed that they're encouraging everyone to go to the dining room for their meals—that's a big plus.'

'Yes, that's one of the things I liked. They give plenty of help, but they expect everyone to help themselves as well. Gran's already beginning to make a few friends.'

'She liked the glass?'

'Are you crazy? After making you fool around for half an hour to make sure it was all hanging in the exact right place? She *loved* the glass, Penn. And it was really nice of Phil to make them for her. I know he doesn't usually do hearts.'

'Maybe we should. They do look very nice with the light shining through them. Perhaps Phil could get Andy to do a few of them.'

'So has Phil accepted the job you offered him yet?'

Penn chuckled. 'He's *doing* the job and I've insisted on negotiating a pay rise with him. Everyone knows he's in charge of the workshop and I dare say he'll let me make that official in his own good time.'

That was Penn all over. Quietly doing the hard work that allowed people to grow, and allowing that to happen in its own way and at its own pace. It seemed possible, in the relaxed atmosphere of their weekends together, that he and Grace might do that, gradually nurturing each other into a new way of thinking about their lives.

When they arrived back at the glassworks, the car park was busy. Grace knew that Penn would be wanting to make one of his unofficial tours of the place, after having been away all morning, and she strolled towards the shop while Penn opened the boot of his car, to sort through the stacks of samples, T-shirts and files for something.

Emma greeted her with a bright smile. 'Everything's under control. I've got an assistant for the day. Phil sent him over so he could see every aspect of the operation, and he's really good with the customers.' She nodded over to where Andy, the new recruit in the workshop, was deep in conversation with a couple. As he talked, his gestures clearly described how the glass bowl they held had been made.

'Penn's on his way over…' Grace grinned back. Emma didn't miss much and she'd clearly put one and one together to make two, but Grace's new relationship with Penn didn't mean that Emma had to report to her. She was a guest here.

Emma chuckled. 'Okay, I'll tell him, then. How's your gran? Okay?'

'Yes, she's good. She really loved the glass hearts that Phil made for her.'

'Mm, so did I. He said he'd make me one…' Emma's head turned as a couple with a large dog, ambling placidly behind them, entered the shop. 'Hang on a minute…'

Emma greeted the couple, before apologising and telling them that they couldn't bring the dog into the shop. The woman remonstrated with her, saying that the dog would be no trouble, and Emma smilingly insisted.

No one seemed to have noticed that the dog wasn't on a lead and that it was gazing up at the light-filled display on one of the shelves. Grace started forward, but before she could reach the animal, it put its paws up onto the shelf, knocking a blue dolphin to the ground. As Emma turned, trying to move the dog out of the way, the glass shelf cracked, sending its contents crashing together and then smashing onto the ground.

Penn first realised that something was wrong when he saw a large dog, bounding through the open door of the shop, followed by a man who seemed to be giving chase.

Then he saw Emma by the full-height window, standing stock still and staring at her arm as blood began to drip down towards her fingers. He dropped the box of T-shirts he was carrying and ran.

Grace was already there, though. As Penn made it to the shop doorway, he heard her voice.

'Can we have some room, please?' The knot of people that had formed around her and Emma began to dissolve in response to her firm tone. 'Andy, make sure no one else has been hurt and that they move out of the shop safely, please…'

Andy took her cue and started to shepherd the customers out of the shop, while Grace wound her arm around Emma's waist, leading her to the chair behind the cash desk and sitting her down, before opening the first aid box that was fixed to the wall behind them. Penn saw dark blood oozing steadily from a wound on Emma's forearm and pushed his way through the people who had congregated in the doorway.

When he hurried over to the cash desk, leaning over to grab some gloves from the first aid box, Grace glanced up at him, the determined heat of her smile searing through him. He passed her a pair of gloves and she pulled them on, turning her attention back to Emma.

'Okay. Emma, you're all right.' She inspected the wound briefly, and Penn put a gauze pad into her outstretched hand.

'Ow!' Emma's face creased in pain as Grace laid the gauze over the wound and applied pressure to it.

'I know. I'm sorry, Em. I have to press hard to stop the bleeding. Now, hold your arm up for me… That's right. Above your head.'

'All this blood…' Emma looked miserably at her stained pink T-shirt.

'A little goes a long way. It looks a lot more than it is,' Grace reassured her.

'You're sure…?'

It was difficult to be sure of anything at this point, but Grace was clearly intent on making sure, untucking Emma's T-shirt with her free hand so that she could slip her hand under the bloodstains and feel for any other injuries. Penn clamped his hand around Emma's arm, freeing Grace up to investigate a little better while he maintained pressure on the wound.

A tear fell from Emma's eye. She was moving from stunned shock to distress, and Penn reached for a wipe, then put it into her hand. 'We've got you, Em.'

'Yeah.' Emma took a shaky breath, dabbing at her face. 'Yeah, I know. Thanks.'

Grace was careful in her examination, making sure that Emma had no other cuts, and taking off her sandals to inspect for any shards of broken glass. Then she shot her a beaming smile.

'You're okay. Don't worry about the blood—it's all from the cut on your arm.' She glanced up at Penn. 'I think it'll need stitches.'

Penn didn't need to look at the cut to confirm it. If Grace said stitches, then the only question in his mind was *how many?* 'Is that okay with you, Emma? I have my medical bag at the cottage.'

Emma stared at him. 'I don't know…' Another tear rolled down her cheek. 'I don't know what to do.'

Grace put her arm around Emma's shoulder, leaning in to explain. 'Penn might be the boss around here, but he can't just tell you what to do about this. He needs your permission to treat you medically. He'll tell you what he thinks is best and then you decide what you want him to do.'

Emma caught on. A little of her playful spirit began to resurface as she turned her head to the security camera, which silently recorded everything. 'Yes, please. I officially want Penn as my doctor.'

Penn chuckled. 'All right. That'll do. Do you feel okay to walk, if Grace is there to steady you?'

'Of course I do.' Emma glanced over to the mess on the floor. 'I'm so sorry, Penn. There's a whole shelf full of glass broken.'

'It wasn't Emma's fault, Mr McIntyre.' Andy had been keeping his distance while they examined Emma, but now Penn heard his voice behind him. 'Someone brought a dog in here and Emma tried to get them to leave, but it jumped up.'

'Thanks, Andy. It's okay, I know that Emma's not to blame. Could you help out by taking charge in here, please? Make sure the door's locked and go over to the workshop and tell Phil what's happened.'

Andy brightened suddenly. 'Yeah, sure. Hope you're okay, Emma.'

'I'll be fine. Thanks, Andy.'

They walked Emma over to the cottage together, and Penn cleared a space on the kitchen table, before wiping it down, while Grace settled Emma into a chair. As he opened his medical bag, Emma craned over to see the contents. By this time, Penn's patients were usually asleep, and he wondered whether Emma was going to want a running commentary on everything he was doing.

'Hey…' Grace quietly laid her finger on Emma's cheek, tipping her head round. 'We'll just let Penn get on with it, eh? I'll keep an eye on him.'

'Can't I watch?' Emma turned the corners of her mouth down.

'I wouldn't want to.' Grace tactfully left out the part about keeping still and letting him concentrate, changing the subject instead. 'Andy seemed very concerned about you.'

Emma nodded, and Penn thought he saw the beginnings of a blush. 'Yeah. He's nice.'

'Any interest?'

That was one way of taking Emma's mind off what was going on, and it seemed to be working. Emma considered the matter, while Penn positioned her arm carefully, before gently peeling the dressing away from the cut. The pressure had largely stopped the bleeding, but Grace was right—it was going to need stitches to heal properly.

'Maybe. We'll see.' Emma flinched as Penn probed the wound a little, and Grace took her hand.

'Nearly done, Em. I'm going to inject a local anaesthetic and then clean and disinfect the cut. Then I'll stitch it.'

Emma kept her eyes focussed on Grace, who gave an encouraging nod. 'Yes. Thanks.'

'All right. You'll just feel a small pinprick…'

'How about you?' Emma seemed determined now not to look and the question was aimed at Grace.

'Me? Oh, you mean do *I* have any interest in anyone…?'

'Yeah.'

Penn wondered if he might just leave, on the pretext that it would take a few moments for the local anaesthetic to work. He straightened, taking a breath, wondering what Grace would say. Her presence at the glassworks was hardly a secret, but the people here had closed around them like a protective family, waiting to be told before they'd admit to noticing anything.

'Yes. Definitely maybe.'

Grace's sudden smile meant everything. They'd taken one more step together and it hadn't hurt at all.

'I don't think that Emma will have too much of a scar, will she, Penn?' Grace adeptly changed the subject again.

'No. Just a hairline maybe. I'll do my best work for you, Em.' Penn's concentration clicked in again.

'There you go, Emma. Benefit of having a top surgeon at your disposal…' Grace smiled at him and Penn went back to the less complicated task of stitching the wound.

Penn clearly had done his best and most careful work, stitching the cut neatly and then covering the wound with a sterile dressing. When Emma protested that she could go back to work now, he reminded her that his insistence he take her home came under his role as boss, not doctor, and he was taking no arguments. Grace took her upstairs to the bathroom, cleaned off the blood smudges that remained and helped her into a new pink T-shirt from the box that someone had picked up from the car park, where Penn had dropped it, and left on the doorstep.

The shop had been cleaned and reopened, and Phoebe had come across from the workshop to fill in. After Andy had asked if he could take his break, Grace had seen him outside in the car park, smiling at his phone and texting. That was probably a sign that Penn would be back soon, and she went up to his office and sat down on the long sofa to wait for him.

'Is Emma okay?' She always felt a thrill when Penn walked into the room.

'She's fine. I gave her mother the list of things to do to care for the wound, and I'll pop in tomorrow to check on her.' He sat down next to her, putting his arm around her shoulders. 'It appears that it would be quite okay for you to come with me, since we're now a definitely maybe.'

'You don't mind?' Grace hadn't been able to resist acknowledging their relationship, and Penn's smile had told her that he was okay with that.

'I doubt it'll be news to anyone here. Do *you* mind?' He was suddenly thoughtful.

'Should I?'

Penn shrugged. 'I don't handle other people's attitudes to my title all that well. I don't see why you should have to encounter that kind of thing because of your association with me...'

Grace laid her finger across his lips. 'Stop, Penn. If we never go out and meet the world then how can we ever really put those things behind us?'

He nodded, hugging her close. 'I like the way you think. By the way...what *does* definitely maybe mean?'

'That I definitely have an all-encompassing interest in you and maybe you feel the same way…' Grace yelped with laughter as he bent her back onto the sofa, pinning her down and kissing her.

'You're in any doubt about how I feel? Perhaps I should reiterate.'

He could reiterate as many times as he liked. Grace would always want to hear it again. 'This is a very comfortable sofa…'

He chuckled. 'Yes, and I'm sure it would work extremely well for impromptu office sex. Sadly, I don't have any condoms in my desk drawer.'

'We could always improvise.'

She felt his hand, tracing a path upwards beneath her skirt. Grace shivered, feeling the warm swell of desire that Penn always created and then used so well.

'Don't get me wrong, I'm all for a little improvisation. But right now, there's nothing I want more than to go the whole way with you, Grace.'

Something stirred inside her. The physical and the emotional falling together into a desire so deep she could hardly contain it.

'I want that too, more than anything. But getting to the cottage…' Someone was sure to stop Penn with an urgent question about something.

'Everything else can wait. This is much more important.' He got to his feet, took her hand and led her out onto the balcony and down the steps. Grace hadn't realised that this secluded short cut existed, and she raced with him to the cottage, waiting impatiently for him to take his keys from his pocket. Then the front door slammed behind them and they were alone.

CHAPTER THIRTEEN

THE LAST THREE weekends had been wonderful. Grace had been busy, working during the week and then coming down to Cornwall to visit Gran every Saturday and Sunday morning. She kept Jessica up to date with all the medical aspects of her progress, and that information was duly passed on to the rest of the family, then the rest of the weekend was her own to spend with Penn.

She'd changed. After Jeremy's betrayal, she'd thrown herself into her work and looking after Gran to the exclusion of everything else. But every time Penn put her first, before everything else in his life, it made Grace feel that maybe she was worthy of a little more than she'd allowed herself to take.

But the practicalities were still stacked against them. Her life, Penn's life, all the things that they both needed to do. And time was running out now, and these idyllic weeks were coming to an end.

She'd met up with Jess, Carrie and Mags for lunch on the Saturday before Gran was due to go home, and they'd discussed and agreed their way forward. When Grace returned to the glassworks, she found Penn hard at work in his office.

'It's all set. Gran will be coming out of rehab this week as planned.'

He nodded. 'That's good.'

'Yes. It's good.' It didn't feel very good, but that was a completely selfish notion. 'Although this is our last weekend together.'

'Grace…?' He held out his hand, and Grace walked around his desk. When she sat down on his lap, he wound his arms around her, pulling her close.

'I feel it too. I'm so pleased that your gran's doing well, and that she's ready to go back home now. But I know it means we'll have less time to spend together.'

'Can we really do it, Penn? I know this isn't a tug of war, but sometimes it feels like it.'

'All I can say is that having someone who's more important to me than anything, has made everything else in my life seem worthwhile. I can't *not* do it.'

He always made her feel that she could take the things she wanted from life. That all she had to do was reach out.

'I love you, Penn. I won't let you go.'

'I love you too.' He kissed her and the impossible seemed to melt away in the heat of his embrace. 'So let's run away. Find a place to spend this afternoon and tonight where no one can find us…'

'Got anywhere in mind? I'll be wanting to dress for the occasion.'

'I was rather hoping you might undress for the occasion. A castle might be nice. Plenty of rooms for us to choose from to undress in.'

Grace laughed. 'Funny you should say that. I happen to know just the place…'

* * *

Gran had been out of rehab for three weeks, and she was doing really well. Grace couldn't say the same for herself.

Two evenings during the week had been harder to organise than they'd imagined. Grace worked two evenings a week, with patients who couldn't come during the day, and Penn never knew if he was going to be delayed. But they'd stuck with it. They'd seen each other at their worst, tired, stressed out or preoccupied. He'd crawled into her bed, late at night and smelling of surgical soap, just so that they could sleep in each other's arms. And still she loved him.

There were phone calls and texts and train rides, sitting together knowing that they'd have to part when they reached Newquay on Friday evening. Sunday evenings were the best time of the week, because they could relax on the train, knowing that they'd be able to spend the night together when they got back to London.

And still they loved each other. When they were together, they lived for the moment, shutting the world out and seeing only each other. If this had taught them one thing, it was that love might not always find the easiest of ways, but it stubbornly refused to give up trying.

After five weeks, Grace could tell that things were taking a turn for the worse, because Penn was sending presents. The first wasn't so challenging—she'd run out of the expensive soap that she'd been given as a gift this Christmas, and then returned home from work on Monday evening to find a large box of soaps, hand cream and body spray waiting for her outside the door to her flat. She'd texted him to say thank you, sending kisses, and he'd texted back immediately, saying that it was his pleasure and that he was looking forward to collecting those kisses in person, when they saw each other.

They'd spent the following evening together, which hadn't felt quite so all-consuming as usual, because they were both tired and Penn was distracted by calls from the glassworks over a large order that Phil wasn't sure they could fulfil. But this was what they'd signed up for, and Grace had told herself that if they could survive this then they could survive anything.

Then the bracelet arrived. Thankfully it hadn't been left outside her front door, and arrived by special courier at the clinic where she worked. Grace had opened the package, staring at its contents. A diamond tennis bracelet, which Penn had obviously put some thought into, because it was difficult to see how a piece of jewellery could be so slim and understated and at the same time so expensive.

Maybe he'd thought it was her birthday. Or maybe the diamonds weren't real. Grace very much doubted that either was the case. It was odd, though, because however much Penn liked giving presents, his were usually more personal. Favourite flowers, glass, coffee made just the way she liked it. This seemed more like a statement, although Grace couldn't fathom what he was trying to say.

She texted him again, thinking carefully this time about how to phrase her thanks. The lack of spontaneity had obviously shown, because he'd texted back, saying that if she wanted something different they could always take it back and the shop would change it.

All the same, Grace wore the bracelet for the train ride down to Cornwall, tucking it carefully into her sleeve in case it drew anyone's attention. He was sitting in his usual seat, and she bent to kiss him and sat down next to him. Penn put his arm around her shoulders, and his scent worked its usual magic. Maybe everything *would* be all right, after all.

'How are things?' Penn glanced at her wrist so fleetingly that she would have missed it if she hadn't been expecting him to do so.

'Things are fine.' She pulled back her sleeve and he grinned suddenly.

'Does this mean you really do like it?'

'It's beautiful, Penn, and it was a very kind thought. I just tucked it into my sleeve while I was walking through the station in case there were any passing muggers.'

'It's pretty well-policed…'

His comment probably meant nothing, and he was just trying to reassure her. But Grace couldn't help wondering if he had a point. She *had* hidden the bracelet, not even showing it to Mia when they'd gone for coffee. It had felt too ostentatious a gift, even if she knew that Penn could well afford it.

'Well, I won't be wearing it on the train every week. I'm going to keep it for best. I wore it today because I wanted to show you how much I love it.' Since when had they had to explain this kind of thing to each other?

'That's thoughtful of you.' His arm tightened around her and she rested her head against his shoulder. 'You don't need to keep it for best. I really wanted to get you something that you could wear as much as you want. We don't get to see each other when we want to, and I wanted to show you that I'm always there for you.'

It all made sense now. The soap, the bracelet. Grace didn't want to throw his generosity back in his face, but diamonds weren't going to fix anything.

'I truly love it, Penn. Even if it does make me miss you even more.'

'And it's a little too much?' Penn voiced the other reason that the bracelet had stayed tucked in her sleeve.

'Maybe…' The carriage was practically empty, but even so she leaned towards him, cupping her hand between her mouth and his ear. 'It's just that all I really want to be wearing is your scent…'

He chuckled. 'Okay, I get it. No more jewellery. But soap's okay?'

'Soap's wonderful and very thoughtful. I won't be needing any more of that for a while, though.'

He gave a mock sigh. 'Fair enough. I don't suppose there's any chance of swapping an afternoon out with one of the others over the weekend?'

'I'd love to, but Jessica's kids are sick and Mags has a deadline so she has to work.' Grace turned the corners of her mouth down.

'Sorry to hear that. You're all under a lot of pressure at the moment.'

'I'm not sure how that's going to change. We've been talking about having a nurse in, maybe just during the night, but it's expensive and I don't know how Gran's going to feel about having a stranger in the house. She doesn't want to go into full-time residential care.' The conversation had been taking place via emails and texts, and had taken up all of Grace's spare time this week. Her flat looked as if someone had broken in and ransacked the place, but she could worry about that when she got home.

'And I guess you're doing the bulk of the investigative work?'

'I understand the system a little better than the others. And I've got a better idea of what to look for.'

He nodded. 'Well, if there's anything I can do to help.'

Grace knew what Penn meant. She probably shouldn't have brought the subject up, but it had consumed her thoughts this week and just flown into her head. And it was out of the question that Penn might help financially, even if he could do so without even noticing it.

'Thanks. I think I've spoken to most of the people I need to speak to now, and I've worked out what benefits Gran is entitled to.'

'Okay. Don't forget that I'm here if you need me.' Thankfully that appeared to be his last word on the matter. 'You're still okay for the train on Sunday? And Sunday night at my place?'

'Yes, and I'm already looking forward to it.' She snuggled against him. A five-hour train journey might not be everyone's idea of a romantic assignation, but she'd learned to love them.

Penn had thought carefully about his preparations for their midweek evening together. No more jewellery. He'd got that message. And probably no more soap for a while, but it could stay on the list for the future. They had to eat, though.

His cleaner had let the caterers in, and when Penn got home from work, he found that she'd ignored his request to just leave everything in the kitchen, and arranged everything beautifully. He scribbled a note of thanks, leaving it in the kitchen for the morning, and lit the candles.

Tonight was going to be a relaxing treat for them both. Instead of racing each other up the stairs and tearing their clothes off, which was admittedly a very strong temptation, they could sit for a while and eat. Talk a little and maybe iron out some of the difficulties that the last few weeks had made obvious weren't just going to go away by themselves. *Then* they could race each other up the stairs and tear their clothes off…

He heard the doorbell and hurried to answer it. Grace was standing outside, her radiant smile bringing sunshine to an overcast evening. She danced up the steps and practically knocked him backwards as she embraced him.

'Glad to see you, too.' He kissed her, feeling all of the warmth that Grace always brought with her when she came.

She'd managed to loosen his tie and get the top two buttons of his shirt undone, before he could find the will to stop her. 'Grace… Not now, Grace.'

Grace stepped back suddenly. 'Is everything all right?'

That was a reasonable question, and right now he was wondering whether everything *was* all right. But rampant, satisfying sex had provided only a scintillating respite from their other problems up till now, and he wanted something a little more permanent.

'Everything's fine.' He took her by the hand. 'Come through.'

It was all laid out. Champagne on ice, and a caviar starter. Then salmon roulade, with salad, which would be followed by a lemon mousse that was still in the refrigerator. The cutlery gleamed, the surface of the highly polished table glimmered in the candlelight, and Grace… Grace seemed more sparkling than all of it put together.

'I thought we could have a nice meal and…maybe talk a little.'

'It all looks beautiful.' Grace smiled and sat down as he pulled out the chair at one of the place settings. There was something a little brittle about her movements, and Penn wondered if he should worry.

He poured the champagne and she took a sip from her glass. 'Mm. This is wonderful. Thank you.'

Sitting down, Penn held his glass out, towards hers. 'To moving forward.'

'Yes. To moving forward.' She tipped her glass against his, looking at the table. 'Are we celebrating something that I don't know about?'

He leaned back in his seat. It was a straight question and he had the straight answer to it. 'I've been thinking a lot about the future, and I really want to be able to spend more time with you. If that's what you want…?'

She smiled suddenly. 'Yes, it's what I want. We don't see enough of each other.'

'We said that we'd work something out and…it's not going to just happen all by itself. We need to *make* it happen. I know that you're in an impossible situation, and I have a proposition for you.'

She took another sip of her champagne, and then a larger mouthful. Something prickled at the back of Penn's neck but he ignored it. Change was hard, and Grace sensed it just as he did.

'I'd like to engage a nurse for your grandmother. Someone well qualified, and who your grandmother likes. It would take the pressure off all of you, and you could go back to being a supportive family and leave the nursing to a professional.'

'But…' Grace pressed her lips together. 'There's more, isn't there?'

At least she was hearing him out. That had to be a good sign. 'Yes, there is. I'd love it if you'd come and live with me here. Or wherever else you want to be. We can go down to Cornwall at weekends—you can see your grandmother and I'd visit the glassworks. But we'd be doing it together. I know that you don't care about my title, and I'm grateful for that. But the way that things have worked out does give me the ability to help out when needed.'

Something was wrong. Grace's smile had become brittle, and she'd already drained her glass, and was reaching for the bottle of champagne to refill it. She never usually drank more than one glass of wine and she liked to take her time over it.

'I know this is a lot, Grace, and we can do it all at whatever pace you want. But it's a way out and I'd really like you to think about it.'

'I don't need to, Penn. I can't say yes to this.'

He'd expected her to put up a fight, but Penn was

confident that he could bring Grace round to his way of thinking. 'Can I ask why?'

'Because you can do all of this. You can snap your fingers, and all of my problems go away. But they're *my* problems.'

Penn took a deep breath. He'd been thinking that he'd found the one woman who didn't care about his title, but Grace did. She might not be measuring up at the castle for curtains, but refusing his help was still a way of judging him for what he was. A lord who wouldn't notice the cost of making sure that an elderly lady was well cared for, and who wanted to give the woman he loved everything.

'I thought that we shared our problems, Grace.'

She was looking everywhere but at him. 'We do, but that's different. I give another little piece of myself to you every day. But that doesn't mean you can take it.'

'Then give this to me.' Penn couldn't see much difference between the two, and it seemed that Grace was splitting hairs, just so that she could refuse the offer.

'I can't, Penn. Not yet. Maybe…some other time. Later.'

'So when it comes down to it, it's all about me being able to afford something and wanting to give it, but you won't take it. You can say that my title and all that goes with it doesn't matter, but that's not what you really think, is it?'

His voice was laden with all the bitterness of a life that had been shaped by rejection. The fear that this was Grace's way of telling him that she didn't want to take that on, and she'd always keep him at arm's length. He couldn't even look at her right now, and he rose from his seat, then walked out into the kitchen to find some cool air.

'That's not fair, Penn.' Grace's voice sounded in the doorway behind him. 'I know you've been hurt and that it's hard to see past that. But I don't care what you are, and if I haven't proved that to you yet, then I don't know how I'm going to. I've been hurt too.'

'You think that I'd…' He couldn't even say it. 'If you don't know by now that I'm different from your ex, then I don't know what more I can do to show you.'

'That's not what I meant. This is about me and you, finding our way and learning how to be together. Letting go of all the things that have hurt us. We have to do the work… We can't just buy it.'

'Stop, Grace. You're being perverse for the sake of your own pride. What's wrong with buying our way into a situation where we can spend some time together?'

Rage began to creep into his heart. Not at Grace, never at her, but with himself for having thought that he could ever make a relationship that wasn't moulded by his inheritance. But still he couldn't quite give up on the dream that had formed in his heart, and the practicalities of that had to be addressed.

'Perhaps we should take a break and talk about this another time. When you've thought about this, then you may see it differently.'

'You mean when I've simmered down, I'll see that you're right and come crawling back. I don't think so, Penn.'

That *had* largely been what he'd meant, apart from the crawling back part. 'Well, maybe I'll see it differently, then.' Penn couldn't disguise his lack of commitment to the idea.

Grace heaved a sigh, tired emotion showing on her face. 'Penn, you wanted me to see the person you really are. And I do. But if that's going to be the case, then Lord Trejowan can't come galloping to the rescue when things get difficult. I have to work things out for myself.'

He shook his head. 'No, Grace, I'm sorry but that's just not acceptable. You're asking me to stand by and watch you struggle when there's a perfectly good solution that's so easy for me to put in place. I can't do that.'

Her eyes filled with tears. Why did she have to make this so very hard? 'Okay. Maybe we should take a break for this evening.' She turned, heading out into the hallway.

What? When he'd said *take a break*, he'd had another glass of champagne and a change of subject in mind.

'Grace, you're overreacting,' he called after her.

'Am I?' She appeared in the doorway of the kitchen again, clutching her jacket and bag. 'Are you going to change your mind about this? Because I'm not, and we can't just agree to disagree.'

He should stop her. The one and only good thing that he had was walking away and he should find a way to stop this from happening.

But Grace was right. They were stuck on opposite ends of a dilemma that would have been difficult for anyone, let alone two people who'd been rendered stubborn by the hurt they'd endured.

'I can't change my mind, Grace. That's not going to be any different tomorrow or the next day.'

'Then I'm sorry, Penn. But goodbye.'

Grace turned away again, and he heard her footsteps in the hallway, before the front door opened and then closed. After all their determination to stay together, they were finally done.

Two weeks. The traditional cure for a broken heart, submerging yourself in your work until you healed enough to face the world again, wasn't difficult. There was more than enough to do even if it felt a bit like wading through treacle. It was a relief to go into the operating theatre, because that at least claimed his whole attention.

He visited his mother on her birthday, taking with him a first edition that he knew she'd love and a bottle of good champagne, which would be similarly appreciated.

'Darling! Thank you so much. You *know* how I adore Dickens, and it'll be such a treat to read this again, with all the original illustrations. And you thought to chill the champagne so that we could drink it straight away.' His mother fetched two glasses from the drinks cabinet, while Penn eased the cork from its neck.

'You look very tired. Are you sleeping?'

'Yep.' When he finally got to bed, that was.

'Is it that wretched glassworks?' Sitting down on the pink velvet sofa, his mother tapped the cushion next to her in an indication that an easy chair would be far too far away. 'I shouldn't say *wretched*, should I? I know your father loved it, and that you're determined to keep it going. You should, for the sake of all the people there, but it's hard work.'

'It'll get better.' Then he could find something else to try and ease the pain.

'I do hope so. Now, I've got a piece of news for you…'

That might divert his mother's attention from how he was. 'I'm all ears.'

'I'm moving to London.'

Penn looked around at the beautifully furnished sitting room. 'To London? Don't you live in London already, or has Maida Vale changed postcodes while I wasn't looking?'

'No, darling.' His mother dismissed the idea with a wave of her hand. 'I mean I'm officially going to take up residence here. I've become very fond of this house over the years, and I never have time to trek all the way down to Cornwall. You'll put me up if I want to visit, won't you?'

Light dawned. 'You mean you want to give up your apartment at the castle?'

'Yes, darling. I never use it and I've decided it's time for me to move on. I'm sure you could put the extra room to good use.'

Penn couldn't think how, since he didn't go to the castle all that often himself. And he really didn't want to go back there now, because the memories of Grace had overwritten everything else about it.

'I don't really have the time.'

'But you *will* have. You just said that things will get better at the glassworks. I know you have mixed feelings about the castle but maybe you'd like it a little more if you put your own stamp on it.'

'Mother, we've been through all of this. I already have a job. I'm a surgeon.'

'You misunderstand me, Penn. I'm not talking about

paint colours and where to put those hideous suits of armour. Use your vision as a surgeon and make changes.'

Maybe the champagne was going to his mother's head. 'It's a castle. We've just had hordes of museum experts traipsing around the place, telling us all of the things we shouldn't change.'

'Well, I'm sure you could use your ingenuity. And think of it like this. Our family has a responsibility to defend the community. That's our true history. I doubt that ramparts are much of a defence against anything these days, so it's necessary to evolve.'

'That's not what you said when I took the place over…'

'I mentioned your responsibilities, because you do have them, and I didn't want you to think that it was all there just for you. In hindsight, I may have overdone things a little.'

'I think it's more likely, in hindsight, that I wasn't listening to you. Or I wasn't ready to understand.' He was ready now. Grace had seen to that. Penn floated the idea and received a smile in return.

'Think about it, will you, Penn?'

'I will. Not right now. Maybe when I've got the glassworks under control a little better.' A thought struck him. 'By the way, that piece I have in my sitting room. I know you said you didn't want it, but does it have anything to do with you and Dad? If you wanted to take it with you…'

'At last! It's taken you this long to realise what it is, has it?'

'The absence of heads was something of a stumbling

block. And the fact it's been hidden away in storage for as long as I can remember.'

'That's because we thought it was a little too explicit for when you were younger. And the heads are there—they're placed alongside our hearts. If you look carefully, you'll see your father's beard in there quite clearly.'

'I'll bear that in mind, the next time I'm down there. You're sure you don't want it?'

'Positive, darling. It's a beautiful piece and something I'd like you to remember him by. Your father and I had a very passionate relationship, you know.'

'Too much information, Mother.' Penn didn't want to think about passion at the moment. It hurt far too much.

'Whatever you say. Anything to tell me on that front, darling?'

'No. Too busy.'

'Make time. I've actually got some news about your Aunt Lillian. I'm sure she won't mind my telling you…'

Penn smiled as he walked away from his mother's house. She could be exhausting at times, but she had a good heart. And she'd made him think.

His mother had made a better job of living with the title than he had. Even though his parents' relationship had ended, there had never been any hint that it was anything to do with their differences in background. And she'd made her own subtle changes to the castle, opening it up and staging art exhibitions and theatre there.

Maybe his mother knew a lot more than he gave her credit for and he should have listened a little more closely when she'd lectured him about his responsibilities when he turned twenty-five. But by then, hurt had already insulated him from the opportunities that those responsibilities brought with them.

Maybe he should have listened a little more closely to what Grace had said to him. He'd offered her financial help, believing that it would solve all of their problems, but what she really needed was room to breathe.

He filled his lungs with air, walking past the underground station in favour of stretching his legs. A plan was forming in his head, and Penn wanted to find out where it might lead…

CHAPTER FOURTEEN

EVERY TIME GRACE boarded the train, she felt an instinctive thrill of excitement. And then she remembered that Penn wouldn't be waiting for her, and she wouldn't be seeing him when she got to Cornwall either. She'd spent the first half hour of her last three journeys, hiding behind a newspaper so that the people sitting opposite couldn't see her tears.

There had been more tears at night. More in the morning, and at unexpected times during the day. At some point she'd be cried out, but that hadn't happened yet.

She loved Penn. She knew that he loved her. It wasn't all his fault either, Grace had to shoulder at least half of the responsibility for this. Gran had said as much when she'd caught Grace crying and insisted on hearing the whole story. The very things that Penn's generous nature compelled him to do, were the things that Grace needed time to come to terms with.

They were both still too bound up with the past. A lifestyle that could have given him freedom was Penn's prison and it would be hers too if she stayed.

Enough. This time she wasn't going to cry on the

train. Small steps. She'd made some decisions in the last three weeks, and life was going to go on, even if it didn't seem that it would ever be as sweet again.

She'd had a call, changing her seat reservation, and when she looked at the carriage numbers, she saw that the shorter car by the ticket barriers, which would be right at the end of the train, was hers. She stopped in front of the doors, pushing the button to open them, and they stayed stubbornly closed, so she walked along the platform to the next carriage.

A guard was loitering at the automatic door, and when she fished her ticket from her purse and showed it to him, he gave her an oddly cheerful smile.

'That's right, Miss. Straight through there.'

'Thank you.'

The carriage was empty, but there were booking tickets on the back of every seat. Hopefully she wouldn't be travelling with a crowd of football supporters, or a boozy group of holiday-makers who were headed to Cornwall for the weekend. And then suddenly, she realised that she wouldn't. Penn had risen from one of the seats.

'Penn! What have you done?' She knew exactly what he'd done. All of those booked seats were for a party of two.

'I wanted to speak with you. To say sorry principally, but there's a lot more. If you don't want to hear it, then that's fine. Your original seat is still booked for you and I won't bother you there.'

Hope almost choked her. Grace looked at her ticket, before marching along the aisle to the correct seat.

'This is the one that's printed on my ticket.'

She was going to cry any moment now. Not the missing him crying that she'd been doing for the last three weeks, but because this was so sweet. A lavish gesture that was all about them, all about the place they'd met and where they'd taken refuge from the world for those precious weeks when love had started to grow between them. All about a piece of his heart that he'd just given to her.

'May I sit with you?'

Yes! Please… Grace didn't dare give in to the pounding of her heart. 'You can sit wherever you like, since I assume that all of these seats are yours. Here's fine.'

He nodded, sitting down. 'I'm not going to apologise for this gesture, Grace. Or for having brought something to eat along with me.' He pointed towards a hamper, stowed away under the table in the group of seats directly across the aisle. From the size of it, he'd brought more than just two rounds of sandwiches.

'Why not?' Grace was trembling now. Everything hung on Penn's answer.

'Because I happen to be a lord with a castle. I can afford to make gestures when something's important, and seeing you means more to me than anything. If you don't approve of that, then…there's always the other seat further down the train.'

She felt her lips quiver into a smile. 'I want to see you too, Penn.'

He seemed suddenly breathless, as if a great burden had been lifted from his shoulders. 'Then you'll stay?'

'Yes, I'll stay. I might even have a sandwich later, if you have any.'

'Lots of them. Can we talk, first?'

Grace nodded. They'd jumped the first hurdle, but there were more to come.

'You were right, Grace, and I was wrong. I wanted to give you everything, but in doing that, I was making all the decisions about what you wanted or needed.' He flashed her a nervous smile. 'I'd like things to be different between us.'

'How, Penn?' Grace was praying that this hadn't come too late. That the changes she'd put in motion in her own life hadn't blocked any way forward with Penn.

'I love you, and I want to be with you. If you'll give me another chance, then we'll be a partnership. We each have something to bring to that, and we'll make our decisions together.'

'Penn, I…' Grace could feel tears pricking at the sides of her eyes. 'That sounds wonderful. But I don't have as much to bring…'

He shook his head. 'That's not true. I understand now how much I could do if I used the resources I've inherited, instead of trying to pretend they don't exist. But I need you to help me with that. Without you, I can't own them.'

The more he said, the more this hurt. Because it all sounded like the life that she wanted more than anything. Grace laid her fingers across his lips.

'That's what I want for you, Penn. But when I said I didn't have as much to bring, I meant that things have changed in the last three weeks. I've given up my job, and I'm going to be coming down to Cornwall for good, to look after Gran. I'm not sure how I can change that in the short term…'

A smile spread across his face. Maybe he didn't understand the implications of what she'd just said.

'I'll move down to Cornwall, then. You'll have some days off from looking after your gran?'

'No! I mean yes, I'll have days off, and I was planning to practise for a couple of days a week while Jess and the others filled in for me. But, Penn, you can't just leave London and move. I'd never ask you to do that. You refused to do it once and you were right to do so.'

'It's not the same. I wouldn't be giving up my medical career. Surgeons are needed in Cornwall just as they are in London. And I wouldn't be swanning around the castle, playing at the role of lord of the manor, when that's not what I want to be. The place has a lot of hidden possibilities, you know.'

The temptation to throw herself into his arms and agree to everything was killing her. Not yet. Not until she knew that this was what Penn really wanted.

'I don't think I spent enough time there to see hidden possibilities.' In truth, Grace hadn't seen anything much other than Penn.

'My mother said something very interesting to me recently. That my real inheritance was to serve and protect the community. My rejection of my title and all that it entails has been keeping me from that. Imagine a rehab centre, built amongst the trees at the foot of the hill to the east. You could practise from there if you wanted. That's just one possibility…'

'Wait. Penn, this sounds…' Like heaven. Crazy enough to work. 'Is this what you really want to do?'

'It's one of many things I want to do. But I'm not here to ask you to partner with me on medical projects. I'm here because I love you and I want to be with you. We can make this work. We'll look after your gran, and set the glassworks on its feet. But the most important part is that we do it together.'

Grace just wanted to hold him, and to kiss him. But there was one thing more she had to say.

'I didn't trust you enough, did I? I felt that I needed time, but I didn't. I've already given you everything and that's not going to change. I'm so sorry, Penn.'

'Then you'll do it, Grace? Give us another chance?'

She wanted to match his trust. Not repay it, because no one was keeping a balance of accounts.

'Penn, I turned you down when you offered to find a nurse for Gran, because I was afraid of ever feeling that I was in debt to someone again…'

'You want to revisit that decision?'

'If the offer's still open. You're right, Gran will be better off if she has a nurse to help us, and a family who can actually be a family to her. I'd still be spending lots of time with her, but it would still give me more time for those hidden possibilities…'

'It would be my pleasure to help make that happen. Thank you for trusting me enough to ask, Grace. I didn't dare offer it.'

This was a dream. Everything that she'd never imagined she might want. 'Is this real, Penn?'

'Say yes and then we'll make it real.'

'Yes, Penn. I love you and I want to be with you. I want to share this wonderful future that we can build together.'

He kissed her hand, and then moved from his seat, kneeling in the aisle. 'Will you marry me, Grace? You're probably going to have to live in a castle, at least for a while, and we'd both have a lot of hard work ahead of us. But I promise I'll love you with every fibre of my being.'

Tears started to trickle down her cheeks. Penn produced a handkerchief from his pocket, with the slight flourish of a man who had brought it along in the hopes that it might be used.

'Yes, Penn. Yes, to all of it, even the castle. We could have a lot of fun in a castle, you and I.'

She bent forward, wrapped her arms around his neck and tried to pull him close. But Penn had other ideas.

'Wait…' He felt in his pocket. 'This has been in my family for generations. Not every Lady Trejowan has worn it. My mother never did because she doesn't like it. But even if you'd prefer to wear something different, I'd like to give this into your safekeeping.'

Grace caught her breath. She'd seen rings like this, elegant twists of gold in a Tudor style. But this wasn't a reproduction—it was the real thing. The gold seemed almost untouched by time and the square-cut ruby in the centre still flashed bright in the sunlight.

'It's beautiful, Penn. I'd be honoured to wear it.'

'It may be a little small. But it's been resized over the years, so I'm hoping it'll fit…' He took her hand, and the ring slipped smoothly over her knuckle, coming to rest securely on her finger.

'Thank you. I'm going to take such good care of this, so that we can pass it on to our children.'

He grinned broadly. 'We're having children?'

'We have time for children, don't we?'

'I didn't know I could ever be this happy, Grace. We have lots of time for children.' He slid the hamper out into the aisle and opened it. 'And some time now for champagne and sandwiches to celebrate.'

'I so wish I could come back with you tonight…' Grace watched as he opened the champagne, then poured it into two flute glasses. 'I can't be greedy I suppose. I have everything else I could ever have dreamed of.'

'I forgot to say. I still have Jessica's number in my phone and I called her and asked if she might be prepared to stay with your grandmother this weekend. We struck a deal, and I have to phone her if she's needed.'

'She's needed. Call her and tell her she's needed. What kind of deal did you strike, and should I be worried?'

'A crate of a nice vintage red from the castle cellars.' He grinned. 'Because we have cellars, and we won't miss it. Jessica doesn't like champagne, apparently.'

Grace laughed. 'No, she doesn't. You know I do, though…'

Penn gave a smiling nod and handed Grace her glass before sitting down.

'To tonight, and all of the other days and nights, for the rest of our lives.'

'Don't forget the train, Penn.'

He grinned. 'And the train that's brought us here.'

EPILOGUE

Six months later

PENN DROVE THROUGH the open gates of the castle, then parked his car beside the entrance to their apartment. While they'd been gone for the day, the great Christmas tree had been erected in the centre of the courtyard, ready for the Christmas celebrations that would be held here.

'What do you think of the honeymoon, so far?' Grace's face shone in the reflected glimmer of the lights on the tree.

'Best ever.' He turned to kiss her.

'Wait until you see what I've got planned for our official honeymoon next summer.' She got out of the car, her breath pluming in the night air. 'Do you think it's cold enough for snow?'

'I wouldn't be surprised.' Penn took her hand and they walked together across the grass to the foot of the tree. 'You're really not going to tell me where we're going?'

'Think sun and sand and making love to the sound of the sea.'

He chuckled. 'That's all I need to know.'

They'd been married on this very spot, two weeks ago. When the huge marquee had been taken down, and the horde of guests had left, he'd spent the best weekend of his life alone with Grace. And then they'd gone back to work and it had turned into the best two weeks of his life.

They'd visited the newly laid foundations of the clinic that was being built in the castle grounds, discussing the work that would start in the new year with the project manager. When he'd left, they'd excitedly paced out the gym together, along with Grace's consulting room and the space that Penn would use when he wasn't working at the hospital in Truro.

Penn had officially handed the glassworks over to the new management team last week, and they'd been presented with an arrangement of glass flowers, each one made by a different craftsperson, to mark the occasion. Phil and Phoebe would be in charge of the workshop and two of the other glassmakers were tasked with finding and training a new generation of craftspeople. An administrator had been recruited, along with a part-time marketing consultant who would guide the new marketing committee in its decisions. Penn still retained a seat on the board of directors, but from now on, the glassworks would be largely self-supporting and run by the people who worked there.

Grace had supervised her gran's journey to the castle for the Christmas break, and spent time settling her and her nurse, Sadie, into the rooms that had been made ready for them. On the other side of the courtyard, he could see two figures sitting at the window, looking at the twinkling lights on the tree.

'Do you think your gran will stay?' He and Grace had chosen her gran's rooms carefully, overlooking the courtyard so that she could see all of the comings and goings, but far enough away that she wasn't disturbed by noise.

'She loves the rooms, and being able to watch the world go by outside. And she can go for long walks inside when the weather's bad. Sadie's definitely up for it, and Gran's already made a list of the things she'd want to bring from her cottage.'

'That's good. It'll take a load off the others, knowing that she's safe here and that we're close by if she needs us.'

'Did you see Carrie's kids in the courtyard, the other day? They were having a whale of a time. Carrie had to practically strong-arm them into the car when it was time to go home.'

Penn chuckled. 'Yes, I did. This is exactly how this place should be, isn't it? A shelter for those who need it, and a place where children can play.'

'Feels like home?' Grace wrapped her arms around him, pulling him close.

'The only one I ever want. Here with you, making our dreams come true. Thank you so much, Grace.' He kissed her, and she snuggled against him.

'I love you, Penn. More each day, if that's even possible.'

Penn smiled down at her. 'I think we've proved that anything's possible, haven't we?'

* * * * *

SINGLE DAD FOR THE HEART DOCTOR

KARIN BAINE

MILLS & BOON

For my lovely neighbours, Stella, Sammy and Miriam.
I'm going to miss you very much. xx

CHAPTER ONE

DEATH NEVER GOT EASIER.

Lily picked up a handful of shingle from the beach, pocketing the frosted, sea-tumbled aquamarine glass and the pottery shards. There were several fragments of blue and white willow-pattern treasures for her to repurpose along with the glass. The Victorians' rubbish and broken crockery, tossed into the sea, was now her treasure. When she had some free time she'd make it into some jewellery...something beautiful. Give it new life.

She pulled her cardigan tighter around her body as the wind began to pick up, but she didn't mind the cold. This was her happy place, where she could forget her worries and concentrate on spotting little gems and giving new life to those broken pieces. It wasn't so easy in the real world.

Losing a patient was always difficult. In her job as a cardiologist, death was not something she could always conquer and she did her best. But events such as tonight's made her job harder than ever, and reminded her of her own mortality. She had chosen this career path to give people a second chance at life but sometimes, through no fault of her own, she didn't even get to play her part.

The ambulance had taken too long to get to their remote village, Glen Nesbitt, on Northern Ireland's Antrim coast. There hadn't been anywhere close by for the emergency medical helicopter to land, even if it had reached the place in time.

In cardiac cases every second counted and, from her point of view, a thirty-eight-year-old mother of two had died unnecessarily. On this occasion the medical profession had failed her and her family with their poor response time. Lily knew she could have saved the woman if she'd got to her sooner and that would keep her awake tonight.

Usually it was thoughts of her father and her sister—of how she hadn't been able to save them. Of her mother, who had died of a broken heart years later, even without inheriting the condition which had stolen half of their little family. Not least the ticking time bomb in Lily's chest which would eventually take her too.

She had inherited the same faulty gene and now, with her confirmed diagnosis of dilated cardiomyopathy, premature death was something she had to consider. DCM left the heart muscle stretched thin, too weak to contract enough to pump blood properly around the rest of the body.

Her sister hadn't had any warning, suddenly collapsing after they'd been racing along the beach, dying from heart failure before anyone had known there was anything wrong. Lily had been the younger of the two but losing Iris at the age of ten years, then her father only days later, killed by the shock, meant she'd grown up from the age of seven as an only child. Then an orphan from the age of seventeen when her mother passed away too.

They'd been unaware of the deadly spectre of the illness haunting their family until it was too late. She didn't know if it had been a blessing or a curse to test positive for the same gene when she'd been young, having lived the rest of her life fearing the same fate as her sibling. Her mother too had feared for her, never wanting her to take part in anything too strenuous or stressful, leading to a somewhat isolated existence.

Although losing her mother too before she'd fully entered into adulthood had been traumatic, it had given her the independence to go to university, to train for a job where she could help others.

Her own diagnosis had come five years ago when she'd begun to experience some symptoms of having the same condition—fatigue, swelling in her ankles and belly. It had almost been a relief when her suspicions had been confirmed after spending her whole life waiting for them to appear, so she could deal with them instead of simply worrying what might happen.

For now, her symptoms were under control with medication, but if they worsened she might need a pacemaker to deliver electrical impulses to regulate her heartbeat. The worst scenario would be if she needed a heart transplant should a pacing device and medication fail to work, and that thought was always at the back of her mind.

It was probably why it was so important for her to make a difference for as long as she could, and why one unnecessary loss was too many.

The sound of sirens and the sight of flashing blue lights blazed through the twilight gloom as a fire engine from the local station raced by. Hopefully they would get there in time to save whoever was in trouble.

The two incidents were uppermost in her mind as she made the short walk back across the beach to her small bungalow, population one, ever since her diagnosis. Relationships had never been easy for a woman who insisted she never wanted children. There had been a few partners who had professed to the same thinking, only to later change their minds as time wore on and they were faced with their own mortality. For her, it seemed selfish to bring another generation into this world, only to pass on the same death sentence her father had unwittingly given her and her sister.

The knowledge of the condition was both a blessing and a curse. Her parents had been able to live their lives freely until illness interrupted it. Lily had been hyperaware of that same illness from an early age and it had affected all of her life decisions. Her career, her relationships and her future were all based around the medical condition and it was the reason she was alone. With no family or significant other to mourn her, she would never leave anyone as devastated as she and her mother had been by loss.

She would do everything in her power for the wider community to avoid that same heartache too.

Charlie 'Finn' Finnegan heard the click-clack of heels long before he spotted the woman who had recently become a royal pain in his backside. This was the first time they had actually met in person but, judging by the phone conversations and email exchanges, they were in for a major personality clash. The local community centre had been commandeered especially for this mediation meeting, all departments keen for them to set aside their differences and co-operate on the matter. It seemed pointless when she had already gone above his head to the Fire Service Group Commander to get the green light for her harebrained scheme after he had raised objections. Nevertheless, he would fight his corner for the sake of his team.

Lily Riordan couldn't have been more than five foot two—a good foot shorter than him—but she seemed to project a much bigger personality. Wearing a figure-hugging royal blue dress which matched her eyes, she exuded confidence. Her loose honey-blonde curls danced on her shoulders with every step and her full red lips were drawn into a tight line, looking as though she was preparing to go into battle. Finn couldn't help but smile when he saw her.

'It's nice to meet you, Ms Riordan.'

Although she shook his outstretched hand she didn't look any happier about this than he was. 'I wish it was in more congenial circumstances. I don't believe in wasting anybody's time, Mr Finnegan, including my own.'

She clearly wasn't one to suffer fools gladly and he already liked that about her. A person who wore their heart on their sleeve was easier to deal with than someone who hid what they were really thinking.

His mind flitted briefly to the dark memories he tried not to revisit too often. Of his wife asleep, or so he'd thought, until he couldn't wake her. He'd known she was tired, having trouble sleeping, but she hadn't confided in him about how much she was struggling with her workload at the hospital. If he had known he would have kept a closer eye on her, monitored the medication she had been secretly taking. Although he would never know if the overdose had been an accident or not, he liked to think she would never purposely have left him and their girls. Instead, he preferred to imagine she'd simply been so tired she had mistakenly taken more than the prescribed dose of sleeping tablets. Either way, the loss had left him devastated and with the guilt of failing his family. To have someone unafraid to tell him exactly what she thought was refreshing and Finn appreciated it.

'I appreciate that, but do call me Finn. Now, shall we?' He stood back to let her enter the room first, with their mediator following behind.

They took their seats on either side of the large table, with the mediator at the head. Leaving them no choice but to face each other. Lily leaned across the table, hands clasped, ready to do business.

'Now, my name is Joe Mussen, and we're here tonight to discuss the involvement of the local fire service in a new cardiac care initiative and resolve any issues or concerns so we can press ahead.' The mediator took out his notes from his bag and set them on the table. Finn wondered if he should have put his thoughts in writing, but Lily didn't seem to have a list of statistics or facts to bamboozle him with. This apparently was just a discussion to iron out any wrinkles, when the hospital board and the fire service had already decided this was going ahead.

Finn did not want to be responsible for overworked,

stressed members of his team when he knew how that could end up. If someone had stepped in for his wife, seeing the adverse effect the extra hours and responsibility was taking on her, his life would be very different.

'So, *Finn*, as local watch commander, the hospital board would prefer to have your co-operation.'

He noted she did not include herself in that statement.

'I don't see why, when it's going ahead with or without my approval.' It had been made apparent to him that he would not have the final say on the matter and, with the good press the scheme was going to generate, his opposition was in the minority.

'That may be so, but they want you involved.'

'Ah yes, the face of the campaign,' he sneered. For some reason the department had deemed him the most suitable for the job. Apparently he would add some gravitas to the campaign or some such nonsense. It was probably the greying hair. There were much younger, more attractive men on the crew than him who would have jumped at the chance. He would rather not have been involved at all but even he had orders to follow. It didn't mean he had to be gracious about it.

Lily raised an eyebrow. 'I don't know about that, but as commander it would look odd if you weren't there for the launch. I will be representing the hospital.'

'It was your idea…' He'd be surprised if she let anyone else take the credit for something she was obviously very passionate about. Finn couldn't fault her for that, but he couldn't agree with her plans. Not at the possible expense of his crew's mental health.

'My idea, yes, but I'm also the lead cardiologist. You

hold the most senior position locally too. They want us both present for the public launch.'

'On Valentine's Day, I'm led to believe. Don't you think that's a bit corny?' He hated the commercialism of the day anyway, but now that he didn't have his wife to celebrate it with he would have preferred to treat it as any other day. Instead, he was supposed to join in some elaborate publicity campaign, no doubt littered with hearts and flowers, to promote this enterprise.

Lily had the decency to blush, her pale complexion taking on an attractive rosy hue. 'That wasn't my idea, but I understand the board wants as much public awareness as possible. The premise of providing emergency cardiac care does tie in with the day, I suppose. Look, I have no desire to be paraded in front of the cameras either, but it's for the greater good.'

He scoffed at that. 'For the greater good' implied someone else had to make a sacrifice. In the past, his wife had been one of many nurses who had given up time with their families to take on extra shifts and look after the sick. She had undoubtedly saved more lives with her selfless attitude, but it had ultimately cost her and her family everything. He did not want the men he worked alongside to make the same sacrifice.

The mediator, who had been silently taking in all they had to say until now, coughed. 'Perhaps we should focus on the reservations you have, Mr Finnegan, and address those one by one.'

Lily cocked her head to one side, waiting for him to begin and listening, a smug smile spreading across her lips. As though she was merely humouring him.

'First, and most importantly of all, my crew are not

medical professionals. Asking them to attend emergency cardiac cases goes beyond the remit of our jobs.'

'We have fire crew with first aid training and defibrillators in local access points. My suggestion is to combine the two. In instances where cardiac patients aren't going to be reached quickly enough by paramedics, we could equip your team to attend and treat emergencies. It could make all the difference between someone living and dying if they're treated before they get to me at the hospital.'

'I appreciate that. However, I have to consider the welfare of my crew. Isn't this opening them up to all sorts of law suits if something goes wrong? It's an extra responsibility none of us signed on for. Which I have repeatedly pointed out to you.' It had been his first reaction to oppose the scheme for this very reason and it still was when he was the one tasked with looking after his crew.

'And, as I have told you on several occasions, they will be given full training in the use of a defibrillator. All that is expected of them is to follow the instructions on the use of the machines. We will also provide additional assistance over the phone until paramedics are in attendance and able to take over. We're not expecting miracles, Mr… Finn. Just a little extra time, which can make all the difference in cardiac care. I understand your concerns, but we are talking about saving people's lives here. I'm sure we can find some way of safeguarding your crew.'

'I'm sorry, but that's not good enough. It will put extra stress on my men, along with the additional hours involved. I admire your dedication to your job and patients but they're not my responsibility.' Finn had enough on his plate with work and raising his two young daughters without the added stress of Ms Riordan breathing down his neck.

'Ms Riordan, can you offer any further support to Mr Finnegan's team from the cardiology department? It could help to have a member of your team available, at least until the scheme is up and running.' The mediator, who had been watching their verbal tennis match across the table until now, spoke up with a suggestion which seemed neither of them could really object to. Much to Finn's annoyance.

'If I, or one of my colleagues are available we could attend the first callouts too. I'll do whatever it takes to make this work.' Lily, of course, jumped in to offer her personal assistance, leaving Finn floundering and grasping for other reasons to object.

'What about the extra work involved? I assume this is a voluntary scheme?' Although he hadn't volunteered his services, it seemed he would be the one to coordinate it all.

'It will be, but I intended it to run alongside your regular shifts.'

'I can't afford for my crew to be caught up elsewhere if a shout comes in.' That meant leaving them vulnerable in two areas and that wasn't going to work for any of them.

'Perhaps we could have one person per shift with a response vehicle dedicated to emergency medical calls, liaising with the hospital team.'

'That's a lot of responsibility for one person and it means I'm a team member down every shift.'

Lily sighed, letting him know she was exasperated with the hurdles he kept putting in her way, but this was what this meeting was for—to find solutions.

'You could put it to your crew and see what they think. I'm sure you will have volunteers. You might even be able to do it yourself.' She was goading him, unaware that he had taken more of a back seat role these days in his new position as watch commander.

It was his job to co-ordinate response to large scale incidents and, rather than the adrenaline rush of running into fires, he got his buzz making sure everyone stayed safe and did their own jobs well. One way he'd been able to reassure his daughters they weren't going to lose him too.

If anyone was going to dedicate themselves to this new position it made sense it would be him, but that would entail working closely with Miss Riordan on a regular basis and he wasn't sure either of them would survive that. One wrong move and he knew she would rip him apart. The thought did nothing to garner his support for her cause.

For two people who were virtual strangers, they'd seemed to get under each other's skin very quickly. It was as intriguing as it was frustrating to Finn, who was used to being the one in charge of everything. Including his emotions.

'Of course.'

Just as they appeared to be making progress, with Finn realising he was fighting a losing battle, the mediator gripped the edge of the table, head bowed, sweat breaking out over his forehead.

'Are you okay?' Lily was first on her feet to check

on him. He stumbled and Finn got out of his chair to go and support him.

'Perhaps you should sit down. I'll get you a glass of water.'

'I'll be fine. I just felt a little woozy.'

'You look a bit pale. Finn's right, I think you should take a seat and maybe loosen your tie.' Lily did her best to convince the mediator to take their advice but he shook them both off.

'I'll be fine,' he insisted and shooed them back to their own seats.

Finn and Lily reluctantly backed away and took their positions on either side of the table again, their gaze never leaving the clearly ailing man, who was dabbing his forehead with a handkerchief.

'Now, where were we?' He shuffled through his papers, then suddenly grabbed his left arm and crumpled to the floor.

'Men are so damn stubborn when it comes to their health,' Lily complained, though she was rushing to help.

'That's why we need people looking out for us. Just as I'm doing with my crew.' He used the moment to reiterate the reason he'd gone to war in the first place. They were both simply trying to do the right thing by others.

'Hmph.' She huffed out a breath as she knelt down beside the prostrate figure of the man who had been sent to corral them. Finn hoped they weren't the cause of his sudden illness.

'Joe? Can you hear me? Finn, he's not breathing.' Lily had already loosened his tie and opened the top button on the man's shirt.

'I think I saw a defibrillator on the wall outside. I'll get it if you can start chest compressions?' He trusted Lily knew what she was doing in that department and he bolted out to get the medical equipment needed to save this stranger's life, calling an ambulance from his mobile phone on the way.

By the time he came back she was pumping the man's chest and counting every compression. 'No response. I need you to follow the instructions on the defibrillator so we can try and get his heart restarted.'

Finn nodded. He had basic first aid training but this was the first time he'd actually had to use one of these machines. It seemed relatively straightforward and once he had undone their patient's shirt he was able to adhere the sticky pads to the skin.

The defibrillator provided vocal instructions for each step and Lily and Finn had to stand back as the electric shocks were delivered to the heart. After each one, Lily checked again for a pulse until eventually they could both see his chest begin to rise and fall.

'Joe? It's Lily. Can you open your eyes for me? Finn, we need to get him into the recovery position until the ambulance gets here,' Lily directed.

After disconnecting the defibrillator, Finn assisted in moving the patient onto his side. Once they were sure he was no longer in immediate danger, they were both able to relax a little but remained on the floor with their backs against the wall, watching over the mediator they'd apparently driven to cardiac arrest.

'I'm going to phone the ambulance again. They should have been here by now.'

Lily gave him a half smile. 'Do you see now how important the response time is for cardiac patients? If we hadn't been here, or had the means to shock his heart, he wouldn't have made it.'

He couldn't argue with the facts and, without time to consider what he was doing, Finn had been part of saving the man's life. When it came down to it he knew that was the thought uppermost in both of their minds and if he had to do it again he would. The burden of responsibility or culpability had not come into the equation and they had both acted purely on instinct. Something he knew the rest of his crew would have done in the same circumstances.

'Okay. You've made your point. Although I think causing a man to have a heart attack just to get your own way was going too far.' He couldn't resist one more tease and was rewarded with an exaggerated sigh for his efforts.

This man would be the death of her. Lily had never met anyone who seemed to enjoy antagonising her so much, or she let bother her so much. Usually, she did not waste energy on people who apparently brought nothing but trouble to her door. If her time on this earth was limited she didn't want to have it taken up with toxic relationships. She was sure they could even have got this project off the ground without Finn's compliance but he pushed her buttons so hard she was determined to show him it would work and get one up on him.

'So, have you had a change of heart? No pun intended.' She afforded him a smile since he had done so much to assist her. Whilst she was used to these sudden life-or-death situations, it was probably new to him. At least outside of his work environment. If he had stuck to his belief that non-medical professionals should not get involved in a cardiac emergency, it would have made things very difficult for her. However, Finn hadn't taken time to consider the consequences, acting on pure instinct to help. Exactly what she had been counting on by including another emergency service in attendance on cardiac calls.

Finn smiled back, and for the first time she noticed how blue his eyes were, now they weren't narrowed at her. The man was fit for his age, in all senses of the word. She guessed him to be in his late forties, his dark blond hair flecked with strands of barely noticeable silver. Yes, he was a handsome man, undoubtedly with a line of women who swooned at his stubborn macho persona, but she wasn't easily swayed by good looks.

It was his willingness to help tonight, despite his reservations, that made her see him in a different light. Though doing so was a futile exercise. If she was ever going to have one last fling, it would be with someone passing through town who she would hopefully never see again, to avoid hurt on either side.

'I'm willing to work together if you are.'

It wasn't a definitive answer to her question but sufficient to get the project up and running at least. Whether they could work together without causing further ructions remained to be seen.

CHAPTER TWO

'IS THIS REALLY NECESSARY?' Lily batted away the heart-shaped helium balloons lining her path but managed to walk straight into the red and pink streamers hanging from the ceiling.

'I think they're keen to reiterate the purpose of this scheme. That it's for heart patients only and shouldn't be abused by those hoping for a lift to hospital appointments or who want us to pop round with a takeaway. Plus it's Valentine's Day so, you know…' Finn's soft voice in her ear caused the hairs on the back of her neck to stand to attention when he was so close she could feel his breath on her skin.

'Oh, I know. Let's bring in all the clichés we can to hammer the point home.' She rolled her eyes. Being deceived by the idea of love and romance wasn't an affliction she suffered from. She left it to naïve young couples who had for ever to fool themselves into thinking it could solve everything. Life, and death, had taught her it only complicated things and made life so much harder. All the people she had ever loved had died and, as for romance, it had brought nothing but heartache when she couldn't give her partners what they needed—children and time.

'Something tells me you didn't get any cards in the post.'

'And I suppose you did?'

'Two, actually.'

More eye-rolling. Not only was he handsome but he knew it. One of the worst traits a man could have.

'Let me guess, one came from a grateful young woman who found herself locked out of her house in nothing but a towel and you came to the rescue? And the other…some impressionable schoolgirl whose class had a tour of the fire station?' Boasting about how many cards he'd received was juvenile, and clearly mentioned to get a rise out of her. He had, of course, succeeded.

Finn laughed so hard she actually felt the vibration through to her very bones. 'Actually, they were from my daughters, but it's good to know what you really think about me. You'll have to take my word for it that I'm not a ladies' man who would take advantage of vulnerable females.'

Lily wished the ceiling would collapse and bury her under the hearts and flowers they were surrounded by for the press call. He pulled his phone from his pocket and proceeded to deepen her embarrassment by showing her pictures of the adorable handmade cards his girls had made. Judging by the handwriting and childish representation of hearts, they were from his very young offspring. She could also see the wedding ring shining on his hand now.

'I'm so sorry. I didn't realise you were married with children. That's so lovely. You must be very proud.'

She had taken something so sweet and turned it into something tawdry. When she was around him she apparently had no filter and said things before she had time to think about it.

'Widowed with children,' he corrected, scrolling through to show her a picture of two gorgeous little blonde cherubs.

Lily's blood froze in her veins at hearing his statement. It had never occurred to her that Finn had gone through something so tragic, and it went some way to explaining his initial reluctance in getting involved. His concerns about the extra time involved, as well as the added responsibility, made sense when he was looking after two young girls who had lost their mother. It made the whole matter more tragic and her heart went out to him and the two little ones left behind in their grief.

'I'm so sorry. I had no idea. Thank you again for agreeing to all of this. I know you must have your work cut out for you already, juggling work and parenthood.' Especially on this particular day, which was likely hard for him anyway as a widower. She didn't know how long it had been since he'd lost his wife, or the circumstances, but she certainly could empathise with the devastation it caused in one's life to lose a loved one.

That he was even able to function was amazing to her, never mind working in such a demanding job and now taking on this new role she'd helped rope him into. Yes, guilt was beginning to poison her feel-good endorphins about setting this whole thing up now she was aware of Finn's circumstances. Would she have backed off if she'd known? Probably not, but she might have been a little more understanding and less confrontational. She knew how his little girls would be feeling—lost, lonely and terrified that they were going to lose everyone they loved. It must have been extremely difficult for Finn to return to his line of work, facing those life-or-death situations every day while promising his daughters he wouldn't leave them too. Lily's heart went out to all of them.

However, Finn simply shrugged, seeming to take it all in his stride. Probably because he had no other option than to carry on with life for the sake of his children. 'My mum helps out with the babysitting, but I just have to get on with things. Try to keep things as normal as possible for them.'

There was a softer side to him when he talked about his family and Lily could see why he hadn't mentioned them before. It was private and a deeply personal matter. One he had chosen to share with her today and she was privileged to have seen beneath that hard, unyielding surface she'd encountered on their first meeting. They both had their reasons for being guarded, but she wasn't ready to share hers just yet. If ever.

'Okay, guys, if you could scooch up closer so I can *try* and fit you both in the same picture, it would be really great.'

'And if you could talk to us with a little respect it would be really great too,' Finn chastised the patronising young photographer rolling his eyes at them. The few words spoken in a measured, firm tone was enough to fluster both the employee of the national newspaper and Lily.

Since hitting her forties it seemed to her she had become invisible to the younger generation and at other times spoken to as though she had lost her faculties. With her credibility as a cardiologist not immediately apparent to strangers, it appeared to her she was judged by the crinkles at her eyes and dress size and found unworthy of interest for today's image-obsessed millennials. She wasn't able to do as much strenuous exercise as she used to in case she aggravated her condition and that, along with the swelling it caused in various parts of her body, meant she wasn't as svelte as she had been.

Pearce had pointed it out numerous times. That was just one of the reasons he was now her ex. Curvy, it seemed, wasn't what all men appreciated in a partner. No matter if it was caused by a medical condition or a fondness for cake. In her case, likely both.

It was difficult to stay buoyed in a world where looks were valued above experience and credentials. A world where even a man such as Charlie Finnegan was dismissed as an 'oldie' and therefore not worthy of respect, despite his service and dedication to the community. Not forgetting how good he looked in his uniform.

He wasn't wearing the whole outfit today, of course, but the smart white shirt and tie ensemble was still hot. It was a uniform of sorts and he exuded authority. Lily hopefully had a while to go before menopause struck but she still had eyes and Finn managed to inspire a hot flush creeping over her skin which took her completely unawares.

It was inconvenient to find him attractive, not only because they were working together but also because he had so much personal baggage. However, it was also a reminder that she wasn't dead yet at least.

'The article will be in tomorrow's paper,' the photographer mumbled before he shuffled off out of sight.

They'd already given an interview to the reporter, recounting the details of the new scheme. Now all they had to do was repeat it all for the evening regional news. They were using the same backdrop for the item, much to her and Finn's chagrin.

'All of this pink and red décor is starting to make me feel queasy,' he whispered as the bubbly TV reporter moved in for her turn at the questioning.

'I know what you mean. It's a bit overkill, but I suppose it'll make for good TV.' Syncing the launch with Valentine's Day gave the press an angle to work with and it was a nice piece to end the usual doom and gloom news roundup.

She heard the rumble of Finn's stomach, followed by a chuckle.

'Sorry. It's been a long day without much of a break for me.'

'Not to worry. This shouldn't take long,' the reporter assured them, beaming. A familiar face on the local television, the pretty young blonde was also much friendlier than the photographer who had preceded her.

Lily and Finn were fitted with their microphone packs and waited as the crew set up the camera and sound equipment around them.

'The worst of it is all the restaurants will be crammed full of loved-up couples and the menu will be twice the price.' She was a tad cynical when it came to love these days. It had eluded her. Or, rather, she had dodged it when it presented itself. In her case it seemed a wasted exercise when she might pop her clogs at any given second.

'All courses with poncy titles like Cupid's Charcuterie and Passion Parfait,' Finn added.

'Served with the lighting down low enough so you can't see the inflated prices on the menu.'

'So cynical. I'm a widower, what's your excuse?'

'Experience.' Let him think she was still a woman about town with admirers who took her out to restaurants on the most expensive night of the year instead of a spinster who would rather cook herself a steak and sit in front of the telly with a glass of wine than be in that cattle market again. Life was too short not to enjoy the things which did give her pleasure and avoid those which didn't. Okay, so she was well past her prime even without the doomed family medical history, but a woman still liked a man to think she was desirable to others even if it was fantasy.

'If you'd like, I could make us something to eat back at the station. I'll be taking the first shift overseeing our new venture and I could show you around?'

The offer of both having a meal cooked for her and seeing around the fire station, on Valentine's Day no less, was a pleasant surprise. Usually she spent the evening on her own, mourning the love life she never had with the help of a bottle of red wine and copious amounts of chocolate.

'That would be lovely, thank you.'

It would be churlish of her to decline simply to save face. He knew she had no one interested in her romantically and there was no need to pretend she might have something else lined up for the night. Besides, she was keen to check out the fire station and Finn's cooking skills.

After his initial opposition, he had been making an effort to set hostilities aside. They seemed to have bonded today over their joint cynicism over the commercialisation of February the fourteenth, and he'd backed her against an obnoxious photographer. She owed him and a thaw in relations would be best if they were going to be working together to make this scheme a success.

They did their bit for the TV cameras and answered all the questions, making the information about their joint enterprise as clear as possible for the general public. By the end of the publicity drive, Lily was emotionally and physically drained but also hungry.

'Are you ready to head to the station to sample my delights?' Finn waggled his eyebrows at her and made her laugh.

'Yes, please.' She'd be glad to get out of this heartfest and relax. Okay, she would've preferred to go home and change first, but she had to remind herself this wasn't a date and it shouldn't matter that she didn't have time to retouch her make-up or put on a clean outfit. They would both have to make do with the navy business suit and white blouse she'd put on first thing this morning. Although changing out of her heels would've been a nice way to wind down, she would have to suffer a little longer.

'Do you need a lift?' Finn stood back and let her walk ahead of him out of the building. As she walked past she was sure she caught the scent of smoke and sweat mixed with soap. Apparently that was her new kink as she found herself inhaling another lungful before realising she hadn't answered his question.

'No, it's fine. I've got my car here.' Thank goodness. If she'd been enclosed in such a small space with him she might have ended up sniffing him like some sort of weirdo.

'I'm guessing you know the way, so I'll see you there.' He left her in the car park smiling like a loon and wondering what the hell was wrong with her.

Finn didn't know how he'd ended up here at the station cooking dinner for this woman when they'd needed a mediator not so long ago. He supposed so much had happened in that short space of time it had left them both reeling. Starting this new work collaboration, doing publicity, not to mention working together to save a man's life had brought them closer in a way he was sure neither of them could have anticipated.

Perhaps it was being of a similar age, relationship status and career path, helping others, which had finally bonded them together but it had become important somewhere along the line that neither of them should be alone tonight. Not that she would have thanked him for it, he was sure. Lily struck him as someone very confident and capable of being on her own. Yet the way the young photographer had spoken to her earlier had angered him almost as much as how easily she had accepted it. Dinner had been a gesture of friendship, an olive branch, and hopefully a foundation for a good working relationship between their departments.

He was also glad the rest of the guys were out on a shout so he didn't have to answer awkward questions about why he was entertaining a woman on site.

'How do you like your steak?' He'd stopped into the

high-end butcher's outside of town so he could offer her something more than a microwave meal or a takeaway, which was sometimes all he felt like making himself at the end of the day. When he was off with the girls he cooked healthy meals and on his shifts here he often made dinner for the rest of the crew. Sometimes, however, cooking for one seemed too much hassle. It had been a long time since he'd shared dinner for two.

'Well done and no comments about how it ruins the steak et cetera. I like it how I like it, and that's preferably without the sight of blood.'

He held his hands up. 'No judgement here. Although I do prefer mine with a little more juice…and flavour.'

Finn ducked from the tea towel which Lily flung at him. She had insisted on helping in the kitchen, even if that only extended to washing and drying the dishes the other guys had left in a hurry and swatting him for making jokes at her expense.

The staff canteen wasn't the most glamorous setting, but this wasn't a date and they'd had enough hearts and flowers for one day. This was simply a shared meal between two people who'd had a busy day and were hungry. It didn't hurt that Lily was good company. He enjoyed teasing her, watching the tiger claw back and give as good as she got. The only females he spent time with these days were his daughters, his mother and those he encountered at work, often too traumatised to hold a conversation.

'Do you bring women back here often?' Lily teased, as though following his train of thought. 'You must get a lot of interest in your fireman's pole.'

Finn paused in the middle of dishing up to raise an

eyebrow at her. It was quite the innuendo to chuck into the conversation at the start of their meal.

Her cheeks flushed that adorable shade of pink again before she narrowed her eyes at him. 'You know what I mean, Finn. No need to get smutty.'

'Hey, I'm not the one talking dirty,' he said with a smirk, setting the heaped plates of steak, chips and salad onto the table under the fluorescent lights.

'I'm sure you're used to it,' she bit back without hesitation. It was true, in an all-male environment conversation got bawdy at times. Finn didn't participate but neither did he take offence when it was all part of the humour which helped them deal with the darker nature of their work.

'I'll admit we do get the odd lonely woman, and man, who gets us out under false pretences. Not to mention the drop-ins we get from people who just like to have a nosy around. I think it's something to do with the uniform.' He shook his head. It never ceased to amaze him what got people hot under the collar.

'I think it's everything to do with the uniform,' Lily muttered as she took her first bite of steak.

It took Finn by surprise that she might be turned on by anything so shallow as appearance. Lily Riordan struck him as someone who would've needed a lot more to impress her than a helmet and a bib and braces.

There was something in that realisation that she was as human as anyone else when it came to physical attraction which piqued his interest. Something he had no intention of exploring. He was only flesh and blood and there were certain physical attributes in a woman he appreciated, all of which Lily encompassed now he thought about it, but since his wife's death he had tried to put those thoughts to the back of his mind. Being attracted to another woman still seemed like a betrayal, even a year on.

'I know some of the younger single guys are happy with the benefits that the stereotypical romantic view of our job brings with it, but I'm not interested. Since my wife died, you're the only woman I've brought here and this is a celebratory dinner for our joint enterprise only.'

He stabbed his slightly bloody steak with his fork and sawed it enthusiastically with his knife. The sooner this was over and they retreated back to their respective departments, the better. He didn't want anyone getting the wrong idea that he was somehow getting back into the market and actively looking for a replacement for Sara. That wasn't going to happen any time soon, if ever, when his daughters were his priority.

'Well, that's me told,' she muttered and took a sip from her glass of water before they both lapsed into an awkward silence, interrupted only by the sound of two people trying to finish their meal as quickly as possible.

Finn was almost glad when the raucous arrival of his colleagues crashed in around them. Almost. When the loud chatter of the men returning reached the canteen door then stopped abruptly as they took in the scene before them, he knew he had some explaining to do.

It was like a farce as the guys stopped abruptly in the doorway, tripping those behind as they stared agog at Lily. She too froze, fork full of steak and salad hovering in the air, as she turned and looked at Finn, waiting for him to say something. He had no idea why he felt embarrassed and guilty. It wasn't as though he had just been sprung making out with her in one of the dorm beds. Even if he had been, they were two grown adults and whether they were having sex or sharing an awkward dinner, it was no one else's business.

'Lads, this is Lily Riordan. The cardiologist who introduced the new defib scheme for us to trial.' He was sure some of the men had probably seen her during the course of the set-up but he thought he should clarify who she was, even if he couldn't explain why she was here now eating dinner with him.

'Ah, right. Nice to meet you.'

'Hi. Any more of those steaks going?'

'Give us a few of your chips, Finn.'

The introduction appeared sufficient to end the stare-off as the men unfroze and invaded the canteen, helping themselves to his fries as they passed by. Lily nodded a hello before returning to her meal. He had lost his appetite since their arrival. There was something about real life disturbing the moment which had brought some unexpected emotions. Primarily guilt. As though simply being seen with another woman, enjoying her company, was something he should be ashamed about as a widower.

'I think there are some sausages in the fridge. I could stick those in the oven and do the rest of the chips for you, if you'd like?' He got up, glad to have a reason to leave the table.

'Cheers.'

'Has the chief has given you a tour of the place?' A couple of the men sat down beside Lily, unperturbed by the scene now they knew why she was here.

'No, he hasn't.'

'I'm sure Ms Riordan has better things to do than look at the mess you lot have left behind.' He'd shared enough with her here tonight, and showing her around behind the scenes at his place of work, where he lived and slept during his shifts away from home, now seemed too intimate.

'I thought you might want me to stick around in case a call came in, for emergency medical support?' She frowned and he could sense her confusion when that was exactly what they were supposed to be doing. Except being around Lily any longer suddenly seemed dangerous to his equilibrium and the life he had been living for the past year.

'It's probably not necessary. I mean I've done the training and the odds of getting a call on our first night are slim.' He positioned himself out in the kitchen, keeping the wooden counter as a physical barrier between them.

'I'm sure you're right.' Lily set down her cutlery and got to her feet, leaving the others to scavenge the leftovers on both of their plates. There was something in her tone which made Finn regret the abrupt end he had brought to their meal. A pained fragility he hadn't expected Lily to possess and that he could have done without being party to.

CHAPTER THREE

'We can cancel if you'd prefer? It is only a courtesy catch-up after all.' Lily was letting Finn off the hook. They had arranged to have an informal monthly meeting to discuss how the project was going, but that was before the awkward dinner they'd shared at the fire station. She hadn't heard from him until tonight, an hour before they were supposed to meet, when he'd called to say he couldn't get away. After the last time they had been together she would be only too glad if she never had to see him again.

The way he'd reacted when his crew had come back during their meal had made her feel about two inches high and she didn't need to be around anyone embarrassed to be seen with her. Life was too short to spend with toxic people and the change in his demeanour had been too obvious to ignore when their dinner had been gatecrashed. It didn't matter that there hadn't been anything going on other than companionship and bonding after their day with the press, she had seen the shame on his face when his colleagues had suspected more.

Her weight or her size didn't generally bother her when she had so much more to worry about—what was going on inside her body. It didn't make his reaction any less disappointing. After seeing him stand up to the patronising young photographer, she had expected more of Charlie Finnegan. That her achievements, her good heart and maybe even her personality meant more to him than carrying a few extra pounds. Although it had apparently been enough for Pearce to stop fancying her. That had been no great loss but she had put more stock in Finn.

If her appearance was all that mattered to him she was sure any business they had to discuss in the future could be done via email or text from now on. Then perhaps she wouldn't let her mind wander where it shouldn't, thinking there was a mutual attraction going on and not simply her appreciation of a fine-looking man. Perhaps that was bothering her more than the idea that curvy women weren't his thing. That she'd mistakenly believed there'd been a spark between them when it was nothing more than wishful thinking.

A lucky escape, she supposed, because Finn was never going to be a safe option for her. He wasn't someone she could ever consider for her casual type of relationships, which burned brightly for a while before she let them fizzle out so she could move on with no regrets or broken hearts. Pearce had upset her with his comments about her putting on weight, but she hadn't loved him enough to cry herself to sleep at night when they'd broken up. She was always careful not to get too involved when she couldn't promise anyone for ever.

Finn was different. He was grieving and he had two little girls to look after. Complications she certainly didn't need in her life. This was an attraction she would simply have to let fade away if she wanted to avoid any emotional fallout.

'No, I have a few issues I want to sort out. There are a couple of teething problems I'd like to talk to you about. Maeve, can you give your sister her doll back, please? No, I don't think she would look better with a haircut...' His voice trailed off as he apparently addressed his daughter in the background. Lily could almost picture the scene and though she was amused at first at the thought of him trying to wrangle two warring tots, her smile soon turned into a frown at the thought he might pass on his superficial judgement on the female body to another generation. She definitely shouldn't be thinking how sweet it was to hear him with his girls either when that was trouble waiting to happen.

'If this is a bad time you can just jot down a few points you want me to look at and pop them in an email.' Then she could end this call and hopefully never have to talk to him again.

'No, I'd rather talk in person. Though I'm having babysitter issues tonight. My mum was supposed to have the girls but she's down with a migraine. I'm merely suggesting a change of venue from the community centre, if you don't mind having two extra distractions? I'll try to get them to sleep before you come over but I can't promise they won't get out of bed again with a thousand and one questions about who you are.'

'Are you sure you'll be okay with that?' She couldn't resist a little dig since the last time he'd had to introduce her to anyone he'd almost died of embarrassment.

'Of course. I'll text you directions and I guess we'll see you soon.' He hung up without giving her any further chance to back out of the meeting now there was a change of venue. She was curious about what was going on when he was inviting her into his inner sanctum after seemingly regretting inviting her into his workplace. It was the only reason why she was grabbing her coat and bag and heading out of the door to make the meeting when she'd told herself any involvement in his personal life was a mistake.

Deep down she knew she was hoping for an explanation for his previous behaviour so she could stop cursing his name. Okay, so it had bothered her a lot that he found the idea abhorrent that anyone could believe they were together romantically, because she so desperately wanted to be wrong about the kind of man Charlie Finnegan was. If he wasn't the shallow Neanderthal she had believed him to be when she'd walked out of the station that night, she knew she was in real trouble.

Because she wanted to like him. Because it had hurt so damn much when he had publicly rejected her. Because she knew she was already ignoring all the warning signs which would normally send her running in the opposite direction.

Finn was a terrible liar. There was nothing about the project that he urgently needed to talk to Lily about or that couldn't wait for the next time he saw her. So far they'd dealt with a couple of emergency calls, both times able to restart the patients' hearts until the paramedics arrived and took over.

It was his conscience which had been bothering him where Lily was concerned.

Looking back on that night at the station, he could

see he'd been incredibly rude. He'd invited her back for a meal then acted as though he couldn't get rid of her fast enough when the boys came in. He wanted to explain, and apologise. Then perhaps he could stop replaying that day together in his head over and over again.

The stuff about not being able to get a babysitter was true though. If he cancelled at such short notice now it wasn't going to help her see him in a better light, it would merely confirm the idea he was flaky and untrustworthy. Something which would not sit well with him in his position in the community. He needed people to trust him, especially those he worked alongside.

Although he would have preferred not to do this at his place with the girls there. They were impressionable and he never brought anyone home, let alone a woman. He didn't want them to get any ideas about who she was or how important she might be in his life. Hopefully he would have them settled in bed before she got here and they would never have to cross paths. Thus still managing to keep his home life and work life separate.

'Teeth brushed, girls.' Finn hustled the two pyjama-clad munchkins towards the bathroom.

'Who were you talking to on the phone, Dada?' The littlest Finnegan also had the biggest ears.

'It was someone from work.' He kicked over the little wooden stool they used for her to reach the sink with her sister and squeezed some toothpaste onto the waiting toothbrushes.

'Is someone coming over, Daddy?' Now she had piqued her sister Niamh's interest, her eyes shining bright with undisguised delight at the prospect of having a visitor in the house. Clearly it had been too long since they'd had company other than their grandmother.

'Uh…just a lady who works at the hospital. I need you girls in bed so we can talk.' He didn't want to lie to his daughters, especially if there was going to be a stranger coming to the house, but he knew this would seem like a big deal to them.

His suspicions were confirmed as his eldest halted brushing her teeth to look at him, toothpaste dribbling down her chin. 'A lady?'

Her astonishment made him smile.

'Yes, a real live lady is coming to the house, but only if good little girls are tucked up under the covers.' Finn grabbed both girls in a bear hug, blowing raspberries on their necks and making them squeal.

He'd taken this for granted when they were babies, working all hours and leaving bedtime rituals for his wife to manage. It was too late to get that time back but he was determined to be with them as much as he could. Not easy as a single parent working shifts, but he tried to be there for breakfasts and bedtimes together where it was possible. He'd moved closer to his mum to have some support when it seemed as though he and the girls would never be normal again. Hearing them laugh, being able to enjoy the simple things in life with his daughters again was a salve for the wound of losing his partner. It would never completely heal, but having his daughters eased the loneliness.

He and Sara had been best friends, childhood sweethearts, together since high school. Thinking they would have for ever together, they had waited until their careers were flourishing before starting a family. It had never occurred to either of them that he would be left alone to raise their daughters from such a young age. He hadn't been apart from Sara since the age of thirteen and living without her had been a struggle for all of them, settling into new routines whilst grieving.

The death of their mother was such a difficult thing for the girls to comprehend at their young age and though there had been plenty of tears and tantrums as they tried to adjust to their new lives, they were managing. It was important, therefore, that nothing disturb their fragile equilibrium. Including the girls getting the wrong idea about him having a female acquaintance at the house.

The doorbell rang and he cursed himself for getting them excitable when he should have been singing them to sleep with a lullaby or reading until they dropped off to sleep. Instead they were running around the house screaming, the pitch of which had risen with the added excitement of a visitor. He had no choice but to answer the door and introduce them to Lily or he would have no chance of ever getting them to settle.

'Shh, girls. Now, we don't want to scare my friend away, so best behaviour,' he warned as he unlatched the door.

The girls nodded enthusiastically, looking fit to burst with the effort of restraint. Once he was sure they weren't going to hurl themselves at Lily like little lemmings jumping off a cliff, he opened the door wide.

'Hi, come on in.'

'Well, hello there.' As Lily entered the hallway she bent down to say hello to the girls, appearing to make their night.

'Who are you?'

'What's your name?'

'Are you having a sleepover with Daddy?'

'Daddy has two pillows on his bed and Mummy isn't here no more.'

As usual, his daughters said exactly what was on their minds, drawing a look of sympathy first from Lily, before she smirked at him.

'Sorry. They have no filter,' he said, trying to hustle them back towards their room in vain as they remained rooted to the spot, waiting for their visitor to answer.

'It's fine. My name is Lily, I'm a friend of your Dad's and no, I won't be staying over. I have a big bed with two pillows to go home to too.'

Little Maeve seemed to contemplate this news before asking, 'Do your girls have a daddy in heaven?'

A frown crinkled Lily's forehead at the question before evening out into a sad smile as she seemed to realise what she was being asked. 'I don't have any children or a husband. I live on my own.'

'Why?'

'I never got married or had babies.'

'Why?'

The question he was asked at least a hundred times a day was now directed at Lily on a loop and where he had to put up with the constant questioning, she didn't. Especially when it was in danger of being too personal and intrusive.

'That's enough, Maeve. It's none of our business.' It was a private matter and though he was curious about her circumstances, he knew what it was like to be put on the spot. These past twelve months had been difficult when people had asked after his wife or enquired about his love life and he'd had to explain what had happened. Information he would not usually have volunteered. Lily had come here under the impression it was to talk about work, not her relationship status.

Still, she didn't appear to take offence or get embarrassed by his inquisitive offspring. 'I just wasn't as lucky as your daddy.'

Lily was smiling, her answer enough to send his two finally skipping off to their room, but Finn had caught the flicker of pain in her eyes as she'd said it. He wouldn't be human if he didn't wonder why a woman like Lily Riordan hadn't settled down with a family of her own when she seemed sad about not doing so. She was attractive, funny, feisty and intelligent, a catch for anyone should she want them, and suddenly he wondered if her past was as tragic as his own.

'Say goodnight to Lily. It's bedtime.' He'd brought her over to apologise, not make her feel even more miserable.

'Aww. Can Lily read us a bedtime story?' His daughters were not about to give up spending time with their new visitor so easily.

'I'll read you a story, the same as I do every night.'

The girls pouted. 'We want Lily.'

'You'll have to make do with boring old Dad.' Finn did not want to get into a battle of wills in front of her, not least because he usually gave in to his daughters' pleas and it would do nothing for his credibility to be seen to cave as easily as he normally did.

'I don't mind reading them a story.' Lily shrugged,

sealing her own fate as his two girls grabbed both of her hands and dragged her towards the bedroom.

'It might get them to go to sleep quicker,' she whispered out the side of her mouth, giving him the impression she didn't want this to happen any more than he did. That gave him some comfort. Lily didn't come across as someone who wanted to inveigle herself into his or his girls' lives at all, so perhaps having her in his home wouldn't be as disastrous as he imagined. He'd say what he had to and she could go back to her place. Conscience salved, working relations smoothed over, no harm done.

Finn followed, though he was aware his presence was unimportant now the girls had a new storyteller to entertain them. For such a small gesture on Lily's part to agree to read to them, it was obviously having an impact, as the girls jumped into their beds without further complaint.

Thankfully these days the prolonged bedtime routine was more about getting extra time under the guise of more stories, requests for glasses of water and, of course, a sudden need for the toilet. For a long time they'd been plagued by nightmares and a fear of the dark, no doubt a manifestation of their grief and loss of their mother.

He'd spent many a night sleeping in the space between their beds, where Lily was sitting now on a pink princess bean bag. Some mornings he would wake to find they had both crawled into bed beside him, and on the nights he'd been on call they'd hardly slept at all, worried he wouldn't come home again. Like Mummy.

Then there were the nights he'd been so lonely, expecting to roll over and see Sara, only to find an empty space. Those were the times he was glad the girls needed him, because they were all that had kept him going. Now they were adjusting to life, learning to live without Sara, perhaps it was time for them all to begin socialising outside of their little bubble. One visitor really shouldn't cause such a commotion.

The girls were enraptured with Lily's storytelling, as was he. Not everyone was as patient with two excitable young children as she had been so far. As she read their favourite fairy tale, complete with character voices and actions, she really brought the story to life. Finn couldn't help but think about her earlier comment about not having children of her own, made all the more tragic by the fact she seemed like a natural mother figure.

Finn didn't know if she had siblings who'd provided her with nieces or nephews, only that she was comfortable being with youngsters. Tonight, that was making his life easier as well as entertaining for her audience.

'And they all lived happily ever after.' Lily closed the book, rolling her eyes at Finn as if to say she didn't believe that was possible any more than he did.

He'd had the loving wife and beautiful family, only to have a very unhappy ending.

'One more?'

'Please!'

'No.' He ignored their pleas, knowing they would keep Lily here captive all night if they could get away with it.

'Can Lily come back another night, Daddy?'

'Can Lily have a sleepover with us?'

Their tenacity was admirable, if exhausting.

'No, now go to sleep and let me and Lily talk in peace.'

They eventually gave up the fight and lay down so he could tuck them under the covers.

'Goodnight,' he said to each of them as he kissed their foreheads.

When he looked up he was sure he saw tears in Lily's eyes, reiterating the sense that being childless was not something she had willingly chosen.

Once they'd left the room and closed the door he let out a sigh. 'Sorry about that. They're not used to seeing anyone else here except my mother.'

'It's fine. They're lovely girls. Very inquisitive,' she said, chuckling.

'They're a handful all right.' Finn led the way back downstairs, heading to the kitchen for a much-needed caffeine hit. He switched the kettle on while Lily took a seat at the breakfast bar, the first face he had seen, other than his daughters', across there in over a year.

'It must have been really difficult for you, raising them on your own, but you've clearly done a good job.'

Lily's unexpected praise and understanding was something Finn didn't realise he needed until that moment and it wedged a lump of emotion in his throat. Since losing Sara he'd done his best to raise the girls the way they'd both wanted, having to take on both parenting roles. He hadn't always got it right, but hearing someone tell him he was doing well meant the world. Lily saw him, saw behind the tough chief façade to the grieving family man struggling as a single parent. She was probably the only one who did and that didn't sit comfortably with him. It made him feel vulnerable at a time when he needed to be stronger than ever for his family.

'I can't say it's been plain sailing, but we have no choice but to get on with things. I have to be Mum and Dad and it's taken me a while to get used to doing all the things Sara did while I was at work. Little things like braiding their hair suddenly seemed so important. I had to watch video tutorials on that one and get plenty of practice before they stopped looking like they'd been dragged through a hedge backwards.'

The mornings had been full of tears and tantrums until he'd got their hair some way close to the way Mummy did it. It had been a learning process, getting to know his daughters' physical and emotional needs following the loss of their mother, but Finn had managed this far and they'd settled into a new normal.

'I can only imagine. Can I ask what happened to their mother? If it's too personal you don't have to tell me…'

Lily wasn't the first person to ask and she wouldn't be the last but it didn't make it any easier to recount the story. He kept his back to her while he made their coffees so he didn't have to see the pity or horror in her eyes as he told the sorry tale.

'Sara was a nurse, under a lot of pressure at the hospital and working long hours. Looking back now, it was obvious she was doing too much. We never saw each other and the girls were practically living at my mum's. Unbeknown to me, she'd been having trouble sleeping and had been relying heavily on medication. I came home one night and found her in the bath. She'd taken more pills than she should have and drifted off… I'll never know if it was an accident or not.'

Although all reports had since recorded it as an accidental death, he would always have his doubts, a worry he couldn't shake that Sara's life had been so unhappy that she had decided to end it. He'd failed her as a husband and in turn failed his daughters. Since then he'd spent every day trying to make it up to them, but nothing could replace having their mother in their lives.

'I'm sure it was, Finn. She would never have intentionally left you or the girls.'

He appreciated the sentiment, but Lily hadn't known Sara or the kind of life they'd had. No matter what anyone said, he knew he'd blame himself for the rest of his life for not being there when she'd needed him the most.

CHAPTER FOUR

LILY DID HER best to maintain her composure, even though she wanted to rush over and hug Finn to within an inch of his life. The whole nature of his wife's passing was too horrific to contemplate. From Sara's obvious distress to the idea of Finn finding her limp body in the bath, it made her want to weep for the whole family. It had clearly been devastating for them all.

She knew what it was to suffer loss, but this seemed all the more tragic given the circumstances and the two little girls left behind. Despite trying to hide his face as he'd told her of his wife's demise, the raw pain was still in evidence when he turned back to hand her a coffee. The deep grooves of worry ploughed across his forehead and the sad tilt of his mouth told of his continuing pain. It was no surprise after everything he'd gone through, and was still living with. All of which she was able to relate to her own situation.

If she had married a man like Finn, gone on to have children, she would have caused the same devastation when her heart condition inevitably claimed her. Further proof it would have been selfish of her to have a family, knowing the heartache she would eventually put them through.

Finn came to join her at the breakfast bar and they sat in silence for a few minutes sipping their coffees before he ventured into some questions of his own.

'You told the girls earlier you weren't lucky enough to marry and have a family of your own. Did you ever come close?'

She supposed it was natural for him to want to know more about her when he'd given so much of himself and his family tonight, but Lily had never really confided in anyone about her personal problems and she wasn't sure she was ready to do so now either.

'Not really. I guess I never met anyone whose future gelled with mine.' That much was true. As soon as a partner mentioned the idea of marriage or children she'd known it was time to get out of the relationship because a future together was something she simply couldn't guarantee.

'You'd make a good mum. You were really good with the girls tonight.'

'Reading a bedtime story is one thing, a lifetime of responsibility is entirely different. Now, I'm sure you didn't bring me over to talk about my desolate love life. You said there were some problems you needed to discuss?' She'd already spent longer in his home than she'd intended and she was worried if she extended her visit any more she would share too much personal information. The reason she didn't was because she didn't want anyone to treat her any differently. Her heart condition didn't make her any less of a person, but not everyone would see it that way. It was easier just to deal with it alone.

She could feel Finn's eyes trying to penetrate through to the truth, but she wouldn't be drawn any further on the subject of her personal life. He stared at her a little longer before apparently giving up.

'I'm afraid I got you over here under false pretences. The project seems to be going well so far. We've had a couple of emergency medical calls, which we were able to assist with until the patients were able to be transferred to the hospital. I actually wanted to speak to you about the other day at the station.'

'Oh?' Lily was glad there were no hiccups to report, but she was confused as to why he'd felt the need to lie to her about it.

'Obviously an apology would have been better if I'd gone to you to make it, but circumstances tonight conspired against that. I…uh…wanted to say sorry about my behaviour that night. I invited you over then…'

'You couldn't wait to get rid of me when your buddies came back,' she finished for him, the memory deflating her previous good mood. Her time with the girls had made her feel wanted, needed, but that was taken away as Finn reminded her of his embarrassment at being seen with her the last time they'd been together.

'No, it wasn't like that. Well, I suppose it was, but not because of the reasons you think.' He became agitated when she challenged him, to the point he managed to knock over his coffee cup, spilling the contents over the counter and Lily. A brown waterfall of hot liquid cascaded into her lap and in her haste to back away she tipped the stool over, landing heavily on the floor.

'Ouch.' She lay dazed on the cool tiled floor, waiting for the pain at the back of her head to subside.

Finn swore before coming to help her sit up. 'Are you okay? I'm so sorry. I'm a clumsy idiot.'

Lily sat up, one hand pressing against her throbbing skull and the other trying to hold the hot, sodden fabric away from her skin.

'I'll survive, don't worry.'

'Can I get you a cold compress or a change of clothes?' He fussed around her, pulling the upturned stool away and mopping up the rest of the spilled coffee.

'I think there's a bit of a lump forming where I hit my head but it's nothing serious.' The last couple of minutes had been a comedy of errors but without the laughs.

She heard Finn rustling in the freezer before he came back with a bag of frozen peas for her.

'This should stop the swelling,' he said, gently holding it against the injury. She flinched at first but the cool pressure was welcome. As she got to her feet, with Finn still holding the bag of peas against her head, they made eye contact and promptly both burst out laughing. It was such a ridiculous situation to have found themselves in and she'd been hurt again, all because Finn was trying to be nice to her.

'So, you wanted to apologise?' She grinned, trying to make light of the situation despite her ruined clothes and head wound.

'I'm not making a very good job of it, am I?' He offered her a lopsided smile in penance and Lily's heart did a weird flip that immediately made her take a step back, putting a little distance between them.

Despite her apprehension about coming here it had

been a lovely night with the girls and she was obviously confusing that cosy scene reading them bedtime stories with something else. Just because she couldn't have a family didn't mean she didn't crave one and she was sure this growing attraction towards Finn was mixed up in that. He was part of this happy image she had of a loving dad and his children. It was a warning that she was getting too close and things would have been better if he'd remained cold towards her instead of trying so hard to be nice.

'Don't worry about it. I should probably go anyway.' She handed him back the bag of defrosting vegetables and sought to make a quick exit before she did something more humiliating than falling off a stool.

'I really am sorry, Lily. For getting you over here, for foisting the girls on you, for spilling hot coffee over you and for making you fall and bang your head. Most of all I'm sorry if I made you feel bad the other night.'

He was following behind her to the door and when she opened it he put his hand against it to stop her leaving, forcing her to turn around and face him. She didn't want to look at him, to have him see the tears welling in her eyes, or see how being reminded of his behaviour had upset her, because none of it should matter. Lily was a strong woman and had been through worse but, for reasons she didn't want to comprehend, the idea of having Finn reject her had hurt bone-deep and she hadn't been able to move past it.

Nevertheless, she sucked it all up and reacted the only way she knew how. 'Listen, Finn, I get it. No one wants to be seen with the fat girl.'

She watched him frown then dip his head as he swore. 'That's not… I don't think that…'

He made a guttural sound and hit the door with the heel of his hand. 'I wasn't embarrassed to be seen with you. I felt guilty about being with someone who wasn't my wife and enjoying the company. When the guys came in, I panicked. It was reality crashing in and making me realise you were the first woman they'd seen me with since Sara, and the shame I felt was from the betrayal of her memory. Of course the boys didn't bat an eyelid, they were simply surprised to see you there, and now I've had time to think it over I realise I overreacted.'

'Oh,' was all Lily could manage, overwhelmed both by the confession and by Finn's closeness to her. She was effectively trapped between his body and the front door, his hand still resting against the frame, caging her there. Not that she could have moved if she'd wanted, frozen by the realisation that he hadn't rejected her after all and the chemistry which she could sense brewing between them was real.

'And for the record, I think you're beautiful.' Finn brushed a stubborn tear away from the corner of her eye and the slightest touch of him against her skin almost stopped her heart. The jolt of electricity which seemed to pass between them stole her breath away.

He hadn't said he thought she was beautiful despite her size, or that she would be pretty if she lost weight, or any of the hundreds of backhanded compliments she'd heard before. Finn was telling her she was beautiful and the sincerity of those words was there in his blue eyes, looking at her as though she was the only other person in the world right now. Locked in this little bubble of longing, Lily couldn't seem to think about anything other than kissing Charlie Finnegan.

They both seemed to be resisting the pull which had drawn them so close their lips were almost touching. She could feel his warm breath on her skin, see his darkening eyes lingering on her mouth, wanting this as much as she did. Then, as if the last thread of restraint had snapped, his lips were suddenly on hers, taking and giving all at once.

Lily was swept up in his arms, the strength of his embrace matched by the ferocity of his kisses. She was lost in the dizzying sensation of passion, of being wanted, and of her own arousal. Finn was creating a need inside her she hadn't felt for a long time, an ache only he could fill, but also an awakening of something she knew to be dangerous. To give in to this lust, this want to be with him completely, was not something which could be satisfied by a one-time surrender to temptation.

She couldn't fall for Finn. He had daughters to think about, girls who had already suffered so much loss and grief to get involved with someone who couldn't be there for them in the future. It wouldn't be fair on any of them after all this time of denying herself a family, to insinuate herself into someone else's. Only to destroy them, the way the death of her father and sister had devastated her. She couldn't let that happen just because she had the hots for the man currently doing his best to kiss her into an actual swoon.

'I'm sorry, Finn. I have to go.' She broke off the kiss and fumbled for the door handle behind her back. If she didn't leave now she knew she would never find the courage to do it again, when being in his embrace felt so good.

'Tiger Lily?'

He wasn't playing fair, bestowing a pet name upon her and fixing her with those lust-dazed eyes. Especially when she was more of a mewing kitten right now than a feisty beast. Any woman would be glad to have him look at her the way he was looking at Lily. With a promise of passion and a whole lot more than fevered kisses on the doorstep. She cursed her father's legacy tonight more than ever, for stealing away her chance of happiness.

'You have your girls to think about and I'm sorry, but I never signed on for family life.'

She wasn't that lucky.

'Lily—' Finn had to take a step back as she opened the door and fled out into the night. It took him a moment to assess what had just happened and come to the conclusion that she was right and he wouldn't go chasing after her. He did have his girls to think of, along with the wife he had only recently lost. His libido and base needs paled into insignificance once he was able to think clearly again.

He closed the door on the dark night and the idea of starting a new relationship with anyone. The screech of tyres signalled Lily's similar regret over their brief lapse of judgement. Even though he'd enjoyed every second of it while it was happening. The sweet smell of her perfume tickling his senses, her soft skin beneath his fingertips and the fiery passion in her kiss were things he wouldn't easily forget. Things he had been fantasising about for some time if he was honest with himself.

They had been growing closer lately, to the point where he had missed her and made up that excuse to get her over here. His first mistake. Not only had he crossed that line between his personal and professional life, but he had introduced her to his daughters, given them reason to like her too. It would be too easy to let her slip into that void Sara had left behind, providing a much-needed female presence in all of their lives.

How wonderful it would be for them all to have someone at home again to love and care for them, to read to them, to talk to, to kiss. Except it was a fantasy he couldn't afford to invest in. Lily had said it herself, she didn't want a family and he didn't want anyone in his life who might possibly hurt his children. Having to end a relationship because he'd jumped in too early would be further damage to their emotional wellbeing and he was already burdened with the guilt of failing them.

No, they would put this lapse of sanity behind them and keep things strictly professional from now on. With things already in motion, hopefully they wouldn't even have to cross paths again. As soon as he returned the coat she'd left behind in her hurry to get away from him.

If Lily hadn't needed the lanyard with her ID on it for work she would have quite happily said goodbye to her coat for ever rather than go back to Finn's place to retrieve it. Even for the shortest spell she'd had in his house, there were too many emotive associations for her to return. Spending that time with the girls seemed to have had a profound effect on her, just as much as giving in to the attraction with Finn. Both occurrences had made her realise what she had given up to safeguard other people's hearts, when hers was aching for that companionship and loving environment she had been part of for her brief visit.

Not to mention the hot encounter she'd shared with Finn before running away from him and those feelings she'd tried so hard to avoid. Who knew all it would take was a widowed fireman to remind her she wasn't dead yet? Charlie Finnegan was as good at starting fires as he was at putting them out.

To save them both from temptation she'd texted him about retrieving her coat, arranging to meet at the station tonight, where there were plenty of other people to keep them out of harm's way.

It didn't mean her heart didn't give a joyful leap when he came down to meet her, dressed in that short-sleeved white shirt that showed off his strong thick forearms which she found inexplicably sexy.

'Hey,' she said, with all the guile of a teenage girl calling on her hot next-door neighbour.

'Hey, yourself.' All he had to do was grin to remind her of what they'd done together the last time they'd seen each other and her hormones partied as if she were eighteen again.

'I'm just here to pick up my coat,' she reiterated, hoping it would excuse the rudeness when she grabbed it and ran in the opposite direction.

He held it out at arm's length, clearly just as eager to avoid their past mistake, and discussing it, as she was.

Before she could make her escape the alarm sounded and the place was filled with bodies and noise.

'There's a fire at a house over on Main Street. Multiple casualties. Paramedics are on their way but we'll be first on the scene,' Finn's colleague shouted over to him, warning that it was probably not going to be an easy shout.

'I should come with you.' Lily didn't have to think twice about it. These were probably people she knew, in her community, needing medical assistance. Any personal issues she had being around Finn were of no importance in the face of a potential tragedy.

'As much as we could probably use the help, you're not authorised. I'll be going in there myself tonight since we're short-staffed and I'm afraid we can't risk anyone else getting hurt.' He was already pulling on his gear, getting ready to organise his crew to face whatever was waiting out there.

'Call me later? Just let me know you're all right.'

Finn nodded and in what seemed like no time at all the engines were on their way, sirens blaring, lights flashing.

The nature of Lily's job meant she usually had some advance warning of what she was going to be dealing with, her patients having been seen and assessed by other medical staff before reaching her door. Here, they were driving into the unknown and her heart was in her mouth at the thought of what might be lying in store for him.

Lily knew this was his job and running into burning buildings was something he did every day, but being here, watching him go, brought it home to her. He could get killed. One night he could head out like this and simply never return to his family, or her. She shuddered at the thought of never seeing him again, and that was when she knew it was too late. She cared for him and there was no going back.

If she hadn't had to come back for her coat she would have found some other excuse to come and see him again. Some things were too obvious to ignore, no matter how inconvenient, and the effect Finn had on her, physically and mentally, wasn't simply going to vanish because she wished it so. Sooner or later they were going to have to address the matter, and her rapid pulse was telling her the outcome she was still hoping to have from that conversation. After all, she was the one to have walked away from the explosive chemistry, not Finn.

Hopefully he would return unscathed and they could take things from there. For now, that was all that mattered.

CHAPTER FIVE

FINN'S EVERY SENSE was engulfed by events. The smell of smoke burning the inside of his nostrils, the roar of the flames, the whoosh of water from the hoses being directed from the ground and the screams of the people inside and outside of the building were unfortunately all too familiar. The imprint of the red, yellow and orange tongues of fire flickering in the darkness would be burned onto his retinas for some time.

Once he donned his mask and breathing apparatus and forced his way inside, it seemed an eternity before he saw anything else. He was calling out for a response, some sign that there was life. All the while moving from room to room, dodging fire and flames. Eventually he moved upstairs and into what looked as though it had once been a nursery, pastel colours smudged black and grey from the devastation of the fire. Out of the corner of his eye he spotted a tiny figure in the cot and he grabbed it up and held it close to his chest. He couldn't see any movement, felt no response, but took off his own mask to cover the face of the child in the hope it would help him or her breathe.

From then on he fought like a lion to get back out of

the house, battling falling debris and pushing through that fierce wall of heat to get outside again.

One of his colleagues stumbled outside shortly after him, his arms around another adult, trying to keep them upright.

'My baby!' The anguished high-pitched scream was the only indication that the person they had rescued was a woman, her entire body and clothes covered in a layer of black soot.

She lunged at the bundle in his arms he could now see was a little girl, no more than eighteen months old. Her long, once-golden locks were streaked with black dirt and grime, her eyes closed, her body still. Despite the urge to retch, thinking of one of his own girls lying there, Finn launched into emergency mode. Falling apart was not going to help anyone now.

'There are two more upstairs,' one of the crew informed Finn as he carried the baby away from the building, shouting instructions to the rest of the men.

With no sign of the paramedics on scene, he laid the child down on a blanket and cleaned away the dirt he could see around her mouth. Thankfully the mother had been escorted away by a well-meaning member of the public so she couldn't see what was going on or hinder his progress.

With no pulse to be found, he had no choice but to begin rescue breaths, willing the little girl to fight her way back to life. His thoughts flitted to Lily and the time they'd had to do this together. Both of their jobs involved saving lives, but when they were dealing with little ones who should've had their whole lives in front of them it brought home how fragile the human body was, and sometimes not even a fireman or a cardiologist could save them.

Finn closed the child's nose using his thumb and index finger. He opened the mouth a little so it was pointing upwards before taking a breath himself and sealing his mouth around the tiny patient's. He breathed steadily, watching for the chest to begin moving, then took his mouth away again. With no response, he repeated the process a further four times.

No sign of life present meant he was forced to begin chest compressions. It was trickier to perform CPR on children and he had to be careful to ensure there was no pressure put on the ribs. With fingers interlocked he began pushing down with the heel of his hand and performed rescue breaths after every thirty chest compressions.

Eventually his prayers were answered and the little girl began to cough. As soon as Finn saw signs of life he reached for the oxygen mask kept in the back of the vehicle to aid breathing. Slowly, wonderfully, the child came round and gave a pitiful little cry. Enough for him to let out a shaky breath, relieved he had been able to prevent one tragedy. It was also sufficient to draw the mother to where Finn had been working on her daughter, tears streaking down her smoke-blackened face.

'Is she okay? Millie? Oh, Millie, thank goodness.' The mother gathered her child into her arms and he left the two of them, calling to attract the attention of the paramedics who had just arrived in the ambulance.

Unfortunately the scene there was not such a happy one. Two figures were now being wheeled by on stretchers by the ambulance crew, one completely covered from view.

Someone passed him a bottle of water, which he took a sip from before splashing the rest over his head and face, his own skin blackened from the smoke he'd battled through to reach the casualties.

'I'm afraid the father didn't make it. He apparently went back inside after raising the alarm to get the son from the upstairs bedroom.'

So much tragedy and pain in one night for a family who had probably lost everything they owned in the fire. The relief of saving the little girl was dimmed by the pain of knowing the grief they would still suffer on learning of their other loss. Finn would have done the same thing again. In fact his entire career was based on him venturing into raging infernos to save others, and one wrong move could leave his girls orphaned. It was something he was aware of every day.

This time it wasn't only the faces of his daughters which haunted him. Lily was there too, waiting for him to come home, and he didn't want to let her down. She was one more thing he had to live for.

Fire was not something exciting and thrilling to Finn but danger, a threat to life, and it had been his calling to do this job the same way Lily had been drawn to work in the medical profession. He wanted to save lives, to prevent death and grief and tragedy, probably even more so now he'd been through so much of his own. Yet he was putting his own life on the line every day to do so and there was no bigger measure of a man than his selfless need to help others. Charlie Finn was a giant among men.

Lily's stomach had been in knots, waiting to hear from him tonight, to make sure he was safe. She had realised whilst sitting staring out of the window into the darkness of night that even if a person didn't have a death sentence hanging over them in the form of a heart condition or work in a perilous profession, life wasn't guaranteed for ever. A revelation confirmed when he had called to say he was okay but that they'd lost someone.

She'd sacrificed her personal life over the years and left herself with nothing, all for some false sense of virtue that no one except her would ever appreciate. A husband, a family and all of those events which happened along the way had been off-limits to her because of her own rules and boundaries. Now she was left wondering if she'd somehow been punishing herself for something beyond her control when she was the only one suffering as a result.

She'd seen young and old alike lose their lives over the years and never equated her life to theirs. However, sitting here tonight chewing her nails as Finn risked his life she was faced with the possibility of losing him. It wasn't something she could prevent, any more than he could predict her inevitable end. Life and death went hand in hand. They weren't things the average person could control or bend to their will. If only she had come to that conclusion years ago, before she'd become this spiky loner who couldn't let relationships stick in case they actually came to mean something.

She was still sitting in the dark, contemplating everything she'd sacrificed for apparently no good reason, when Finn arrived at her door.

'Hey,' he said, leaning into the doorframe, that lazy smile making her even more regretful about the life she had denied herself to this point.

'Hey.' She opened the door wide and walked away, letting him follow her inside. 'I wasn't expecting to see you tonight. The phone call was enough. I just wanted to know you were safe.'

'I thought I'd call in on my way home. You seemed as though you had something on your mind tonight and I thought you might need to talk to someone.'

He could add being perceptive to his list of superhero qualities, along with his selflessness.

'You're the one who has been through a traumatic event tonight.'

'Maybe I need someone to talk to,' he said and plonked himself into one of her armchairs, frowned, got up to switch on the light and sat down again.

'Something wrong?' She knew losing someone at work stuck with you, regardless of age or circumstance, but was surprised he'd chosen to come to her.

Finn sighed. 'It's just reality hitting home that none of us are ever promised tomorrow. That, despite all my precautions or desperate need to be around for my daughters, I can't control fate.'

'Tell me about it,' Lily mumbled.

'No, you tell me about it, Tiger Lily. There's clearly something bugging you.'

'Why do you keep calling me that?'

He gave her a cheeky grin in response. 'When you're riled your claws come out, Tiger Lily.'

'I'm a vicious cat?'

'No, you're defensive, lashing out when anyone gets too close, but I'm prepared to brave the scratches to get to know you better. I owe you for helping get my kids to bed, and I can tell there's something going on with you other than forgetting to pay your electric bill.' He was trying to make a joke about the weird sight he'd found on arrival, the house in darkness with her sitting here like some dormant spirit just waiting for someone to haunt.

She took a deep breath and prepared to share the secret which had ruled her adult life, then perhaps she would be able to move on into her afterlife.

'I never had children because I have a genetic heart condition, dilated cardiomyopathy. I lost my father and sister to the disease and it devastated me. Iris was only ten and I guess my dad was still young at forty-two when he died. I decided it was better for me to be on my own than to ever put anyone through the grief my mum and I suffered. I didn't want to bring more lives into the world, only to hand them a death sentence either. So I've concentrated on my career and any relationships have been short-lived.'

Finn had been listening intently, his forehead furrowed into a frown. 'Surely loving you means accepting whatever the future holds together?'

It sounded so simple when he said it, but she had never been with anyone she thought she couldn't live without or who was prepared to take on her medical problems when she explained her circumstances to them. She was fine for a fling but long-term she was not a safe bet.

'Perhaps I've never been loved,' she joked, though the truth in those words struck deep. It wasn't something that she'd let bother her before now, telling herself that was the way she wanted it. Love made things complicated and painful and she'd done her best to avoid that. The result being that she now had no one in her life to turn to for the comfort and support Finn was giving her now out of pity.

'I doubt that.'

She ignored his attempt to soft soap her. It wasn't necessary. She knew the woman she'd been, and she'd purposely made it hard for anyone to love her. Including herself at times.

'Anyway, sitting here tonight, waiting for news on whether you were alive or dead, made me think and you're spot on, we're not guaranteed anything in life except death. I've realised that tonight, perhaps too late. I've sacrificed having a normal life for…for nothing.' She threw up her hands, the futility of it all suddenly overwhelming her, her eyes filling with liquid regret for the woman she could've been.

Finn reached across the gap between them to take her hand and reconnect. 'I'm so sorry, Lily. You can still live your life to the fullest. Better late than never, eh?'

He tried to make a joke because he didn't know what else to say or how to process the bombshell she'd just dropped. Outwardly she appeared to be a self-contained, confident professional woman. No one would have guessed that inside she was so troubled and fragile. It showed a lot of trust in him that she was opening up to him like this. Even if it was sounding more alarm bells for him.

His reasons for coming over tonight hadn't been entirely selfless. He had known there was something on her mind but he'd also wanted to see her again.

It had been a long night. He was used to that, but every loss was one too many and he always felt it, down to his very soul. More so since losing Sara. Another widowed partner, more children left without a parent and enough tears shed to put the fire out which started it all in the first place—a scenario he wouldn't wish on anyone.

It was all part of his chosen career, but it was something he would never get used to. As in all emergency services, death was something they were supposed to compartmentalise to let them continue to function in their job, but a person would have to be inhuman not to carry some residual trauma after an event like tonight. Lily had been the one person he'd wanted to see to give him some comfort. She understood the job, and him, better than people he had known for a lot longer.

'Do you ever have any regrets?' Either she didn't hear his comment or she chose to ignore it, changing the subject completely.

'Who doesn't?' he said with a yawn, the events of tonight catching up with him too. It would only be a few hours before the girls would be up, looking for their breakfast, and he wanted to be there this morning more than ever.

'If you'd known your wife would die when your girls were so young, do you think you would have still had a family?' She turned to look at him now, but the shock of hearing her question must have registered on his face as she added, 'Sorry. That was insensitive of me.'

Finn didn't know what had prompted that. Perhaps it was the untimely death they had witnessed tonight, or another reminder of the family she'd never had, but it was clear Lily was the one with regrets. However, the mere mention of his wife and everything she had left behind plunged that dagger of pain straight back into his heart. It was a loss he would never be able to explain or get over.

He strengthened himself against the tidal wave of memories flooding back. Their wedding day, the birth of the girls. Then the devastating memory of finding her in the bath, lifeless in his arms as he cried for everything they had lost.

'I can't imagine ever being without my girls, and we had some good times. So I guess the answer's yes, I would still have had our girls even if we'd known our time together was going to be short. It's better to have lived our life together for as long as we had than never to have experienced the joy of having our family.' It might not be the answer she'd wanted but it was the truth. He had the good memories of their time together, which he hoped some day would overshadow the bad ones. As for the girls, they were his everything, the reason he got up in the morning and their happiness more important to him than his own.

Lily promptly burst into wretched, messy tears. This unravelling was such a contrast to the composed adversary he'd first encountered at that mediation meeting, he couldn't help but rush to her side, desperate to provide her with some comfort. He needed to do something for her which didn't involve pulling her into his embrace and kissing her tears away.

Although he was honoured that she had shared a very personal issue with him, it had reminded him of why he shouldn't be here offering her a shoulder to cry on. If that was all he was doing there wouldn't be a problem, but this constant craving to be with her, this longing he felt when he was with her, couldn't go anywhere. Now, more than ever, he had reason to fight this growing attraction to his Tiger Lily. She'd given him all the ammunition he could ever need to avoid getting entangled with her.

He didn't know a whole lot about her condition but it had been enough to take her sibling, a parent, and rule her life this far. Enough to disrupt the lives of him and his daughters. It might seem insensitive, and he felt for Lily and everything she had gone through, but he had to protect his girls from any further pain. He could be a friend to Lily, a colleague, but anything more than that, knowing her circumstances, would mean inviting heartache into all of their lives. Judging by her past relationships, she didn't need that any more than he did.

Yet he still wanted to do something to comfort her instead of ignoring her pain. The last time he'd done that he'd lost Sara and he wouldn't—couldn't—go through that again. He wouldn't fail another woman he cared for.

'Why don't I run you a bath and make you a cup of tea? That's my mother's cure-all.'

Lily looked at him as though he'd suggested getting in with her. As much as he would like to, he was thinking more along the lines of making her comfortable so he could go home and avoid any further temptation.

'Why would you do that? You're the one who was

working and went through a very traumatic experience by the sound of it.'

'I had a quick wash and change before I came over. Is it too much to let me do one nice thing for you, Lily?'

'Does that include the tea-making?' she asked, already looking a little brighter.

'Of course.' Finn headed straight for the bathroom and set to work, adding a selection of fancy oils and potions to the big bath tub. It was the perfect way to help her relax, along with a cup of tea or a huge bar of chocolate. Whichever brought those much-needed feel-good endorphins he usually got simply from being with his daughters after a tough shift.

He filled the bath until the foamy bubbles were in danger of spilling out onto the bathroom floor and went in search of Lily.

'All ready when you are, madam.'

'Thanks, Finn.' He could just about make out her smile, but all he could hear was sadness. There was a rustle as she unfurled herself from the foetal position she'd been in on the sofa and got to her feet.

He handed her the towel he'd extracted from the bathroom closet and made sure not to touch her again. The last time he'd got too close and crossed that line between wanting and having he'd sent her running. Lily needed support and that was all he should be offering.

Thankfully she took the towel and headed towards the bathroom without another word or look which would make him think twice about letting her bathe alone. Once he fulfilled his promise of making her a strong cup of tea his job would be done and he could go home with a clear conscience where Lily Riordan was concerned.

CHAPTER SIX

ALL LILY WANTED to do was crawl under the bedcovers and never come out again.

Liar.

What she really wanted was for Finn to carry her there and give her such a good time she would never have to think about everything she had missed out on over the years.

Instead, she stripped off and sank into the warm bath he had kindly drawn for her. The bubbles crackled in her ears as she lowered herself under the water and tried to wash away the realisation she'd thrown her life away.

Lily thought about her own grief when she'd lost her father and sister, and of Finn's words. He would rather have lived with the pain of his loss and had the happy times than never have started his family at all. The same was probably true of the victims' loved ones tonight. It all went to show she had been living a lie this whole time. She hadn't been trying to protect anyone but herself by not getting close to anyone. Now she was all alone and when her time finally came she wouldn't even have those good memories of family or relationships to cling on to.

Full of self-pity, and mourning the life she might have had, she couldn't stop the tears from falling. She sat up, clutching her knees to her body, the closest she could get to a hug when she had pushed away everyone who had ever got close. Including Finn. Only the other night she might have let herself experience one evening of pleasure, of belonging, but the moment she'd thought it could lead to something she'd run out. He was only here now out of pity, knowing she didn't have anyone to go home to the way he did.

She sobbed as though decades of self-denial, loneliness and regret had finally bubbled to the surface, and she worried she might never stop. It was too late for her to find love, to be loved the way she longed for, and it was her own fault.

Finn added sugar to the tea, hoping it would help with whatever else was ailing Lily tonight. It wasn't going to solve her problems but he hoped the gesture would make her realise she didn't have to go through whatever this was alone. Perhaps if he'd done the same for Sara, been there to run her bath and bring her a cup of tea when she'd needed it, things might have been different.

He intended to leave the tea outside the bathroom door and was ready to knock when he heard noises from inside. Listening to the gut-wrenching sound of Lily crying, great heaving sobs which seemed to come from her very soul. Whatever she was going through, it was obviously raw and painful and something she shouldn't be dealing with alone.

'Lily? Are you all right in there?' He knocked gently on the door and waited for a response.

The crying stopped but she didn't reply. He tried knocking again but the ensuing silence brought back those dark memories of his wife's last moments. That deathly quiet, the horror which had met him on the other side of the door and desperately trying to get her body out of the water. He didn't want to ever feel that powerless again.

'Lily, if you don't answer I'm coming in, so you might want to cover yourself up.' He braced himself with a deep breath, holding that oxygen in his lungs until he was sure she was all right and he was able to release it.

The sight he found, whilst still upsetting, was a relief. Lily was hugging her knees, rocking in the bath, silently crying her heart out. He set the cup of tea down and went to her, kneeling at the side of the bath. It was clear she didn't want to talk, but he wanted to show her she had someone who cared about her and who would be there when she was upset.

Since she hadn't screamed at him to get out, Finn took it as a sign she was comfortable with him being here. He took a sponge from the edge of the bath and dipped it into the bathwater, gently wiping away the tears coursing over her smooth skin. He squeezed the sponge and let the warm water cascade over her back. Lily closed her eyes and let him bathe her, a privilege from someone who was usually so guarded around him.

He lathered some shampoo into her hair before rinsing it off again with clean water. When he was sure he'd done all he could for her and he saw her fingertips begin to prune, he held up a large towel for her. He turned away to protect her modesty as she stepped out, then he wrapped her up like a burrito and swept her easily into his arms. She didn't protest but wrapped her arms around his neck and snuggled into his chest. He wondered when was the last time anyone had shown her a little love, when she seemed so in need of it.

'Where's your bedroom?'

She lifted a hand to point, but even that seemed to require too much energy. It was as if the events of the night, and whatever emotional turmoil was going on inside Lily's head, had completely physically drained her. In all their previous encounters she had given him the impression she would rather die than accept help, yet here he was, bathing and carrying her to bed like a helpless child.

He set her down on top of the mattress, still clad in her towel. If they had been a couple he wouldn't have thought twice about helping her get ready for bed and putting her under the covers, but he thought he had probably seen more of Lily than she would usually be comfortable with as it was.

'If you need anything at all, just call or text me. You have my number.' He didn't like leaving her like this, looking so lost curled up on the bed, her wet hair clinging around her face, make-up washed away to make her appear younger and more vulnerable than ever.

'Stay with me. At least for a little while.' The plea reached deep inside to play a lament on his heartstrings, making it impossible for him to walk away now. There was no way he could leave her here like this. He'd never forgive himself if anything happened to her too. What harm could it do to offer her some company and emotional support? They both knew nothing could happen between them, no matter the temptation of being in the same bed.

'I'll have to be back before the girls get up,' he said, climbing onto the mattress beside her. As she tucked her head in under his arm, he kicked off his shoes and closed his eyes. All he was doing was providing a little comfort. Once she was asleep he'd let himself out and check in with her again later. In the meantime, he'd rest his eyes too. It had been a long, tiring night for both of them.

At first Lily wondered where she had woken up, a large wall surrounding her and preventing her from getting out. Then it moved and she heard a little snore, reminding her she was in bed—with Finn. She lifted her head to glance at him. He looked at home in her bed, filling the side of the mattress which usually served to remind her she was alone. Thanks to Finn, during one of the lowest points of her life, she hadn't been.

Whatever did or didn't happen between them from now on, she would always remember the kindness he had shown bathing her, lying here with her, and showing her a compassion she had never known before. He had been so tender and understanding, letting her cry it out while supporting and taking care of her.

She didn't know how to explain what she'd gone through last night to herself, never mind Finn, but if it had shown her anything it was that every second in life counted and she had wasted so many. All this time on her own, pushing loved ones away in an effort to avoid hurting anyone long-term, had been a kind of self-flagellation. A punishment she had bestowed upon herself because she believed her medical condition made her unworthy of the life everyone else took for granted. The tears last night had been a kind of mourning for everything she'd denied herself—a partner, children, love.

She was hoping this wake-up call hadn't come too late. The man beside her was amazing, in public and in private. If she hadn't been so stubborn they might have had something. *No*, she reminded herself, *too much baggage.* It was one thing deciding she might have got it wrong where relationships were concerned, quite another to take on a widower with two small children. She might have had a revelation but she still had to consider the feelings of others. Her fate hadn't changed simply because her mindset about it had.

'Morning.' Finn's voice was husky from sleep as he caught her watching him.

'Hey.' She had that momentary feeling of embarrassment from recounting earlier events which usually came after a night of raucous partying. Unfortunately, she did not have the excuse of alcohol or high spirits to explain away what had happened.

'How are you feeling?' He rolled over onto his side, propping his head up on one elbow, and her heart gave a little flutter. He was gorgeous as well as kind and compassionate. The complete package. For someone who could allow herself to take on a ready-made family.

'Better. Thank you.' If he hadn't come to her door last night, Lily would probably still be sitting in the dark, crying and feeling sorry for herself. She'd had her moment and he'd been right there with her until it had passed. It wasn't lost on her how generous that had been of him, sacrificing that time with his daughters to comfort her. A sign that he might have some feelings towards her too, even if there were many reasons why he wouldn't act on them either.

'Good. I was worried about you.'

'Sorry for keeping you away from your family.'

'Don't be silly. It was more important for me to know you were okay. Besides, the girls will still be asleep.'

Lily wasn't used to having anyone put her first, including herself. It was nice. Especially when she knew how devoted he was to his children. When she thought about the circumstances and how worried he'd been about her she could have slapped herself. He'd told her about his wife and how he'd found her lifeless in the bath. Lily's pity party must have brought back traumatic memories for him. It was no wonder he'd been afraid to leave her on her own, probably convinced history would repeat itself.

'I shouldn't have made you worry. It was incredibly selfish of me.'

'You were upset. You don't have to apologise, Lily. I'm simply glad you're okay.'

'It just seemed to hit me last night about how much of my life I've wasted. You said you would rather have had that short time with your wife than never being with her and it touched a nerve. That love you had for her, the strength of love that man had for his son to go back into that fire… I'll never have that and it's my own fault.' She didn't want to get morose about it again but every time she thought about the people she had pushed away, the opportunities she might have had, it was impossible not to have that ache in her chest for the life she could have had.

'It's not too late, you know.' He was trying to be optimistic on her behalf that she might still meet someone and fall in love, but it seemed too little too late. What was the point of getting into something now, when she was past her best and heading for middle age?

'I'm over forty, fat and set in my ways. It doesn't make me a catch.' She could just imagine sticking her profile pic on one of those dating apps and getting tumbleweeds in response.

'Stop saying that. I don't like it when you talk about yourself like that. You're beautiful.'

She cringed at his words. 'You don't have to say things like that to make me feel better. I know what I am, Finn.'

He huffed out a breath, but she wasn't trying to frustrate him. Lily was simply saying what she believed was the truth. She'd spent her youth building her career, batting away potential love interests, and now the bloom had well and truly faded she couldn't expect to be snapped up simply because she'd decided she didn't want to be alone any more.

What was worse, Finn was the first man who'd ever made her regret her life choices and she'd blown any chance she had with him by telling him about the ticking time bomb that was her heart.

'Why do you think you're not worthy of love, Lily? Who put that into your head?' It was the second time she had brought up the subject of her weight and he couldn't understand the reason behind the issue. People came in all shapes and sizes and it wasn't a reflection of who they were on the inside. Not that he had a problem with the way Lily looked. Other than the fact he was attracted to her and couldn't seem to bring himself to leave her bed. Lily was usually so confident in everything she did he couldn't help but think this insecurity about her appearance had been a seed planted by someone else and it had grown like an unruly, intrusive weed. He'd certainly never given her cause to think she was anything other than beautiful when he had difficulty keeping his hands off her most of the time.

'Oh, just an ex.' She tried to dismiss it as a non-event but Finn wasn't so easily fooled when the painful memory was blazing so clearly in her eyes.

'Uh-huh. So you were with some waste of space who didn't appreciate you for who you are and you've lived every day since looking at yourself through his eyes? Why would you even give him thinking room in your head?' Finn's body tensed when talking about someone he'd never met but was prepared to take to task for everything he'd done to hurt this woman.

'I guess Pearce is tied in to that whole time of getting my diagnosis and how it made me feel about myself. I did pack on a few pounds because of the condition but in hindsight the weight thing was probably an excuse so he didn't have to support me through my illness.' She snorted.

'He was fun for going out to bars and dinner parties with but he would never have made a good partner long-term. Probably why I got together with him in the first place. I didn't want someone for any more than that. At least until I had my condition confirmed, then I could've done with someone to support me rather than make me feel worse about myself.'

'He sounds like a real swell guy,' Finn emitted through gritted teeth. It was no wonder she had a complex if she'd been getting criticism at home during such a challenging time. That, wrapped up with her diagnosis, explained why she'd projected her insecurities onto him after that first dinner, and why she'd assumed the worst of him.

'Listen, that Pearce doesn't know what he's talking about. You are gorgeous, *my* Tiger Lily, and I wouldn't be here or saying these things if you weren't special.' He had to be honest with her and himself about the feelings he had for her. They both deserved that much at least after the loss and heartache they'd gone through, now they were finding solace in one another.

Lily's circumstances might have been different but he was sure she wasn't any less lonely than he had been since losing his wife. At least he had the girls, even if he sometimes felt as though he was acting the part as a parent, putting on that brave façade in order to hold things together when he was falling apart inside. Lily had no one and seemed to think that was her fate because of something beyond her control. She didn't see herself the way he saw her—fierce, kind, an amazing doctor and a beautiful person. There were a million reasons why they shouldn't be together, why he shouldn't be tempting fate by lying in her bed, but that didn't stop the wanting, or the need to show her she was worthy of loving.

'Really?' Lily looked up at him with such disbelief it was Finn's undoing.

If she wasn't going to listen to what he was telling

her, he'd have to show her. He tilted his head and kissed her softly on the lips. A taste which only made him want more. She was fiery and sweet, tender and passionate, all in one kiss. Everything he could want.

Lily pressed her body closer to his so he could feel her warmth even through his clothes. He wanted more, but that came with risks he wasn't sure either of them should really be taking.

'Do you believe me now?' he asked, his voice, his body, his mind, all pulsing with desire for this woman lying next to him, who didn't realise how beautiful she was, inside and out.

She opened her eyes and he all but drowned in her sapphire gaze. 'Hmm, I might need a little more persuading.'

That uncertainty seemed to have disappeared during the course of the kiss, replaced with the confident Lily he knew better. A greater turn-on, if it had been needed. She wanted this as much as he did.

He kissed her again, this one building into something more passionate and urgent with every passing moment. Their lips clashing together, tongues searching for one another, hands grabbing each other, so they could be as close as possible.

'Is this okay?' He broke off the kiss to get her consent before they went any further, knowing she was vulnerable and not wanting to take advantage of that in any shape or form. If he thought for one second she wasn't sure he would put a halt to proceedings, no matter how painful for him.

'Yes. Make love to me, Finn.' Lily instigated the kissing this time, and began tugging his T-shirt up his chest. All the confirmation he could have wished for to make the next move.

Goodness knew he wanted to, but lust could only blind him to the reasons he shouldn't for so long. He let out a groan of frustration.

'We shouldn't be doing this.'

'Why not? Don't we deserve to have some happiness, Finn?' She reached up to cup his face in her hands and he knew she needed this as much as he did. He also knew she had as many reasons not to get involved with him too.

'I'm not denying that, but a relationship is a complication neither of us need right now. We're both going through…a lot. I appreciate you being honest with me about your problems and honestly, to the right person that won't matter, but I have the girls to think about. I can't bring someone into their lives, it will only confuse them.' He rolled away from temptation, trying to compose himself and think clearly without lust clouding his judgement.

Lily shifted onto her side to look at him. 'We don't have to rush into anything. This is just between us. I'm not asking for anything serious, Finn. I don't need the complications. But I do want you.'

She grabbed the front of his shirt and pulled him down, kissing him full and firm on the lips, marking her territory and her desire all at the same time. His head was buzzing with the implications and the pleasures of taking this further.

He wanted Lily too, but they both knew her medical issues were something he would have to be wary of if she became part of the girls' lives when they'd already suffered so much loss. She was making this easier by taking the idea of a serious commitment out of the equation, but was that the kind of man he was? The truth was he didn't know. He'd never had a one-night, or a one-morning, stand with anyone. Never even *been* with anyone other than Sara.

'I'm not denying the feeling's mutual, but I don't want things to get messy. I can't promise you anything, Lily, and we still have to work together.' He didn't want to trick her into believing there could be more to this than sex and risk hurting her when it became apparent he wasn't offering her anything more than that.

'Hey, I'm not asking for a wedding ring. It could be a one-time thing.'

'To get it out of our systems, you mean? Does that ever work?'

'It works for me.' Then Lily's hands were tugging at his shirt, urging him to get naked. She wanted to live in the moment instead of worrying about the future, encouraging him to do the same. He couldn't tell her not to live her life based on what-ifs, then do the same thing himself.

He liked Lily, he was sure she liked him back and that should be enough for now. Sara was gone but he still had many years ahead of him and he didn't want to be alone for ever because of loyalty to his deceased wife. Lily was the first woman who had made him rethink the idea of facing the rest of his life alone and, even though they were staying away from the idea of commitment, he had been without joy for long enough. Something he knew he could find with Lily, for however long they had together. He couldn't keep his life on hold for ever. Every now and then he had to act on impulse, on his feelings, and right now they were telling him to get naked.

He stripped off his shirt and Lily leaned into him, kissing her way across his collarbone, her feather-light touch driving him wild, so barely there it made him question if he'd felt it all.

She grew bolder the more she explored his chest with her mouth and, when she reached his nipple, washing her tongue over the sensitive skin until all of him was standing to attention.

'Lily, it's been a while for me. I don't want to peak too soon. Besides, I'm supposed to be the one making love to you.' He rolled her over onto her back with a primitive groan. There was nothing he wanted more than to fill her, to experience that ultimate joy of forging their bodies together as lust consumed them, but they both needed more. He wanted this to last, to enjoy one another for as long as they could. Once reality dawned there was no way of knowing what would happen between them.

He kissed the skin behind her ear, revelling in the little gasp it elicited. She was so responsive to his touch it made him want to investigate further, find all of her sensitive spots and pleasure her until she was spent.

Slowly, he untucked the towel and unwrapped Lily's voluptuous body so she was lying there like a delicious candy, making his mouth water.

As she bit her lip and her breathing became rapid, he could see she was nervous about being so exposed to him, so he took off the rest of his clothes, leaving them both naked, with nowhere to hide. Not that he would want her to. Despite her self-deprecating comments about her figure, Lily was everything he had fantasised about. Those feminine curves and full breasts had been the reason he'd questioned his ability to remain celibate for the rest of his life. He was a red-blooded male with a fire burning inside him to have her every time he saw her and he couldn't believe he was lucky enough to bring that fantasy to life.

'You're making me anxious, staring at me like that. Come here.' She tried to pull him back down, to cover her body with his, but Finn hadn't finished his perusal of her sexy figure.

He shook his head, grinning as he lowered his head and began to kiss his way across her skin. This time he was determined to get the upper hand where Lily was concerned, leaving her at the mercy of his attentions, and hopefully her own orgasm.

Taking the weight of one breast in his hand, he teased her nipple until it was straining for the attention of his mouth. Dutifully, he sucked the tight pink bud, leaving Lily moaning a plea for more. As he licked his way around the dusky areola, he pinched her other nipple between his fingers and she bucked beneath him, writhing in ecstasy.

He was loath to leave the sensitive nubs of her full breasts but there were so many other places he wanted to explore he didn't want to miss anything. Trailing the tip of his tongue down her torso, he moved further down the bed, and down Lily's spreadeagled body, until he came to that little patch of curly hair nestled between her thighs. She sucked in a sharp breath and, before she could exhale, Finn plunged his tongue into her wetness. After her initial shock, her limbs went limp and she seemed to surrender to everything he was doing to her. A clear sign she was enjoying it as much as he was.

He gripped her soft thighs to give him purchase as he drove deep inside, tasting and teasing until they were both panting for more. That desire to make her come hastened his pace, his tongue licking and swirling as he sought her orgasm like a man possessed. Giving her no time to think or come down from the high of her obvious arousal, he sucked on that most intimate part and found her breaking point. Lily cried out as her climax coated them both and Finn could wait no longer to claim his satisfaction too.

He slid his throbbing erection into her slick heat and gave a muffled groan with his face buried in the crook of her neck. It took him a moment to regain his composure and resist the urge to give in to his pleasure too soon when it was something to be savoured. Lily felt so good he wanted to stay there for ever.

'Are you okay?' He was aware that it had been a while for her too and he didn't want to do anything she wasn't ready for, regardless that her body was responding so readily to his every touch.

'I'm good.' She chuckled, that jiggle of her body against his stimulating him further.

With Lily's permission he was free to continue his pursuit, striving to reach that pinnacle of ecstasy himself. Lily was a willing participant on the journey, her every kiss on the lips, and squeeze of her inner muscles around his rock-hard shaft, urging him closer to release. He pushed inside her again and again without restraint, his breathing and pace becoming frantic. Lily's eyes were locked onto his, the intensity of what was happening between their bodies reflected in her dark pupils. He watched as she bit her lip, as her forehead furrowed and her mouth fell open, a cry of ecstasy piercing the dark room, and he could hold back no longer. The wet rush of her orgasm as she tightened around him ripped a roar of elation from his chest and he poured inside her.

In that moment nothing else mattered except how she'd made him feel. Complete. Given the chance he would happily spend every second of every day here, their bodies entwined and fitting perfectly together. He was content, he was happy, and he was a very lucky man.

CHAPTER SEVEN

LILY HAD BEEN rendered speechless. Not only was she out of breath from their physical exertions but she was lost for words after what they'd just shared. Neither of them had apparently seen it coming, yet she was sure they'd both been fighting it for their own reasons. Now Finn was lying here, looking at her with a silly grin on his face as if he wanted to do it all again.

Usually—though it had been a while since she'd shared a bed with anyone else—during this post-coital awkward stage, she tried to cover up. Once the passion of the moment had passed she became aware of her lumps and bumps on display. Finn's hungry gaze emboldened her so she was quite happy to lie naked on top of the covers. He was a boost for her self-esteem and seemed to accept her not only for how she looked on the outside, but also the challenges she was facing in the future.

Of course sleeping together was no promise of anything beyond getting their breath back, but for now it gave her hope all wasn't lost. He had shown her she could still be wanted and didn't have to be alone for however long she had left on the earth. Being with Finn had helped her move from despair into ecstasy and it would be heaven if she could have this on a regular basis, though she was aware he had responsibilities she wasn't a part of, and had no desire to be.

'As much as I would like to lie here with you, I'm going to have to get home for the girls.' Finn vocalised what she knew was coming, but still didn't want to happen. It meant she would end up alone again.

'I know, I've taken up too much of your time.'

He scowled at her. 'I am definitely not complaining. Believe me, I'm sorry I have to leave.'

The little bird of hope which had been flapping its wings in her chest since the moment he'd kissed her took flight, soaring dangerously close to the sun. Despite her current euphoria, she had to be careful not to get too carried away or she might get burned. She'd been protecting herself for so long. Now that she had opened herself up to the idea of romance and relationships, a rejection could scar her for ever. Although they had given in to the attraction on the basis that this was a one-off, Finn had given her the confidence to at least believe there was a chance for more, and a reason to query the possibility.

'Do you think we could do this again some time?'

Finn smiled and dropped a lingering kiss on her lips. 'I would like to but, as I said before, I'm not ready to get into a relationship.'

'We don't have to be anything serious. We can keep it casual. I don't think either of us is ready for anything more than that. I mean, I'm not going to beg, but the offer is there. We're both adults, with needs. This could be good for us.'

She wanted the best of both worlds—great sex without having to make any serious commitment. That was a step she wasn't ready to take, and certainly not with someone who had two young impressionable girls. She'd seen how excited they'd been when she'd turned up on the doorstep. Not only did she want to avoid upsetting them, but she was keen to dodge an insta-family situation. After spending most of her adult life keeping people at arm's length it would be a shock to her system to suddenly find herself playing stepmother to someone else's children. For now it would be enough to simply continue seeing Finn in private.

'Tempting, very tempting…' he muttered against her neck, kissing and nibbling at her skin, and she wasn't sure he was even listening to her.

'Finn… I thought you had to go.' Lily saw no point in getting her worked up if he was going to leave her here, alone and frustrated.

'I'm sure we can manage another thirty minutes. Who needs sleep anyway?' With a growl he captured her mouth with his and she could feel his hard member already pressing against her thigh.

'A whole half hour together? Then why are we wasting a single second?' If this did turn out to be their one and only bedroom tryst, she wanted him to remember it and think of her as more than the doctor who'd had a breakdown in her bath.

This time she straddled him, determined to make the most of their time together. She ground her hips against him, the lower half of her body grazing along his. Finn cupped her breasts, kneading the soft flesh and playing with her nipples until she was wet and ready for him.

Taking him in hand, she teased the tip of his erection along her inner thighs before sinking down along his shaft. He filled her completely, making her gasp with the satisfaction of feeling him inside her. Her body instinctively took over, rocking slowly against him at first and gradually picking up speed. She braced her hands on his chest as she rode him and it wasn't long before his hands were on her hips as he thrust up to meet her in response.

The pressure of her impending climax was already building and she was powerless to resist it, having experienced it once already and knowing that utter bliss of finally giving in to it. Everything Finn did to her body reminded her she was very much alive and though it had let her down in some areas, sex could still be an important part of her life. Although she was sure she would only ever want it with Finn.

He sat up then, took one of her nipples in his mouth and tugged it between his teeth, sending a tidal wave of arousal shooting through her and leaving her at his mercy.

Finn took advantage of the distraction and switched places so she was the one now lying flat on her back. He kissed her fully on the lips as he pushed inside her, giving her exactly what she needed. They climbed the peak together, bodies in synch, hot breath mingling, eyes locked onto one another. When she reached her orgasm Finn followed close behind. It was as though they knew exactly what the other needed, perfectly in tune, even their chests rising and falling in harmony.

'I'm done with you now. You can go,' she joked,

knowing they couldn't delay his return home any longer. It wouldn't be fair on him or the girls.

'Glad to have been of service.' He jumped out of bed and collected his clothes from the floor before disappearing off to the bathroom.

Lily watched his naked backside as he walked away and gave a contented sigh. She'd had no idea when she'd come up with the idea of the fire brigade working with the hospital that they would end up here. Perhaps if she had the project would have gone ahead without her because this feeling she had was something she'd been trying to avoid for a long time.

She was falling in love with Finn and she knew it would only end in tears. Most likely hers.

'I don't want my hair in a ponytail, Daddy. I want to have it down, like Lily.'

'Fine.' Finn gave up trying to style the hair of a fidgety five-year-old and simply put a clip in the front to keep it from falling in Niamh's eyes.

'I've been hearing a lot about this Lily,' his mother piped up from the corner of the room. It was a rare Saturday morning off for him and they had planned to go out for the day. He should have been prepared for the inquisition, especially when he'd been so late coming from Lily's a couple of days ago.

They'd both been busy with work since, but had kept in touch with a few sexy text messages. There was no denying he'd enjoyed their night together, but this was new territory for him. He didn't have any regrets about sleeping with Lily, but he did have to pause and think about what they were doing and how it might affect his children. Some time apart from her would clear his head so he wasn't constantly thinking about how much he wanted to do it all over again.

'She's the cardiologist I'm working with on this new scheme. I'm sure you saw her on the TV with me.'

'Oh, that's her? She's very pretty. And unmarried, I hear.' His mother helped Maeve into her coat and pretended that she was simply making casual conversation rather than fishing for information on her son's personal life.

She had been very vocal of late about how he should be getting back out there to meet someone so he didn't spend the rest of his life alone. Something he'd had no interest in until he'd met Lily. His mother would be over the moon to know he had found a woman he liked, more than liked if it wasn't too scary to admit to himself. However, that was the problem. Finn didn't want his mum, or anyone else, to get carried away by the fact he'd met someone when he couldn't predict what, if anything, it would lead to.

'She's also a very busy doctor.' He wasn't about to give his mother reason to think she should be buying a hat for their wedding. She meant well, but Finn didn't need the added pressure of his mum interfering in his love life.

It was still strange to even think he had one after the death of his wife, and something he needed to get used to. At least by keeping things casual he could back away if it turned out he wasn't ready even for that.

'Uh-huh. Well, the girls like her…'

'Lily read us bedtime stories,' Niamh added in support of the idea that she would make a suitable match.

It would definitely have made a difference if the children hadn't taken to her, but they were clearly fans already. That would put him under more pressure to make things work if their budding relationship should ever be made public.

'She's a very likeable person. Now, are we ready to go?' He opened the front door to chivvy everyone out, and hopefully put an end to the conversation.

'Okay, okay, I'll drop the subject—'

'Good.'

'Suffice to say, you're still a relatively young and handsome man and this Lily seems like a nice, child-friendly woman. I know you loved Sara, but she would want you to be happy. When your father died I swore I'd never want to be with anyone else, but it has been lonely, Charlie, and maybe if I'd been able to open my heart again I would have had a different life.' His mother shrugged her shoulders and for the first time Finn noticed a sadness in her usually twinkling blue eyes.

He was so used to having her support, a babysitter and agony aunt on hand, he'd never really wondered if it was a fulfilling enough life. Children by their very nature were selfish, only thinking about their wants and needs, neglecting those of their parents, and he included himself in that group. Since his father's death when he'd been very young, she'd spent her days looking after him, and now her granddaughters too. Finn had taken it for granted, but now he was made to question if that life would be enough for him in the future.

It was going to be a balancing act between his love life and family life and he needed to get things right when he'd messed up so much with Sara.

'I'm sorry if I've never said this, Mum, but I appreciate everything you've done for me and the kids. I don't know how I would've got through this past year without you, but we're good now. If you ever need time out or there's something on that you want to go to, please just say. I don't want to stop you living your life.'

He grabbed his mum into a bear hug, which quickly became a pile-on as the girls flung their arms around them too. They didn't even know what they were hugging for, but they were such loving little girls they didn't need an excuse for cuddles. Their sensitive, caring nature was even more reason that Finn didn't intend to drag them into his relationship with Lily. He didn't want them to get too attached, the way he already was.

Lily checked her phone again, but there hadn't been any messages from Finn today. Usually she didn't have any problem resting when she had some down time but she was restless and not hearing from him had put her on edge too. Every ping notifying her of a message had put a smile on her face, knowing it was another saucy comment from her sexy fireman, but now she was worried he was cooling off.

In the heat of the moment they hadn't been able to get enough of each other, but perhaps now he was back in family life and they'd had time apart he'd realised even a fling wasn't feasible. At least she'd been upfront with him about her heart condition, even if it had put him off the idea of anything more serious between them.

It wouldn't have been the first time, but she'd thought Finn was different. He'd told her accepting her should mean accepting that part of her which had ruined every other relationship, but only time would tell if he was ready to make any sort of commitment to that uncertain future before her. Or if she even wanted that.

For now she would go to her happy place and dressed accordingly. Wearing her puffy waterproof coat, wellies and her scarf wrapped well around her neck, she set off out of her door for the seashore.

Lily closed her eyes and listened to the gentle lapping sound as the tide washed out over the sand and soothed her soul. She didn't need anyone or anything when she was out here. Although she would be lying if she said she wasn't still waiting to hear that sharp ping connecting her with Finn.

So much so, she thought she'd imagined him calling her name.

'Lily?'

She opened her eyes seconds before she was body-slammed by two tiny figures.

'Lily!'

'Hey, you two…three.' She spotted Finn walking towards her too. So she hadn't imagined him after all.

'Four,' he said as an older woman walked out from behind him. There was no introduction needed as the family resemblance was apparent. With the same fair hair and brilliant blue eyes as Finn and his girls, this had to be his mother.

'What brings you all here?' It seemed a tad out of character for him to bring his entire family to her doorstep when he'd been concerned about keeping his daughters at a distance from her lest they got too close. Even more so when she hadn't heard from him for a while.

'The girls wanted to come to the beach. I…er…didn't know you'd be here.' He looked as though he'd been caught red-handed doing something he shouldn't, but he'd been to her house and knew she lived only a few metres away.

She frowned, not quite understanding what they were all doing here or how she was supposed to act around them. Especially when his mother was here too. Whilst she doubted Finn had shared anything about the time they had spent together, she couldn't be sure what he had told her about the nature of their relationship. He certainly appeared uncomfortable to have run into her on her home turf.

'It is a small town, I guess.' She was at a loss as to why he was being so cool with her now. Yes, it was awkward meeting for the first time after they'd had sex, and having his mother and children witness it, but as far as she was aware she hadn't done anything to warrant getting the cold shoulder. Given the nature of his recent messages, she had assumed they were going to continue seeing each other at least. Now she wasn't so sure.

'We're going to get ice cream. Daddy said we can have strawberry sauce and chocolate sprinkles if we're good.' Niamh's enthusiasm for the treat made it seem likely it was her sole reason for suggesting this particular location. It might have been more comfortable for Finn if he had simply taken them to an ice cream parlour from the outset.

'You're lucky girls to have such a lovely daddy. Enjoy your ice cream.' She extricated herself from the girls' grasp and, with an uncertain smile for Finn, she began to walk away.

'Can Lily come too, Daddy?'

'What's your favourite ice cream, Lily?'

Niamh, then Maeve, blocked her escape route, closely followed by their grandmother, who stepped in front of Finn, who seemed temporarily struck dumb by the situation they'd found themselves in.

'Yes, do come with us. The girls have been talking about you non-stop since you called to the house. I'm Finn's mother, Josie, by the way, since he hasn't bothered to introduce us.' The elegant older woman's smile was welcoming and friendly, unlike her son's at this current moment.

'Lily Riordan. It's lovely to meet you.'

'I've told you Lily's a very busy woman, Mum. I'm sure she has better things to do than get ice cream with us.'

It was the look of disappointment on the girls' faces as much as Finn's attempt to get rid of her which made Lily contradict him. 'I'm never too busy for ice cream, and I would love a mint choc chip. What's your favourite flavour?' She took the girls' hands and walked towards the ice cream van she knew would be sitting in the car park nearby for all the beach-goers.

'Strawberry.'

'Chocolate. That's Daddy's favourite too, but Granny likes boring old vanilla,' Niamh shared along the way.

'Everyone has different tastes. If we all did the same things all the time life would be boring. I mean, sometimes you want something you probably shouldn't have and that's okay too.' Lily spoke loud enough for Finn to hear too and she hoped that he would pick up on her allusion to guilty pleasures. Perhaps that was what she was to him and she didn't care as long as he would tell her what was bothering him. Not knowing what was going on in his head was as bad as being ghosted.

'Why don't you and Charlie go and get us a seat and the girls and I will get the ice creams?' It was Josie who gave them the space to talk and Lily wondered how much she knew. If Finn's thunderous expression was anything to go by, probably not a lot, she imagined.

They walked in silence over to the only picnic table which wasn't occupied by ice-cream-covered children and fussing adults yet.

She wanted to get straight to the point rather than tiptoeing around the subject when they only had a limited amount of time alone.

'Are you regretting what happened the other night?'

Finn flinched then glanced behind him as though worried someone had heard. It didn't bode well for their future as a couple.

'No…not exactly. It's just…the girls being here…it's making things awkward.'

'They don't have to be. All right, neither of us was ready for a meet-the-parent scenario, but it's not the end of the world. I've met your girls before, and all we're doing is having an ice cream together. If you want me to leave, I'll go before they come back.' She didn't want an accidental meeting to spoil what they had together when she was so looking forward to the next time they got to be alone.

Finn stretched out across the table and grabbed her arm before she could go. 'That's not what I meant, not what I want.'

'No? What is it you do want then?' She was finding

it hard to swallow, her mouth suddenly dry as he looked at her with that same predatory hunger she'd seen on his face before.

'You.'

It was the answer she'd hoped for, yet it still made her insides flip as though she were on a big dipper. She'd never needed a man to want her as much as Finn, simply because she'd never needed one as much. That look in his eye, the tight grip on her arm and the longing in his voice were confirmation that their time together hadn't been a one-off.

They both wanted to do it all over again.

CHAPTER EIGHT

FINN SWORE UNDER his breath. With Lily looking at him the way she had the other morning in her bed and his family coming towards him, he was torn over how to act. All he wanted to do was take her somewhere private and kiss her senseless. Well, more than that, but neither of them were exhibitionists. Instead, he let go of her arm before either the girls or his mum saw and got their hopes up.

'We got mint choc chip for you, Lily,' Niamh announced proudly as her ice cream melted over her fingers.

'Thank you so much.' Lily beamed, taking the proffered treat.

Finn took his from Maeve, who didn't seem as enthusiastic as her sister in the delivery.

'They were fighting over who got to give Lily her ice cream,' his mother explained, as if there were any logic involved. She gave him a knowing look, suggesting there was more going on than sibling rivalry. He had to look away, sure she would see right through him as well and realise that he and Lily were more than work colleagues too.

'Why don't we go for a walk to the park and eat these on the way?' He was already on his feet, unable to watch Lily licking her scoop of mint choc chip without his imagination going into lewd overdrive.

The girls didn't need much persuading but his sudden request did draw questioning eyebrows from his mother and Lily. Nevertheless they acquiesced and soon formed a short crocodile walking in single file along the narrow pathway leading to the play area, with Finn bringing up the rear.

'I can make some excuse and leave you all to it if you want.' Without drawing the attention of the others, Lily had slowed her pace and hung back to speak to him.

'Why would I want that?'

She rolled her eyes at him. 'It's kind of obvious you're uncomfortable with me being here. Admit it.'

'Yes, I'm uncomfortable, but not for the reasons you think.' As soon as he saw an opening he took it. With his mum occupied supervising the girls, who'd run ahead to go on the climbing frame, he grabbed Lily's hand and pulled her into the trees lining their route.

'What are you doing?' She laughed as he backed her up against an oak tree whose thick bushy branches provided sufficient camouflage to keep them hidden from view.

'What I've wanted to do from the moment we saw you. From the second I left your bed.' He captured her mouth with his, greedily drinking her in like a man who'd just been given water after a month in the desert.

'In here? Really?' She laughed again as he began kissing her neck, his body already on fire for her.

Lily's giggle did little to dissuade him from letting his libido rule his head.

'We'll have to be quiet or we'll end up the talk of the town,' he muttered against her skin, with no intention of keeping quiet. There was something about being with Lily which made him reckless and gave him the same adrenaline rush as running headlong into a fire. It was exciting and dangerous and he couldn't seem to give it up, despite the risks.

'Yeah. Oh, look, your ice cream is melting.' Lily leaned over and licked the stream of liquid chocolate running down his hand, and he knew having a physical relationship would be easier than not having her in his life at all. And infinitely more enjoyable.

'Sod the ice cream,' he said, taking her cone and tossing it, along with his, onto the grass so he could take her properly in his arms and kiss her thoroughly enough to prove himself worthy of her.

She tasted fresh and minty, her tongue cold in his mouth, but everything about her was making him hot. He knew he had to put the brakes on before they careered completely out of control.

'Sex in a public place is probably not something two forty-something pillars of the community should be doing.'

'Hmm, but it feels so good.' She reached down and took a firm hold of his burgeoning erection, to make him groan.

'You're trouble, you know that, Tiger Lily?' He took a step back and adjusted himself so he could be seen in public again without being arrested for lewd behaviour.

She pulled him back for a quick peck on the lips before making her way back onto the path. 'Yeah, but you can't keep away from me, can you?'

No. No, he couldn't.

Lily couldn't believe he'd done that. Not that she was complaining when she was almost skipping along the path like a teenager. Finn made her feel like that. Carefree, that nothing mattered except being with him. It was dangerous, she knew that, but she figured she was due a little fun. A sexy interlude to boost her ego couldn't do any harm as long as they kept things casual. It was bound to fizzle out eventually. This scorching passion they'd ignited couldn't burn for ever, but she would fan the flames until there was nothing but ashes left between them.

'Hey, girls. It was lovely to see you again but I'm going to head home. Thanks for the ice cream.' She caught up with the rest of the family to make her excuses and felt a little guilty when they begged her to stay. Then she caught Finn's gaze again, that blatant want reflected so brightly it turned her insides molten, and she couldn't wait to get away. To be somewhere private, where they didn't have to hide what it was they wanted from each other. Physically, at least. She was trying to block out how much she was emotionally investing in him because it would spoil everything.

''Bye.' Lily waved to Niamh and Maeve, whose interest had now been captured by the recently vacated swings.

As she passed Finn she whispered, 'You know where I live,' and walked away. A little hip sway with every step because she knew he was watching her and couldn't resist teasing him the way he'd done with her, kissing her when he knew they couldn't do anything more without risking being seen.

She'd barely had time to take her coat off and freshen up at home before he was ringing her bell.

'That was quick. Won't the girls wonder where you are?'

'Mum's taking them back to her house to bake cupcakes. I'll suffer the consequences of their sugar high later, but it's worth it if I get to spend time with you.' He didn't wait for an invitation, pushing her back inside and closing the door with his foot.

'Careful, it's beginning to sound as though you like me,' she teased, glad that his awkwardness around her hadn't been because he was growing tired of her already. Quite the opposite when he couldn't seem to get enough of her, already kissing the side of her neck, hitting all her erogenous zones at once.

'Hmm, maybe a little bit.' He was nibbling that little bit of skin just behind her ear which undid her every time and sliding his hand up under her dress.

She let out a helpless sigh, unsure how long her legs were going to hold her up if he continued to wreak havoc on her body. 'Do you want to take this into the bedroom?'

'I'm good here. You were right, it's nice to try something different every once in a while.' He flipped her round so she was facing into the wall as he hitched her dress up and pulled her panties down, cold air hitting her naked backside.

Finn pushed up against her so she could feel the hard bulge in his jeans-clad crotch and a tsunami of arousal crashed through her body, obliterating everything but the need to have him.

'Finn—' It was a plea to show her some mercy, to relieve the ache pulsing in every part of her. She was relinquishing control of her body, trusting him to take care of her.

'I want you so much, Lily,' he whispered deep in her ear, turning her on to the point her clothes felt too restrictive. It was a relief when he released her from the fabric prison, cupping her breasts in his hands, rolling and pulling her taut nipples until she was grinding her body back against his, trying to drive him to the brink of insanity with her.

The sound of him unzipping his fly signalled her victory. A short-lived triumph as he slid his fingers between her thighs and into her wet core. Lily moaned as he stroked her, his fingers filling her, stretching her, taking control of her orgasm. He brought her there quickly and she had to brace herself against the wall as it slammed into her.

There was no time to come down from that high as Finn nudged her legs apart and pushed into her with a quick thrust.

There was a time and place for slow and gentle and one for plain old lust. They were both ready for something different.

She'd convinced him a fling was the way to go because she knew that was all he could give her. A good time. And boy, did he.

She was beginning to want more of an emotional connection, more of a relationship and more of Finn.

But for now she would take what he was giving her. Absolute pleasure.

His hands were on her hips as he pounded into her, his breath quickening in her ear as he drove them both over the edge. Finn slammed his hand against the wall as he released the full extent of his desire inside her with a groan.

If a physical relationship was all that was on offer she would grab it with both hands when it made her feel so good. Sure, there would be a time when she was alone again with only memories to keep her warm at night, but it was preferable to the life she'd had before Finn had shown her what she'd been missing.

A husband, a family and good health might not be in her future, but she would settle for an unbelievable sex life and whatever time she could get with this man who reminded her she was alive every time he touched her.

She turned around and he kissed her, his tongue softly stroking hers a contrast to the fast and furious lovemaking of only moments ago. She wasn't averse to either and his seemingly insatiable appetite for her, at least on this base level, was enough to convince her that this was enough. For now.

How was he ever going to give this up? The thought of never holding Lily again, kissing her, making love to her, was something he didn't want to contemplate. Yet by the very nature of the arrangement they'd entered into, this couldn't last for ever.

'Well, that was certainly different.' His voice was as shaky as the rest of him following their encounter. Lily made him feel things, experience things he'd never had before. This passion, this fire was something rare, he knew that, but it was also something they'd found together.

Only time would tell if it would burn itself out or blaze like wildfire, out of control and a threat to life. His.

Lily flashed him a grin as they fixed their clothes. 'Good different?'

'Definitely. I mean, I'm not sure these old bones would hold up to doing this all the time...'

'Trust me, you've still got the moves.' She chuckled, shaking her head.

He had to admit the ego boost was nice, but it had a lot to do with his partner too. When he was with her his age didn't matter because she had given him a new lease of life. One he was enjoying and couldn't see without her in it.

'Do you want to go for a coffee or a walk or something?' It seemed backwards to ask her out now after what they'd done together, but it would have been cold to simply zip up his trousers and leave. Besides, he wasn't ready to be without her company just yet.

'Sure. Let me get my coat.' Lily had studied him for a moment before she answered, as though she was trying to figure out if it was a genuine offer. It was disappointing that she doubted his sincerity. He'd agreed to this casual arrangement to prevent any sort of relationship interfering in his home life, but that didn't mean he was merely using her for sex. Despite it being Lily's idea, he didn't think that was all she was getting out of it either. If that was the case she wouldn't even have entertained the idea of coming along with the family today.

She liked the girls and he was pretty sure she liked him for more than his middle-aged body too.

Lily's bungalow was right on the edge of the shore. The perfect place to get some fresh air and a head clear of all thoughts of the bedroom. Or the hallway, or the number of places he could quite happily make love to Lily. It was important for her to know this was about more than sex to him, even if he couldn't afford a serious emotional entanglement.

'It's peaceful here. No screaming or crying or endless questions.' Finn loved his daughters but there was very rarely any quiet time to be found. Work too was a constant source of noise. Even when they weren't dealing with an emergency call, the station was full of men clattering around.

Lily smiled. 'Well, I don't have two young children bending my ear but I still enjoy being out here. It's as though nothing else matters and you can simply let the sound of the sea wash over you. Sorry, is that too tragic?'

'Not at all. I get it. Sometimes it's nice not to have to think about anything and just be. I never did go in for the partying and clubbing, or the need to be living it up all the time. I always enjoyed the quiet life.'

It might sound boring to some, but it had meant more to him spending time with Sara than being out on the town. Some men might have gone back out on the single scene after losing their wife, but that had never been more important to him than spending time with his children. That was why he'd never expected to meet another woman. This thing with Lily had taken him completely by surprise and he was still trying to process the implications of that when she was such a big part of his life now.

'I have to admit, I was the party girl when I was younger. Probably because I didn't think I had a long-term future and I thought I should experience everything life had to offer, all at once. I studied hard but I played harder. Never settling in one place too long with anyone in case something happened. There was no one to intervene. By that point I'd lost my mum too. Now I'm all about the quiet life, content to see out my days picking sea glass off the shore on my down time.' She bent down and stood back up, clutching a tiny speck of dark blue glass he would never have spotted in such a vast, stony expanse.

'Part of an old perfume bottle,' she exclaimed, as though she'd just discovered the Crown Jewels lying on her front doorstep.

'I can see you as a wild child, drinking shots and going to foam parties back in the day.'

'Hey, I could still do all that. If I wanted to.'

They were grinning at each other, but Finn knew there was an undercurrent of 'what if?' beneath their admissions. What could have happened if they'd met each other at that time? He didn't regret his life before her, he'd loved Sara and had his girls as a result, but there might have been a point when the timing would have been right for him and Lily. Where a proper relationship could have been possible.

'I never wanted to. Sara and I were childhood sweethearts. Getting married and having children is what's expected when you're together so long. I dare say it had something to do with me losing my father at such a young age too. I never knew him but the loss created a need for that stability of a family around me.' Whereas in Lily's case she had actively pushed against the idea because of the way hers had been taken so tragically from her.

'It's funny how these things shape you, influence the decisions you make.' The sad note in her voice and her wavering smile suggested there was nothing remotely funny about the choices she'd been forced to make as a result of her childhood. He couldn't help but pull her in for a hug. Although he was swamped with them daily from his girls, he was sure it was a long time since Lily had one.

She folded easily into his arms and they stood on the beach for a while, his head resting on top of hers as the waves continued to crash in around them.

It wasn't until much later that he realised anyone could have seen them. The more startling realisation was that he didn't care, because in that moment a hug was what both of them had needed more than anything.

CHAPTER NINE

'So, YOU CAN rest assured if you ever have to deal with a cardiac emergency you are not on your own. Either the ambulance service or the fire brigade will be there to assist you.' Lily climbed down from the podium to a round of applause. She and Finn were still on their PR campaign, this time in the local high school, informing the younger generation of what to do in case of an emergency.

Finn stepped up to the microphone again, after already giving his talk on fire safety, and now came the dreaded Q and A session. In her experience of these things, most teenagers were too embarrassed to ask further questions in front of their classmates and those curious enough to do so were inevitably teased mercilessly about being a swot.

'Thank you, Dr Riordan. Now, does anyone have any questions?'

A few titters and mumbled voices sounded in the assembly hall before one brave, sassy student called out, 'Do you do hen parties?'

Ever the professional, Finn answered, 'Only if they're on fire.'

The headmaster walked forward at that point to glare daggers at the group of young girls who appeared to have taken a shine to the mature fireman, and Lily couldn't blame them when she was completely smitten with him too.

'I think that will do for today. Thank you, Mr Finnegan and Dr Riordan.' He began a round of applause and Lily was relieved their little presentation was over for another day.

A member of the Parent Teacher Association who had asked them to speak today led them to the staffroom, where they were honoured with tea and biscuits.

'I'm sorry about that little outburst. Teenagers and their hormones, eh?'

Finn looked a tad embarrassed as the matter of his fan club was raised by one of the ruddy-cheeked members of the PTA hovering with her cup of tea in hand.

'No harm done,' he mumbled and sipped at his tea.

'There's something about a man in uniform that makes us all a bit giddy.' She winked at Finn before she took off again and Lily nearly spat out her own tea.

'We really should see about setting up a proper fan club for you. Maybe even get a calendar printed. I'm sure it would make a lot of money for charity, judging by the number of female admirers you seem to attract.' Lily was teasing him but she was suffering from an attack of jealousy jabbing sharply at her insides. Seeing other women fawn over him was a reminder that she had no real claim on him when their relationship was a non-starter. She was nothing more than his good-time girl, and who knew that would last if someone else came along who could offer him more than an uncertain future?

It was her own fault that he saw her now as nothing more than his secret lover when she had been the one to suggest it. At the time it had seemed the only way to keep him in her life, but the longer they spent together the more she yearned for something more. The co-operative between their departments meant they were working closer than ever, which was as frustrating as it was enjoyable when she couldn't touch him or kiss him for fear of being discovered. She didn't know how long she could continue being someone's dirty secret.

As far as any of the residents knew, Finn was a widower and available. Even now there was a group of the mums whispering in the corner and shooting furtive admiring glances in his direction, probably wondering if they stood a chance with him. Lily was so insecure about the nature of their relationship even she couldn't be sure.

Her paranoia was interrupted by the bushy-haired school secretary rushing into the room. 'Headmaster, there's an incident with one of the students. She's on the roof and refusing to come down.'

There was a clatter of china as everyone abandoned their tea to go and investigate, including Lily and Finn. They stood in the playground with the group of children who had also gathered, staring up at the small figure standing on the edge of the roof.

'That's Ruth Harlow. What on earth is she doing up there?' The headmaster, though clearly concerned for her safety, seemed more annoyed than sympathetic with the young girl.

'I've phoned for the emergency services. Apparently she was very upset today during PE. I think she's been told she can no longer take part in competitive sports.'

Recognition dawned deep in the pit of Lily's stomach. 'She's one of my patients. I had to give her the bad news this week. Let me go and talk to her.'

Ruth had been upset when she was advised her heart condition was going to limit her sporting activities and Lily had referred her for counselling, as well as making future appointments to check in on her. Apparently that hadn't been enough to look after her mental health.

'You're not going up there, Lily.' Finn's command was unexpected and unwanted, making her hackles rise as he tried to tell her what to do.

'She's upset. I know what it's like to have to live with an illness limiting and controlling your life. I'm just going to go up and sit with her until the emergency services get here. She shouldn't be on her own.'

Lily went to move and Finn grabbed her by the wrist.

'I don't want you to overdo it by climbing up there. That's my department.'

She prised his fingers from her arm. 'I know my limits, Finn, and I know my job. You have no say in my life. After all, it's not like we're in a serious relationship or anything.'

His mouth tightened but he didn't argue with her. How could he? There was little point pretending there was more to their relationship than just sex because he wanted to pull rank.

'At least let me come up with you,' he insisted as the caretaker brought over a ladder and propped it against the wall.

'Fine, but keep your distance. I don't want you to interfere.' Lily began her ascent up the ladder, cursing her choice of dress and heels, which were totally inappropriate for climbing, especially with Finn following close behind.

'Ruth? It's Lily Riordan. I'm just coming to check you're okay.' She tentatively stepped over to the edge of the roof where Ruth was now sitting, her legs dangling over the edge. A glance back told her that Finn was close but still managing to give them some space and privacy.

'It's not fair,' Ruth cried, shuffling closer to the edge.

'I know, sweetheart. You don't know this, but I have a heart condition myself. I had to stop competing in sports too, and I know it seems like the end of the world now but you will adapt.' There was no choice, other than to spend the rest of your days bemoaning the fact you'd been dealt a rotten hand in life. Something she had done for a while before deciding medicine was the new route she was going to take.

'I'm not good at anything else. Stupid heart. Why does it have to be me?'

'I can't answer that, but you're not alone. I'm sure we can find you some support groups, with people your age who have the same condition for you to talk to.'

Sometimes it made all the difference to simply get your worries off your chest. Despite her current beef with Finn, she was glad she'd confided in him about her illness and her fears rather than internalising it all and feeling worse. She had been annoyed that he'd tried to use her condition as an excuse to wrap her in cotton wool, but in hindsight it was nice to have someone who cared about her.

'It sucks.'

'It does, but it doesn't have to rule your life. There'll be other hobbies and interests, I promise you. We'll do everything we can at the hospital to help you live as normal a life as possible.'

'I didn't know you had a heart condition too.'

'See? With treatment it can be managed and no one has to know. Hopefully, with a few adjustments, you can live as normal a life as possible. I will do everything I can to help you.'

The irony wasn't lost on Lily about the manner of their conversation, advising someone else about not letting their illness define them. She ought to take a leaf out of her own book and the advice of a certain fireman standing not too far away about living in the moment instead of getting bogged down in her fears about the future. And Lily only wished her sister had been given the same opportunities her patients had these days.

'Promise?' Ruth looked up at her with big trusting eyes.

'I promise.' She crossed her heart, vowing to Ruth and herself to help her through this difficult time.

Ruth looked down at the assembled crowd. 'I didn't mean to cause a fuss. I just wanted somewhere quiet to go so I could think straight.'

'Don't worry. Everyone will be glad you're safe. That's all any of us want. Now, can we get down? I'm not very good with heights.'

Ruth attempted to get to her feet but slipped on the

loose gravel lining the roof. She landed with a thump before Lily could get to her.

'What…what happened?' Now disorientated, Ruth was lying on her back. She touched the top of her scalp and flinched when she saw the blood dripping down her fingers.

'You've had a fall. Don't try to get up. I need to take a look at you.' Lily didn't want to panic her, but the blood from her head injury was quickly turning the gravel around her deep scarlet.

As she parted the teenager's hair gently she could see the wound, deep enough to warrant a couple of stitches, but that wasn't the main concern. Lily knew the girl was on anti-coagulant drugs for her condition, which meant her blood wouldn't clot. It explained the vast pool of blood spreading out to stain the gravel like a gothic halo around her head.

'My head hurts.' Ruth reached up again, but Lily stopped her from touching the injury site.

'You've had quite a knock, but I don't want you getting that wound infected. We have to stop the bleeding so I need to put pressure on it, okay? It might hurt a little.'

Ruth nodded and Lily reminded her to try not to move. She was afraid there could be other damage apart from the superficial. Apart from neck or spinal damage, there was a chance she could have a subdural haematoma, blood on the brain, which could require surgery.

'Finn?' she yelled, knowing he wouldn't be too far away.

He was at her side in seconds.

'What happened?'

'Ruth slipped and hit her head. Can you get an ambulance here? In the meantime, I'm going to need a cold compress and a first aid kit with dressing and bandages to try and stop the bleeding.'

He didn't even take time to answer before he was off in search of the required items.

It was a positive sign that her patient was alert and talking, her breathing apparently normal. However, as she was losing so much blood there was a chance of Ruth going into shock with her vital organs not getting enough oxygen. She needed to elevate the girl's legs to improve the blood supply, but there was nothing around to prop her up and she needed to keep applying pressure to the head injury.

Thankfully, Finn turned up in record time with everything she needed and more. 'What can I do to help?'

Lily could have kissed him there and then. 'We need to keep her warm and lift her legs up to get the blood circulating sufficiently around her body.'

'I brought some blankets. They should do the job.' He tossed the first aid kit over before covering Ruth with one of the blankets he'd commandeered. The second one he rolled up to prop under her legs. Then he helped her dress the wound.

'We make a good team,' she told him, her feelings for him swelling so deep inside her she might just explode. He was there when she needed him at work. If only the same could be said out of hours. She only got to see him when he wasn't occupied by his other priorities.

'That we do.' He was looking at her exactly the way

she wanted him to, until her insides were melting and her brain was playing a montage of their best bits.

It was obvious she was falling in love with this man, probably even to Ruth, who was lying between them watching their interplay with a knowing smile. She likely imagined this to be some romantic fantasy where they'd found love and were about to live happily ever after. But as much as Lily wanted her patient to have a normal life, it was probably too late to have one herself.

It took the paramedics some manoeuvring to get Ruth safely into the back of the ambulance, leaving Lily and Finn to make their own way down again.

She made the mistake of looking over the end of the roof and completely froze. 'Finn? I can't move.'

Her feet felt as though they were cemented to the roof, her heart was racing and her vision was blurry, the ground seeming to rush up to meet her.

'It's fine. I've got you.'

He walked over and took her hand. Lily buried her head in his chest, afraid that one wrong move would have her plummeting to the ground.

'Only you would come up onto a roof to save someone else even though you're afraid of heights.' He wasn't mocking her, his voice low and soothing.

'I don't think I can get back down.'

'I'm here for you,' he said, releasing her from his embrace to coax her over towards the ladder.

She took several unsteady steps as he led her by the hand, but she couldn't find it in her to set foot on the first rung. 'I can't do it.'

'Okay, you asked me to trust that you knew how to

do your job, now I'm asking you to do the same.' All of a sudden he was bundling her over his shoulder as though she weighed nothing at all.

Lily let out a startled scream. 'What if you drop me?'

'I won't. You'll have to trust me.'

That was half of Lily's problem. She'd spent so long on her own it was difficult for her to trust anyone not to hurt her, either emotionally or by dropping her head first from a school building. If they were ever going to have anything more than a meaningless fling she knew she had to open her heart and trust he wasn't going to do her harm.

'Okay, but don't expect me to keep my eyes open.'

That made him laugh as he slowly and carefully walked the two of them back down to solid ground. The round of applause from the spectating pupils and teachers still watching let her know when it was safe to look again.

If it wasn't for all the eyes upon them and Finn's need to keep her secret, she would've kissed him. Instead she had to settle for a simple thank you. Any further gratitude would have to wait until they were in private again.

Finn wanted to kiss her stupid and make her promise never to scare him like that again, but it wasn't in keeping with the nature of their relationship. He'd already ticked her off by crossing the line to express his concern about her going up there. Thank goodness he'd been there and she'd put her faith in him to get her back down again.

It was proving tricky to keep his feelings at bay for Lily when she evoked so many in him. So much for keeping things casual when he was already so invested in what happened to her.

'You should let the paramedics check you over.'

Lily tutted. 'I'm fine. Just a case of the wobbles. It's you who probably needs pain relief after carrying me all that way.'

He gave her a sideways glance that he hoped conveyed his annoyance at her for talking about herself that way again. It seemed to do the trick as she simply smiled at him and made no further reference to her weight.

'You had a shock. I want to make sure you're all right, that's all.'

'And I appreciate it, but I'm fine. I've been looking after myself for a long time.'

Finn got the impression she was telling him to back off, that his concern was straying beyond the boundaries of a no-strings fling, but he couldn't help himself. He didn't want anything bad to happen to Lily. He cared for her. Perhaps more than he'd be willing to admit, or than was appropriate for their arrangement. He was in deep and trying to keep her at arm's length wasn't working out so far.

It only made him want to be with her more.

CHAPTER TEN

'I'M...GOING...TO...have...to...go,' Finn repeated in between snatched kisses as he tried again to back out of the door. Although it was very tempting to stay when Lily only had a sheet to cover her naked body. Something which only a short time ago they had both been wrapped up in.

'It's torture watching you walk out this door every time we get five minutes together,' she said, clutching the sheet to her chest, her hair still mussed from their time in her bed.

'I'd like to think it was more than five minutes, but I hear what you're saying. It would be nice to actually spend the whole night together, instead of me sneaking over in between shifts and the school run.'

It was exhausting juggling this double life, yet he didn't want to give any of it up. His family, work and Lily were all important to him, but they were all separate entities demanding his time. When he wasn't working the night shift he was splitting his time between being with the girls or Lily.

It was almost as if he were having an illicit affair, lying about where he was so he could jump into bed with his lover, even though he didn't have a wife to cheat on. Lily had been great about the whole thing, understanding about his need to protect his children and spending quality time with them. Keeping things casual had been her idea for that very reason, but it wasn't fair on her either.

A fling was a compromise so they could be together without putting any expectations on each other, but he didn't feel good about simply walking away from her after they had sex. As though he was simply using her, when the connection they had was much deeper than purely physical.

'I don't see what alternative we have.' Lily sighed. 'Unless you're talking about breaking up?'

'No, of course not.' His response was automatic because the last thing he wanted was to lose her when being with her was the best thing that had happened to him in a year.

Since being with Lily, he'd rediscovered himself again and an enjoyment in being alive rather than merely enduring it for the sake of his children. It made him want to be with her even more and there was only one way he could have that without detracting from his other responsibilities.

'What if we move things on from our casual status?' He closed the door again, prepared to at least give the conversation the extra time it deserved.

'What do you mean?'

'I mean, I'm enjoying the sex, and being with you, but not the sneaking around.'

'Really? I thought that was what's making it exciting for you. You know, having sex when and where we can manage it. In the cab of the fire engine when the rest of your crew are asleep was my particular favourite.' She was grinning at him with that same naughty glint in her eye she'd had when she'd turned up at the station that night wearing little more than her lingerie under her overcoat. Under the guise of discussing their 'project', they'd steamed up the windows of the rig that night after a whole twenty-four hours apart. It seemed they simply couldn't get enough of one another, and that wasn't easy to manage when they had so little time together.

Lord help him, but he was reaching for her again. Getting the requisite eight hours of sleep didn't seem so important when she was slowly unfurling that sheet to give him a glimpse of everything he would be leaving behind simply so he could be in his own bed when his girls woke up.

'Trust me, there hasn't been a single moment with you I haven't enjoyed, but I want to do everything.' He took his jacket off again before pulling Lily back to him.

'Everything?' she asked, eyebrows raised.

'Everything. Dinner, walks along the beach, vegging out in front of the TV. All the usual things couples do when they're together.' He hitched her legs up around his waist and carried her back towards the bedroom.

'So we're a couple now? I thought you were trying to avoid that.' With her arms wrapped around his neck, she was kissing her way along his jawline and nibbling on his earlobe. Doing everything she could to test his restraint. Not that she needed to when he was a willing participant.

'Yeah, well, I'm getting greedy where you're concerned. How about it? You want to go steady with me?' He was teasing to cover his own anxiety surrounding the question.

It was a big step for him to commit to something more with Lily. Though it had been her suggestion to keep things casual, he'd agreed in order to protect his girls. He worried that if they got too close to Lily and things didn't work out it would be his fault, but they couldn't keep hiding for ever. The only way they could spend real quality time together was if they brought everything out into the open, but that would entail a commitment neither of them had signed on for. It would mean being more to one another than bed buddies because he would only risk his family's wellbeing if he thought they could make it as a couple.

He set Lily carefully onto the bed and waited for her answer. It was only then he realised she might be the one to end things if she didn't want their situation to get any more serious than their need for frequent sexual release.

'Are you sure? What about the girls? I know you didn't want them to get confused about what was going on between us, and you're already aware of my medical situation.' She was reminding him that more was involved than waking up together in the same house or having family meals together.

'Dilated cardiomyopathy—I know, I've been looking into it. I know you lost your father and sister suddenly, but you've had a warning. You've got time to make whatever changes are going to be necessary to keep you around for a lot longer. I read you can get a pacing device to regulate your heart.'

It had been on his mind for a while, knowing he was

falling deeper for Lily every day. He'd wanted to look beyond what she was telling him, what she believed, to see what *could* happen. So they could all be prepared.

'Someone's been doing their research, but it's no guarantee that the same thing that happened to the rest of my family won't happen to me. Are you really willing to take the chance that some day I might simply drop dead too?'

Lily was being brutal about her own possible demise, but Finn knew it was a defence mechanism. She was trying to put him off the idea of getting into a proper relationship in case he did change his mind further down the line and hurt her as a result. He knew because he had the same worry.

The only way they were going to get through this was to think logically instead of basing their future on fear. There was treatment available, if and when Lily needed it. They could both stop using her illness as an excuse not to get close to one another. The time had come for him to open his heart again and stop being afraid that history was going to repeat itself. Lily was the most vibrant, clever woman he'd ever met and so far there had been no indication that there was anything wrong with her other than that same terror he harboured of losing another loved one.

'We're all going to die some time, Tiger Lily. In the meantime, we should make the most of the life we do have. That's not to say we have to rush things, we can just take it one day at a time and let the girls get used to having you around before we make any grand announcement.' Daddy having a girlfriend could cause all kinds of hysteria. Either they would love it or hate it and he'd prefer to build up to it gradually rather than shock them with this big change in their lives.

'I think we can manage that. Let's say dinner or even a night at the cinema the next time you're free?'

'It's a date. Until then, perhaps we can have a little more *casual* fun,' he said, pulling his shirt back over his head and climbing onto the bed with her.

'I thought you needed to get home for some proper sleep?' Lily shuffled in against him with no apparent intention of letting him go again.

'It's overrated. I can think of much better ways to spend my time,' he said, suddenly finding a new burst of energy.

'I know I said you should live your own life, Mum, but you're not giving me much notice. I have to get to work for my shift.' He was already running behind today after staying over at Lily's this morning and being late getting the girls to school. His mum was the only one who could babysit and without her he was lost. This was stress he did not need.

'I'm sure Lily would help if you asked her. She's such a nice woman and the girls love her.'

If he didn't know better he'd swear his mother was engineering this for Lily to spend more time with his daughters. They hadn't discussed it but he got the impression his mother knew there was something going on between him and Lily and she was trying to push it further.

'Daddy, Niamh is all wet.' Little Maeve was tugging on his shirt, trying to get attention, and he just knew there had been some catastrophe in another room. At least it was a distraction from his mother's matchmaking plans. He knew Lily would come if he asked, but it would be taking their relationship to a new level by getting her to help with his daughters. It could prove too much too soon for all involved. Yet he wasn't sure what choice he had at this moment in time.

'I'll have to go, Mum. You have fun and I'll talk to you tomorrow. I'll sort something out here, don't worry.' He ended the call, trying to sound positive for his mother's benefit even though he had been left in a real bind. That was the thing about trying to do everything on his own, he had no one else to turn to for help.

The sound of glass smashing sounded from the kitchen.

'Niamh? Don't move. I'm coming.' He rushed in to see her rubbing her eyes, standing in the middle of the room, water, glass and juice all around her.

'I was just trying to get a drink, Daddy.' Her bottom lip began to quiver and Finn gathered her up before the tears began to fall.

'I know, sweetheart. We'll go and get you cleaned up. Maeve, don't go into the kitchen until I get all the glass swept up, okay?'

'I know you have to go to work, Daddy. I wanted to show you I could look after me and Maeve if Granny can't come.' She was clinging onto his neck as he carried her to the bathroom, clearly stressing about his problems. At her age she shouldn't have to be taking on the responsibility of her younger sister and he knew it was a reflection of his struggles since losing their mum. It was about time he opened up and let someone in again, for their sake as well as his own.

He thought about Lily and everything they had shared in the early hours of the morning. She had agreed to venture into something more than they already had together, but he wondered if asking for her help now was overstepping the mark.

In an ideal world he and Lily would be perfectly suited, she'd fit easily into the girls' lives and they'd all live happily ever after. The reality could prove somewhat different. She had her reasons for not wanting anything serious and had gone to great lengths to ensure she didn't have anyone in her life to worry about. It would be selfish of him therefore to expect her to slip into his family now because it suited him. Besides, only time would tell if he was truly ready to get into another relationship. They both had baggage they weren't keen to dump on the other. However, this was an emergency and he was looking for a favour, not for her to sign adoption papers.

'Don't you worry about it. I'll phone a friend and see if I can get them to come over.'

'Lily? She could read us another story and stay for a sleepover.' Niamh was muffled as he stripped her wet nightdress over her head to dry her with a towel and give her some new PJs to put on.

It was funny that Lily was the first person to spring to his daughter's mind too. Although it could have been merely because she was the only person he had allowed into the house since Sara's death.

'We'll see. I'll have to phone her. You two brush your teeth.' He squeezed toothpaste onto their brushes and ushered them closer to the sink, while debating whether or not he should ask Lily for help.

There was no question that he wanted to see her again, even though he had to get to work, but he didn't want to be trying to rush them into something too soon. It was probably for the best if he did make out this was more of a favour he was asking of a friend in an emergency than a lead into their new relationship and keep them all in their comfort zone.

He called her number as he wandered into the kitchen to begin the clean-up of the mess his daughter had caused trying to prove she was able to fill the void her mother had left. It wasn't down to Niamh, or Lily, or anyone else to prove themselves as a replacement for the wife he had lost. Sara was gone and he had to move on with his life. Hopefully with Lily in it. If he didn't scare her off tonight.

He was simply in a predicament, and one that could easily be solved if he was brave enough to ask for help.

Lily walked in on a scene of chaos at Finn's place. When he answered the door he was holding Niamh's hand with Maeve on his back, her arms wrapped around his neck. He was carrying a bag full of rubbish with a mop tucked into his arm.

'Thank you so much for coming over.' The relief was palpable as she took the cleaning equipment from him to lighten his load.

She was glad he had thought to call on her for assistance. It showed a trust in her she knew he didn't give easily and said a lot for their budding relationship. Although she was wary of it being too soon to be introduced to his daughters now as someone other than a friend of their daddy. For them and her.

She'd spent a lifetime safeguarding against this kind of thing happening, of getting close to people. Now, not only was she involved with Finn on a deeper level than either of them had expected, but she was insinuating herself into his family. His trust, his optimistic belief that they could work through all of their issues was heart-warming, but that could make it all the more painful if things went wrong. There was nothing she wanted more than to be with him, to have that normal life most people took for granted. Experience had taught her differently, so she remained cautious, and could only hope for the best when Finn was risking so much for her.

It was clear how much he'd loved Sara and that he would take a bullet if it meant protecting his kids. The fact he was willing to take a chance on her, on them, showed a faith in their relationship she prayed she could match.

'It's not a problem. I'm not on call tonight and spending the evening reading to your girls will be more fun than sitting in front of the TV on my own all night.' She'd been pleased to hear his voice on the phone, even if it was to ask her to babysit. He could have played it safe and kept her and his girls separate so as not to confuse matters, but he was taking the next step. The best thing she could do was take it with him.

Now she was here she knew she would love having some time with the children, getting to know them. It would bring her closer to Finn, the place she most liked to be.

'They can stay up for a little while and you can have my bed for the night.'

'Is your mum okay? I know she usually minds the girls for you.'

'To be honest, I think she needs a break. We've relied heavily on her this past year.'

'I'm sure she's loved every second being with her granddaughters. Now, Niamh, if it's all right with your dad, I've brought some stuff to make our own jewellery.' Lily wasn't going to simply put them to bed without any interaction, she wanted to make an effort with them. To show Finn she was willing to lower her defences to try and make this work too.

'Fine by me as long as no one ends up down at the station needing rings cut off because they're too tight and stopping the blood circulation.' He saw Lily's raised eyebrow. 'It happens.'

'I promise, no emergency visits to the fire station.'

Niamh swapped her father's hand for Lily's and Maeve clambered off her father's back to take her other hand, neither apparently having any misgivings about her being here in place of their grandmother.

'In that case I better get moving.' Finn kissed each of his daughters on the cheek and reached up and did the same with Lily. She hadn't expected any display of affection in front of the girls, and she wasn't sure they'd even seen the swift goodbye kiss, but it meant the world to her. He was ready to move on if she was and there was a chance for more than a fling with Finn, maybe even a life.

'What did you bring?'

'Can we see?'

The girls were tugging at the zip on the bag of materials she'd brought.

'We'll take it into the kitchen and spread everything out on the table so you can have a look.' With the last-minute plea for help she'd thrown some pieces of sea glass, craft wire and some necklace cord in her bag in the hope it would keep two small children entertained until bedtime.

She made sure to cover the table with some old newspapers so as not to ruin Finn's furniture with scores or scratches before emptying out her treasures. The girls, who had taken their seats at the table, were wide-eyed as the sparkling green and blue glass pieces tumbled out before them. To a small child they probably looked like precious jewels and when Lily found them glinting on the shore that was how they felt to her. In reality they were nothing more than chunks of bottles churned in the sea for decades until they were smooth, as she explained to the girls. Still, they turned the pieces of sea glass over in their fingers as though they were priceless.

'Go ahead, you can pick whatever colour you like.' Lily chose a small aquamarine piece, while Niamh went for a darker sapphire colour and Maeve clutched the large piece of deep green in her hand as though it were a real emerald.

Lily wound some of her craft wire around the sea glass to keep it secure, before adding jump rings for the cord to go through. She let the girls do that bit themselves, threading the pendant onto the necklace, so they were part of the process.

'Ta-dah!' She held her finished piece up for the girls to see but took a sudden rush of blood to the head, making her feel a little dizzy. It was probably low blood sugar, she concluded, since she had skipped dinner to get over here as soon as possible. Once the girls were in bed she would see if Finn had anything to eat in the fridge or even order a pizza.

'Are you okay, Lily?' Niamh watched her, a frown marring her forehead.

'I'm fine,' she replied with a smile, sorry she'd worried the child over nothing.

'Look at mine, Lily.' Thankfully little Maeve offered a distraction, holding up her chunky necklace for them to see.

'Good for you. Well done.' Lily helped fasten it around her neck and Maeve admired herself in the mirror after climbing down off her seat to get a better look.

'Can we make one for Daddy?' With her own necklace securely around her neck, Niamh was now choosing something for Finn.

'I'm not sure your daddy would be able to wear one to work. Why don't we make him a key ring instead?' Lily rummaged around in her bag of bits and pieces until she found a key ring fob. Knowing Finn, he wouldn't want to upset the girls and would wear the necklace to please them, but she could imagine the ribbing he would get from the other guys. At least a key ring was something practical.

Niamh pondered the idea for a moment before snatching up a frosted white piece of glass. 'I want to give him this one.'

'I want to help too.' Maeve came bounding over and selected another sizeable green bit.

'I've already picked Daddy's.' Niamh tried to elbow her sister out of the way, which prompted Maeve to push back. Lily knew she had to step in before their sibling rivalry got out of control and there were tears before bedtime. Finn would not be best pleased if his daughters went to bed upset.

'Why don't we put both on? There's enough room for two.' It might make the gift a bit clunky but she was sure he wouldn't mind.

She held out her hand to collect the two pieces they'd chosen and the girls managed to set aside their hostilities once more.

'You pick one too, Lily,' Niamh encouraged, the sweet way she was trying to involve Lily in their little project making her tear up.

How nice it would be to be part of this lovely family, enjoying time with the girls when Finn was working and spending nights with him when he wasn't. This was everything she could have wished for, but she worried that the spectre of her illness would eventually appear to spoil everything.

She could argue that their father would only want the gift to come from his girls but she didn't want to upset them. Once they were asleep she could always remove her contribution. So she picked out the rare piece of red from among the sea of blues and greens. It reminded her of Finn. The colour of his passion, and a one-off.

She focused on twisting the wire around the glass, making little cages to keep them protected and secure. If only there was such a thing for the heart, she wouldn't worry about getting close to this family in case it shattered.

As she hooked the last piece onto the key ring she experienced a momentary lapse of concentration, her brain seeming to switch off, causing a micro blackout.

Nothing serious, but another reminder that she should get something to eat.

'Okay, girls, you'll need to take your necklaces off in bed but you can wear them tomorrow.' She wasn't going to take a chance on them getting tangled up in their sleep.

The pair groaned and reluctantly took off their new creations. Lily left them on the table beside the key ring for Finn in case they tried to sneak them on again in the middle of the night.

'Will you be here when we give Daddy his present?'

'I…er…don't know, Niamh, but I'm sure he'll be thrilled when you give it to him.' They hadn't discussed the morning's arrangements so she didn't know if he wanted her to stick around in order for him to get some much-needed sleep, or go back to her own house. In an ideal world she would get to crawl into bed beside him for a cuddle, but she knew they were a long way from doing that when the girls were in the house.

The girls reluctantly left the table and Lily stood up to go and tuck them in. That strange light-headed sensation made her reach out to steady herself on the table, only this time it didn't go away. She was fighting to stay on her feet, her body swaying on trembling legs. The last thing she heard was the girls calling out her name, then darkness swept in and claimed her.

CHAPTER ELEVEN

FINN WAS PUTTING his stuff in his locker when his phone rang. Seeing it was his home number, he imagined it was Lily phoning for some advice on getting the girls to bed. No doubt they were running rings around her, completely hyper about having her to stay with them. He had a brief moment of panic in case there was something wrong, but he was sure if that had been the case she would have called him on her mobile.

'Hello? Lily? Is everything all right?'

'Daddy?'

Finn's heart dropped like a stone at the sound of his daughter's voice and his whole body went on high alert, anticipating bad news. Perhaps they hadn't got along as well as they had all expected after the last time and he'd rushed everything with Lily, upsetting the girls.

'Niamh? Where's Lily? What's happened?'

'Lily's asleep on the floor. I think she hit her head.'

Finn was already on his way back out of the door, signalling to his colleagues that he had to go. The only thing worse than hearing his daughter's frightened voice telling him Lily had had some accident was the sound of his youngest crying in the background. He should never have left them.

'Can you try and wake her, sweetheart?' He listened, phone wedged between his ear and his shoulder as he got into the car, hoping it was nothing too serious.

There was a bit of fumbling on the line and he could hear Niamh calling Lily's name. He could imagine his two young daughters sitting either side, trying to rouse her. It broke his heart. When he'd found Sara it had almost killed him too. He didn't want his daughters to have to go through that at such a young age.

'Lily won't wake up, Daddy.'

'Niamh, I need you to hang up the phone. I'm going to call an ambulance then I'll phone you straight back. I want you to take your sister into another room and wait for me. I'll be home as soon as I can, okay, sweetie?'

'Okay, Daddy.' That little voice, so full of fear, was a sign he had failed his children again. He'd dismissed Lily's concerns about her illness and how it might impact on others, focused on getting what he wanted and nothing else.

She'd tried to warn him of the consequences of getting involved with her, had spent years avoiding relationships through fear of anyone getting hurt. All he'd been able to think about was being with her, giving her the impression they'd deal with anything come what may. He hadn't even asked her how the condition affected her or what he needed to know about it. Now his daughters were suffering the consequences.

Lily was strong. Whatever had happened or caused this blackout, he prayed she would get through it. He phoned for an ambulance on his hands-free device and gave them his address. There wasn't much more information he could give them when he was in the dark himself. All he knew was that Lily needed help and his daughters were there on their own.

His phone rang as he pulled up outside the house. There was no sign of the ambulance so he sprinted towards the front door as he answered it.

'Finn?'

'Lily?' He walked into the living room to see her standing with the phone to her ear.

'Finn, I was hoping to catch you before you left the station. I'm so sorry to have caused all this commotion. Niamh told me an ambulance was on the way so I've cancelled it.'

They both ended the call as they spoke face to face. She looked pale and he wasn't convinced she didn't need some medical assistance after all.

'Sit down. What happened? Where are the girls? They were very upset when Niamh called me.'

'They're in the kitchen having some hot milk and chocolate biscuits. I thought they could use a little treat after the scare I gave them. It was nothing serious. I think it was low blood sugar or something. I hadn't had my dinner before I came around. I'm so sorry.'

'Did you hit your head when you fell? How long were you out for?' Finn knew in the case of a head injury there was a chance of concussion and they couldn't simply dismiss what had happened as a mere inconvenience.

'I have a bit of a lump at my temple but I don't think I was unconscious for very long. The girls were so good phoning you and getting help, even if I don't really need it.' She was trying to convince him he was fussing over nothing but he wasn't taking any chances.

'My number is written down beside the landline in case of emergencies. The girls know they can reach me any time. Let me take a look at that head of yours.' He moved closer to her and she lifted the curtain of hair so he could see the injury for himself.

'Still, I don't know if I would've had the presence of mind to call for help at that age. Ow!' She winced as he brushed his thumb across the raised lump forming under the skin.

'You'll need a cold compress on that. I'm not sure I've got any frozen peas left. Honestly, you might have to start carrying an ice pack around with you at this rate.' It was the second time she'd had an accident here and he would have to think seriously about leaving her on her own with the girls in case something happened again, for all their sakes.

'I'm sorry we had to drag you away from work for nothing.'

'Better that than coming back to see you being carted off in an ambulance. Are you sure you don't want to go and get yourself checked out at the hospital?'

She shook her head. 'Honestly, I feel fine, and I know all the signs to look out for when it comes to concussion.'

'Well, sit down and I'll bring you a glass of water. I'll just go and see to the girls first.'

'Of course. Tell them I'm fine and I'm sorry I gave them such a fright.'

'I'm just glad it was nothing serious.' Except one day it might be. With the hours he worked, who was to say it wouldn't happen again? Only next time it could be much worse. It might seem heartless but he didn't want to put his girls at risk of the trauma he'd suffered as an adult. Lily understood that. It was exactly why she'd chosen not to have a family of her own and he should have listened to that when she'd told him.

The girls were sitting quietly at the table, clutching their bedtime toys, with their bedtime snacks uneaten. It was obvious to him, if not Lily, that the incident was playing on their minds still.

'Where are my brave girls?' He opened his arms and the two came running at him full pelt for a hug.

Clinging to either side of him, he scooped them up so they rested on his hips, their arms around his neck.

'I'm glad you're home, Daddy.' Niamh buried her head into his chest. Not usually needy, she was clearly needing a little extra TLC tonight.

'Lily fell.' Maeve looked very earnest as she told him about their eventful evening.

'I know, sweetie, but she's feeling much better and she's sorry for worrying you. You did very well, Niamh, phoning me and taking care of your sister, but I think it's bedtime now.' He carried them to their room and deposited them one by one into their beds.

'I was scared, Daddy. Lily was lying on the floor and I couldn't wake her up, no matter how hard I tried.' Niamh was still sitting up recounting the events and it would be a surprise if she got to sleep at all tonight. There were sure to be nightmares and tears and he doubted they'd stay in their own beds for too long, seeking comfort elsewhere.

'I know, honey, and I'm sure it was scary, but you

did a good job. Try not to think about it too much. Lily is feeling a lot better. She just forgot to eat tonight and it made her faint.'

'That was silly. She'll get sick.' Niamh's cross face made him chuckle. Clearly his mealtime lectures about eating properly had hit their target. Perhaps he'd have to start monitoring Lily's eating habits too, or distance himself from them altogether.

'I'll tell her. Now, I'll leave the light on so you can read for a little while. I'm going to stay home tonight so you don't have to worry about Lily getting sick again.'

Niamh bounced up off the bed to hug him again.

He was sure he could get cover for one night, not wanting to leave the girls when they were so upset or take a chance that Lily might have another 'turn'.

''Night, you two,' he said, backing out of the room.

''Night, Daddy,'

'Night-night, Daddy.'

Those two little girls were relying on him to keep them safe, to guard them from all the horrors of the world outside those bedroom doors, and he would do everything within his power to do so. He was all they had and they were his world. He couldn't put their peace of mind at risk for anyone. Not even a woman he could be falling in love with. His need for love and companionship and everything he could have with Lily had to take a back seat. He had to prioritise Niamh and Maeve.

'How are you feeling?' He fetched a glass of water before going back into the living room to check on Lily.

She gave him a half smile. 'I've told you, I'm fine.'

'No headaches or nausea?'

'I'm just tired.'

'You can stay in my bed. I'll sleep on the couch.' He felt a responsibility to keep an eye on Lily tonight in case anything else happened. He was unwilling to leave her on her own because it suited him and potentially put her life in danger. Whether what had happened tonight was due to her heart condition or lack of food, she had hit her head and been unconscious. He couldn't send her home in case her condition worsened in any context.

'Don't you have to get back to work? I wouldn't want to get you in trouble.'

'I've got someone to cover for me. I'm needed here tonight. Listen, Lily.' He took a seat across the room so he wouldn't be distracted from what he had to say by the scent of her perfume or the heat of her body. 'Tonight has made me think about what we're getting into. I know you said this was nothing to do with your heart condition but it was enough to scare my girls, for them to worry about you. Niamh should never have had to phone me like that.'

'I said I'm sorry, Finn.' She didn't need the guilt piled on when she was already beating herself up over it.

'I know it was me who said we can't live our lives based on what-ifs, but I'd forgotten to take my daughters into account and therein lies the problem. When I'm with you I forget about everything else.'

'And you can't take the chance that some day they'll have to grieve all over again. I know.' Tonight was a dizzy spell through lack of food, tomorrow it could be something more serious and he didn't want his children always on alert, worrying that something was going to happen to her. She understood that when it was exactly the way she thought, the way she used to approach life. That caution had been tossed aside the second she'd fallen for Finn.

'Perhaps we should leave things the way they were, on a casual basis.' He was trying to find a compromise, a way of being together without anyone getting hurt, but it was asking the impossible.

'That's not going to work, Finn. I think this has run its course. You need to focus on your girls instead of being distracted by me.'

'Are you telling me we're over?'

She didn't want to look at his face when she could hear the hurt in his voice. This had been on the cards from the moment they'd got together. At least an early breakup would be easier to get over than another premature death and the girls would never have to know anything about it.

'I think that's for the best. It was only supposed to be a bit of fun and I think we're both past that now.' Somehow Lily managed to get to her feet even though her entire body appeared to have turned to jelly. All of that happiness and contentment she'd experienced in bed with Finn only the night before had now been snatched away from her, leaving her with nothing.

'You don't have to go.' Finn reached out to grab her hand but she didn't want him to touch her in case she made a scene and burst into tears.

She backed away out of reach. 'I do. I've caused enough upset and upheaval for one night.'

'Lily, we can still be friends. You don't have to run away.'

'I don't think we can, and yes, I do.'

She couldn't be around Finn and not think about the time they'd spent together, about what could have been. If it hadn't been for this damn illness blighting her future as well as her present she might have been a part of this family. As always, all she could bring to the relationship was fear and upset. She should never have believed anything else. Then perhaps her heart wouldn't be shattering into a million pieces at the thought of being without Finn and the girls in her life. In the short time she had come to know them, they had become such a big part of her life. They made her happy. Now, even the thought of them made her sad.

She couldn't blame Finn for wanting to protect them. Her foolish mistake had frightened the girls and dragged him away from work, concerned for them all. They couldn't live the rest of their lives like that, worrying, waiting for the day she got really sick. She should know when she'd spent her entire adulthood doing just that. This family had been through enough grief and she couldn't add to it.

On her way out she grabbed her coat and overnight bag from the hall where she'd left them.

'I'm sorry. For everything.'

Finn didn't try to stop her.

CHAPTER TWELVE

'COME ON, NIAMH, your gran is waiting for you,' Finn yelled up the stairs for the third time in an attempt to get his daughter moving.

'I can't find my necklace. I'm not going until I find it.' His eldest's temper as she stormed away from the top of the stairs was probably only a sample of what he had in store for him when she hit her teens.

Finn sighed. 'We may as well get you strapped into your car seat in the meantime.'

Maeve skipped out of the door ahead of him playing with what looked like a lump of kryptonite hanging around her neck. They'd been obsessed with those necklaces Lily had helped them make and he didn't think it was merely because they thought they looked pretty.

He had been fielding questions about Lily ever since that night and why she hadn't been back. It was clear they had built a rapport with her quickly and the attempt to spare their feelings had come too late. Now they were all missing her.

He'd swapped worrying about the future to obsessing over the past. In particular the time they'd spent alone. If he was ever going to think about being with someone again they couldn't possibly hold a candle to Lily. She'd opened up a whole new side of him he'd forgotten existed. If he'd ever really explored it before she'd come into his life.

He'd loved Sara, they'd been together since they were teenagers. She was his first love, the mother of his children and he'd never stop loving her, but he'd had something different with Lily. His relationship with Sara had been expected, their marriage something they'd drifted into because it had seemed the next step to take after being together for so long. Not that he regretted a second of it when it had given him his beloved children.

With Lily he'd found a passion not only for her but for life again too. She'd been understanding about the girls, about the loss of his wife and how afraid he was of them all being hurt again. To the point of leaving him. He hadn't even tried to stop her.

In hindsight, he could have taken the time to research what the condition meant, what he could do to help her and plan ahead. Instead he'd accepted it was over because he was afraid of what it would mean for him otherwise. Now he was lonelier than ever, knowing what he could have had with Lily if he hadn't been so afraid of taking a chance on love again.

'When is Lily coming over again, Daddy?'

'I told you, Maeve, Lily won't be coming over to the house any more.'

'Why?'

'She's very busy,' he lied, clipping his daughter securely into her seat.

Maeve pouted. 'You said we could have a sleepover but we didn't.'

'Lily wasn't well. She wanted to go home to her own bed.' He didn't enjoy lying to his children but what was the alternative—telling them he loved Lily so obviously he'd needed an excuse to push her away? Deep down, he knew that was why he'd acceded to her decision to end things so easily. He'd fallen hard and fast but had been afraid of getting close then being left alone again. The big brave fire-fighter had been frightened by the prospect of love.

'I found it, Daddy.' Thankfully Niamh appeared so he didn't have to keep answering her sister's questions and learning way too much about himself in the process.

'That's good, Princess. Now, get in the car.' He was manning the line for emergency cardiac care tonight and he didn't want to be late. Especially when he'd already had to call for cover recently.

Niamh was admiring her necklace, twisting the piece of sea glass in her hands. 'Isn't it pretty, Daddy. Lily said it was the same colour as your eyes.'

His heart gave an anguished cry at the reminder of Lily in their lives. In a way, despite his efforts, they were already grieving her loss. Not only had she been a great lover and companion to him, she'd been good with the girls. Patient and entertaining and as close to a mother figure, other than their grandmother, as they'd ever hope to find. The possibility of giving the girls a maternal influence, something they would have cherished no matter how long they had together, had been stolen from them.

'It's beautiful, like you.' He dropped a kiss on Niamh's head and hoped that would be the end of the conversation.

'Do you still have your present too, Daddy? Can I see?'

Apparently he'd been mistaken.

'It's here, on my keys.' He dutifully held up his bunch of keys with the homemade fob attached. Now he was cursed forever with the reminder of Lily since the girls insisted on seeing it every time they left the house.

They had presented it to him the next morning after Lily had gone home, upset that she hadn't stayed the night after all. He'd known who'd chosen which piece on sight. The monstrous green rock could only have come from his magpie youngest who liked shiny bling, the sensible dark blue would have been Niamh's choice and the fiery red jewel could only have been from Lily.

He was sure she'd chosen the colour deliberately, a symbol of her feistiness, her passion and the love he'd been too cowardly to admit to, and he hadn't even had the opportunity to thank her.

It was a spurious reason to see her again and he'd be extremely lucky if she would even talk to him, but he was missing her so much that he had to at least try. Anything more than that was probably wishful thinking but maybe, just maybe, she was missing him too and realising what they could have had together if only they'd been as brave in their personal lives as they were in their professional ones.

When the call came in Finn had that familiar rush of adrenaline but also an attack of nerves. Fire-fighting he was used to, it was his job, but he wasn't a heart doctor like Lily. However, they had agreed to attend these emergency medical situations when the ambulance wasn't expected to make it on time. He prayed he would.

'Charlie Finnegan, I'm with the fire service,' he said to the man who'd opened the door.

The frown followed by the look of panic on the man's face was to be expected in the circumstances.

'It's not the fire brigade we need. I told them on the phone it's my daughter—she collapsed and we can't wake her up.'

'I know. In circumstances like this, where we're able to get to the scene first, we're authorised to provide medical assistance until the paramedics arrive. Now, where's your daughter?' He hustled past the concerned parent with no time to lose if he was going to be able to do anything to help save the child.

'She's in the living room with my wife.'

Finn hoisted his equipment onto his shoulder and headed for the front room, where he found the young girl lying on the floor, covered with a blanket, cradled on her distraught mother's lap.

'Sally? Wake up for Mummy, sweetheart!' the woman cried, but garnered no response.

Finn could see the girl's lips already had a tinge of blue, a sign of cyanosis, meaning a lack of blood flow or oxygen.

He set to work with his equipment. 'I'm Charlie Finnegan from the fire service. As I told your husband, I'm here to offer medical assistance until the paramedics get here. Now, I'll need you to gently set Sally's head on the floor and give me some space to work on her.'

The mother did as instructed even though she was still very tearful. 'She said she felt dizzy… One minute she was standing there and the next she just collapsed.'

'She has a very fast pulse, that's probably what made

her dizzy. This defibrillator will hopefully shock her heart into a normal rhythm.' He opened the child's shirt and attached the sticky pads to her chest.

'Is she going to be okay?' It was the father who asked the question Finn was dreading as he went to comfort his wife.

'We'll do our best to make sure she is.' He was speaking on behalf of himself and the paramedics, though for now it was all on him.

As the device delivered a shock to the little girl's body he thought of his own daughters in the same situation, hovering between life and death. They were all that had been keeping him going since he'd lost Sara, until Lily had come along. With her in his life he hadn't been simply existing but living and enjoying life.

As directed by the voice on the defibrillator, he continued with chest compressions until it was time to deliver another shock.

'Stand clear.'

He thought of Lily lying there some day at the mercy of a machine, with no one else around her. She deserved so much more. Especially when she gave so much of herself to help others, even as far as giving up on the idea of a family to save loved ones from heartache. All she had received in return was rejection and a lifetime of loneliness. Okay, so she mightn't be sitting in every night mourning the loss of their relationship and if there was any chance of getting it back he wanted to try. Life could end at any moment, at any age and it didn't make sense to waste any of it through fear of the unknown.

The defibrillator advised again to begin CPR and Finn focused on the little girl before him. In the midst of the chest compressions he heard the sirens and was relieved that he had done everything he could to keep Sally alive until they got here. He'd had all of the training, of course, but it was a bit like being a trainee again, afraid one wrong move could cause a loss of life.

Finn waited for the defibrillator to reanalyse Sally's heart readings and she suddenly began blinking, a little colour beginning to come back into her features.

'I've got her back,' he yelled to her parents, who'd gone to let the paramedics into the house, and moved Sally into the recovery position.

The group consisting of relieved parents and paramedics came rushing into the room and Finn was able to take a step back.

'Thank you so much.' The father gave him a bear hug which nearly knocked him off his feet.

It seemed trite to say something like 'You're welcome' or 'Just doing my job, folks', so he said nothing other than filling in the first responders with the details of the incident.

He stood waiting with the parents, watching the medical team stabilise Sally, invested in the little girl and the rest of the family. Helping to avoid the pain he and his girls had suffered was a reward for his hard work. Yes, he'd been reluctant at the start of the project, but if this was the outcome, relief instead of devastation, then it could only be a good thing.

Once more his thoughts turned to Lily and how she dealt with people hovering on the brink between life and death every day. She was the bravest, most altruistic person he'd ever met in his life and a man would be lucky to be with her. Or extremely stupid to have pushed her away.

'We're going to transfer Sally to the hospital now. They'll run some tests and work out the best treatment for her.' The paramedics carefully rolled her onto a stretcher and escorted her out to the waiting ambulance. Her parents climbed into the back, holding each other's hands and talking to their daughter, telling her everything was going to be all right.

It didn't seem right to him to simply walk away without seeing this through to the end. As an emergency key worker he knew he shouldn't get personally attached. For peace of mind it was important to be able to separate work life from everything else or he would never be able to switch off his emotions, but this was his first call-out in his new role.

'Do you think I could go with you? I just want to make sure she's all right.' He stopped the driver just as he was climbing into the front of the ambulance.

'Sure. I think you've earned a ride along.'

With the green light to extend his role this once, Finn took a seat up front with the driver. It was only when they were on their way to the hospital, sirens blaring, lights flashing, that he thought about the possibility of seeing Lily again. His own pulse rate began to soar with hope that his relationship with her could be restarted if he worked hard enough on it too.

'Dr Riordan, we have a nine-year-old girl in the emergency department I'd like you to take a look at, if you have time?' The phone call from the consultant in A&E came at the end of Lily's shift. She had nothing to go home for, so one more patient wasn't going to make a difference.

'Sure.' She listened to the summary of the child's presenting symptoms before making her way down to see the little girl for herself. There were a number of conditions which could have caused her tachycardia but they wouldn't know for sure until they ran all of their tests. Whatever the results showed, she would most likely be under Lily's care so she thought it better to get acquainted now, when they were both in the same building.

Since splitting from Finn she'd been spending most of her time at work, trying to keep herself occupied so she wouldn't wallow in her own misery for too long.

Things not working out in her personal life wasn't a new concept but this hurt because she'd got close to Finn's family as well as the man himself. She'd let herself believe it was possible to have it all for however long she was in this world, only for a sharp dose of reality to stab her in the guts.

Being with Finn, her illness had been the last thing on her mind. Somehow he'd made her forget all the bad stuff she thought was her lot in life, to live in the moment. It had been fun until she'd started to believe they could have more than a casual fling. Now she was mourning not only their relationship but the future she'd seen as part of a family. The closest she would ever get to being a mum or having children of her own.

Finn and his girls had already been through a lot with Sara's death, and she represented the possibility of having to go through the trauma of losing someone all over again. She couldn't do that to them. She shouldn't have done it to herself. Lesson learned. Falling for someone wasn't a cure-all, simply a mistake. A painful one it would take a long time to recover from, if ever.

'Hello, I'm Dr Riordan, the cardiologist.' She had to push her own heartache to the background as she walked into the cubicle in A&E.

It was her job to prolong the life of her patients and give them the chance to have everything she couldn't. Scant consolation when she'd had to go back to her old status quo, knowing what she could have had if fate hadn't run up and tapped her on the shoulder to remind her that wasn't her life, it was someone else's. Whether it was the one Sara had left behind or the one a future partner for Finn had waiting for her, it didn't matter. It shouldn't matter because it wasn't any of her business. Their time had simply been a pleasant interlude and she'd got carried away.

'Hi. I'm John, Sally's dad. Can you tell us what happened or if it's going to happen again?' He was rightly concerned, as was the mum, she supposed, who was sitting by the side of her daughter's bed, clutching her hand.

'That's what I'm here to find out. We're going to admit Sally onto the ward to monitor her overnight and we'll run some tests to see what's going on. Once we have a diagnosis I'll be working with you to give your daughter the right treatment to keep her happy and healthy.' It was a big promise, but one Lily was confident she could deliver. If only her future had been laid out for her the way she hoped to do for Sally, she might not have been so afraid to face it. Now it was too late for her to make up for lost time and lost love.

'We're just grateful that fireman was able to get to our place until the ambulance arrived. If it wasn't for him, Sally might not have made it.' The father was clearly grateful for the intervention, but the new information caused Lily to pause reading the girl's chart.

'A fireman? You must have been a candidate for the new crossover scheme. Glad to see it's working.' She didn't need to brag it had been her baby when knowing it was doing the job of saving lives was sufficient reward. It did, of course, make her curious about who had been the crew member who had saved the little girl's life.

'Yes. He used the defibrillator and did CPR until the ambulance arrived. By all accounts, Mr Finnegan's the one who saved Sally's life.'

Lily's quickening pulse betrayed the idea of her remaining unmoved by the mere mention of the man.

'I'm glad to know the scheme is working the way we intended and that Sally here is doing so well now.'

'We owe him everything,' the mother added and her words brought tears into Lily's eyes from both pride and sadness for the man she seemed destined to be reminded about for ever.

'If you'll just excuse me, I'll go and chase up those blood tests.' She exited the cubicle quickly but the opportunity to get some space from Charlie Finnegan was lost as she ran into him in the corridor.

'Lily? What are you doing here?' He was dressed in the same short-sleeved shirt with the fire department logo and black trousers outfit he'd worn for the photoshoot on the first day the project had launched. It seemed a lifetime ago now.

She cleared her throat before she spoke in case it came out in a squeak. 'I was called down to look in on your young patient, Sally. Her parents have been singing your praises.'

His cheeks turned an endearing shade of pink. 'I just did what I was trained to do. If it wasn't for you I wouldn't have been there at all.'

Whilst Lily appreciated the shared glory, it was killing her standing here making small talk, pretending things were okay, when her heart still felt as though it wasn't done breaking.

'I'm glad it's working. It makes everything worthwhile.'

She went to leave but Finn moved to block her path.

'Can we talk?'

His simple request sent her insides haywire, her stomach in knots and her heart thumping in anticipation of what he had to say. She was too raw to handle it if he said anything nice to her. It would only be another reminder of everything she'd lost, of all the things she couldn't have. She was destined to be the one standing out in the cold for ever, looking in on the cosy family she'd been denied from an early age.

'Not here. We can go to my office.' The busy A&E department wasn't the place for a heart-to-heart over their failed relationship.

Lily ordered up the necessary tests for Sally with a note for the results to be sent to her as soon as they came back.

'Is she going to be okay?' Finn asked as they made their way back up to her room.

'It's too early to say what caused her episode tonight,

but I'm sure with the right treatment she'll be able to lead a relatively normal life.' She couldn't believe they were standing in the middle of her office discussing a patient as though they'd never crossed that professional line and ended up in a relationship, no matter how short-lived it had been. Every time she saw him she was going to be reminded of their time together, and how unfair life was that they couldn't still have that. If this was the new normal for them, it sucked.

'That's all any of us want, isn't it?' Finn was looking at her with a strange hangdog expression. He had no right to look at her that way. After all, it was his family she was protecting in all of this.

'Not all of us can have it, though.'

'Why not? Who's to say you can't lead the life you want too?'

'Um...doctors, biology...fate.' It wasn't fair of him to put her through this, upsetting her all over again.

He sighed. 'I know you were just thinking about the girls when you put an end to everything. It's the only real reason I can think of as to why you'd give up on us'

'How are they?' There was no 'us', so she saw no point in referencing it.

'Missing you.'

Another punch in the gut. She was missing them too and didn't need the extra guilt, feeling bad that she'd disappeared out of their lives without a proper explanation. 'That's not fair, Finn.'

'I know, but it's true. We're all missing you.'

'What exactly is it that you want? I'm supposed to be working.' The only way she'd ever been able to protect herself was to keep everyone at a distance and it was about time she returned to her tried and tested methods. Albeit too late to save her poor fragile heart from another blow.

'To say I'm sorry I didn't fight hard enough.'

The vicelike grip his words had on her squeezed the oxygen from her lungs.

'For what?' she managed to gasp with her last breath.

'For us.'

She took a seat at her desk to ensure she didn't give a repeat performance of her dramatic collapse.

'Are you okay?'

'I'm fine. I'm not some delicate flower that's going to fall apart at the slightest touch.' The last thing she wanted was for him to think she was about to collapse again, even if her legs were a little wobbly beneath her.

'I know, you're my Tiger Lily.' He cocked his head to one side and smiled and she was glad she was already sitting down because that would surely have been enough to make her fall to the floor again.

'Not any more,' she reminded them both.

'I know you're still hung up about what happened in front of the girls and yes, it was a shock to everyone but we're over it. There's no reason to keep beating yourself up over it. People get sick all the time. They recover or they live with it. That's life. You don't need to hide yourself away from the world, punishing yourself and those who love you. We can get through this together.'

Love. Together.

The words swam around in Lily's head, making her dizzy and almost steering her off the path she was determined to walk alone.

'I'm moving away, Finn.' She'd toyed with the idea

and now, seeing him again, she knew it was the only option. Especially now he was trying to make the impossible work. She couldn't run the risk of running into him at work every now and then, and having this painful reminder of what they'd had every time she saw him.

'What? Where? When?' The heartbroken expression on his face was unmistakable when it was the same one she saw in the mirror every day.

'I think it's best for both of us to make a clean break. I'll look into getting transferred as soon as possible. I'm sure I won't have trouble getting a position at another hospital.'

'So it's not a done deal then? Won't you think about staying for me? I really think we could make it work. I know you care about me, Lily, and you know I love you. At least if we're honest about that, this time we can at least try.'

Finn knelt down beside her chair and took her shaking hand.

'Is this a proposal?' She snort laughed, trying to hide her nerves over what was happening.

'What if it was? What would you say?'

'I'd tell you to stop being stupid. I've told you, I'm moving on and you should too. Who knows, maybe you'll meet someone else.' Lily snatched her hand away.

'I don't want anyone else. We're good together, Lily.'

'*Were* good.'

'Tell me you don't love me and I'll walk away right now.'

'What would that change, Finn? I'm still me, with all the baggage no one can help me carry.'

'I should have supported you. I'm sorry I didn't do

more to make you think we could talk over your fears. I guess I was still trying to protect myself too.'

'Why now? What's happened to cause this sudden change of heart?' She folded her arms across her chest, a defensive move against the words she was afraid would cause more damage to her already battered heart. It would be easy for her to get carried away by the idea of living happily ever after again, but reality had a way of crashing in and spoiling things. In this moment, in the wake of his life-or-death encounter with Sally, he might be running on adrenaline and the idea of mortality. Eventually he would remember hers would come sooner than most and cause him to think twice.

'Tonight made me realise life isn't guaranteed for any of us. Sally, Sara, the father who died in the fire that night—no one knew what was in store for them any more than we do.' He was gesticulating wildly, his eyes wide, and he was giving off a vibe of absolute excitement, as though he had just made some incredible breakthrough. It was something she'd dared not to search for herself. Hope.

'And if I die and leave you and the girls traumatised? That's what will happen, Finn, we both know it. I've lost my father and my sister, you've lost Sara, and it's something you never get over.'

'That's true, but our time together is something to cherish, isn't it?' He rested his hands on her shoulders, forcing her to look at him. 'Whatever time we have together is precious and we shouldn't waste it when we never know what tomorrow will bring.'

'Have you been overdoing the country songs?' She arched an eyebrow at him, trying to make light of what he was saying, afraid the sincerity she could see blazing in his blue eyes would make her believe it all, but anything had to be better than being alone with this aching hole in her chest where her heart used to be.

'I'm serious. Any of us could go at any time and I don't want to waste another second without you. Sara and I put off a lot of things believing we had for ever. You and I know different, so what's the point in being apart any longer?

'I was afraid of actually admitting that I was in love with you because it meant being vulnerable to getting hurt again. I let you walk away because of my own fears, but I'm willing to take that chance if you are. If you're open to the idea, I'd like to take the next step and for you to move in.'

Lily's eyes almost popped out of her head they were so wide with incredulity at the commitment he was willing to make to her.

'You mean move in with you and the girls?'

'Yes, with me and the girls. I'm not sure you're ready to live with the rest of the crew at the station.'

'I don't know… Some of them are very fit…'

Finn frowned at her before breaking out into a goofy smile. 'I know I'm older, not as fit as the others and have my fair share of issues too, but I love you and I want a future with you. What do you say, Tiger Lily—are you willing to take a chance on love? On me?'

'What if it doesn't work out? What if I get really sick? The last thing I want to do is cause you or the girls any pain.' That went for her too. She didn't want the promise of a relationship, only for him to bail out when things got tough. If that was the case she'd rather be on her own than deal with heartbreak on top of her illness.

'One of the things I've learned about you, Tiger Lily, is that you do everything you can for your patients. You never give up. Now I'm asking you to do the same for yourself, and us, and keep fighting. We can't predict the future and it seems such a waste to throw what we have away on the basis of what might happen. I love you, you love me, and that's all that matters for now. Move in with me and we can build on that.'

Asking her to live with him was something she knew he wouldn't take lightly when it meant being part of his family. Finn would never do anything to hurt his daughters, and that included moving a stranger into their home, into their lives, on a whim. He would have thought carefully about the impact it would have on them by inviting her to stay permanently. It was a huge gamble for him to take and if Lily wasn't prepared to do the same she'd be alone for the rest of her life because she would never love anyone the way she loved Finn.

She thought about the years she'd wasted just existing, the time she'd spent with Finn and the girls, and there was no competition. There was only one place she wanted to be.

'Take me home, hot stuff.'

Finn kissed her long and hard, making up for the time they'd spent apart. When she was in his arms she believed anything was possible and now he was offering her a future together she knew she would fight hard against anything that threatened to take that away.

Her heart might not work as well as some, but it belonged entirely to Finn and if love was enough to keep it beating she'd live for ever.

EPILOGUE

'ARE YOU GOING to be my new mummy?' Little Maeve was standing staring at Lily with her head cocked to one side, face screwed up in concentration.

'Shh. You're not supposed to ask things like that.' Big sister Niamh bustled in with a scolding and tried to wrangle the curious flower girl away.

'It's okay. You're both bound to have questions. This is as big a deal to you two as it is to me and your daddy.' Lily wished Finn were here to be part of the conversation but they had decided not to see each other until the wedding and she didn't want to leave the girls wondering what would happen once they were officially married.

She carefully smoothed her dress before sitting down and patted the bed for the girls to come and join her. They'd spent the night in the hotel room together, with Finn staying down the corridor. Lily's quality time with the girls was always special and they'd had fun putting on face masks and ordering room service.

They always enjoyed girls' nights, something they'd started doing on a regular basis since she'd moved in. It was a way of bonding and they were keeping her young at heart with their endless energy and enthusiasm. Both Niamh and Maeve seemed to be enjoying having another female in the house. Whilst she didn't have much experience with children, she was able to braid their hair and paint their nails, which their father apparently hadn't managed to do adequately since they'd lost their mum.

After only six months of living together Finn had proposed, keen not to waste whatever time they had together. He and the girls had brought her breakfast in bed that morning with a handmade card from the girls with *Will You Marry Us?* written on the front. She'd watched Finn drop to one knee by the side of the bed, holding out a beautiful diamond ring, through happy tears. Of course he'd consulted his daughters before asking when it would affect their lives greatly, and of course Lily had said yes because she loved them all.

Now they were all here in paradise, or Bali to be precise, for their wedding. There was a party planned back home when they returned for friends and colleagues but they'd both wanted the day just for their little family to enjoy. That didn't mean they hadn't gone all out on the outfits. After all, she only planned to do this once.

Not wishing to overdo the frills and froth, she'd opted for a more age-appropriate white satin slip dress, overlaid with a layer of embroidered tulle. Being with Finn had helped her learn to love her body the way it was so she was happy to showcase her best assets in the V-neck of the tailored bodice.

Niamh and Maeve were a big part of the ceremony and the day so they'd had fun choosing their outfits, simple white satin shift dresses with bands around their waists in their favourite jade-green and deep blue colours. They were all wearing the sea glass necklaces they'd made and Lily was looking forward to a stroll along the beach with the girls later to find more treasures.

For now she was content just being here with them, helping them transition into this new family which would include her.

'I'm going to be your stepmother. I'll never replace your mum, but I'll be here whenever you need me. I love you and your dad very much.' She had to choke back the tears, overwhelmed by the occasion and the realisation that she was finally getting that fairy tale ending she'd thought would never happen for her.

'Do we have to call you Mum?' Niamh, the older of the two, who would have had more memories of her mother, asked and Lily wondered how long that question had been bothering her. She'd tried not to force herself into their lives, despite how quickly her relationship with Finn seemed to have moved forward. Thankfully they'd accepted her and she'd done her best to keep the memory of their mother alive so they would never forget the woman who'd brought them into the world.

'You can just keep calling me Lily. Nothing's going to change at home except that I'm going to be Mrs Finnegan now.'

For some reason that made the girls giggle and her heart was full at the sound of them being so happy on such a special day.

'We should go and meet your daddy before he goes and marries someone else.' Lily got up before she started crying and ruined her carefully applied make-up.

Taking the still giggling duo by the hands, she made her way from the hotel down onto the beach.

Finn was standing under the floral arch the hotel had kindly erected for the ceremony. He looked gorgeous in his cream linen suit, sleeves rolled up to show off his tanned muscular forearms and white shirt opened at the neck, giving her a peek at his chest. She couldn't wait to spend the night alone with her husband and thankfully her future mother-in-law was in attendance and taking on babysitting duties tonight.

Lily couldn't wipe the smile off her face as she walked across to meet him at the edge of the sea. It was as perfect a wedding as she could ever have hoped for.

'You look beautiful,' he said as she came to stand beside him and kissed her on the cheek.

'So do you.'

That made him smile but she meant it. Freshly shaven and wearing a suit, or skin smudged with smoke when he was in uniform, he always looked good to her and she knew he always would because she loved him so much.

They said their vows before the celebrant and exchanged rings, then Lily turned to her young bridesmaids.

'I have rings for you too since I'm marrying the whole family today.'

The girls were jumping up and down, fizzing with excitement as she slipped the tiny rings onto their fingers. It was a gesture she'd discussed with Finn to show her commitment to his daughters and a promise she would be there for them. Something she intended to do for a long time.

'I now pronounce you man and wife…and family.'

The celebrant didn't have to give Finn the go-ahead to kiss her as he took her in his arms and melded his lips with hers. It was difficult not to get carried away when she hadn't seen him since yesterday, but she enjoyed their first kiss as a married couple as much as every other. For the first time in her life Lily considered herself a very lucky woman.

Their smooch was interrupted by a flurry of colourful confetti raining down on them, followed by the joyous sound of the girls' laughter.

'Hey, you two. Come here.' Finn swung the girls up so he had one balanced on each hip and leaned in to give Lily another peck on the lips. Then the girls leaned over to kiss her on both cheeks. Finn's mother, who had shed a tear or two during the ceremony, came over to hug them all.

It had taken a scarred fire-fighter and his family to mend Lily's broken heart so she could finally start living.

* * * * *

MILLS & BOON®

Coming next month

SECRET SON TO CHANGE HER LIFE

Alison Roberts

'I tried every way I could to contact you,' Brie said quietly. 'But it was weeks after you'd left. Your phone was disconnected. You never responded when I tried to message you on social media. Nobody knew where you were.'

'So you just gave up?'

'It was during those weeks I found out that the baby I was carrying had spina bifida.' Brie's tone changed. She might deserve Jonno's anger but she wasn't the person he thought she was. She hadn't set out to lie to him. 'My priorities kind of changed at that point.'

That silenced him. Brie walked ahead and found another stick to throw for Dennis. Then she turned.

'I never expected to see you again,' she said. 'But when I'd had a bit of time to get used to you turning up out of blue, like that, I did try to tell you – the day I came to your apartment.'

She could hear the echo of what she'd said to him then, in spite of the background shriek of the seagulls. She knew Jonno could hear it as well.

I had to come…There's something I really need to tell you, Jonno…

They both knew why she hadn't ended up telling him that day.

'You could have told me well before then. Like when I asked you if you had any kids.'

'Oh… yeah… Right after you'd been telling me how thankful you were that you didn't have any dependents? How do you think that made me feel?' Brie's voice hitched. 'I was still trying to get my head around it myself. How was I going to tell my son that his daddy was back in town but might not want to have anything to do with him because he had better things to do with his time? That he wasn't even planning to be around long, anyway. He was going to get rid of the last tie he had here and then he'd be gone again. Forever. Probably on the other side of the world in Australia or New Zealand.'

'I said those things because I didn't know,' Jonno countered. 'Do you really think I'm someone who'd walk away from a responsibility like having a child? That I wouldn't care?'

Brie swallowed hard. Of course she didn't. 'Maybe I was hoping that one day, Felix would be able to find you.'

Continue reading

SECRET SON TO CHANGE HER LIFE

Alison Roberts

Available next month

www.millsandboon.co.uk